THE NIGHT CRAWLER

STEWART CLYDE

Copyright © 2025 by Stewart Clyde.

Published by Hunt Press in 2025.

The moral right of Stewart Clyde to be identified as the Author of the Work has been asserted by him, in accordance with the Copyrights, Designs and Patents Act 1988.

All rights reserved. No part of this publication may be reproduced, stored in a retrieval system, or transmitted in any form or by any means without prior permission in writing from the publisher.

First published in 2025 by Hunt Press.

First published in Great Britain.

All characters are fictitious and any resemblance to real persons, living or dead, is purely coincidental.

For Ema & Henry

"If you talk to God, you are praying; If God talks to you, you have schizophrenia." —Thomas Szasz

1

THE HARDEST HUMAN TO kill is a cop. He knew from experience. Harder still is getting away with it. As soon as a cop is killed, the whole nest of uniformed police, like so many black ants, start moving—springing into action. Getting busy 'catching' the guy who did it.

Hell, it didn't matter if they caught the guy or not. What mattered was that they cracked heads—and re-established their dominance. You don't kill cops. If you do, we make your life so you don't want to live it anymore. Capisce? You'll wish you never lived. That's how they think. The one thing, though, about cops—especially homicide detectives—they liked to drink. Killing people wasn't easy. Not morally, you understand, more from a technical perspective. Even more difficult was killing a cop. Why? They're big, brash, and full of brawn. Plus, they come pre-loaded with a gun. And they know how to use it. It's probably the most difficult prey. A cop. They're hardly ever alone. If they are, they're always highly suspicious. Less so if they were drunk, though.

He knew something about this one cop, though, which helped. He'd stalked him for weeks. The guy's name was John Marshall. He liked to gamble. Bet on the horses. He liked to trawl the street hookers and force a little protection money from the pimps. And he liked to drink. No other animal would take something that dulled the senses and reverted man to the level of dumb beasts. Cops do. Calves to the slaughter. Innocently waiting for a metal bolt to shoot out and penetrate their brain. The truth was that cops like Marshall deserved to die. They were practically begging for it. They deserved to die to protect the victims in cases they just ignored. Or worked so badly that the suspects walked. Or just didn't give a damn about solving it. Getting close to a cop takes time and cunning, like bowhunting a deer that can think.

He equated this service to society—the whole damn tapestry of it—to writing a script or a song. It's done in a vacuum. Secretly. Without anyone knowing anything about it, until, finally, with much trepidation, you release your masterpiece to the world. Then, and only then, does one receive the acclaim. The notoriety. The analysis and publicity. The trick was to stay hidden and keep the mystery alive for as long as possible. Then, when they finally discovered you, you received celebrity, like the great killers of the past. It was a strange dichotomy, like Yin and Yang. He deeply desired the celebrity, but to achieve it, he had to suppress that desire and remain in the shadows for as long as possible. Still, that's not to say one cannot have fun while doing it. It was a game, after all. And so, the long labor of love continued.

Now, if the hardest person to kill was indeed a cop, how do you get away with it?

"Hello, Johnny."

"The hell do you want?" the detective said and swayed. He had a little spittle on his lip and lifted his chin so he could see out from under his droopy eyelids.

The hell, indeed.

2

THE SMELL OF DEATH. It hung in the crime scene air. It was a stench she'd never get used to. It clung to her like a new lover.

Special Agent Caitlin Sandling had seen enough of these by now to know what to do. She'd come prepared, took a tin of ointment out of her jacket pocket, and twisted the lid off. She dipped two nitrile glove-covered fingers into the menthol balm and wiped it under her nose and on her nostrils. She saw Detective Michael Benson of the Baltimore Police Department watching her from under his bushy eyebrows and tight-lipped. He didn't give much away. He reminded her of a caveman. One wearing an ill-fitting suit. He was one of the good ones.

Silently, she held out the small tin of balm and held two fingers under her nose, showing him how to apply it. He held up his hand to decline. She shrugged and screwed the lid back on.

Sandling stood in the darkness of a narrow hallway of a walk-up apartment on the outskirts of Annapolis, Maryland. People in white hazmat suits were moving around the small space. The constant flashes of crime scene photos left spots in her vision. On her right, the door to the bathroom was blocked by crime lab techs, so she and Benson went into the bedroom. The place was a mess. Pink and blue neon lights from an advertising billboard for a condom brand shone through the threadbare curtains and shimmered off the bed sheets.

How fitting, Sandling thought bitterly. She held up her pen-sized flashlight and switched it on. The white light beamed into the blackness ahead. She passed a kitchenette on her left and followed Benson into the bedroom. A crime lab tech was taking pictures on his haunches at the end of the double bed. Sandling looked down at the bed as the camera flashed. The whole room lit up in a grungy snapshot. Seared into her mind's eye were the cheapness and dirtiness of the scene. The duvet was in a heap at the foot of the bed. The sheets had stains and marks on them. The shiny-black bedside table had a mirror on it covered with lines of crushed crystal meth. She saw torn black lingerie— a bra and thong, strewn on the bed next to an upturned designer clutch. The contents looked like they'd been scattered haphazardly. A single Christian Louboutin high-heeled sandal was lying on its side. Someone was in a hurry.

Sandling walked behind the lab tech as he took another picture. He looked up at her and acknowledged her with a nod. Sandling stepped to the window, pulled the curtain open, and looked down at the street.

It was 3 A.M., yet the streets were thick with cars and people. She could see prostitutes on the sidewalk and groups of men hanging around vehicles and alleyway entrances. The streetlights gave off a strange yellow glow, and she could see a small crowd of onlookers. The local police were keeping them at bay.

Detective Benson walked up and stood beside her, leaned toward the glass, and looked down at the street. "Want to get a bite after this?" Benson asked. Sandling ignored him. When her silence made it awkward enough, he asked, "What's that smell?"

"Clorox," Sandling said, without looking at him.

Benson glanced at her like he was impressed. And then over his shoulder at the lab tech.

"I saw a bottle lying next to the bath," Sandling said.

"He dumped about five of them in the tub with her," the tech confirmed.

"Why'd he do that?" Benson asked Sandling. She shrugged and shook her head.

"Could be shame, trying to clean away the evidence, could be some kind of ritual. Part of his fantasy."

"Sick fuck," Benson said like he was trying to sound tough.

Sandling thought it was bravado in place of anything useful to say. It was a disturbing crime scene. Not the place for quiet contemplation even though that's how she felt.

"No, it smells like something else to me. Did he fire a handgun? I smell gunpowder," Benson said.

Then they heard someone call out, "Detective, you'd better come and see this."

They glanced at one another, then turned away from the window and followed a slight, short woman in a white hazmat suit to the voices. Two other forensics staff members were already waiting in the kitchenette. They pointed at a plastic ice cream container.

"There's some in the microwave too," one said.

"What is it?" Sandling asked from the doorway.

The short woman turned around and asked, "Who are you?" She was snippy.

"Detective Benson, Baltimore PD," Benson said from behind. "This is Special Agent Sandling."

"Right, well, you shouldn't be in here."

"What is it?" Sandling asked again.

"See for yourself," the woman said, opening the microwave door wider. The inside of it was smeared in blood. There were two bits of fatty-looking flesh in there. Benson lifted his hand to his mouth like he might throw up. He turned away and went down the corridor. "He removed some of her organs. Looks like he tried to cook and eat some of it."

Sandling felt dizzy, like she was having an out-of-body experience. It was her mind trying to defend itself. She took a deep breath and composed herself. "What's in the Tupperware?" Sandling asked.

One of the forensics guys tilted the ice cream container. "He collected her blood."

Sandling gasped and didn't dare breathe.

"Looks like he drank some," the forensic guy said.

"You worked anything like this before?" the woman asked her from behind a surgical mask.

Sandling ignored her stare. "What about the body?"

"You'll get your full report when it's ready, Special Agent, um ..."

"Sandling. Who're you?" she asked, trying to avoid looking at the contents inside the microwave.

"Rachel Luca," the woman said. "Deputy director of crime scene sciences."

"What about the body?" Sandling asked again, this time meeting Luca's eyes.

She sighed, giving in, and said, "This way." Sandling followed her into the cramped bathroom. "Give us some space," Luca said to the others, and they filed past her. Sandling's breathing was shallow, and her heart was beating in a heavy, steady thump.

"We found her face down in a mixture of chlorine and cold water," Luca said. Sandling looked down at the body. It was face up. Sandling could see the look of pained horror frozen on the gray and blue corpse's face.

"These are major knife wounds," Luca said, indicating wild-looking slash and tear marks on the torso. With one huge, gaping incision from the victim's chest to her belly button. Parts of the victim's intestines were hanging out in the slimy water. She looked away, nauseated.

"It looks like some internal organs have been removed from the body cavity and hacked at," Luca said. "We'll analyze them and let you know which ones. Some of her body parts are missing. Her left ear, her left pinky finger. There are at least a dozen stab wounds to her left breast - we'll have more detail after the examination."

"What's that in her mouth?" Sandling asked, staring at the victim's face.

Luca looked at her. "Animal feces. We found a litter box, but no cat. He stuffed it in her mouth. Can't tell if it was pre- or post-mortem yet. I'll let you know."

"Thanks," Sandling said and felt disgusted by the action of having to thank her for needing to carry out that task. "When did this happen?"

"Hard to tell. Best guess right now, a few hours ago," Luca said. "Less than twelve. We'll get a more accurate time from the lab."

"Who found her?"

"Anonymous report. Probably her pimp. We can check."

Sandling stared blankly at the blood-streaked tiles behind the bath.

"You think she was a prostitute?"

"Don't you?"

Sandling didn't respond.

"Anything else?" Luca asked, still looking at the side of Sandling's face. She shook her head. Benson appeared in the doorway.

Sandling glanced over her shoulder at him and said, "No. We'll get out of your hair."

"Look, if it's any consolation, judging by the amount of crystal meth she probably wouldn't have realized what was happening until the very last moment. She would have been out of her mind. Horny as hell and euphoric as a wet dream, not in a—"

"Are there signs of penetration?" Benson asked.

"Not with his penis," Luca said.

Sandling lifted her fist to her mouth and cleared her throat.

"Sorry," Luca said. "Gallows humor. You need it in this trade. We can't tell right now. We'll know more after the screening but the bleach may have nullified our results."

"Come on," Benson said to her.

Sandling grimaced and nodded. "Thanks," she said to Luca and walked out feeling the strain of the scene.

"Special Agent Sandling," Luca called after her. Sandling stopped and turned. "I hope you catch the bastard."

"Let's get out of here," Benson said to her and Sandling turned and followed him out of the apartment and down the brightly lit stairs without really seeing anything.

As they reached the bottom of the stairs and walked out into the street, a uniformed cop approached them, wide-eyed and out of breath. "Come on," he said to Benson, "You've got to see this, sir."

"What is it?" Benson asked the officer as they walked. Sandling skipped a little to catch up to the big-striding men. They went around the corner of the block, and the officer said, "It's down here."

"What is?" Benson asked again.

"Another body," the officer said.

"Who are you?" Benson asked him.

"Grady, sir."

"Who found it?"

"I did, sir. I was checking the perimeter and canvassing. I shone my flashlight down the alleyway here," Grady said, gesturing towards a dark alley with his arm. There were a couple of other unformed officers standing opposite some dumpsters. "I saw a pair of shoes. I went to check it out, you know? Maybe the guy saw something or heard something."

"You did well, Grady," Benson said.

"Can we take a look?" Sandling asked.

Benson glanced at her and said to Grady, "Go and get forensics over here."

"Already done, sir; they are on their way."

"Let's go take a look," Benson said to Sandling.

As they walked up, the other uniformed cops stopped talking and took a step away from the body. Sandling looked down at the man lying there. Her eyes started at his head and slid down his body to his feet. He wore a purple hat with a white feather tilted down, covering his face, and buried in a fur coat. His shoes were white-and-black leather brogues polished to a high shine.

"That'll be her pimp," Sandling said.

"He's a night crawler," Grady said under his breath.

"What'd you say?" Benson asked, and Grady glanced at him.

"Oh, sorry, sir, I just—"

"No, repeat it. What did you say?"

Grady swallowed hard and said, "He's a night crawler, sir."

Sandling and Benson's eyes locked.

"Well, Grady, if that nickname leaks to the press, at least

we'll know where it came from, huh?" Benson said, turning to him.

"Yes, sir," Grady said just as two crime scene technicians in white hazmat suits walked up to them.

"That'll be our cue," Benson said to Sandling. "Let's go."

3

SANDLING RESTED her head against the passenger window and watched the streetlights pass by. Late-night radio played in the background. Benson spoke as he drove. He must be feeling better, she thought. She felt worse.

"I know this great late-night breakfast place. It's not far. We'll go there and talk—"

"What'd you make of it?" Sandling asked him.

He stopped talking, and she saw him look at her from the corner of her eye.

"Another crazed drug attack," Benson said. "Isn't it?"

"You think it's drugs that made him crazy?" Sandling asked and lifted her head off the glass.

Benson shrugged. "I mean, don't you? There was enough Tina there to kill a small horse and who knows what else she has in her system. Wouldn't be surprised if we found GHB too."

"A foal," she mumbled.

"Huh?"

"Never mind."

"No, tell me."

"A small horse is a foal."

"Okay," Benson said. "I could've meant a fully grown small horse, like a Shetland Pony."

"Sure."

"Okay. Anyway," Benson said. "That's what it was, right? Drug-crazed killing. That's what I saw."

"What about the body parts in the microwave?"

"They'll probably find it's minced beef or something ..." He didn't sound convinced.

He's in denial, she thought. "So, you don't think it was her blood he was drinking?"

Benson didn't reply. It grossed them both out. Too disturbing to think about. They rode along in silence. Sandling put her head on the glass and watched the streetlights again. She was tired. Benson parked and got out. She followed him across the street to a brightly lit, late-night diner.

"Cop joint," he said to her over his shoulder. She could see two other uniformed police officers sitting at a table near the entrance. Sandling went and sat in a booth in the back, put her forehead on her hands, and rested on the table. Benson ordered the food. Usually, crime scenes made her ravenous, but this time, she didn't have much of an appetite. When he came back, he said, "Waffles. They're famous for them here."

She sat up, studied him briefly, and said, "Thanks."

He was holding two coffees and put one down in front of her. She picked it up with both hands and took a long drag on it. Benson checked over his shoulder and bounced his knee. He looked agitated.

"You okay?" Sandling asked as she shook a sugar sachet and tore it open.

"Yeah, you?" Benson said.

"You left the scene in a hurry ..."

"I had to get out of there," he said. "How can you stand it?"

Sandling shrugged and poured the sugar into her coffee.

A dull-faced, tired-looking waitress brought over two plates. They were piled high with waffles, whipped cream, and extra syrup. She placed them down on the table. "Can I get you anything else?"

"No, we're good," Benson said, and she turned and walked away. "Dig in," he said and picked up a fork.

Sandling took her utensils out of the paper napkin. The thought of all that sugar suddenly seemed appealing. Benson cut his waffles into quarters and used the fork to shove a mouthful of waffles and whipped cream into his mouth. He grunted and moaned and nodded. Sandling laughed.

"What?" he asked around the mouthful of waffle and folded another quarter into his already full mouth before licking his fingers.

"Hungry?"

"Sure, aren't you?" he said.

The two cops at the other table got up to leave. Benson turned towards them and said, "Have a good one, fellas." They gave a little wave and sauntered out of the place. Sandling put a fork full of waffles into her mouth and closed her eyes.

"Good, right?" Benson asked.

She nodded. "Mm-hmm," she said. Better than she expected. She was more a savory girl than sweet. Maybe she was hungry after all.

"How're you finding it?" Benson asked.

She was chewing, opened her eyes, and put her cutlery on the plate. "It's yummy."

"No, I mean, the assignment. Baltimore, you know? The whole deal."

She wiped her fingers on her napkin as she watched him and thought about how to answer the question. Sandling had put in for a transfer. After the furor around the Skinwalker killer case died down and Carver left the hospital to heal, she formally requested reassignment away from the Sofa Squad and away from Carver. Not that she felt like she'd earned it after stopping Edward Derange. It was more that she couldn't stand to be in the same room as her team leader.

One of her psychology professors said something she now profoundly understood: People are hurt most by deception. Humans don't process betrayal well. They can't handle being lied to or having the rug pulled out from beneath them by people they trust. *That just does them in*, he'd said.

That's how she felt—done in by it all. She'd been sure that Deputy Director Gibson would support her desire, and Gust—at the very least—wouldn't try to stop her. It seemed as though, between them, Gibson and Carver had come to a compromise. The deputy director was suddenly her biggest fan because she'd captured a killer and put the Behavioral Analysis Unit front and center of stopping crimes by serial killers. Politically, it was a great look for her. Gibson convinced Sandling to take on this case in Baltimore as a stopgap while they processed her move away from Grant Avenue.

So, for now, Sandling was still technically part of the Manassas resident agency; she was just working as a field agent and liaison seconded to the Baltimore PD to support them with another suspected serial killer case. She'd agreed to it, but after having been in Baltimore for about five weeks, she started to feel that perhaps she'd made a mistake.

Gibson told her all the right things to make her stay for now. In retrospect, as the sweet whipped cream and crispy waffle melted on her tongue, Sandling realized that Gibson was buttering her up. Gibson talked about how she admired her for her bravery in saving the hostage and killing Derange. She said how Sandling reminded her of a younger version of herself and how, as women in the male-dominated world of the FBI, they needed to stick together. Gibson made it seem like she would take Sandling under her wing, nurture her, and feed her on regurgitated nutrients of officialdom to strengthen her career. Sandling could see now that meant putting her on assignments to move her out of the gravity of Carver's orbit and closer to Quantico again, where the real action in behavioral analysis was.

Gibson said Sandling—with the right guidance—had the potential to be a future deputy director of the BAU. She just needed to build up her hours on cases in the field and prove that catching Edward Derange wasn't a one-off. The only thing Sandling was sure of was that Gibson, through her training in psychology, knew how to press buttons, knew how to play politics, and knew how to get people to do things they didn't want to do.

Sandling watched Benson as he ate. Stuffing it in his mouth and smiling like a five-year-old. He was burly, rough around the edges, but a good guy from what she'd seen. He still had a boyish charm. He also seemed like he needed to let loose now and again, blow off some steam. He was assigned as her liaison after she'd joined them. It wasn't far from Manassas, but it felt as distant as Mars. It was an alien planet to her. She had no experience of the culture of a city police department. Benson was helping her adjust, though. She preferred to stay in the background anyway.

She looked at the dimple on his chin and coarse-looking

stubble and wondered how many days of growth it had been. Probably one, maybe less than a day. Under the table, she unconsciously touched the place where her wedding band used to sit. It was just the bony part of her finger now, but sometimes, it felt like it was still there. She still felt the guilt.

"You thinking about the case?" Benson asked. He was looking at her like she had that far-away look on her face. She came back and felt the glare of the fluorescent lighting again.

"Sure," she said.

"What about?"

She shrugged.

"Did you notice anything missing?" Benson asked her.

She shook her head.

"Nothing from the purse?"

"Clutch."

"Money?"

She hadn't thought about it. "We don't know if any money was missing."

"Yeah, but come on!" Benson glanced over his shoulders and said quietly, "A working girl like that has cash on her." Sandling just looked at him. "From all the johns," Benson said.

"Like, *duh*. Thanks for explaining what you meant, Detective Obvious," she laughed at herself and him. He was so serious. He was usually so laid back. Acted like it, anyway.

"Okay then, Agent Obscurity," he said with a glint in his eye. Sandling furrowed her brow, confused.

"You think it's the same guy?" he asked.

There was no doubt in her mind it was. "Could be," she said.

"Oh, come on!"

"What?"

"I can see that you think it is."

"How?"

"You have a look ..."

"A look?"

"You have a knowing look."

"What does that mean?"

"Holier than thou," Benson said.

"Christ! Really? Thanks ..." she said and scoffed.

"Forget it. I can just tell, okay?"

"Fine. Let me ask you this," she said. "How could it possibly be a different suspect?"

"Different *modus operandi*."

"Different how?"

"The first one was a family. This was just one girl."

"Thank you."

"For what?"

"Not calling her something crass, like a *hooker*," Sandling said.

Benson shook his head and raised his eyebrows. "I would never ..."

"Okay. But what about the wounds?" Sandling asked. "Both female victims were the targets. Both had massive injuries. Both are from a bladed weapon of some sort. The nature of the attacks—the removal of organs, the violent hacking of the abdomen."

"Yes, but the drinking of the blood? That didn't happen at the first crime scene."

"That we know of," Sandling said. "Maybe he took it with him the first time. Maybe it was a hassle. Didn't like the idea of carrying around a pint of human blood."

"Or driving around with it."

Sandling was silent and bit her cheek, almost glaring at him.

"You think he walked?" Benson asked.

She shrugged. She was tired, but the suspect she pictured was disorganized, impulsive, careless, and apathetic to the point of being blasé. The only thing that didn't fit was the pimp. That implied planning ...

"So tell me your theory then," Benson said.

4

SHE THOUGHT ABOUT IT. Benson held his fork like a spoon and scooped a big mouthful of waffle and cream into his gaping bazoo. He smiled at her, knowing that it looked a bit ridiculous. She smiled back. He licked his thumb and spoke around a mouthful of waffle, "Explain it to me then ... your thinking."

"My thinking?"

"About the scene."

"The scene or the case?"

Benson shrugged. "I don't know how it works."

"What works?"

"This whole profiling thing. You know?"

"It's a bit ..." She looked away and bit her lip.

"Complicated?"

"Yeah."

"For a dumb cop like me," he joked.

She gave him half a smile. "If the shoe fits," she said and shrugged innocently.

"How does it help, then?" he asked.

"You really want to know?" Sandling asked.

He nodded. "Try me," he said. "Give me an example."

She was dubious. She'd never had anyone take the idea of profiling seriously. When they did—more often than not—they found it threatening to their procedural and forensic way of working. Everything in the world was expected to be pragmatic, formulaic, and process-driven. Especially in the FBI. It was the nature of bureaucracy. However, behavioral analysis required a certain amount of morbid creativity and a sick enough imagination to make it useful.

"An example?" she asked. "As in, off the top of my head?"

"Sure."

"Okay," she thought about it and checked over his shoulder to see if the staff or customers were within earshot. There was no one else in the place. "Going off the top of my head, I'd say our unsub is a white male. Undoubtedly under thirty-five, but probably somewhere between twenty-four and twenty-eight. If you saw him, you'd see a person who looked like they had scurvy."

"Scurvy?" Benson asked and smiled.

"You know, like malnourished."

"Yeah, but *scurvy*! Who has scurvy?"

"Hey," she said, "I knew a boy in high school who only ate ketchup on white bread and got scurvy."

"Jeez, I thought that was only sailors in the seventeen-hundreds."

"It was, and this one boy at my high school."

They smiled at one another and he waved his fork like a conductor and said, "Go on, continue."

"Hell, I don't know. If you went to his home, it would be like a rental abandoned in a hurry. The other thing is, maybe an obvious one, he has at least one mental illness. It's severe. He may have been treated for it in the past."

"We know he uses drugs," Benson said.

"I was thinking the same," Sandling said. "Why he uses

them, it's hard to say exactly, but he's probably on amphetamines—"

"Wouldn't he have taken the Tina with him then?"

"Good point," she said and looked down, thinking.

"Hold on ..." Benson said. "You got all that from one walk through the crime scene?"

"There's more," she said.

"Sorry—go ahead."

"You knocked me off my stride," she said, glanced up at him, and felt self-conscious.

"No, it's great. I'm sorry. Please, keep going."

She'd been thinking about the guy with scurvy from her high school. "It's obvious, but I'd say he's a loner. You know, that weird guy at school that nobody talks to. Doesn't associate with anybody, maybe only his parents—if he has any. But he spends a lot of time by himself."

"Homeless?"

"No. He has a home. I'd guess he's even employed, or, if not, he probably gets some sort of disability cheque. I'd say if he has a job, it's blue-collar. Garbage man, something like that ..."

She sat and looked at him. He was staring at her and finishing his mouthful of his cream. She could tell he was trying to choose his words.

"Hell, I'm impressed, Agent Sandling."

"Give me a break!"

"That sounds pretty precise."

"It's pretty general," Sandling said and shrugged. "I have my reasons," she said. "But we've reviewed enough cases to know that this is a sexual homicide."

"Sexual homicide?" Benson said. "We haven't seen an autopsy yet. There's no evidence that he's committed a sex act."

"It's not *only* defined as a sexual homicide if he jerked off at the crime scene ... It's because of the way the crime is linked to his fantasies. As deranged and obscure and *crazy* as they might be - it's all to do with the state of his mental world, not the physical one. That's why we use psychology to catch them," she said, raising her eyebrows. "And why he has to keep killing."

"Why?"

"Because the physical world can never be as rich and perfect as his fantasy. His performance is never as clean or precise. He has to try again to turn his fantasy into a reality."

"Hmm," Benson said. "Sounds pretty la-di-da to me."

"La-di-da?"

"Yeah, you know, a bit complicated."

"Esoteric?"

"Sure."

"It is a little bit."

She had to give it to him, it was. Didn't mean it wasn't real, though, or that it didn't work. They'd proved it did.

"Why do you say he's white?" Benson asked.

"We know most of this kind of violence committed by males - and they don't usually cross racial lines. It's white on white and black on black. Serial killers don't generally stray outside of their own race."

"Serial killers, huh?"

"Yeah," she said, saying it out loud for the first time. "If I'm right, that's what this is."

"If you're right?"

"Sure."

"So it might not be."

She gave a little shrug again. There was the possibility, she could acknowledge, but in her mind, it was a certainty. The problem was that the FBI didn't deal in certainties; it dealt in probabilities. Of this, though, she was certain.

"Interesting," Benson said. He was thinking. "Okay, so

now you've told me all this; what are we supposed to do with that information? Stop people in the street who look too skinny?"

"No, think about it, okay? Even just knowing his age, race, and complexion means you can eliminate big segments of the population. That wasn't a white residential area but the victim was white, which means that maybe he would have stood out. Maybe somebody saw him and your cop buddies should be canvassing the bystanders in the area ... It *narrows* down the suspect pool."

"Okay," Benson said, more convinced. He pushed his plate away from himself. "What else can you tell?"

Sandling used her fork to twirl through a dollop of whipped cream on her plate and thought about it. She could go into making the distinction between killers who were logical and prepared and those who were messy and random for him. The organized versus disorganized spectrum. She knew from looking at that crime scene that this was not an organized killer. It was not someone who stalked their victims, acted methodically, and followed a process to avoid leaving clues and getting caught. But there were inconsistencies in her thinking.

"I think he's disorganized, but I'm also confused."

"How come?"

"The pimp ..."

"What about him?"

Profiling textbooks suggest this is someone extremely disorganized with a full-blown and serious mental illness. They've likely become more unstable over a long period. Someone who'd ripped up the body of the victim in such a savage way that he'd probably been ill for a decade or more. That's what it took to develop the depth of psychosis that would result in this senseless, violent murder. That's what Sandling knew.

"It implies planning," Sandling said. "Like he knew which pimp to target. He knew how to neutralize her protection."

She stared into the distance, lost in thought again.

"Come on," Benson said. "Let's get the bill. I need to get back to see the kids." He stood up and looked down at her. "And the wife." He took his wallet out of his pants and looked into it. He pulled out a note, put it on the table, and glanced at Sandling again. "Or, maybe not so much. She doesn't exactly care for me at the moment."

"In what way?"

"My presence."

"I need to get back to Virginia," Sandling said. "There's some stuff I need to follow up on."

"You're gonna miss the autopsy?"

"When are you going to see her?"

"The victim? Tomorrow, hopefully, maybe the day after."

Sandling moved her mouth from side to side as she thought. "Maybe I can go back to Manassas after that …"

"Attagirl," Benson said. "Come on, let's get out of here."

5

Rachel Fox had a problem, and she didn't like problems. Problems made her uneasy. She had a low tolerance for uncertainty, which made her anxious. When she was anxious she chewed the inside of her cheek. She didn't like the taste of blood. Sometimes, she chewed it raw and got that metallic tang on her tongue. She had her over-ear headphones on while listening to heavy psychedelic trance music. If anyone else was in the office they'd have heard a tinny thumping bass coming from her headphones. She glanced over her shoulder like she expected to see someone. It was still empty and dark. The only light on was the glare from her computer screen.

"Shit," she said to herself and checked her watch. 3 A.M. She wondered if her grandmother was okay, whether she'd had something to eat, and whether she was worried about her. She'd just worked sixteen hours again. The program she'd built to analyze crime scene photographs was almost finished.

Fox had been helping Sandling with a new case. Something was happening up in Maryland, and Deputy Gibson had asked Sandling to consult on the case. They'd asked for her by name because of the publicity she'd received after the Skinwalker case.

Fox was busy reanalyzing evidence to find anything that might have been missed. Her mind drifted as she thought of Special Agent Sandling. Fox was keen to follow in Sandling's footsteps. She always felt a warm glow of admiration in the pit of her stomach when Special Agent Sandling walked into the room. She seemed to have so much elegance and grace. She seemed so poised. This was everything Fox felt she wasn't. Knew she wasn't. She wasn't good with people.

The Federal Bureau of Investigation logo melted away on the computer screen, and she pulled herself towards her desk. She started to flick through the crime scene photos her program had analyzed, looking for any anomalies. She'd noticed during her time at the FBI that the local forensics teams at crime scenes rarely took pictures under UV black light. So instead of going through the bureaucratic process of trying to create a memorandum, circulate it, and get traction with middle and upper management—she designed a program. It could manipulate the digital images they received in the FBI database and convert them to something that used an algorithm to highlight the places where ultraviolet or infrared lights should be used. It was a way to show her superiors where they could revisit the crime scenes to gather evidence or as justification for sending forensic techs back to the scene with UV camera equipment. She called it CrimeSight.

Instead of being seen as something potentially useful—or revolutionary—when her previous boss found out she'd spent her time building this software program, she was reprimanded for wasting agency resources and not "doing her job," as they said. Something she still resented. She found it hard to look at the pictures. She was biting her cheek again.

Last Thursday, Annapolis residents woke up to the news of a triple homicide. Truly horrifying murders. At 6 A.M., a neighbor discovered three bodies in a beautiful white-painted suburban family home. The deceased included Evelyn Monmouth, she was thirty-five. Her ten-year-old son, Derek, and a man named Robert F. Rimsby, who was forty-seven. He was believed to be a family friend. Their relationship status was unclear. Monmouth's seven-year-old nephew, James Parsons, was also missing.

He was assumed to have been abducted by the killer. All of the dead had been stabbed to death. As Fox could see from the pictures, Evelyn was the primary target of this insanity. She was badly slashed up. It looked like whoever did this had done it in a rage. The killer had then escaped in Mr. Rimsby's maroon station wagon, which was found abandoned in a ditch not far from where the crime scene was. Local detectives could find no clear motive for the crime. Nothing had been taken. Evelyn Monmouth was a separated mother of two; her other child lived with her husband and survived. For Fox, these were some of the most grotesque and senseless images she'd ever seen. She was used to trawling the dark web late at night where anything and everything goes - nothing came close to what she was looking at. She took a stick of strawberry gum from a little silver wrapper and popped it in her mouth. She chewed loudly with her mouth open and shook the cobwebs out of her head. She felt disgusted. And she felt angry. Angry that somebody had made it so she was now forced to look at these pictures. She'd been over the police report more than once, but now she was looking at Evelyn Monmouth's body.

She was found naked on the side of a bed, her body covered in stab wounds. Two large crossing cuts on her abdomen left loops of intestines partially protruding. The lab report showed that her internal vital organs had been hacked and stabbed. There were dozens of stab wounds all over her body, including vicious cuts to her face and her anus. Fox wished she hadn't read the forensic report. But she had, and so she knew that the rectal swab showed the presence of a large amount of semen. At least when they caught him, he'd be easy to identify, she thought grimly.

Finally, the FBI logo on her screen dissolved, and the CrimeSight window popped up, letting her know the program had finished analyzing the pictures. Since she'd been sequestered to Sofa Squad, she'd started using CrimeSight differently. Instead of showing places where UV photographs should be sent, CrimeSight was analyzing visible stains, patterns, and blood spatter in non-UV crime scene photographs. The benefit was that instead of a human combing through hundreds, even thousands, of images, the machine could do it—faster and more thoroughly than a dedicated team of people could. That's why she loved machines—she understood them. They were precise, ordered, and reliable. They didn't complain. She didn't understand people. Her social awkwardness had driven her to develop CrimeSight ... it meant she didn't have to rely on a team of slow, emotional humans who did and said things that she couldn't begin to fathom.

Fox checked over her shoulder almost expecting someone to be in the dark but no one was there. She was still alone in the office listening to loud trance music through her headphones and chewing strawberry-flavored gum. She looked at the computer screen and clicked her mouse on CrimeSight to review the annotated images her software program had highlighted for further investigation. As she scrolled, she stopped at a picture of the mattress in the master bedroom where Evelyn Monmouth had died so horrifically. She gasped when she saw it and swallowed her gum. She kept chewing her cheek and tasted a little blood. She gagged, unsure what to do next. She checked her watch. Her boss, Gust Carver, was usually nice enough to her. Last week he'd taken her aside to have a little chat—as he called it—about when it was appropriate to call him outside of office hours. She'd stood there silently and awkwardly listening to him explain that 3 A.M. on his personal number wasn't appreciated. She was allowed to call if it was important enough, he'd told her. This was important. Usually, when she called, he was awake. Sometimes, he didn't even seem to mind. They would talk a little. Neither of them was very good with people, she felt. She needed to get back to her grandmother. It was a sudden feeling she had. She wanted to check that she was safe. All of this murder and mayhem made her emotional and drained. She felt tired. She used her forearm to sweep everything off her desk and into her black backpack. She locked her computer. Shoved another stick of gum in her mouth and left the office. She took a deep breath, dialed Carver's number, and descended the stairs two at a time.

"Hello?" Carver's groggy voice answered.

"Morning, Special Agent Carver. It's—"

"What time is it?"

She hesitated. "It's three fifty-three, sir."

"Rachel," Carver said. "Please, just call me Carver. Or Gust. Hell, I'd even settle for chief or boss."

"Of course, Special Agent Carver."

"No ... I mean can you just call me ... Oh, it's not important." He sighed.

"Have I done something wrong again?"

"No, it's not you. You're fine. It's me. Forget it."

"How can I forget something that's just happened?"

Carver was silent. Fox pushed her way out of the

building and onto the car park. There was dead air on the line. "Could I tell you what we've found, please, sir?"

"How can I help?"

"I need to talk to you about something I—something CrimeSight found—about the slaying in Annapolis."

"Oh, that. That's Caitlin's case," Carver said.

"Yes, sir."

"Why're you calling me about it?"

"I'm helping her with it."

Carver was quiet. She felt the tension but wasn't sure what it was about. That creeping uncertainty she felt. She couldn't try and decipher it—she didn't have the people skills—and she couldn't blurt it out to ask him directly. So she just stewed in it. Was it about her dedicating time to helping Sandling with a case that wasn't part of Sofa Squad? Or was it something else, like the bad blood everyone was getting covered in because of the tension between Carver and Sandling after the Taxidermy Killer case? She didn't know.

"I'm not sure I can get involved," Carver said. "Could you talk to Special Agent Sandling about it?"

"Caitlin?"

"Yes," Carver said. "That's what I meant."

Fox stood next to her motorcycle and put the key in the ignition. She waited for Carver to speak.

"What's it about?" Carver asked.

"There's a pattern on the victim's mattress. It seems intentional."

"Call Sandling," Carver said.

"Okay," Fox said and hung up.

As the line went dead, Fox stared at her phone, fighting the familiar sting of disappointment. Carver had been polite, sure. He always was. But there was a distance in his tone, a coolness she couldn't quite bridge. It was the same with everyone. Colleagues, superiors, even people like Sandling, who at least seemed to tolerate her. They didn't see her, not really. They saw her algorithms, her data models, and the stuff that made her useful. But when it came to actual interaction, she always felt like an outsider looking in, like she spoke a language no one else cared to learn. Maybe why she preferred working alone in the dark, poring over crime scene photos and numbers. At least there, things made sense. People, though ... People were messy and unpredictable. They never quite added up the way they should.

She put on her motorcycle helmet and swung her leg over the seat. She started the bike, rested her sternum on the fuel tank, and sped away from the Grant Avenue offices.

6
___

CAITLIN SANDLING SHUT her motel room door and kept her hand on the knob and rested her forehead against the wood. She closed her eyes. She felt drained. She felt exhausted. She felt like she could sleep for a week, but she knew that wasn't going to happen. Probably wasn't even worth resting for the few hours she had to herself. Detective Benson had just dropped her off. They were going to meet the coroner to attend the autopsy later that day. So she would sit and brood and ruminate on what she'd seen. She knew she would. There was no way to avoid it. She turned around and rested her shoulders and the back of her head against the door. Her eyes were still closed, and she saw strobe-like flashes of the mutilated bodies in her mind's eye. Stab wounds. Bite marks. Viciously torn skin.

She opened them and reached for the light switch on the wall. The brown and orange motel room lit up in a soft yellow light. It had distinctly 1970s-style decor, and she dreaded thinking about the dust lurking in the fabric.

"How are you doing? Did you miss me?" she asked Mr. Bam-Bam, her worn, torn, and beaten-up teddy bear that she kept with her. It was the last childhood present her dad had given her. She knew it was childish, but she couldn't bear to part with it. It would be like cutting off her arm if she removed a piece of her memory of her dad. Besides, Mr. Bam-Bam was better company than any man she'd ever known. He never left. He always listened. He was always there. Anyway, he was a good substitute for her cat, Minx, for now.

She took a hot shower and washed the stench from the crime scene from her hair. She picked up a heavy cardboard box from the nightstand and dropped it on the bed. She sat down next to it wearing an oversized white T-shirt that said 'Happiness' in sunshine yellow on the front and wrapped her wet hair in a twirled towel so she looked like a soft serve ice cream. She took the lid off the box. Her job was to try to find something—anything—that would link the crime scenes and the unknown suspect. She'd only known Detective Michael Benson of the Baltimore Police Department for a few days. She considered him easygoing to a fault but a good cop. Even he was skeptical about whether it was the same suspect. People like to think in boxes that all serial killers follow a pattern. That wasn't true. What was true was that different mental illnesses manifested differently in each killer. Some were precise and methodical. Calm in the face of authority. An ability to plan and execute their plans. Killers like Zimmer and Derange. Others, like her unsub, were haphazard. Seemingly did not care if they were caught or not. They probably didn't think they were doing anything wrong and didn't care if they made a mess or left traces of themselves. Each was just as difficult to catch as the other for different reasons. Her job now was to prove to Benson that it was the same man. If she could do that, he could help her convince his skeptical colleagues. The people who would decide on the best strategy for getting this guy before he roughly butchered any more innocent civilians.

Just then, her cell phone rang. She checked her watch and answered it.

"Special Agent Sandling, this is Rachel Fox from the Manassas resident agency office."

"Yes, Rachel. Hi—"

"May I speak with you about something urgent about your case?"

"Sure," Sandling said. "Is everything all right, Rachel? It's four in the morning."

Fox paused and said quietly, "Is this not a convenient time?"

"No, it's fine. I'm up. I was just at another crime scene connected to the case—"

"He struck again."

"I think so ..."

"You can't tell for certain?"

"It's the same MO, but the detectives out here are dubious."

"Check under the mattress," Fox said urgently.

"Excuse me?"

"Check under the mattress," she said again, frustrated.

"Okay. What am I telling them to look for?"

"It looks like a drawing," Fox said. She sounded uncertain. "I need to show it to you. He's burned something—used some sort of chemical to burn something—into the mattress. Like a marking—"

"You're sure?" Fox was silent, and Sandling realized it was a redundant question. Rachel Fox didn't make mistakes. She didn't guess. She didn't suppose. She used statistics and probability in her judgments. She was mathematically precise in her reasoning. "Forget it, Rachel, I believe you. It's just an expression."

"Why does everyone keep telling me to forget something they've just talked about? It's impossible. How do you do it?"

Sandling heard the tightness in Fox's voice, the slight quiver at the edge of her question. Fox was always like this —bluntly straightforward—but there was something else, too. An intensity that bordered on discomfort. She could almost see Fox's mind working. Overanalyzing everything, dissecting words and meanings in a way that didn't come naturally to her. The pause stretched, and Sandling realized Fox wasn't just asking a simple question. She was genuinely puzzled, maybe even frustrated, by something that seemed obvious to everyone else.

"Who else told you to forget it?"

"Special Agent Carver."

"You spoke to Gust about it?"

"Special Agent Carver, yes."

"Why him?"

"He's in charge."

"Yeah, but it's my case. *Our* case. Remember?"

"How could I forget?"

"Indeed," Sandling said.

"You sound irritated, Special Agent Sandling. Are you?"

"No, Rachel, I'm not annoyed, or at least—it's not you. It's me and Gust, you know ..."

"No."

Sandling was fingering a loose thread on the brown floral bedding with her fingernail.

"Rachel?"

"Yes?"

"When will you be able to send the photograph of the burn mark over?"

"First thing this morning," Fox said.

"Thanks, you're a star. We're seeing the autopsy this afternoon. It would be great to have it before then."

"Okay," Fox said, and the line went dead.

"Hello? Foxy?" Sandling said and then looked at the

phone. "Bitch hung up on me," she said to Mr. Bam-Bam. She shook her head, smiled, and called Benson. It went to voicemail.

"Hey, Mike. It's Cate, sorry to call ... um, yeah, anyway. I just got off with one of my colleagues in Virginia. Do you think the crime lab techs are still at the scene? We need pictures of the bed. The killer might have left a mark on the underside of the mattress. Anyway, call me when you get this."

She tossed her phone against the pillows and put the lid back on the box of case files. If Fox was right, she would have to trawl through gruesome victim photographs looking for similarities in barbarity. Maybe it would have her reliving the images of the dead in her head.

Her eyes started to feel heavy. She climbed under the covers and propped Mr. Bam-Bam next to her. She stroked his head and felt the familiar threads and indentations. Her mind drifted. She didn't want to end up an insomniac like Carver. Nearly everyone she knew who worked serial homicides fell victim to severe situational stress. Sandling had started seeing a therapist after she'd shot Derange because the post-traumatic stress was giving her nightmares. She'd had a fast and unexplained loss of weight, and she wasn't heavy to begin with. She'd had all the tests. There was nothing physically wrong with her that they could find. She knew people who'd gotten bleeding ulcers and suffered attacks of anxiety so severe they thought they were having heart attacks. Zimmer once told her that killing—as a vocation—was hard work. She was starting to see that catching killers was just as hard—if not harder—work to endure than carrying out the bloody murders.

It wouldn't be forever, though, she told herself. "Right, Bam-Bam?" she said out loud to the teddy bear. "It won't be forever. Just 'til we push hard enough to get out of Grant

Avenue and back to the big show." But time was slipping through her fingers, and every minute that passed felt like another chance wasted. She could feel the weight of it pressing down on her. The latest victim was just another notch in the killer's belt, but how many more would there be? If they didn't find him soon, there would be more bodies, more blood, and doubts about her ability. Derange had easily slipped through the cracks before she caught up with him. She couldn't let that happen again. Not this time. If she failed, it wasn't just another statistic. It was someone's life, but it was also hers. The thought gave her anxiety and made her breath catch in her throat. Her lingering fear of her own incompetence haunted her.

She was still unsure of herself, lacking confidence, but she knew she wanted to prove herself to Gibson and, deep down, probably to Carver. Maybe to herself, too. She could do it. She could be an effective field agent. She could help other people like her who'd lost loved ones to the insanity stalking the streets. She could keep others safe, but when she closed her eyes, she saw shapes and figures. The gray-blue three-dimensional heads and faces of victims hovered in her mind like some kind of Big Brother figure on a screen. It was no use. She couldn't sleep. She threw the covers off with a sigh and got up.

"Right," she said. "If Benson isn't going to return my call, I'll go back to the crime scene myself."

7

SANDLING WAS KNEELING next to the bed where the prostitute had died. She held a UV flashlight between her teeth as she tried to lift the heavy mattress. It was completely dark in the apartment except for the streetlights and neon signage shining through the window. The crime scene investigators had long since cleared the scene, removing the body from the bathroom.

They also seemed to have taken all of the other evidence, including the plastic ice cream containers filled with human blood and the pieces of flesh they'd found in the microwave. She did not doubt that this insanity had tasted a bit of his victim's flesh.

She heard a noise and quickly glanced over her shoulder. She was looking down the narrow corridor leading to the front door of the walk-up apartment. There was nobody there. But the combination of kneeling, trying to move the mattress, and her deep-seated fear of the dark heightened her nerves. Knowing that serial killers often returned to the crime scene didn't help. They wanted to relive the experience and reimagine a fantasy. It kept her on hyper-alert and the tall coffee she'd sunk on her way over. She was buzzing.

She'd gained access with keys, checked out from the duty sergeant on her way over to the scene, and ducked under the yellow police tape that the local PD had left in place. She realized she hadn't locked the door. She hadn't planned to stay long, but the thought crossed her mind that she should lock it while she was alone in the killer's fresh kill site. The light was turning from dark blue to grey outside the windows and she could hear the faint sounds of the city starting to come to life. There were even birds chirping in the distance as the sun rose. She wanted to hurry before the rising sun made it too light for the black light to be effective on the stains at the scene.

Sandling put her sweaty, blue nitrile-covered hand on the mattress and pulled herself up from her knees. She was struggling to get a grip on the ground. She stood up and tried to remember her health and safety training about keeping her back straight and her knees bent for lifting heavy objects. She wedged her fingers underneath the heavy spring mattress. She squeezed her core, drove her heels into the ground, and grunted. She hoped she wouldn't let one slip as she pushed the mattress toward the ceiling.

"Come on!" she muttered, flashlight still clamped in her teeth. The mattress bowed in the middle and started to lift, and she bent her head to see under it. She angled the UV light with her jaw to see if she could see the markings that Foxy had found at the first crime scene. Just as she thought she could catch a glimpse of something, she heard a scrape of a boot and a tapping sound behind her. Someone said something that sounded like, "Hey! What're you doing here?"

She dropped the flashlight from her mouth and the mattress from her hands. In one movement, she spun toward the door, pulling her .38-caliber revolver from her hip holster as she did. There was a tall, heavily built figure in the corridor. The silhouette raised its hands as she yelled, "FBI! Freeze! Down on the ground!"

"Hang on, Caitlin. Whoa, there, it's me! It's Benson. Calm down."

Sandling was breathing heavily, blood whooshing in her ears, and her heart racing in her chest. She raised the muzzle to the ceiling and said, "Michael! It's you, thank God, you scared the bejesus out of me. What the hell are you doing here?"

"Hey, hey! You called me, remember? You left me that voicemail. I went to find you and the duty sergeant told me you checked the keys out, so I came to see if I could help. You weren't answering your phone."

She touched her jeans pocket and realized that her phone was on silent. "God, sorry, I nearly shot you."

"Yeah, I'm aware. What, did you think I was the perp returning to the scene of the crime?" He flashed her a grin.

An odd thing to say, she thought, as she holstered her weapon. "Of course, I did ... that's what they do."

"What the hell are you doing here alone then?" Benson asked.

Benson rubbed the back of his neck, his easygoing demeanor faltering for a second. He hadn't told her much about his personal life, but it was hard to miss the signs—the way his phone stayed on silent mode, the way he kept glancing at it like he was waiting for a call that never came. He always showed up for work and always did what was needed, but there was something else behind the grin, something darker. Maybe that's why he was here now, at this ungodly hour, standing in the middle of a crime scene when he should have been at home with his kids. Maybe he needed this case more than he'd admit.

She glanced over her shoulder at the light gray outside the window.

"Come here," she said, "We're running out of darkness. Help me lift this. I need to check under the mattress for a marking."

8

Augustine Carver walked into Charles Village Pub on St Paul Street in Baltimore. It was one of those long, wooden, low-ceiling joints. Brightly lit game machines to his left. Rows of booths ran to the back. An array of bottles behind the bar. Television with baseball and the volume turned down. The heavyset bartender glanced at Carver as he entered. One of the regulars, a thick guy in a faded ball cap, took a swig of his warm-looking beer and followed the bartender's gaze.

Carver was looking for an old partner of Elizabeth Webb. A man called Barney Brexler. He was the heavy-set guy in the oversized suit sipping on his pale ale at the far end of the bar. Carver could see his cheeks were red and his face pockmarked. Brexler was built like a cartoon bull—powerful and squat. He walked up and pulled out the bar stool next to him. Brexler looked slowly up at him. His eyes narrowed in recognition. They were watery, hidden under bushy eyebrows, and deeply inset into his face.

"Hey, Bull," Carver said. "It's Augustine Carver, you remember me? Mind if I sit down?"

Brexler looked straight ahead and said, "No," out the

corner of his mouth. He was bristly, his manner like course grit sandpaper.

"As in, no, you don't remember me or don't mind if I sit down."

"Both," Brexler said, more grunt than an actual word.

Carver sat down, hanging his arm casually off the back of the chair, and looked at this fading detective. His top button was undone, and his tie dragged roughly to the side. He looked like he was in here for the night, for a proper session, but that's probably every night, knowing Brexler, Carver thought.

"We, ah, ran into each other a while ago when I was an undercover narco."

Brexler glanced at him again and gave a shake of his head.

"I know you?"

"Not anymore, I guess; it was a long time ago. We were both young men."

"Tell me about it."

The bartender wandered over. "Get you something?"

"Uh, give me a tonic water," Carver said. Brexler took a big swig of his beer and shook the glass. "And another pale ale for Mr. Brexler, please."

"You got it," the bartender said.

Brexler watched the ball game and Carver helped himself to a handful of peanuts from the counter.

"You gotta be crazy eating peanuts off the bar, don't you, Rob?" Brexler said to the bartender as he brought the drinks over.

"Why's that?" the big bartender asked.

"Think about it," Brexler said. "Guy goes to take a leak, gets piss on his hand, doesn't rinse it under the tap. Comes back to the bar and fishes around in the peanut bowl the

43

same hand he's just pissed on. Now you go eat the peanuts and you get this guy's piss in your mouth. Am I right?"

The bartender shrugged. "Maybe," he said and moved away. bartender didn't want to be around Brexler any longer than he had to, Carver thought.

"Enjoying the peanuts?" Brexler asked Carver. His eyes were like slits. Carver could tell he was in a foul mood.

"What's the matter," Carver said. "You don't wash your hands after you take a leak?"

"What do you want?" Brexler asked, picking up his new beer and taking a long, slow pull.

"You knew Elizabeth Webb, right?"

Brexler swallowed, his voice straining against the cold ale, "Yeah, what about it?"

Carver leaned back and looked over Brexler's shoulders. "Mind if we grab a booth? Something I gotta ask you."

"Suit yourself," Brexler said and sighed as he got up. He followed Carver to a booth in the back and set his glass down before heaving himself onto the bench.

"Okay," Brexler said. "You bought me a drink. You got my attention. 'Til I finish it anyway. What's it about? And hurry it up. You're cutting into my drinking time."

"Elizabeth Webb had a sister, Jessica—"

"Has," Brexler said. "Just 'cause she's dead doesn't mean they ain't sisters anymore."

"Fair enough," Carver said. "Do you know her? Did Elizabeth ever mention her to you?"

Brexler belched quietly and said, "Maybe, so what?"

"I'm helping Jessica out."

"With?"

"Nothing certain yet. Just trying to get a lay of the land here. I was hoping to talk to you about Elizabeth a little."

"First of all, stop calling her Elizabeth. You got me? People called her Webb or Webster or Liza sometimes ...

Second, you told me your name, but you haven't told me who you are."

Carver gave him half a smile. "You're right, Bull. It's been a long time. Listen, uh, I owe Jessica—Spider—a favor, all right? That's all I'm doing here right now. Trying to get a few details."

"You federal?"

Carver nodded slowly and said, "Not here in an official capacity. Just doing a favor for a friend."

"You're friends with her now?"

Carver shrugged.

"She still thinks it was murder?"

Carver stared at Brexler for a moment. He'd come right out with it. "Why, do you?"

Brexler took another gulp of his beer, put his glass down, wiped his hand along the back of his mouth, and said, "I'm done thinking about that. I'm done searching for 'what ifs' and 'maybes,' all right?"

"Bull, that glass in your hand tells me maybe you aren't done with the questions but that you're trying to forget them." Brexler didn't reply. "Believe me, I know," Carver said. "I've been there. That's why I drink tonic water now. You get me?"

"Yeah, I got you."

"Why'd you say murder?"

"That's what Jessica has you out here looking for, isn't it? *Murder*."

Carver didn't know what he was looking for right now. He just wanted to get a better feel for Detective Elizabeth Webb as a person from the people who spent the most time with her before she died. After Jessica visited him on his yacht, he'd spent a few days thinking about what she'd said. Initially, his gut told him not to get involved, especially since Jessica had connived to determine—illegally—who her sister donated her organs to. One thing was clear to Carver, though: Jessica Webb wasn't about to let this drop. She phoned him a couple more times in the days after her visit, and eventually, Carver went to see her at her apartment.

She called it her apartment, but when he went in, it looked a lot more like a corporate filing facility. Piles of bankers' boxes were stacked against the walls, and a huge corkboard with images, clippings, and papers were stuck to it with brass pins.

She had very little furniture and what she did have looked like it came from garage sales or stuff she'd found in the alley behind her apartment building. To say that she was obsessed was an understatement about the time, energy, and effort she continued to plow into getting to the bottom of her twin sister's death.

Jessica Webb had meticulously taken Carver step by step through what she'd gathered about her sister. Cases she was working, people she'd spoken to, relationships she had within the department, outside of the department, the lot. She had plenty of information and it seemed compelling. Especially when presented by somebody as enthusiastic and as committed as Webb. Carver felt like there were still holes in the theory, though. Maybe something was missing in her logic, perhaps clouded by her passion. That didn't mean she was wrong. It just meant that Carver had to be careful about taking what she presented at face value. He felt he needed to get closer to the source, and that's why he found himself in this stale-beer-smelling, Irish-rock-playing, lonely-old-man bar in central Baltimore.

"Do you think she was murdered?" Carver asked.

Brexler held his gaze with his bloodshot, watery eyes. His bottom lip hung open. Then he shrugged and said, "I used to."

"Why?" Carver asked. "What changed?"

"Something I found out after ..."

"After what?"

"After I started looking into it."

Carver leaned forward. "What did you find?"

"Something about her father." Carver silently watched Brexler, waiting for him to continue. "What are you really after?" Brexler asked him.

"Anything to do with Liza's case file you might still have."

"We'd have to go back to the office for that," Brexler said.

Carver sat upright. "You mean you still have her files?"

"Boxes of the stuff," Brexler said. "Boxes full. How do you expect me to throw that away, huh?"

9

"How long were you partners for?" Carver asked Brexler as he followed him through the quiet Baltimore Police Station Headquarters.

It was already late evening, and most of the daytime staff had headed home. There were just a few of the night crew around. Uniformed officers hanging about with coffee mugs, chatting in hallways. They eyed Carver up as they saw him and gave Brexler a courteous nod as the pair passed by.

Carver heard them saying, 'What the hell is Brexler doing here this late?' and 'bars must have closed early' and laughing - when they thought they were out of earshot. Brexler didn't react. He held one of the doors open for Carver to enter and said, "About two and a half years."

"How was your relationship?" Carver asked as he entered Brexler's office. He turned to look at the weathered homicide detective and saw him shrug. He sensed Brexler wasn't comfortable dredging up old memories of Elizabeth.

His voice cracked as he said, "We were like family. She was a younger sister to me. I mean, we spent every day together ..." he stopped speaking. Carver got the message.

Brexler had one of those long and wide metal desks. It

sat in the corner of the room. He went behind, pulled his desk chair away, and got onto his knees.

"You keep those files under your desk?" Carver asked as Brexler grunted and pulled the reinforced cardboard boxes from under. Perhaps Carver had misunderstood the relationship or the effect that Elizabeth's death had had on her partner. She'd died over two years ago, so why was this guy keeping her boxes of files under his desk?

Brexler lifted them with a huff and dropped them on the desk, one after the other. There were two. They looked heavy and full. Brexler took the lid off, and Carver moved closer to look inside. Although it looked haphazard, they were filled with papers, files, and photographs.

Brexler put his hands inside one of the boxes, on either side of the documents, and lifted them.

"This is all I got," Brexler said, dropping it on the desk. "There's all sorts in here. All of the stuff Detective Webb was working on."

"I was expecting you to take me to the evidence room," Carver said. "Why have you got all this stuff under your desk, Bull?"

"Evidence? This isn't evidence, Carver. This is what Webb was working on when she died. This is all the stuff I collected that I thought might help in piecing together what happened or at least understanding her state of mind. Anything ..." Brexler looked at Carver with sincerity on his face. "I lost months to this. I was reprimanded. My caseload fell off a cliff. I was so focused on this stuff."

"So what's in here? What did you find?"

"I don't know. There's a diary. She was supposed to meet somebody the night she died. It's all in there, annotated."

He held up a hard-covered ledger with colorful posted notes along the side and held it out to show Carver his work.

He'd been through and cataloged and categorized everything.

"You sure put a lot of time into this, Bull," Carver said and saw Brexler swallow and give him a hard look with his wet, pinkish eyes staring directly into his. "It was hard going back then, Carver. I don't know if you know what it's like losing somebody close. I'm sure you do. Being in this game for as long as you and I have."

Carver shrugged. He knew. Of course, he knew.

"I guess I was in shock—disbelief—back then," Brexler said. "Maybe I still am." He said it more to himself. A moment of quiet self-reflection. "It was just such a shock, you know. She was so full of life. She loved the job. We were working on cases. Nothing about her behavior or how she acted suggested that she was on the brink of taking her own life. It took me a while to come to terms with that. That's why it's not in the evidence room. This wasn't treated as suspicious. My gut told me back then that something was wrong, but, you know, I'm not ashamed to say I saw a therapist - and everybody I spoke to said that maybe I was just too close to it, right? I couldn't see the wood for the trees. Maybe I didn't know her as well as I thought." Brexler paused, thinking. "And, yeah, that's it, I guess."

"Mind if I take these with me?" Carver asked, gesturing towards the boxes.

Brexler kept looking at Carver, then down at the boxes. He swallowed and cleared his throat.

He harrumphed. Something was sadly amusing to him. "You know it's kind of lame to be so personally attached to a box of papers, but strangely, this is all I've got left of her ..." Brexler said. "There's even some personal items of hers still in there. Things that were collected from the car where they found her. I didn't know what to do with most of it. I couldn't bear to part with it. You should probably take it and see what you can do with it and, when you're done, give it to her family," Brexler said and looked back at Carver.

"Back at the bar, you said that you found something, you know, stuff that made you accept that perhaps it was suicide," Carver said. "What was that? What did you find that changed your mind?"

"Oh yeah, that," Brexler said. He reached into the other box, flicked through some papers, and pulled out a thin file. He held it out to Carver.

"What's this?" Carver asked as he took it.

"I didn't know until quite late, but some of the stuff in here was kind of a sideshow that Webb was working on. Again, as I say, I feel a bit dumb now for not realizing sooner. Perhaps because I didn't speak to her about it at all the whole time we were together? Anyway, I found out that her father did it ... you know? Took his own life. He was also a homicide detective, right? Family business, kinda. It turned out Liza was working on a cold case that her father had also been working on.

"What was the case?"

"A spate of disappearances. Young women. They were treated as suspicious. He was sure that there was a serial killer out there, and ultimately, it seemed like it drove him a bit mad—staring down into that abyss. And that's why he took his own life."

"And was there a serial killer?"

Brexler shrugged.

"Right, so you think this had something to do with why Liza took her own life? Like it was a psychological trait in the family?"

Brexler moved his head from side to side. "Not exactly that," Brexler said. "It was more the similarities between the two suicides," he said and cleared his throat. "Have a look in that folder that I just gave you."

Carver opened the faded Manila folder. Inside was a small, cream-colored card that looked like it had been rolled into a straw. Although it was flat now, the edges were still raised, showing where it had been rolled.

"They found that in the car with Liza," Brexler said.

"What is it?" Carver asked.

"It's a line from a Sylvia Plath poem. You know her?"

He did. Plath was a famous American poet who took her own life in her twenties by sticking her head in an oven. She was considered one of those rare geniuses, gone too soon.

"Owl's talons clenching my heart," Carver said.

"Huh?" Brexler grunted.

Carver shook his head. "Doesn't matter. That's how Plath described her depression."

Carver read the printed lines on the card to himself:

AND I A SMILING WOMAN.

I AM ONLY THIRTY. AND LIKE THE CAT I HAVE NINE TIMES TO DIE.

"Hmm," Carver said and looked up at Brexler. "And you say they also found a Plath quote with her father?"

"Not *a* Plath quote," Brexler said. "The *same* Plath quote. Not only that, she typed it on the out on the same old typewriter her father used."

Carver furrowed his brow. "Really? Where's the typewriter now?"

"Fuck knows. Probably at her mother's house along with all of her father's possessions. I visited her, you know, *after* ... Father's office was still the same as the day he died. His widow couldn't get over it, either. Grief is strange, isn't it?" Brexler said.

"And the suicides?" Carver asked.

"They were the same," Brexler said. "Carbon monoxide poisoning in a car. The only difference was her dad used his service revolver right at the end, and she didn't."

10

Sunlight glinted off the electric-blue reflective glass that wrapped around the state's Office of the Chief Medical Examiner building in Baltimore. Sandling squinted and turned her eyes away. She followed Detective Benson through security, showing their badges at reception and down the wide, fluorescent-lit corridors to the basement.

"Cold down here," she said and shivered. It smelled sanitary. Formaldehyde and wiped-down bleach.

As they walked down the corridor, a middle-aged man with salt-and-pepper hair, wearing a navy suit and speaking into his cell phone, approached them. "Yeah, I just spoke to him," the man said. As he approached, he nodded and said, "He knows our stance, Scott."

Benson slowed, following the man with his eyes as he passed. He stopped and turned, looking after him as he walked away.

"What is it?" Sandling asked.

Benson pushed his eyebrows together and lifted his index finger in the direction the man went. "That's the mayor of Annapolis. Gary something ..."

"Buckland," Sandling said. Benson raised his eyebrows,

impressed that she knew. "What was the mayor doing here before the investigators?" Sandling asked.

Benson shook his head, "I don't know. Let's go."

He pushed through some double doors into a long, rectangular, white-tiled room with stainless steel fridges. A man in full surgical scrubs stood near one of the fridges holding a clipboard and checked his watch. "You're late, Detective Benson," he said.

"Sorry, Doc," Benson said and lifted his palms. He gave him a mischievous, up-to-no-good grin.

"You'll have to sign in and put on PPE," the man said. "The body is ready for you, so make it snappy."

Benson turned around with a boyish grin and said, "Come on, better get a move on. They have a backlog of about two hundred bodies waiting to be autopsied."

Sandling nodded hello to the medical examiner and followed Benson out the way they'd come. As they pulled on blue surgical scrubs and put on hairnets and facemasks, Benson said, "That's Victor Weeding, chief medical examiner."

"Oh," Sandling said.

"I'll introduce you. Good guy. Serious."

"Okay. Well connected, too," Sandling said. She felt apprehensive.

"What do you mean?"

"It's not every day you get the mayor visiting you at work, is it?"

"Oh, yeah. I wouldn't worry about it. It's a high-profile case, though, right?" Then, "You ready?" Benson asked.

Benson looked a little worried about it, though. He was good at hiding it behind his lighthearted demeanor. They went out of the changing rooms. She hated hospitals. She hated seeing dead bodies. She hated it even more in morgues. It was gruesome and disturbing seeing them at a crime scene but at least they felt natural. The cold, hard sterility of a coroner's office removed all humanity and identity from them. She worked with people and their psyches. The external world gave insights and showed life through their behaviors. Here, they were just slabs of meat without heartbeats. More movie props than humans. Something to be studied. Their past, their hopes, and their dreams didn't matter anymore.

"Wait," she said, putting her hand on Benson's upper arm to stop him. "Don't mention anything about last night."

"Why?"

"Let's see what the medical examiner thinks first."

Benson thought for a second, "Okay," he said. "Let's go."

He scribbled their names in the visitor's book as they passed and went through the same swinging double doors as before.

"This way," Dr. Weeding called, leading them into a low-ceilinged stainless steel room. It was cramped and cold, with extractor fan casings dotted around above and behind them. Sandling could see the shape of the body under a blue plastic sheet.

Dr. Weeding spoke, glancing at the autopsy report in his hands. "It's as bad as they say."

"We saw the body at the scene," Benson said.

"We didn't examine it," Sandling corrected him. Benson looked at her and then at Dr. Weeding.

"This is Special Agent Caitlin Sandling."

Dr. Weeding didn't look up from his notes. "Then you'll know what we're dealing with," he said.

"Same guy?" Benson asked.

"Toxicology came back positive. High levels of methamphetamine and traces of fentanyl. She was heavily under the influence - which impaired her ability to resist."

"She didn't fight back?" Sandling asked.

"There is some evidence of defensive wounds," Weeding said and looked at her for the first time. "Skin under the fingernails. Wounds on her hands and wrists."

Sandling swallowed. Her breathing was shallow. She kept having flashing images of the assault in her mind's eye.

"She still Jane Doe?" Benson asked.

"We have a positive ID on one Alice Waters, also known as Candy Floss - her street name."

"Hooker," Benson said knowingly and looked at Sandling nodding. She rolled her eyes. She caught Dr. Weeding watching her. He looked back at his file.

"Is that what killed her, Doc, the drugs?" Benson asked.

Dr. Weeding furrowed his brow. "No, detective," he said curtly. "The cause of death was not the drugs. She died from exsanguination and shock due to the multiple stab wounds and the ... violent removal of vital organs."

Sandling felt uncomfortable. She glanced at the body covered partially by a blue sheet.

"You wanna see her?" Dr. Weeding asked. Sandling swallowed and gave a slight shake of her head.

"Okay," she said, but the word got stuck in her throat, and she cleared it and said more loudly, "Yes, please, doctor."

She didn't know what she wanted to do, but she felt like she needed to see her. See her to understand her. Understand her to know her. Know her to learn who might want to hurt her. Sandling was taking long, deep breaths.

Doctor Weeding carefully peeled back the sheet. Her skin was a blue and purple hue. She looked like porcelain. Or something the Greeks carved out of marble. She didn't seem real. She wasn't anymore, Sandling thought, just a shell.

"But who were you?" she said.

"Excuse me?" Dr. Weeding said. Benson was looking at her. She realized she'd said it out loud.

"Were there signs of forced sexual assault?" Benson asked. Sandling felt it was his way of saving her embarrassment.

Dr. Weeding glared at Benson, "Sexual assaults by their very nature are forced, Detective Benson."

"I know that Doc; I'm just asking if she was, you know ... like at the previous crime scene."

"I'm not sure I know what you're referring to ..." Dr. Weeding said.

Sandling was staring at Alice Waters' statuesque face and her perfect skin. She looked so at peace, like she was asleep. "A previous victim, Evelyn Monmouth, was sexually assaulted. They found semen in her ..."

"Her what?" Dr. Weeding asked, his tone indicating he wanted them to spell it out

Sandling and Benson glanced at one another. Was he serious? He wanted them to spell it out. Too much time staring at dead bodies all day. It was a cliche but Sandling couldn't get past the idea of the type of people who wanted to do jobs like this. She'd seen her fair share of dead bodies recently, though, too.

"Her anus," Sandling said.

"I wasn't aware of that," Dr. Weeding said.

"Who handled the previous autopsy, Dr. Weeding?"

He checked his notes but said, "I'll have to get back to you."

"Aren't you the chief medical officer?"

He glared at her.

"Do you know the backlog of autopsies we have? You're lucky I was able to amend my diary to lend some weight to your investigation."

"We appreciate it, Doc," Benson said and gave her a look telling her to knock it off.

"It was the Monmouth case. Do you know it? It was in the news. Hard to miss."

"Yes, I'm familiar with it, special agent. I just don't know which of my team carried out the previous physical investigation."

"Okay. But you don't think the two crimes are linked?" Sandling asked him.

"No. Why? Do you?"

Sandling didn't respond. She wasn't expecting that. To her, the signs linking the two murders were striking. How anyone could overlook the similarities between them struck her as suspicious. Dr. Weeding must have seen her expression because he quickly said, "Of course, I'll have to check the medical examination notes from the previous crime to be sure, but in my mind, the victim profile and the nature and method of the attack differ significantly from the victims at the residence. I'll take, for instance, his attempt to at least conceal the evidence by bathing her in chemicals for one thing; the other is that there were no obvious signs of sexual assault, although it's difficult to tell, judging by her profession. I'm sure she might have had some rough johns in her time, and there is some scarring which is indicative of that. Added to that, I would say that overall, this crime is more choreographed and planned."

"Really?" Sandling said, surprised. "You think that that crime scene looks like someone that was organized?"

She could tell Dr. Weeding didn't like her tone, so he stopped talking and stared, burning holes in her.

"What about the blood and containers filled with meat?" Benson asked, emphasizing the word meat.

"Yes, well, those turned out to be from the victim."

"Did they? Hell," Benson said, "I was sure it was going to turn out to be ground beef."

"No, no, certainly not ground meat," Dr. Weeding said. "The perpetrator appears also to have drunk some of the blood, from what I understand from the forensic report."

"Same as at the previous scene." Sandling said, "Tell me, Dr. Weeding if you come across many vampire killers in your time?"

"What exactly you're trying to imply, Special Agent Sandling?"

"I'm not trying to imply anything. I'm just asking you how common you think it is to have two crime scenes that are different perpetrators, both with signs that somebody has consumed human blood?"

"Fairly uncommon, I would think."

"That's what I thought."

"I wasn't aware they'd confirmed he'd *drank* blood at the Monmouth murder scene," Dr. Weeding said.

"They showed he'd collected it and potentially transported it somewhere," Benson said.

"But not drank it?" Weeding asked.

"No," Benson admitted.

Sandling closed her eyes. She was in disbelief. She couldn't understand what she was hearing.

"Hold on," she said and opened her eyes. Dr. Weeding was looking at her. "Is there some sort of agenda here?"

"What do you mean?"

"Are you actively arguing that the case scenes aren't linked?"

"That's the line we've decided to take."

"Who's we?" Sandling asked. Her face turned to one of sudden realization. She snapped her fingers. "Now I get it."

"What is it?" Benson asked.

"The mayor," Sandling said, then looked back at Dr. Weeding. "That's what the mayor was doing here. He was speaking to Scott ..."

"Scott Dixon," Benson said. "Mayor of Baltimore."

Dr. Weeding didn't speak. He swallowed and made a show of flipping the papers over his clipboard.

"No fingerprints or other DNA evidence at this scene, Doctor?" Sandling asked.

"Another reason we're treating this as separate. No fingerprints here. No semen. No sexual assault."

"Lack of evidence isn't evidence of something else, though," Sandling said and scoffed. She was miffed. "You can't prove a negative."

"All right then," Dr. Weeding said. "If it isn't a sign that it's someone else, what is it?"

"Careful, Doc," Benson said out the side of his mouth with a smirk. "She's a brain surgeon, like, legit. She's a doctor of psychology herself."

Dr. Weeding wasn't moved or impressed. He was looking impassively at Sandling. She could sense what he was thinking. This one is going to be a problem. She wondered how deep the rot of corruption went.

She chose her words carefully. "Detective Benson and I appreciate your opinion, but we've got some new information that we haven't been able to share with you yet. We have strong evidence to indicate the same perpetrator."

Dr. Weeding shook his head and scoffed.

"What?" Benson asked.

"What's the evidence?" Dr. Weeding asked.

"We'd prefer not to disclose it at this time," Sandling said.

"I see," Dr. Weeding said. He was not impressed.

Benson covered for her, "Just until we've had it independently verified, Doc, right? We wouldn't want to jump to conclusions."

Sandling glanced at him, and he shrugged.

"Okay, well," Dr. Weeding said, checking the next page of autopsy notes on his clipboard. "There is one other thing about the victim. She had bruising on her left forearm and what looked like an old cigarette burn on her inner wrist. Recent bruises too—consistent with a struggle, but not necessarily from the killer."

"I mean, it kind of goes with the territory," Benson said, looking at Sandling.

"You think the pimp did it?" Sandling asked.

"It's a possibility," Dr. Weeding said with a shrug. "I can tell you these women don't exactly live gentle lives, Agent Sandling. That's why it's never easy with these cases. There's a good chance she argued with her pimp or one of her regulars, or maybe a new John and it got out of hand ..." Sandling furrowed her brow. This was a lot of speculation for a medical examiner. "Maybe one got rougher than she expected," Dr. Weeding added.

Sandling cocked her head to the side, "Would you mind telling me what you and the mayor of Annapolis were discussing earlier?"

Dr. Weeding's face hardened. He was staring her down. Sandling stared right back at him.

"I think what she means is ... is there a lot of political heat on this one?"

Without taking his eyes off hers, Dr. Weeding said, "Detective, I'm required to give you a briefing on the autopsy. Would you like me to continue with the briefing?"

Benson nodded. "Yes," he said.

"It could explain the defensive wounds you were so interested in. For all we know, she was already hurt before she ran into her killer, or it was the same man. Women like her don't tend to make it out clean."

"Women like her?" Sandling repeated, her tone harsh.

Weeding gave her a flat look. "Yes, women like her. Prostitutes, streetwalkers, call them what you will. Their lives are full of risk. If it weren't this killer, someone else would've gotten her, eventually. It's tragic, but it's the reality of life on the streets ..."

Benson shifted uncomfortably. "Okay, Doc. Let's not get too cynical here. This is still someone's daughter."

"Sure," Weeding said, but his tone was dismissive. "But let's be honest. You've got limited resources. Claiming you're chasing a serial killer who targets people on the fringes of the social tapestry is not going to win you any prizes or sympathy. Maybe that's why the mayor's so interested in this case?" Dr. Weeding said sarcastically, "He's got to defend the amount of resources spent on keeping upstanding members of this community safe."

Sandling's jaw clenched. "What exactly are you implying?"

"I'm not implying anything, Agent Sandling," he said, the faintest smirk curling his lips. "I'm just being realistic. You're chasing a ghost; meanwhile, this city's resources are stretched thin. It's worth asking whether you should focus your attention elsewhere."

"We're on the trail of a serial killer, Dr. Weeding. Every victim is worth the effort. And if you don't believe that, maybe you're in the wrong job," Sandling said.

Dr. Weeding raised his hands mockingly, clipboard in one. "Relax, Agent. Just offering my perspective."

Benson stepped between them, his tone light but firm. "Okay, okay. Let's not turn this into a thing. Doc, thanks for your time. We'll let you know if we need anything else."

"I'll be outside," Dr. Weeding said, gave a curt nod, and walked toward out, leaving Sandling and Benson standing near the examination table.

"What the hell was that about?" Benson asked after he was out of earshot.

"You didn't hear it?" Sandling said, still glaring after the medical examiner.

"Hear what?"

Sandling shook her head. "What's his agenda? Why was he trying to steer us away ... Pushing the pimp, or killer-John theory, acting like these crimes aren't related. And what was all that about the mayor?"

Benson frowned. "You need a cigarette," he said.

"I don't smoke."

"Maybe you should. A cigarette after sex will take the edge off ..."

Sandling didn't say anything. She just stood there looking at him until it became awkward. Benson lifted his fist and cleared his throat. They were both aware that they were standing rather close to each other and right next to a murder victim's naked corpse.

"I just don't trust people who act like the victims don't matter."

Benson sighed. "He's just full of himself. He's important. Let's focus on the facts. Weeding might be a jerk, but that doesn't mean he's hiding anything."

"Maybe," Sandling said. "He would fit the medical knowledge of human anatomy angle."

Benson gave her a skeptical look. "Is a schizophrenic, though?"

"He said himself it was two different killers," she said and shrugged and turned on her heels.

As they left the morgue, Sandling couldn't get Weeding's comments about the mayor, his dismissive attitude, and his seeming eagerness to deflect suspicion out of her head. None of it felt right. For instance, why was the mayor of Annapolis on the phone with the mayor of Baltimore while visiting the chief medical examiner? Technically, Weeding fit the profile she was forming of the killer, except for his lack of insanity.

11

Rachel Fox woke up with a start, sitting bolt upright in bed. She had the nightmare again. The one where she was drowning. She was so little, her grandmother said it never happened, but she could feel the icy grip of the Tumen River pulling her under. She touched her wrist to feel her pulse, closing her eyes and controlling her breathing.

She pressed her fingers to her wrist, feeling her pulse, then closed her eyes. Slowly, she breathed in, then out. The pounding in her chest eased, but the memory of her dream lingered.

The door creaked open. Her grandmother, quiet as always, stepped in. She was old, with lines deep on her face, and her eyes dulled with fading time. But she smiled. She always smiled. Her grandmother was the only precious thing in her life.

She didn't need to say anything. Her grandmother sat on the bed, resting her hand gently on her shoulder.

"You had it again, didn't you?" she asked, voice soft, knowing.

Rachel nodded, her throat tight. "It's nothing. Just a dream." But she knew it wasn't just a dream. It was the river.

The cold. The fear. The memory of crossing from North Korea into China. She was so little, barely old enough to understand what was happening, yet old enough to remember the terror of it. The water was so cold. Her grandmother said it didn't happen like that, but Rachel still felt it. She always would.

She stood, pulling her hair back into a rough knot.

Her grandmother stood up and said, "I'll make some tea."

That was her remedy for anything in life. '*Oh dear, never mind, I'll put on a cup of te*a.' Fox heard the pot whistle, and her grandmother came padding back in and handed her the cup. Steam curled into the cool morning air and she relaxed at the smell of it. She took a sip, the warmth steadied her. Maybe it was an elixir for all of life's ills.

"You don't need to worry," her grandmother said, her voice firm, though the smile stayed on her lips. "You're safe now. I made sure you'll be safe."

"I need to get ready," Fox said and got off the bed.

As she prepared breakfast, her mind drifted back—as it always did—to their escape from North Korea. She could still see her mother's beautiful, frightened, determined, lovely face as they waded into the river's frigid waters. Debris rushed past. Her mother held her so tightly that she thought she might not be able to breathe, and she whispered words of love, hope, and encouragement as they fought further out into the current. Her mother had given everything to ensure her daughter's safety. She sacrificed herself, pushing Rachel to the shore with her last ounce of strength before being swept away in the rushing waters. Fox had a lump in her throat, and tears welled in her eyes. Her heart ached with the emotions she felt, so she did what she always did, what she'd been instructed to do. She pushed it deep, deep down, and refocused on the task at hand—any task—to help control her feelings.

Fox made her grandmother another cup of tea, adding just the right amount of honey. They sat together, eating in comfortable silence. Her phone buzzed on the table. She glanced at the screen—an email from Sandling. Her heart skipped as she read her instructions for the day.

"I need to go," Fox said, finishing her breakfast quickly. She helped her grandmother with her medication, trying not to let the worry in her eyes show.

"Don't be concerned about me, Lisa. Just do your best at work," her grandmother said, squeezing her hand. She always called her by her given name. She felt her grandmother understood why she needed to feel like someone else and keep her work persona separate.

Fox nodded, a lump forming in her throat. "I will, Halmeoni," she said, the memories of their escape still fresh in her mind. She remembered the nights spent hiding in the forest and the fear of being caught by border patrols. Just as her mother had always been there, guiding and protecting her, now it was her turn to protect her grandmother.

Rachel checked her email one last time, grabbed her backpack, and headed out the door. Her thoughts about her past switched naturally to her work life, the trouble she'd gotten into as a teenager for hacking into the Pentagon. The thrill of proving she could do it, the fear she felt when the NSA tracked her down. Instead of prison, they'd recruited her, but it hadn't worked out. Now she was with the FBI, her last chance, they'd said. Otherwise, jail. She couldn't let that happen. This had to work.

She arrived at the office. She always felt the Sofa Squad's workspace was organized chaos. Fox headed to her desk, setting up her workstation. She exchanged glances with her teammates, her social awkwardness kept her interactions safe and muted. She logged into her computer and noticed Sandling across the room, deep in conversation. Fox felt a fluttering of nervousness, her admiration for Sandling tinged with something more. She was something to aspire to.

Fox had a hidden determination—the same determination her mother had—that brought her here. She wanted her mom to be proud of her.

Now, she was safe and immersed in her work. The logical, structured world of programming languages was a refuge where everything made sense. She lost herself in the job Sandling assigned her, and the outside world faded.

12

CARVER SAT on the 1970s-inspired brown leather sofa in Jessica Webb's childhood home. Out of politeness, he accepted a china cup of instant coffee and stirred it while taking in the time capsule of Mrs. Margaret Webb's life.

Since her daughters left home and her husband had shot himself, she was alone. That didn't stop her from putting on a 1950s-style housewife dress in periwinkle blue with bright red lipstick and freshly curled hair.

She smelled musky, and so did the rest of the home. It was spotless, though. The orange and cream-colored kitchen contrasted with the mauve and faded sunflower-yellow tones in the rest of the house. Carver perched himself on the edge of the sofa, feeling out of place and conscious that he didn't want to scar the fragile-looking features of Mrs. Webb. She had a brave face plastered under her foundation, but when he'd glance at her eyes, he could see the trepidation and fear of a mental hostage.

Carver glanced to his right at Jessica Webb. Her brow was furrowed, and she looked at her mother with concerned eyes.

"This is Augustine Carver, remember? He's the one who's helping me with Elizabeth's investigation."

Carver looked back at Mrs. Webb, but she didn't return his gaze. Instead, she squared her shoulders and put her hands, one on top of the other, on her crisscrossed knee, and with an air of impertinence, said, "Well, I'm not sure what all this is about, Jessica, you know I prefer to keep the family's business private, and the last few years have been distressing enough."

"But Mom, he's here to help; we need to get to the bottom of this."

"No, we don't, Jessica. *You* need to get to the bottom of this. I'm at peace with the way things are."

"No, Mom, you don't—"

Carver held up his hand to restrain Webb. She closed her mouth, clenched her jaw, and looked down at the brown carpet in frustration. Both knew now wasn't the time or place to get into it.

"I'm sorry to intrude, Mrs. Webb, and I completely understand that you'd prefer us not to be here. I've lost family too, and I know the kind of toll it takes."

For the first time, Mrs. Webb looked at Carver, and her expression relaxed a little.

"Do you?" she said. It was a genuine question. She seemed to be warming up to the strange man that her black sheep of a daughter had brought home, talking about her dead husband and her dead child.

We're just looking through a few of Dad's things," Webb said, pulling a frustrated face.

Her mother closed her lips and said quietly, "What sort of things?"

"Just a few files and boxes from one of his prior investigations," Carver said.

"You think my late husband's work might be relevant to a case you're investigating?" Mrs. Webb asked.

Carver nodded slowly and glanced at Jessica as he said, "Yes, I do, ma'am. From what I understand from your daughter, your husband was a hell of an investigator."

Mrs. Webb narrowed her eyes and asked, "Which case is it? Not the one that killed him?" She closed her eyes tightly, and her eyelids fluttered as her eyes darted underneath. "I really don't want to talk about it," she said and sighed. She's onto me, Carver thought. She opened her eyes. And Carver sensed that she *did* want to talk about it. She stuck him as a vulnerable narcissist—hypersensitivity, passive-aggressive behavior, full of resentment, depression, and a deft user of guilt in manipulation—and someone who relied upon their victimhood to get others to give them attention. She was desperate for it. It is a hard situation. This woman had experienced real loss. But how much of a role did she play in her husband and daughter putting guns in their mouths?

"Carver?" Jessica Webb said.

Carver cleared his throat and snapped out of it. Carver-trance. Mrs. Webb was staring down her nose at him with her mouth in a pout.

"Sorry, I-uh, was lost in thought."

"You were saying, Mrs. Webb?"

"I said I didn't want to talk about it."

"What was the case that you thought killed him?"

"Which one didn't," she scoffed. "He worked all the time. Never here for the family. For his children," she gestured and glanced at Jessica like she was saying, 'Case in point, see how she turned out. ' That little movement, almost imperceptible in a conversation, stung Jessica. Carver sensed it. She looked downcast. "But that last case," Mrs. Webb scoffed again and moved uneasily in her chair, brushing an imaginary piece of lint off her skirt and sucking her cheeks. "The serial killer one. He believed—convinced himself— there was a serial killer who'd been operating for decades in the area. I didn't want to hear about it. All that blood and guts. It's disgusting. But he wouldn't let it go. He became reclusive. Hid from his family. Absolutely no help in the end. And it killed him. Didn't it, sweetheart?" Mrs. Webb asked her daughter, looking for validation.

Jessica shrugged. "I don't know, Mom," she whispered.

"Speak up; nobody can hear you."

Jessica looked at Carver, she was tired. Her eyes begged for his help. Her mother sucked her teeth. Carver pursed his lips.

"Do you still have the files?"

Mrs. Webb held his gaze as they examined one another. She interlocked her fingers, put them on the front of her knees, and rocked herself slightly as she said, "You know, I did keep them."

"What?" Jessica asked, "Why didn't you tell me you kept his work files?"

"Well, your sister was the detective, Jessica, not you, and she expressed an interest in them before you. And I figured, you know, what the hell, let her have a look. I think Elizabeth took some and made copies of some, but whatever was left of your father's is in his study. I don't go in there. I never used to go in there. I occasionally dust, but you'll find that just as he left it, he was always tidy, a bit of a neat freak, anyway. And he always told me I have no business going through his things, so I leave them be." Jessica lifted the back of her hand to her mouth and sniffled. Mrs. Webb saw it and reacted by getting angry as a defense mechanism. "Is that so wrong of me? Is that so wrong of me, Jessica? Why are you tearing up? Act like a grown-up. We have company."

"Come on, Carver," Jessica said and stood.

"Just where do you think you're going?" Mrs. Webb asked harshly.

"To get what we came here for," Jessica said.

"And what might that be? Your torturing me with these memories isn't enough?"

"We're not torturing you, Mom, *jeez*. We're trying to solve Elizabeth's murder!"

"Your sister committed suicide! Like her coward of a father!"

Jessica stormed off. Carver felt he was getting an idea of what growing up in this home must have been like. Mrs. Webb softened.

"Talk to her for me, will you? I can't seem to get through to her. She's in denial, isn't she?" She waited for Carver to respond.

Before he stood, he said, "Thank you for the coffee, Mrs. Webb."

"Oh, call me Margaret," she said with a wave of her hand.

Carver could hear Jessica rummaging through boxes in her father's office. "You've been a big help," Carver said and motioned that he was going to join Jessica in searching through the records Mrs. Webb had kept. Carver heard her sniffle trying to hold back a tear. She lifted her chin and shook her hair out. Carver stopped and turned.

"Sorry to ask this, Mrs. Webb, but did you keep James' suicide note?"

Mrs. Webb blinked back her tears and looked up at Carver. She was expressionless. "I'm sure it's amongst his things," she said. "I don't throw things out. I mean, despite wanting to, how could you throw something like that out? It's hell living here, Mr. Carver. It's hell."

. . .

The late Detective James Webb's office was narrow and short. The book ended with a floor-to-ceiling glass cabinet filled with boxes of files and memorabilia. It had an imitation pine, prefabricated-style office desk running the length of it. James Webb had framed pictures of his daughters and his family. Some were taken down at a lake, no doubt happier times. Carver could imagine him sitting in his office, working hard on his cases, glancing up and smiling at the photographs he liked to look at.

Jessica was in there, hunched over, pulling boxes from the floor and loading them on the desk. She was muttering to herself. After glancing at Carver, she said, "I think I found something that might be relevant." They had sifted quickly through what they needed and, instead of staying there to study it, decided to load the car up for the two-hour drive back to Manassas.

Mrs. Webb stood on the porch with her arms crossed, watching them take her husband's belongings. She pulled the tissue from her sleeve, dabbed her nose, and wiped under her eyes, trying not to let her mascara run. As Jessica walked past her, mother and daughter averted each other's gaze, trying not to engage.

Carver, collar open, tie pulled down, fell into the front passenger seat and felt the sweat from the effort of carrying boxes under his armpits and along his top lip. Jessica climbed into the driver's seat. Carver looked at her and wondered if she was okay to drive but thought maybe it was better not to say anything. Then, as she started the car, Carver said, "Between your apartment wall full of boxes and the stuff I got from Brexler and now your dad's files, we should have everything to start sifting through what we need to put the pieces of the puzzle together. What did you say, kid?"

Jessica looked in the rearview mirror, adjusted it, and spent a few seconds watching her mother standing at the top of the steps. Then, she looked forward and drove off without a word.

13

THE PREVIOUS EVENING, Sandling had begrudgingly called Carver. Even though, when she thought about him, she still got a stabbing sensation of betrayal in the pit of her stomach. The idea that he'd lied to her. And lied about knowing her father. Hell, he'd worked with him and had conveniently forgotten to mention it. Not only that. He's put her in harm's way. He sent her in there—with a monster—alone and unarmed because he *hoped* Hermann Zimmer would use it to his advantage.

He'd bet that Zimmer would work out who she was while knowing that the Ripper was the prime suspect in her father's murder. His words he said to her that night—the night she shot Derange—played over and over in her mind like a vinyl record as it skipped. "I didn't tell you because I didn't know how you'd react. We needed you. We *need* you ... If I told you that Zimmer killed your dad, you wouldn't have been the same with him, it would've thrown you off," he'd told her as they stood under the flashing red and blue lights.

Thrown you off. That's what he was worried about. Her performance. Her little psychology show for the madman. To his credit, it'd worked. They'd caught the bad guy. But how far was Carver willing to go to catch them? All the way. He had no qualms about using people in his team to get ahead, so why shouldn't she? After all, he was the great Augustine Carver ... may as well play him at his own game.

It went to voicemail, and she didn't leave one. He didn't call her back. She hadn't spoken to him directly in a few weeks. She didn't miss it.

She wanted to tell him she needed to brief the team on her current case. This killer was driving her beyond simply working with local law enforcement. She was getting sucked into it. She could feel herself drawn in like debris swirling around a plug hole.

"Have you talked to Deputy Director Gibson?" she imagined him asking her. No, she hadn't. After she saw the mayor of Annapolis walking out of the morgue in the basement of the medical examiner's office, she didn't know who to speak to. And her concerns about outside interference were growing. All she knew was she needed help from the team. They had broader skills than her, and she needed them to get her out of Grant Avenue and away from Augustine Carver.

She'd gotten to the office early like she always did. She wasn't sleeping much. She checked just in case, making sure Carver wasn't asleep in his office. Sometimes, he just passed out and didn't bother to go home.

He wasn't there. That was new for him, she thought. It was nice to be back in the office. She hadn't thought she'd have missed it as much. The sun shone through the bank of windows and onto each desk. The roughness of the carpet and the dullness of the decor were familiar and comforting.

Being out on assignment, working in a strange city with strange people, and sleeping in strange beds left her restless and on edge. It was nice to be home. Even if it meant seeing Carver, she felt she didn't have the whole picture yet. The case was too violent for her to feel like she could step away from it and see the complexity. Approach it unemotionally. Be detached from it. That's why it was better for profilers to sit behind desks and help field agents with investigations from the shadows. She preferred that. But going out on jobs supporting local law enforcement was a way for her to get back into Gibson's good books and back to the main show. Not be trapped out in the sticks under the tutelage of someone she despised. And she wanted redemption and a chance at the big time again. After all, what would her dad think of how things turned out? He'd feel let down, she thought. Then she heard the front door of the building slam far away and the familiar thud and stomp of footsteps as the gang came tramping up to the Sofa Squad's third-floor office.

Sandling swiveled in her chair as the main door to the office opened and she saw Penny Maudmont and Rachel Fox walking in shoulder to shoulder. Penny was smiling and talking about something. They were followed by Frank Hornigen and Toby Underwood. There was no sign of Carver.

When Penny saw Sandling, her eyes lit up, and she went quickly to her desk saying, "Oh-my-god, oh-my-god, oh-my-god," and put her hand to her waistcoat and smoothed it down. She tottered up to her with open arms and said, "Come here darling, hug me, golly it's so nice to see you, it's been ages, how are you doing? Wait, don't say anything; we have to have a proper catch-up, you can tell me all about it."

"Hey Penny," Sandling said, smoothing her ruffled hair from Penny's bearhug. She took a deep breath. The energy was lovely but on a very different level from how she was feeling. She saw Fox standing next to her desk, and Fox gave her a faint smile and lifted her hand a little. She seemed shy and awkward but also happy to see her, which was nice.

"Hey Caitlin, welcome back," Frank said in his usual

calm and measured grandfatherly tone. "Nice to have you aboard the good ship USS Sofa Squad again."

She gave him a chuckle and saw Toby lift his chin to acknowledge her. He said, "Hi Caitlin, how's Baltimore been? Carver told us you were working up there. It sounds like a hell of a case. I was reading about it on my way in. " He held up a copy of a folded newspaper.

"Hey, Toby," Sandling said and gave him a wave. She'd forgotten how much she liked these people that she worked with. The truth was that after the previous case where she'd shot Edward Derange and freed an Atlanta Supreme Court Judge's granddaughter, she'd gotten caught up in the whirlwind of the after-effects of the case. There'd been so much publicity, internal recognition, gossip, and distractions. She felt like she had forgotten about the people who helped her to solve that puzzle in the first place. The people in this room were the ones she was trying so hard to get away from. And now she realized she was back, not because she wanted to be but because she needed their help. It seemed like they missed her, but it didn't seem like her absence had affected them and their lives - which shouldn't have come as a surprise.

She looked around and asked, "Where's Augustine?"

Toby took his satchel off his shoulder and said, "Carver's been investigating a case with Jessica Webb out of state."

"Webb, the journalist?" Sandling asked.

"Right, you know the one who helped you get the bait in the paper," Penny said, helpfully.

"Yeah, of course, Penny," Sandling laughed. "How could I forget? Not like I think about it all the time! You know what I mean? It's on my mind every five minutes or so ..." Sandling looked down and away.

"Oh, *sooorry*," Penny said and tutted at herself, "I didn't mean to bring back bad feelings, I was just trying to be helpful."

"As usual," Sandling said under her breath. "Does anybody know if Carver's gonna be back?"

"Yeah, I think he should be back later on today," Frank said.

"Why?" Penny asked, "Do you need to speak to him?"

"Something's come up," Sandling said in a non-committal way.

Toby looked at her quizzically, "What's happened, something on the ground in Baltimore?"

"Well, yeah ..."

"That case sounds crazy," Toby said.

"It's starting to look a little like that," Sandling said, with a faraway look. She was tired.

"What's up?" Frank asked.

"A little bit of trouble with some of the higher-ups," Sandling said. "The case is also a little tricky, to be honest."

She looked at Fox and said, "I could use some help from you guys, but I don't know what you're working on, and I need to get sign-off from Carver first, right?"

Penny shrugged and looked at the others. They were quiet. Sandling felt the tension. It wasn't good for the team. Things hadn't been the same since she'd shot Edward Derange.

THE DOORS OPENED, and they turned to look at Carver as he walked into the office. He stared at his phone, holding it between both hands and mouthing the words as he read something.

"Morning guys," he said casually, "How're you all doing?" He was distracted and in a hurry. He glanced up briefly as he made his way to his office. When he got halfway across, he realized nobody had said good morning to him. Everybody was just standing there, staring. He stopped, looked up from his phone, turned around while putting it back in his pocket, and asked, "What?"

Everybody kept looking at him. Then he noticed Sandling. He swallowed and smiled and said, "Ah! Caitlin was just the person I wanted to speak to. What's going on in here? You guys are all acting strange."

"Not strange, boss," Maudmont said, "Just having a quick catch-up with our long-lost colleague here."

"Sure, well, okay, don't make it too long or too sentimental. We've got work to do ..." he said.

"Gust, I need to talk to you about something to do with the case in Baltimore."

"Yeah, I figured as much," Carver said. "Otherwise, you wouldn't be looking at me with those doe eyes, like a puppy asking for a biscuit."

"Hold on a second," Maudmont said, jumping to Sandling's defense. "She hasn't been in the office in weeks. You guys are barely talking, and now you're treating her like just another piece of furniture. Come on, Augustine, you know her better than that; I mean, you know *us* better than that."

"Hold on, hold on, hold on," Carver said, "Woah! Work is work, you know, and life is life, and I'm sure we've all got more important things to be getting on with than some family feud, don't you think? Everything is fine. Right? Caitlin?"

She didn't respond. The room grew tense, and everyone shifted awkwardly in place.

Carver finally said, "I've got something I need to talk to you guys about, too. So, how about this? Let's do something we've never done before—start fresh, like a regular field office with a morning briefing. We can discuss our cases and what's going on. How about that?"

"Okay," Sandling said. She liked the idea and appreciated that he wasn't brushing the issue aside. At least by overlooking the mess, she could get on with life in a professional, platonic way. In other words, enduring being around Gust—only for as long as she had to.

14

THE TEAM WAS GATHERED around the front of Sandling's desk. Even with everyone standing around, she couldn't help but watch Carver. Her eyes were drawn to him and she felt like she was rubbernecking at a car crash. Sandling wasn't sure if he'd managed to stop drinking after his downward spiral from the Skinwalker case. He didn't smell like he had, but he did look like he hadn't taken a shower in a few days. Carver had a look on his face somewhere between anguish and *I'd rather be anywhere else right now*. He stood at the back with his hands in his pockets as Sandling debriefed the team on her case.

She stood beside a flip chart and wrote keywords about the case as she spoke. She would flip over to the next page as she moved on to another aspect of the investigation. While she'd been explaining the whole case to the team, she noticed Rachel Fox flinch and wince a couple of times, especially when she was describing the extreme violence and hacking motions the killer used to torture his victims— more than kill *just* them. It was medieval savagery of the cruelest kind. It was an insane type of rage that the killer used, and Sandling saw Penny Maudmont looking like she was going to throw up and looked quite scared. Toby Underwood was looking down a lot, and Frank Hornigen just took notes. His expression never changed. Carver crossed his arms. Sandling knew his keen mind was absorbing every detail. She finished up and asked, "Any questions?"

The Squad looked like they had a few.

"How are local law enforcement handling it?" Carver asked. Sandling swallowed and shrugged as she put the lid back on the marker pen and said, "I'm working with one guy, a detective called Benson. He's handling it like it was just like any other day, but I don't think they grasp the extreme danger this guy poses to civilians." She glanced up at him. "I don't think there's a huge sense of urgency—and there should be. I had a bit of a run-in with the medical examiner. I think there's politics involved. They don't want to admit or think about the possibility that it's just one killer."

"Makes sense," Hornigen said.

"What do you mean?" Sandling asked.

"Well, politicians never want to admit there's a hunter of humans on the loose in their city. It makes them look bad," Underwood answered for him.

Sandling saw Carver shrug in agreement. "Yeah, but that doesn't help the case. And find the killer," she said.

"No," Carver said, uncrossed his arms, and stepped forward. "But it's one of those variables we must deal with to solve this thing. So, what help do you need from us?" he asked.

Sandling looked at him briefly before taking the cap off the green marker and flipping the chart paper to a fresh page. "I need help with this," she said and started drawing. First, she drew a big circle, then, from memory, sketched out the outline of something that looked like a strange M shape with another ring in the center.

"What the hell is that?" Underwood asked.

Sandling turned to face them. "First thing I need to say," she said and looked at Rachel Fox, who was already looking at the ground, and seemed like she wished she could hide. "I don't mean to embarrass her by giving her a shout-out, but I owe this to Rachel for the work that she's been doing."

"Hmm. Wait, what? You've already been working on this case, Rachel?" Carver asked.

"Don't be mad at her, Gust," Sandling said sweetly. "She was helping me out. And, as you see, it's paid off."

"How exactly?"

"Because this is the evidence that we need to prove to the politicians and law enforcement that it's the same guy."

"Okay," Carver said, intrigued. "Go on ... and sorry, Rachel, don't be concerned. I was just surprised that's all."

Rachel was still looking at the ground, but she nodded in acknowledgment of Carver's words.

"Rachel was diligent and spotted something that forensics hadn't. This is a pattern—from what we can see on the photographs—of a symbol that's been burned, using some sort of chemical into the mattress at both crime scenes."

"Burned in without setting the place on fire?" Hornigen asked.

"Yes," Caitlin said. "Exactly. A flammable chemical was used to create the effect. We could smell it when we went into the crime scene, you know like a phosphorus smelling ... something, but he's going to great pains to conceal it."

"But he's also leaving his markings at the crime scenes, like a dog," Hornigen said.

Sandling didn't like the comparison, but she agreed with him. "Yep," she said. "Maybe he's marking his territory in some way." Sandling looked to Fox again, "Um, Rachel, you'll be glad to know that I've got Baltimore forensics going and taking UV pictures of the mattress so that we can analyze them in more detail."

"So they're taking samples to trace the origin of the chemical used?" Underwood asked.

"Exactly," Sandling said.

"I don't know if that's going to get you anywhere ..." Carver said. "It's a long shot. Also, chemistry isn't exactly our specialty. You'd be better off focussing on the symbolism and what he's *trying* to tell us about why he's leaving them at the scene."

"Well, yeah, exactly, and I don't have the research capacity or the time to dedicate, so I was hoping I could get some help with this," Sandling said while looking at Fox. Rachel was still looking at the ground, but she popped her head up and said right on cue, "I can help! Sorry a bit loud," then much quieter, "I can help."

"Okay," Carver said and stepped back. Sandling could tell he was done with the brief. "That's one element that we've got to look at."

Sandling looked at him, waiting to hear more, and the rest of the team also turned towards him. He was ashen and looked a little worried. Now that he had everyone's attention and they were all looking up, he seemed to realize he had everyone's attention and cleared his throat.

"Uh, Caitlin, may I speak with you in my office, please?" he asked.

15

SANDLING FOLLOWED Carver into his office and shut the door. He didn't need to close the blinds because they were always down. On the floor at her feet were the same boxes of books about serial killers and criminal investigation that had been there the first time she'd stepped through the threshold and met the Bureau legend, Augustine Carver. He stood in front of the blinds as if looking out the window for a moment. He turned around, and his worried expression shifted slightly. It softened when he looked at her, and she could sense the melancholy and regret he felt, which made her uncomfortable. She looked away, avoiding his gaze. She didn't want any small talk, and instead of Carver asking, 'How are you? How are things going? Is everything okay?' they just stood in silence and let the small talk happen in a vacuum.

"You know what that burned engraving means, don't you?" Carver asked. His tone was flat, and his voice low, like he was in a restaurant and didn't want the table beside them to hear their conversation. She swallowed and shook her head and said, "No, I don't, because it was one of the things I was hoping to get help with by coming back here."

"We can see what we can do," Carver said.

Sandling thought it was non-committal. "Penny will be able to help direct traffic and organize the roster of what's going on."

Sandling nodded and said, "Thanks, Gust. I appreciate it."

"How are you holding up? That case sounds pretty terrible."

"I'm okay," she said, and felt like she'd told a lie. She was feeling a little out of her depth, and if she was honest with herself, happy—or relieved—that she could talk to somebody about it who understood what it was like, even if she hated him.

"What're you working on?" Sandling asked and immediately regretted extending the olive branch.

Carver looked pleased and said, "Did the team mention something?"

"Something, yeah," Sandling said.

"It's kind of complicated. I'm not sure if it's a case yet. I've just got a pile of boxes from Jessica Webb. She asked me for help with her sister's death."

"I see," Sandling said, hoping that that was the end of the conversation. "Anything to go on?" She asked and bit her tongue. She couldn't help herself; she was too inquisitive. What was Augustine Carver working on? She always wanted to keep tabs on it, which was also the natural state of an FBI special agent to be looking over at everybody else's lunch and wondering if they should try to get some for themselves.

"Fourteen dead detectives," Carver said, summing it up. "That's what we've got between Jessica's investigation, something her father was working on before he died, and some boxes I prized from Elizabeth Webb's office."

"Is that normal?"

"I don't know," Carver said. "It sounds like it's high, but with the pressures of the job and the cases they were working ..."

"What were the cases?"

"Each was involved in a missing persons case."

"Suspicious?"

Carver half shrugged and slightly cocked his head. She could feel herself getting drawn in. "Just so we're clear, I'm also going to ask the team to get involved with this one, so you're going to need to share resources," Carver said. She looked into his eyes but didn't respond. "But, as you said," Carver continued, "the first thing is to work out whether that number is an anomaly or not ... And I had a favor to ask you in return."

Sandling felt a pit of dread open up in her stomach and a sudden wave of anxiety like she wanted to fall through the floor and get out of there.

"What is it?" she asked, her throat dry. Her voice cracked a little.

Carver pressed his lips together, looked down, and took a small step forward like he was searching for the right words.

"Listen, I know you've been seeing a therapist," he said and looked up at her. Here it comes, she thought. Forget the Carver-trance. Here came the *Gustzooka*. How had he found out that she was seeing somebody? Her mind flicked through the possibilities. It stopped, like the Wheel of Fortune, on the face of Deputy Director Bronwyn Gibson—the person who'd recommended the man she'd been seeing about her psychological and emotional state.

She felt a tightness in the base of her throat. She'd been seeing somebody since soon after the shooting. Not the typical Bureau provided professional advice, and it wasn't something mandatory. She decided that even psychologists sometimes need therapy, and maybe her shooting the Skinwalker suspect was the culmination of a couple of years of dread and disappointment stemming from her failure at the academy. Her demotion to Sofa Squad. The loss of her marriage. And all those happy holiday snaps she thought that she'd be taking with a man she still loved.

"Okay," Sandling said meekly.

"It's nothing personal," Carver said in a way that made her feel like he knew exactly how personal it was. "It's strictly business. And I'm sorry, but he is the preeminent figure in his field ... He studied rates of cop suicides and has been published in journals."

"Just say it, Gust," she said. She was resigned and tired of his drawn-out, kind of apologetic tone. She wanted the '*Who-the-hell-cares?*' Carver back. That was better than this version, walking on eggshells around her. Something she didn't need.

"I'm surprised you saw him ..."

"Here we go," she said, picking up on his tone. "Look," she said, "before you say anything else, all I know is he got recommended to me, and he was local to where I was assigned, in *Baltimore*. You know, Johns Hopkins is a good university and the Bureau has a good relationship with them."

"Yeah, I know all of that," Carver said, putting his hands up and showing her his palms. He didn't want to fight. "I know all that. I did have a word with Deputy Gibson about this, and that's how I found out that you were seeing him. But I'm standing here asking you if it's okay for us to go and speak to him about these detectives' deaths, you know?" He gave her a soft look. "It might be nothing. Statistically, he might show us those numbers are within the expected attrition rate for cops, say."

"That's a polite way of putting it," Sanding said, imagining all those cops sitting in their cars, putting the barrels of their service revolvers in their mouths and pulling the trigger.

"Yeah, well," Carver said, "It's not something I feel that comfortable talking about."

Oh, yeah? You tried death by serial killer? she thought. Which is more or less noble? she wondered unconsciously. She could feel the tension, like the opposing forces between two magnets. She wanted to get out of the office as much as he wanted her absolution.

"Why did you say *us*?" she asked.

Carver hesitated and looked at her, trying to choose his words. "I think it would help if you were there to explain to Dr. Blackwood that it was professional and not linked to your sessions. Also, maybe you could help me build a rapport so he would understand that you have my blessing ..." She didn't say anything. "Hey," Carver said throwing his hands up, getting defensive now. "I'm just telling you as a personal courtesy."

She was quiet and pushed her tongue in between the gaps of her molars, as she always did when she was thinking.

"Professional?" she mused.

"Personal," Carver said.

"No, Gust," she said. "We don't have a personal relationship. Let's be clear about that." She felt a knot in her throat and could see what she said pained him. "All right," Sandling said, letting him off the hook. Suddenly, she felt braver and a bit taller. She stood up straight, puffed out her chest a little, and looked directly at Gust. He had a bemused expression on his face.

"If I do this for you, what are you going to do for me?" She asked. "I need Rachel Fox on the case with me."

"Part-time," Carver said.

"Full time," Sandling countered.

"Fifty-fifty," Carver said.

"Seventy-thirty," Sandling said. "Final offer."

Carver looked to his left, thinking, and said, "Okay. Deal. You drive me to see Dr. Blackwood, and I'll let you have Rachel Fox as part of the case. But she's still a Grant Avenue asset, and I might need to recall her."

"Drive you?" Sandling said. "I mean, I can come and make the introduction, but I wasn't planning on staying." She didn't want to be stuck in a car with him.

"My chest and arm are still giving me trouble," Carver said, touching his shoulder and then rolling it while wincing. Sandling also winced. Of course, he would pull out his ace. The gunshot wound.

"Fine," she said, "deal."

She felt like she should step forward and shake his hand, but also that it would be too cringe-worthy. There was a brief moment between them as they looked at one another —like they were acknowledging all the things left unsaid— and then Sandling quickly jumped in.

"Okay, thanks, Gust. I'll see you later," and made for the door.

"Wait, Cate, sorry, there's something else I need to talk to you about."

She stopped and turned. "What is it?" she asked.

"That iconography. That *symbol* at the crime scene."

"What about it?"

"It may be nothing, may be something, but I wanted to show you just in case."

Carver walked over to one of the cardboard boxes on the floor near her and pulled it open. He ran his finger over the spines of a few files and pulled out an orange one with a white tag on it.

"What's this?" she asked and looked at the file.

He went to his desk, and she followed him. He opened it up and pointed to a black and white photograph of a hand-drawn image and a note underneath. "Does this look familiar?" Carver asked.

Sandling stared at it. She was trying to overlay it in her mind with the burn marks they'd found on the mattresses.

"Where did you get this?" she asked and glanced up at him.

"That's from the Peninsular killer case," Carver said.

She gasped and covered her mouth. Her eyes were wide. She was shocked.

"You see it too?" Carver asked.

"I thought you said you killed the Peninsular killer."

"I did," Carver said. "But—"

"And Zimmer's in prison, so it's not him. None of this was ever leaked to the public?"

"No," Carver said, "As far as I know. This is someone else. I mean, it—might—be a coincidence, but it's something you should look into."

No shit, she thought. "This is crazy," she said, staring at the photograph. She felt like something from the past had risen from the dead. Carver was watching her carefully. She could feel him looking at her.

"You know what you have to do, though, right?" Carver asked.

She furrowed her brow, confused as to what it meant. "I don't know what those symbols are, but the burns in the mattresses at each scene—it flips the narrative on its head," Sandling said.

"He's not as disorganized as the initial crime scenes would have suggested," Carver said. It was more an open-ended statement than a statement of fact. He was testing her.

Sandling shook her head slightly and said, "It doesn't make sense. We missed the initial iconography in the first scene—"

"But he would have had to know what he was doing," Carver said, "And have the right materials with him and time to leave his mark on the mattress."

"Exactly," Sandling said, "Which doesn't gel with the rest of the murder."

"No, brutal, isn't it?" Carver said.

Sandling swallowed but didn't reply. The violence and destruction were graphic enough without her reliving it in Carver's office.

"There ... there might be someone who could help you with this ..." Carver said.

Sandling knew instinctively whom he meant.

"They moved him," Carver said. "Gibson told me. He's in a maximum security prison now, not Hotel California anymore."

She wondered if that was meant to make her feel better about it and thought, *please don't let it be who I think it is.* "If he's in solitary confinement, he would be more susceptible to making a deal," Carver suggested, his intonation rose on the word *deal*. He was really trying to sell this idea to her, she thought.

She shook her head and said, "I don't know, Gust, I just don't know ...." She'd already been seeing Dr. Blackwood once a week for three or four months, and maybe she was just starting to feel better. Now, he suggested she arrange an interview with a certified sociopath.

"Gibson said she'd support it," Carver said, "I'm just throwing it out there as an option. It worked last time, and we're getting a lot of heat from the mayors. Annapolis *and* Baltimore."

Click, everything fell into place for her. Politics, again. Was she just a pawn in all this? She wondered. And whose game was she playing here? Gibson's, Carver's, or Hermann Zimmer's?

16

EVIL LITTLE BASTARDS. *We see them*. There they are. Progeny. Vile, disgusting offspring of the mutating glut of cellulite. Eyes scanning. Darting. *Stay alert, stay alive*. See the gap-toothed smiles on the children's faces? *We see them*. Bobbing up and down and round and round. The sick smell of salty sea air. It makes me want to hurl. *Need peace*.

A child is screaming. My finger is on the little button. *We put it there*. Above their heads is a camera. *They'll find out, they'll see it!* No, they won't. They won't know about it. Pressing the button very lightly. No sounds. No clicks. *God, I'm afraid*. Shut up! Be silent. Stop being such a sissy. *You sound just like daddy*. This is what we do. This is the safety net. They won't get us here. Leaning on the control box we watch them drift past, like sushi on a conveyor belt. *Need solitude*. A morsel. A snack. A payout. *What a sick society*. They'll get what they deserve.

Pulling my black ball cap down to cover my eyes. *Is that dad looking at me? Does he know?* Goddamn bastard. He doesn't know. Keep taking pictures. See the bright lights flashing red and white and yellow on the carousel? See the expressions of the plastic horses change? They're screaming.

Not the children, the horses. They're in pain. I feel it. *Can you feel it?* They're just fucking plastic horses. No. The universe is pulsing through them. *Are they sending us a message?* The patterns—they *mean* something. *Everything means something.* If you look closely enough. The lights stretch and twist, reaching for us, morphing into a face like that painting. *The Scream.* Yes. They can't touch us. Not when we have the symbols. *But we left them, the symbols.*

The parents are too nearby to do it right now.

"Christ almighty," we blurt. *It was under our breath.* Stand up straight. *He approaches.* The fat controller.

Randy Guzzi walked over to us, waving his clipboard in one hand, waddling along. Monkey-see and Monkey-do are with him too. *As usual.* Always flanked by his assistants *cum* muscle. They're brutalists. Look at him. *Disgusting.* With his stained white vest tucked into his grey track pants. Balding, short, round, and he was the boss. *Our boss.*

"Wacha doin' *Crows-feet*," Guzzi called out. "Staring all googly-eyed at the little kiddies, again?" He let out a laugh. *Forced.* The Monkey-boys joined in a little over enthusiastically to the same joke he made every time we spoke. The ride stopped. Glance over. See a few parents gave us a dirty, side-eyed look, and picked their kids up off the screaming plastic horses. They hurry away. The horses stopped screaming. *Thank God.*

"Thanks, come again!" Guzzi called out and waved over to them. "Assholes," he said quietly. The Monkey-boys grin at one another. *Assholes.*

"Good one, Guzzi."

"Huh? Whaddya say, Crowe?" Guzzi turned to Monkey-see and said, "What do they say about all the killers having three names?"

"Dunno boss," the meathead said.

"I'm about to tell you, nitwit. You ever noticed? Lee Harvey Oswald, huh? John Wilkes Booth, eh?" Guzzi asked.

"Who's he?" Monkey-do asked. Guzzi ignored him.

John Wayne Gacy.

"And now we have Victor Harlan Crowe—Crows-feet—the prim and proper carousel conductor."

"You sure are good at handling that ride," Monkey-do said.

"Thanks," we mumble. Can't look him in the face. Stare only at his chest. He's wearing a tight T-shirt. *Vanity.* Bet it hides the blood well. *We should get some.*

"Huh?" Guzzi cut in. "You're always mumbling, Crowe. Whaddya say?"

We gaze at the fat Guzzi now. *He saw something in our eyes.* He looked afraid. He swallows.

"What do you want, boss?" Spoken clearly like a Victorian.

Guzzi looked at the clipboard to avert his eyes. *He's scared.* He smells it on us. *Shut up.*

"You're working a double," Guzzi said.

We shake our heads. *No.* "I have somewhere I need to—"

"Listen, mumbles, I can't hear you but it looks like your mouth is moving. I only want your head to move up and down while you nod at what I am saying."

We started nodding. *Does he control us? Can he read our minds?* It's all real. *Or it's all fake.* That's one of the benefits—*and there aren't many*—of insomnia. You know when you don't sleep? *Can't sleep.* What's sleep? Haha. We shake our head.

"Okay, I can do it."

"Damn right you can do it," Guzzi said and turned to go. *Relief.* Then he turns back. "And where the hell is your company polo?"

We looked down at our checkered shirt. *Damn*. Oh, well. Must've forgotten again. "Laundry day."

Guzzi shook his head and pulled a face which said, '*You? Laundry?*'. "At least undo your top button. Why you gotta have it buttoned all the way up, huh? I'm starting to think you might actually be one of those triple-barreled name guys we talked about. Don't ever let this guy buy a gun, am I right?" Guzzi glanced at them. "You look like someone who'd shoot up a school."

We would. The Monkey-boys laughed. *Unconvincing*. A crowd of people are waiting for the ride to start. *They're watching us*. They're just looking at the commotion. *They read our thoughts*.

"Come on," Guzzi said to his muscle.

They left. *The blood is sacred, but they waste it*. We won't waste the blood. Voices whisper. *Where?* Do it, do it now. *No, not yet*. Wait for the right moment. *Yes* …

17

SANDLING WAS STILL ARGUING with herself as she made her way towards the prison. She'd sworn never to speak to Hermann Zimmer again. She gripped the wheel tight so her knuckles turned white and she swore at the cars around her. She was talking herself into it. "It's just this once, Cate. Once and never again."

She knew Gibson wouldn't be pleased if she shirked her responsibility but this wasn't about her superior. Her curse was that she was incapable of doing a half-assed job. No matter how much she hated it or wanted to cut corners, she couldn't. It was her working-class Irish blood she told herself. But she knew better than that. It was the deep-seated need to please the person who'd left her behind. Who she felt on her shoulder, looking down on her, observing her path through life. How do you go about pleasing someone that isn't there?

"Ugh, snap out of it," she yelled and honked the horn at a cyclist. "Just get in and get out," she told herself. "Confirm it isn't him. They aren't linked. And be on your way."

Time to face the madman's music.

. . .

SANDLING SAT at a small interview table. She was in a cell at the end of death row that was used nominally as a Chaplain's Quarters. An iron-gated room for penance, forgiveness, and final reflections. It was the sort of room used for giving the Last Rites to men being sent away to have their organs stopped until they died by lethal injection.

The Chesapeake Detention Facility on East Madison in Baltimore looked like two giant brick shipping containers stacked one on top of the other at a port. This was a supermax that housed some of Maryland's most dangerous inmates. It also was the new home of the infamous serial killer Hermann Zimmer, who was more infamously known as the Californian Ripper and Zimmer the Ripper, as the media anointed him.

She'd been through the invasive and intimidating security protocol to enter the facility, signing away any liability should she experience assault or injury during her visit. She also gave up her handgun and her badge and was instead given a plastic tag with the bad passport-style photo printed on it with her particulars. Although the duty clerk said she should keep her ID hidden unless asked for it by a member of staff in case one of the inmates got hold of it.

The death row was empty of prisoners and was away from the rest of the inmates. They decided to let her use the old chaplain's quarters because if the other prisoners found out Zimmer was speaking to the Feds, he'd be branded a rat. His life would be in danger. It was no secret that in state lock-up, Zimmer's life was already in danger because of his past exploits. Violent criminals had their own code.

Your run-of-the-mill convicts, murderers, thieves, gangbangers, and drug dealers found pedophilia and acts against minors beyond the pale, even for them. Zimmer still commanded fear and respect, but there was a definite threat to his life in the general prison population. He was crazy.

Sandling often wondered if the authorities used that as an excuse, the threat to his life, for keeping him separate because they were afraid he might infect the rest of the population with his particular brand of madness. And so, despite the power that Zimmer wielded from a psychological perspective, he'd been kept away from everyone else. He was alone the majority of the time. He exercised for one hour a day by himself.

As she was being escorted up to death row and the chaplain's office by a young, spotty prison guard, he told her the warden had signed off on Zimmer being allowed to use the quarters to speak to his lawyers and prepare his appeals cases.

"So in many ways," the guard said, "This feels a lot more like Father Zimmer's quarters than the Department of Prisons Chaplain's office." He was smiling as he said it. *Father Zimmer*, Sandling noted. The moniker didn't appeal to her. If anything, it was an ominous sign of things to come. The guards were already paying homage to the serial killer in their midst.

As she sat alone in the dim office she jumped and flinched at the loud metallic banging and screams that echoed down the corridors from the rest of the prison below. In front of her on the shiny metal table was a folder that contained a single photograph. The gate at the far end of death row slammed open. She heard the slow shuffle of a prisoner in restraints. She tried to stay calm, but her frayed nerves were on edge. The whole situation seemed like she was reliving some long-forgotten nightmare with no idea whether she was dreaming or whether she would ever wake up.

Then, like a gargoyle come to life, the man she most feared, the man she'd promised she'd never see again, was standing in the open cell doorway. He was at least a foot taller than the prison guard escorting him. He was pale, and gaunt, but still had a gridiron straight back, and looked like his sinewy body was made from cables. He looked powerful. If he ever decided to take somebody down, Sandling assessed that he could easily subdue the guard with a deft wrap of his steel chain. Zimmer would be able to pull tight and squeeze for a long time before he tired.

Zimmer didn't say anything. He didn't look at her. He was staring straight ahead. A model prisoner, Sandling thought.

The guard said, "Ma'am," and nodded in acknowledgment to Sandling. She just sat passively but with heightened expectation, waiting for the procedure of moving this dangerous man from point A to point B to be over. The prison guard indicated the chair next to the metal table and looked Zimmer in the eye to show him he should enter. Zimmer did so without saying a word.

Eurgh. He reeked. He smelled like somebody who spent days in the same sweaty institutional clothes, in the same small steel box, with no safe way to get a thorough wash.

The prison guard stood at the entrance for a second, looked at Sandling, and said, "When you're ready to leave, you just press the red button here on the wall behind you ... Press it once and someone will come up and escort Father Zimmer back to his cell. You'll be free to go after that. Any issues, just give us a call."

"Thank you," Sandling said, glancing quickly at the guard. She was too wary and took her eyes off Zimmer's face. His pale blue, almost translucent eye held her with a steady gaze like an electric current. One thing she knew beyond any doubt was that Zimmer was a keen observer. He never missed anything. A look. A sensation. Something implied but left unsaid. He was a master manipulator. And highly sensitive to others' psyches and emotions, like most sociopathic serial killers are.

The guard left. When they heard the gate at the end of the empty death row shut, Zimmer's eye slid over and he looked at Sandling. His expression was blank, and he leaped slightly forward, feeling uncomfortable because the chair was a bit too small for him.

"Hello, Hermann," Sandling said. Her voice sounded okay to her. She darted her eyes around his face, looking for any semblance of recognition or emotion.

Zimmer clicked his tongue and said, "First name terms from the start, Agent Sandling. How very far we have come. A remarkable evolution," Zimmer looked up, lifted his hand, and gestured around the converted cell. "Welcome to my new digs, Cate. Seems like another world—an *other* world—since we last spoke."

"I would ask how you're finding it, but—"

"That would be the polite thing ..."

They looked at one another for a moment. Zimmer broke the staring contest. He gave her a Cheshire cat grin and said, "And well done you, also. You broke your cherry, as I understand it."

At first, she was confused about what he was referring to. Then it clicked. The look on his face, the vileness behind his eye. He was talking about her killing a man.

"It's not the mile-high club, Hermann, though, is it?"

"No, dear Cate, that it's not. It's so much better, don't you agree?"

It made her feel ill. It pained her. Here she was pretending to share a moment of empathy about taking a life with a convicted serial murderer. She wasn't going to do it.

"No, what I mean is, it isn't something to be proud of. Don't you get that yet?"

Zimmer's sickening smile stayed stuck on his face. "Nevertheless," he said. "It's so significant, wouldn't you agree? It's not losing your virginity as much as gaining your stripes."

"You think it's a promotion?"

"There's no going backward in this life, young Caitlin. Forwards is the only way."

"Why don't they call it gaining your womanhood rather than losing your virginity, then?"

"Isn't Religion a vile thing," Zimmer said with a glint in his eye. "Purity and purification is all."

"Tell that to an obsessive-compulsive germaphobe housewife," Sandling countered.

"I'm more of a yin-yang man myself," Zimmer said.

"Meaning?"

"There's always some evil in the most good and a little good in the most evil," Zimmer said and winked at her. It was such a strange sight, seeing a one-eyed man blink at her. Especially one like this.

"It's never just one thing or the other ..." Sandling said and lifted her fingers to her chin contemplatively. Hermann Zimmer was actually giving her some perspective, ironically, she thought.

"Anyway," Zimmer said.

His voice brought her back. She read the impatience on his face. She didn't want to make Zimmer angry. Keep them calm. Keep them talking. Keep them light and positive. "You were asking about my new digs?"

"Yes," Sandling said.

"Better for us not to speak about it," Zimmer said. "It makes me hot under the collar."

"It's part of the reason I'm here, though," she said, and her voice croaked. She was dying for a sip of water and struggling to hear Zimmer above the noise. She thought there was some electric buzz around them but it was her blood rushing in her ears. Her heart was beating like a drum. She felt hot. She didn't want him to smell it on her … the fear.

"Let's have some small talk anyway," Zimmer said. Sandling was surprised. Taken aback even. Hermann Zimmer wanted to chat. "Shoot the shit, as these oafs say."

He looked around like he was trying to locate a fly on the ceiling. "I'm sure this place has listening devices. They'll probably put something in my food now. Spit, no doubt. I'd better be careful."

She'd not seen him like this before. Paranoid. Under his eye—even under his missing one, which was now made from glass and sat motionless in its socket—had dark rings under it. A lack of sleep. A lack of exercise. A lack of rest.

"You think I'm imagining it?" Zimmer asked.

She didn't know what to say. Keep it professional. Keep it tight. What would Augustine Carver do?

"We have a question to ask you."

"Just one?"

"One important one, yes."

"When you say 'we,' to whom do you refer, Cate? Augustine and yourself, or Behavioral Analysis at Quantico?"

It was a good question, she thought. Knowing Zimmer—as well as she could know a delusional psychopath—she knew he was probing for weakness. The answer would tell him a lot about a lot of things. Depending on what she said, he would know where she was, whether she'd moved up in the Bureau. Whether Carver was alive, injured, working, or retired. And what the aftereffects of his little human chess game were.

"A bit of both," Sandling said.

Zimmer smirked with half his mouth. His eye glinted. The glass one looked ahead, dead and unmoving.

"Whatever became of Dr. Forsmith, that quack over at Patton State?"

Sandling shook her head. "I'm afraid I don't know, Hermann."

"You remember what we said about lying?"

"Yes."

There was a second of pure energy between them like some connection had been made. A crossing of the Rubicon. No way back from here.

"You're not enjoying prison?"

Zimmer's posture changed. He seemed unsure whether Sandling was goading him, and his demeanor was hostile. He flicked between moods with the click of a finger, like that. It scared her. She thought about leaving, but she couldn't. The gate at the end of the hall was locked shut.

"Do you have another one on the loose?" Zimmer asked.

"Yes," she said. He smiled. It made her feel sick to think that he enjoyed knowing there was someone out there killing people for sport.

"Tell me about him," Zimmer said.

She put her hand flat on the folder on the desk. "First, tell me about these."

"What have you got there?"

"Pictures."

"Are they of the victims?" He showed his teeth in more of a snarl than a smile.

"No."

"I'll take a look, but no more. Tell me about him ..."

"What do you need to know?" Sandling asked.

"Really, Cate? You know the moves to this dance already. It's a Foxtrot, not a *fucking* Waltz." She shuddered as he swore. It was so violent coming from his mouth. A little spittle stuck on the corner of his mouth. He wiped it away with his sleeve.

"How many have been killed?"

"Two so far," Sandling said. Lying.

Zimmer watched her closely with his single good eye. "Just getting started then, isn't he?"

"That we know of."

"How does he do it?"

"First look at the file."

Zimmer flopped his head to his shoulder and watched her. She squirmed and cleared her throat. God, it's hot in here, she thought. She daren't remove her jacket.

"What're they calling him?" Zimmer asked.

She shook her head. "He hasn't been anointed by the press corps yet," Sandling said.

"What are you calling him?"

She didn't want to say. "The medical examiner called him the Incubus killer."

Zimmer lifted his hand to his chin. "Hmm. Let's see; a male demon who fucks women as they sleep ... how interesting. So, he's a necrophile?"

Demon was right, she thought. He's also a cannibal, kidnapper, and serial killer.

"That's what the report of the autopsy says."

"A real lunatic then," Zimmer said. No hint of a smile.

The light in Zimmer's eye danced as she watched him. Even though she was sitting opposite one of the most insane men she'd ever encountered she could appreciate the irony of Zimmer's statement. She wondered if it was a genuine attempt at wit or whether he truly lacked self-awareness.

"You could say that," she said. She felt a tiny prick of pleasure that she hadn't risen to the bait. This wasn't a conversation as much as a challenge of wit. A chess match of the mind. Emotion and control were important above all else.

"Show me your file."

Sandling opened the cover. She showed him one image and kept the others hidden. Rachel Fox used her image analysis software and digital research wizardry to pull together a briefing pack on the symbols and what they could mean. Of the list of possibles, Sandling had been most swayed by this one. She spun it around so Zimmer could see. He squinted his right eye and leaned in. She studied his blotched, sagging face and thinning, greasy hair. Zimmer stared at the image.

"Okay," he said. "What about it."

"What is it?" Sandling asked. Her tone wasn't inquisitive though, it came out challenging, and Zimmer heard it.

"Don't tell me you don't already know," Zimmer said.

Of course, she knew. But what it *meant* was another thing altogether. It was important enough to the case that it brought her to a maximum security prison to rekindle her relationship with Zimmer the Ripper. And similar enough to the blood-drawn symbols found at the Peninsula killer scenes—while also different enough—to make the mystery of their similarity a dark alley she knew she had to go down.

Although the burn marks were rough and rudimentary, this was the shape and lines that Fox's software program managed to isolate. It was known as the Eye of Horus, and it was usually placed inside a pyramid or triangle. It was also known as the Evil Eye.

"Do you recognize it?" Sandling asked.

Zimmer kept watching her. She could almost see his mind working.

"Of course," Zimmer said.

"From where?"

Again, he paused, unsure of exactly her meaning. His mouth inclined just at the edge in a grin.

"I see," he said. "Remind you of someone?"

"Does it remind *you* of someone?"

"I'm not sure," Zimmer said. "I'd need some time to think on it. Ruminate."

"To scheme, you mean."

"Come, come, dear Cate," he said in a tone imploring her not to break the rules of their game.

"Time is the one thing we don't have, Hermann."

"While it's the only thing I have, my dear. Time is the only thing I have. All the time in the world."

Sandling pursed her lips. And there we are, she thought.

"That's how this works, Cate, you know that. Still want to climb into bed with me?"

"I thought they were just cots in here?" Sandling said.

Zimmer smiled. Audacious. She knew she would pay for that one. Maybe not now, but later. Zimmer knew it too.

"Tell me about the image, please?" Sandling said, touching the folder.

"Give me something in return first."

"You know I can't do that."

"What? The—*special*—agent can't pull some strings?"

"Tell me about it," Sandling said, standing her ground.

She wasn't giving territory to him early this time. She wasn't as naive as she was before.

"The Eye of Horus, you mean?" Zimmer asked.

She looked at him impassively. Not showing her cards this time either. So he did know what it was. It was a start. Now, did he know what it meant and whether it linked—at all—to the killings in California?

"What does it mean?"

Zimmer sighed. "Are you testing me, Cate? After I was the one who pointed you in the direction of young Edward Derange?"

She felt a pang. Zimmer bringing it up. The whole agony flashed inside her.

"Of course not," she said. It came out as a whisper. She cleared her throat.

"Did you know then," Zimmer said, "that Horus used his eye to restore his dead father, Osiris, to life?"

Renewal, Sandling thought, okay ... "Did he?" she asked.

"Indeed," Zimmer said. "To bring about *Maat*. You know what that is?"

Sandling shook her head.

"Did you do any reading on Ancient Egyptian religion before coming here?"

She didn't answer, taking her berating like a good little schoolgirl in front of the wise and powerful teacher. Deference could be a powerful tactic in a negotiation. She shook her head. Sometimes playing dumb was the right thing.

"Maat is cosmic balance, Caitlin," Zimmer said. "The gods provide harmony—so long as truth and justice are maintained."

"Okay," Sandling said, only half following him.

"Do you see?" Zimmer asked. She didn't say anything. "Maintaining Maat is a reciprocal relationship—if one upholds Maat, the universe remains in balance, if one disrupts Maat, well, chaos ensues. As I'm sure your new peregrine knows only too well."

"I see," Sandling said. And she did. Zimmer felt like their Maat was out of balance.

"One hand washes the other," Zimmer said.

"What do you want?" Sandling asked looking up at Zimmer.

"You're not as drawn as I am, Caitlin," Zimmer said. "But it looks like we're on the same diet, special agent."

"Are they not feeding you, or are you not eating?"

"They feed me, but this way I get to have a trip to the medical center every few months so they can put me on an IV and force a tube down my throat. It's the little pleasures, don't you think?" Zimmer bared his gums, showing her. He had nubs for teeth. A bulging protruding pink gum. Sandling unconsciously pressed her lips together, closing her mouth.

"Gingivitis, Caitlin. They won't let me floss. Barely let me use a toothbrush. It's inhuman."

Zimmer was older now, she thought, but his hands were still big and powerful. Sandling had often imagined him bent over the open skulls of the men who'd sought his professional help. He was the only man who claimed to understand them. Who claimed to know how to stop the headaches.

"My father had four wives. All of them were aged between fourteen and sixteen when he met and married them," Zimmer said. "My mother was last. Her family moved to San Francisco from a small hamlet in Austria. My father is American, I am American. I deserve to be treated as an American. I have rights."

"Your father the serial killer?"

Zimmer raised an eyebrow. "So Augustine told you?"

Sandling didn't respond. "And now the truth is out in the open," Zimmer said. "More ties that bind, don't you agree?"

The little girl her daddy left behind and all alone wanted to ask him, *why'd you do it? Why'd you take him away from me?* But she knew she couldn't. What good would it do? Zimmer could already read the pain on her face no matter how much she tried to hide it. She just left the elephant standing there in the corner of the prison cell.

"You want me to ask the warden for better nutrition?"

Zimmer considered it for a moment.

"They've taken away my writing tools. They're killing me, slowly. It's time to start on my memoirs," he said. "Have them bring me some writing paper and a fountain pen, with some ink. I should like to write."

"A pencil," Sandling countered.

Zimmer acquiesced. "And something to sharpen it with."

"I'll see what I can do."

Sandling leaned to her left and pressed the button on the wall. She heard it buzz far away. They sat in silence. The tension was palpable. No one was coming. After a minute—which seemed like fifteen—Sandling pressed the buzzer again. Despite forcing herself to stay calm she felt a cloud of apprehension drift over her face. Zimmer, so in tune with the psyches of others, picked up on it. Another chance for him to show his power.

"Don't worry, Cate. It's prison routine. If you check the time, you'll notice they're in the middle of a shift change. A prison is like a hospital or a regiment, everything is done by the clock. It could be a long time until they're ready to come and get you out of here ... A long, long time."

She felt her breathing shallow. Her heart rate quickened. Her pupils dilate. In contrast, Zimmer seemed to relax. He leaned on the back of his chair and kept a still gaze over

Sandling. He was much bigger than her and not locked to the table between them. She wouldn't let that happen again. If there was to be a next time. He could be on her in a flash of handcuffs and prison jumpsuits.

"How do you think they'd react if they came in here and found your head sitting on the table?" Zimmer asked.

She was trying not to panic. She couldn't run. Where was she going to go? The gate at the end of death row was locked. She'd be screaming for her life.

"Doubt anyone would be around to hear you scream even," Zimmer said. He tiled his ear and said, "Listen. Quiet. Isn't it?"

There were no sounds. Only car engines, far away. The occasional distant slam. He'd choke her out and no one would even know.

Sandling cleared her throat. "Yes, you'd kill me, Hermann. Easily. We both know that. But what then? What about the Maat? How are you going to get your writing paper and your quinoa?"

"Maybe, but imagine the kudos from my fellow inmates if I smoked a hot little FBI agent," he said and licked his top lip. "I see the headlines now: 'Zimmer the Ripper strikes again.' The legend reborn."

She swallowed and made her voice hide her panic. "You could try, Hermann," Sandling said. "But as a federal agent, I don't need to make an appointment, I don't need to ask permission to see you, and I don't have to give up my weapon. Do you think I'd come in here unarmed? Especially when I'm left alone with you?"

Sandling had to say something to get Zimmer's mind off the idea of killing her before the prison guards came to release her. The last part was a lie, but she knew he was like a dog with a bone. He wasn't going to let go of the idea. And like a seed planted in rich soil, that idea would only sprout and grow and his fantasy would develop until it was the only thing he could think about. That's how these sexual crimes happen. Deeply ingrained fantasies that are richer and more real than anything else in their lives. She swore at herself. Never again would she visit him alone. In a way, she felt this was all Carver's fault. He should be here with her and he wasn't. Just then, she heard a loud buzz and a key slide home in the large metal gate. Oh, thank God, she thought. Zimmer smiled. He could sense the relief in her.

"Perhaps next time, Special Agent Sandling," Zimmer said as the footsteps grew louder. The guard appeared. He gave Sandling a nod and said, "Ma'am."

Zimmer stood and held his hands forward for the guard to guide him out of the cell. "I'm already looking forward to our next chat. Don't keep me waiting too long …"

18

"Longpig," Rachel Fox said as she read the words on the screen. She looked over her shoulder into the dark living room to check she wasn't disturbing her grandmother, who was asleep in her armchair.

Fox couldn't get over the idea of eating another human being. She'd been trawling the internet for information and come across some disturbing stuff. She'd so far learned that the term 'longpig' was borrowed from the infamous cannibal tribes of Papua New Guinea. It was what they called human meat. There were references to it on all sorts of depraved websites devoted to sadomasochism, bondage, and eating other humans. She swallowed and made a *gulp* sound. Her mouth was dry. Normally, her grandmother's presence was comforting, but now she worried she might wake up and glimpse the horrifying content on the screen. She took a swig of her Diet Coke and leaned towards the monitor.

The thought of a cannibal roaming the greater Baltimore area was enough to laser-focus her inhuman ability to concentrate on one thing and one thing only. Running through her mind as she worked was the question of why she was so captivated by the cannibalism side of it. Was it tied to her aversion to anything but the blandest foods? If it wasn't white, soft, and textureless, she couldn't force herself to eat it. She didn't eat animal products. Not that she was a vegan. Her grandmother—who she lived with and looked after—had learned to fry up a floured white fish that she could swallow in one bite if she held her breath and did it quickly and without thinking.

Fox was already six hours into a dark web internet trawling session and wasn't about to stop any time soon. She might go and pull the covers over her head when the sun poked up. There was a whole underworld of people, all over the globe, who were into this stuff. On one side, those fascinated by the idea of being killed, butchered, and eaten; and on the other, people who were consumed by the idea of eating human flesh. Fox was reading about a fifty-five-year-old German man—who went by the handle *Caligula*—who met a sixty-year-old Polish truck driver on the dark web at a site called ... "Zambian Meat," Fox said out loud.

Caligula then took this man to the cellar of a bed and breakfast he owned and strung him up, slashed his throat, collected his blood in an old paint tin, and spent the next five hours butchering his corpse. Fox felt ill and took another swig of her Coke to wash the smell and taste of old paint mixed with blood out of her mouth. Okay, Fox thought, guess I'm looking for a site called *Zambian Meat*. She started typing Z-A-M-B-I-A-N-M-E-A-T into a secure browser for surfing the oil-black pirate-infested waters of the dark web. She stopped breathing. The banner of the website was two men roasting a woman on a spit. Fox couldn't wrap her head around the idea of a cannibal in Baltimore; she was now struggling to grasp what she saw on the screen. She'd seen all sorts of things on the internet and been fine, but this was harrowing. How was it that these sites even existed? But ... there it was right in front of her. She just had this hunch that *if* this unsub was a cannibal, as the crime scenes suggested, he *must* be the real person behind one of the usernames on this site. It made total sense. So, what was she after? She wondered.

What she needed was enough to present to the Carver, Sandling, and the Sofa Squad. She'd have to get enough evidence to convince the team that a cannibal was trawling the streets of the city, and he was active on a forum of sick individuals with sick fantasies about making their sick ideas into reality. The only difference was, while most 'Longpigs' were looking for a 'master chef' to fulfill their fantasy of being eaten—kind of like a dating app for cannibals—there was only one willing party in the way the unsub was going about it.

He'd want to brag, though, right? Most serial killers do —whether to the papers, the police, or the public. If she could convince them, maybe she'd be in line for some field work, too. It happened for Sandling, why couldn't it happen for her? She had ambitions. It was the first step out of Grant Avenue and back to the life and career she wanted.

Fox made an account—*HungryFox25*—and became a member of *Zambian Meat*. She went deep into the murky well. People wanted to be killed—not just killed, slaughtered, like an animal—and there were people who would do the slaughtering. First, she had to learn their terminology— this sub-dialect of twisted cannibal slang. A 'chef', she learned, was a seasoned cannibal. A 'master chef' was a cannibal who could also butcher and prepare the human flesh. It was severe. She felt disgusted but also a tingling excitement, which was weird. Still, she didn't want to know more than she absolutely had to.

The first thing she needed to do, besides engage on the forum to build up a history of activity and gain their trust, was to narrow down the field of potential suspects. She needed to separate the twisted fantasists from someone who was a dangerous, deranged predator and killer of human beings. The obvious thing would be to focus only on the master chefs. People who claimed to butcher and consume other people. As wild as it sounded to her, she knew it happened. She'd read about another case in Germany where a cannibal was serving a life sentence for murdering, dismembering, and eating a computer technician at his remote farmhouse. The cannibal neatly packaged the 225 lb victim into little baking paper-wrapped parcels and ate him over the following year. When they caught him, only about a quarter of the victim's flesh was left in the freezer.

"I wonder how he was preparing it?" Fox said to herself, and then she felt a suspicion that it wasn't acceptable to wonder about that. Was it a stew or casserole? Was he frying it? She wondered if he was a good cook and a cannibal. With her headphones over her ears, she dove deeper into the depths of *Zambian Meat*, determined to drag her suspect into shallower waters.

19

CAITLIN SANDLING DROVE SLOWLY through the tree-lined streets and red-brick buildings of Johns Hopkins University. Carver sat in the passenger seat beside her. The whole drive over, he'd been switching intermittently between glancing out of the window and glancing at her out of the corner of his eye. He was waiting for an opening, she'd thought. A chance to speak. She didn't want to give it to him.

She could feel him looking at her. This was strictly business for her. A quick introduction to her Bureau appointed therapist and she could move on with her investigation. She had both hands on the wheel, gripping it a little too tightly, as he tried to ignore him. His body—just *there*. She didn't like his proximity. His presence felt invasive, making her tense up. Like David, her ex-husband had when she touched him towards the end. A mild revulsion. Maybe it was Carver's smell that revolted her. She didn't like the laundry detergent he used—she doubted he used a fabric softener—to wash his clothes. Damn it, she thought. Now, she had her ex-husband on her mind. No, she thought, it wasn't weird to be thinking about him. After all, they were on their way to Dr. Blackwood's office. And, naturally, her former husband had come up during their sessions. They were high school sweethearts. And—typically—David Sandling was a local high school hero. Captain of the you-name-it ... football, baseball, and wrestling teams. Just a local guy living his life on a high. He didn't even really need to try. It came so effortlessly and easily to him. She was in complete adoration. And she became attached to the comfort he provided. Physically, he could protect her. When he had his big bear arm around her, with his hand wrapped into the crook of her shoulder, she felt something she hadn't felt since she was a little girl running into her daddy's arms. She felt safe. She felt protected. She felt like somebody cared. And that was exactly what Dr. Blackwood picked up on in one of their earliest sessions. Her unhealthy relationship with men was because of the death of her father. The realization flashed like a spark in the middle of a dark wood. It shouldn't have. In retrospect, it was the most obvious thing in the world. Not bad for a doctorate in psychology, huh? she thought. But wasn't life always like that? It was always the best accountants who were the worst with money. Or the most conservative financial advisors who take the most personal risks. The human animal's behavior was a strange thing out in the wild, she thought. Her present case. That cannibal thing ... if nothing else, proved her hypothesis.

She felt Carver glance at her again and instinctively reached for the volume knob on the car stereo. The truth was that Carver was in better shape than she'd seen him in a while, pain from his gunshot wound notwithstanding. Maybe she was the one facing a slippery slope, not him. She felt less healthy. Drawn out. Like somehow she'd started drying out in the sun. She turned up a little bit of classic country as Carver said, a little too loudly, "So you went to see Zimmer yesterday?"

"Yeah," she said and gave him a straight-faced smile. "I'd rather not talk about it."

She didn't want to seem rude—or maybe she did—but she wasn't in the headspace to be talking about Hermann Zimmer right now. Now that they were talking, though, she might as well keep going.

"Listen," she said. "There are a few things I wanted to discuss. As you know, I'm seeing Dr. Blackwood professionally—recommended by the agency—but still, I feel like I'm starting to make progress there so ..." she looked across at him earnestly, "... so please could you *try* and be nice to him? He's actually helping me, and until this thing of yours becomes an official investigation, I don't want you to mess with my sessions."

"Hell, *mess with your sessions,* but okay," Carver said and gave her a single nod. "Of course, sure thing, but this *is* an official investigation, Cate. Right?"

She clenched the steering wheel even tighter. "Even so, could you just be—"

"Nice?" Carver ventured a guess.

She wanted to say a little less like *you*. Too late. They were here. She pulled in front of a squat rectangular red building and saw the words Gilmore Hall above an arched entrance. She stopped in front of a black wrought iron gate that had a sign saying, 'no parking at any time' on it and unclipped her belt.

"Is this where you come for your sessions?" Carver asked.

She shook her head as she pulled the keys out of the ignition. "No, I head into town. Dr. Blackwood has a treatment room in the city."

They climbed out. Sandling squinted into the sunlight and looked around. She liked the sensation of being back on a college campus. The vibe was serene. She wondered if it was the lack of urgency or responsibility. The whole leafy-green aura made Johns Hopkins feel like a library—quiet and contemplative.

"Do you know where you're going?" Carver asked.

She didn't respond. They'd soon find out. She walked under the Gilmore Hall arch and climbed some brick stairs until she saw the Department of Psychological and Brain Sciences above a door. She spoke to a middle-aged receptionist and took a seat against the wall. No need to show her badge. Carver followed her lead but left a spare chair between them. They'd been waiting around ten minutes and staring at the same saying, embroidered in lace in a small, square frame: *Small minds talk about people, medium minds talk about things, big minds talk about ideas.* It sounded good. Accurate even. But the longer she sat there looking at it, absentmindedly biting her cheek, the more she thought it was hogwash. Talking only about ideas made you an idealist, while ignoring people showed a lack of real-world understanding. It was an apt quote for academia where they had little ceremonies and bits of official-looking paper to congratulate one another on their 'ideas'. Practicality be damned. No need to let real life intrude on your 'thinking'.

She looked up when she heard a creaking floorboard above them. "Dr. Blackwood is ready for you now," the receptionist said just as Sandling saw him at the top of the staircase. He lifted his hand and said, "Come on up," then turned and disappeared.

Carver trudged up the stairs behind her. The closer they got to his office, the more nervous she felt, like a schoolgirl summoned to see the headmaster.

20

Augustine Carver and Caitlin Sandling stood just inside the doorway of Dr. Blackwood's office. He didn't look up at them. He was busy writing something on his notepad with a fountain pen. The office was longer than it was wide, with floor-to-ceiling wooden bookcases on each side of them. There were two leather chairs in front of Blackwood's large mahogany writing desk and, behind him, bay windows that looked out over the greenery of the Johns Hopkins campus. The thing that caught Carver's eye was a painting hanging behind Dr. Blackwood's desk, almost touching the ceiling. It was oil on canvas, but the picture was mesmerizing. Done in thick swabs of black, maroon, and purple. It seemed like a dark sunset. The picture was a mirror image in two halves, like an evil-looking bunny from a Rorschach test. It was open to interpretation about what you saw. The paint swirled and drifted and moved in patterns which, although Carver didn't believe in the analysis of art like this, almost led him to try and read into the mind of the artist as a troubled. *Messed up, I guess you'd say*, Carver thought. He saw Dr. Blackwood staring blank-faced up at him. His expression turned into a smile.

"Caitlin! Special Agent Carver, come in and sit down."

Dr. Blackwood stood and tucked in his shirt and hiked his suit trousers up a little. He took a step forward and extended his hand. Carver took it. They locked eyes.

"Dr. Blackwood," Carver said by way of acknowledgment.

"Please, call me Edmund."

Carver saw that he was tall and wiry-looking, but his grip was strong, much stronger than Carver would have expected from a nerdy academic. They released each other's hands, and Carver pulled his chair. He looked at Sandling and said, "Dr. Blackwood was the lead psychologist on Zimmer's medical tribunal."

"Oh, I didn't know," Sandling said quietly. "I wasn't there for that." She sounded like she was processing all of this new information. Now, it made sense to Carver why she'd been so coy and dismissive about making the introduction.

"You didn't mention it?" Carver asked Dr. Blackwood. He was sitting down again, holding his fountain pen like he was about to take a deposition.

He had on his permanent, polite smile. "To be honest, I thought you knew," he said to her. "I also didn't think it relevant to your sessions." It was said forthrightly and dismissively, like he was trying to get out of a conversation with a neighbor. Carver was looking up at the painting again. He couldn't take his eyes off it. Blackwood noticed him looking and half-turned to acknowledge it, and said, "Strange and impressive, isn't it?" and glanced at Carver.

He didn't reply immediately, but then he nodded and said, "Yes, it is. Very strange."

"It was done for me by one of my first patients as a trainee clinical psychologist during my apprenticeship. Part of his treatment, which was revolutionary at the time—at least for me—was to try and alleviate some of his more dire symptoms with a combination of pharmacology, clinical psychology, and what we ended up calling 'art therapy'. He ended up being quite good, this one, you know. Most of them can't draw for peanuts; excuse my French. But this guy had a semi-stable family relationship, and his mother was into the piano, so he could play. I guess he had something of an artistic bent."

"That was your American Psychiatric Association paper," Carver said. "I remember it caused quite a stir in the community at the time." Dr. Blackwood looked suitably smug but played it down, trying to be humble. Carver could see that it still tickled him to have people remember his work.

"What is it?" Carver asked.

"I'm sure you can tell, can't you? It's a patient's interpretation of his mental illness."

"What does it mean?" Sandling asked.

Dr. Blackwood dropped the corners of his mouth and gave a slight shake of his head. "I have no idea. We never spoke about it. It was the last time I saw him, he handed me this without saying a word. A memento, if you like, of our sessions together. He made a very impressive recovery," Dr. Blackwood said. "But luckily, as I say, the patient had a loving family to take care of them and make sure they stayed on their medication."

"Are you still in touch?" Carver asked.

"Heaven no," Dr. Blackwood said and glanced back up at the picture, "It was so long ago now. His mother was given custody of him, and I believe they left the state." Dr. Blackwood smiled politely. "It's just a nice little anecdote for people," he said. "Students come to see me, and it's a living, visceral, tangible experience with an outside world they'd all like to be a part of, do you understand?" He looked at Carver from under his eyebrows.

"Mm-hmm," Carver said, trying to look pleasant. There was a moment of silence, but just before it became awkward, Dr. Blackwood said, "So, in your official capacity, special agents, what is it you think I can do to help?"

Carver and Sandling looked at one another, each checking if the other wanted to take the lead. "You mentioned a paper you wrote, Dr. Blackwood, on art therapy."

"That's right," Blackwood said and nodded as Carver spoke. He was watching him intently.

"You also wrote a different paper on police suicide, if I'm not mistaken? *Mystery Within*, I believe it was called ..."

"Understanding police suicide, yes, mm-hmm," Blackwood said. "We compared rates of suicide of fighter-fighters and military personnel."

"Interesting," Carver said. "And what did you find?"

"Excuse me—if I may—is this regarding a case you're working on?" Blackwood stared at Sandling as he spoke to Carver. "Caitlin wasn't too forthcoming with the details."

"We're in the preliminary stages of an investigation," Carver said.

"Ha!" Blackwood said and leaned back in his chair. "You always were one to keep your cards close to your chest, weren't you, special agent?" Carver shrugged. "Is it an investigation into police suicides? I thought the Federal Bureau of Investigation had strict remits about when and how they go about getting involved in cases," Blackwood said.

"Yes, well, as I say, we're in the evidence-gathering phase of our investigation."

"And you wanted me to consult?" Blackwood sounded eager. "I have some experience, as you know, working hand in glove, so to speak, with the criminal justice system."

This is what Carver was afraid of. These so-called

experts always wanted to take more rope than he was willing to give.

"Thanks, Dr. Blackwood, but—"

"Call me Edmund, please."

"... that might be an option in the future. In the meantime, would you be willing to discuss some of your findings and impressions of your findings with us?"

"Relating to the police suicides?"

"Yes," Carver said and felt himself getting frustrated.

"Of course! Fire away."

Just then, there was a light tapping on the door. It opened. Sandling turned to look, Carver lifted his hand to his eyes and massaged his temples.

"Ah, Abigail, come in, come in," Blackwood said. "Abigail, these are Special Agents, Carver, right here," Blackwood indicated to Carver. He turned and smiled. "And Sandling, they're here to talk about some of the research we're doing, isn't that right?"

"I'm so sorry to interrupt you, professor," Abigail said.

"No, don't be silly. Never mind," Blackwood said and sounded pleased to be able to show off his standing to an impressionable young student. He'd love to set the tongues in the department and around campus wagging, Carver bet. Dr. Blackwood addressed the special agents now and said, "Abigail is one of my finest grad students. She helps me with all of my research these days."

Carver turned to glance at the girl again. She was of average height with average looks. She had mousy-brown hair, parted in the middle, and hazel eyes concealed by thick-rimmed black spectacles. She was carrying a stack of books and a thick file and holding them close to her black knit top. With a plaid skirt and black leather shoes, she looked more like she was wearing an expensive private schoolgirl's uniform than someone in grad school. She was looking at the floor and pushed her specs back up to the bridge of her nose.

"I just wanted to let you know I was next door working," she said quietly to Dr. Blackwood.

"Of course, no problem. See you later then, Abigail." She turned and went out, shutting the door as she left.

"Charming young woman," Dr. Blackwood said and smiled. "Just come to think of it," he continued, "Perhaps there would be a chance to add to our paper, or even write a new one, depending on how the case develops?"

Carver was watching him. Strange fellow, he thought. He didn't want to make any promises.

"What can you tell me about them?"

"Police suicides?"

"Yes."

"Well," Dr. Blackwood said and held his hands in prayer close to his mouth, and stared down at his desk, "Police officers in the United States are a fifty-four percent higher suicide risk than the general population, for a start. They're constantly exposed to severe, traumatic events. They suffer fivefold the rate of post-traumatic stress disorder when compared to ordinary civilians. They work more, sleep less, and because it's shift work and irregular hours, their family lives suffer." Dr. Blackwood glanced up and said, "I fear I am preaching to the converted, though."

"Go on," Carver said, shrugging off the implication Dr. Blackwood was trying to make about him and Sandling.

"Of course, easy access to firearms significantly raises the likelihood of fatal suicide attempts, sadly."

That sparked Carver's interest. "That's what I was thinking," Carver said.

"What?" Dr. Blackwood asked.

"About the firearms ... do you have data on methods of

suicide? Does anybody record how someone tries to take their own life?"

Blackwood pursed his lips and thought for a moment. He shook his head. "No—it is an interesting perspective—but no, I don't think the method was widely recorded. We can go back and have a look, though, if that might be helpful. I can have Abigail reassess the data."

Carver was thinking.

"Why, might I ask, are you investigating police suicides?" Dr. Blackwood asked. Carver looked into his eyes. Watching him. When Carver still didn't respond, Dr. Blackwood filled the silence, "Unfortunately, something we're up against is that many of the statistics and records are unintentionally doctored under the cultural and instinctual understanding the police have to protect the institution. It's one of those things that everybody knows about, but nobody talks about. It's the same with emergency room doctors. The suicide rate is about four times the national population; did you know that?"

Carver's trance broke, and he shook his head and said, "No, I didn't know that."

Dr. Blackwood checked his watch. "Shoot," he said. "I have a faculty meeting starting now—I'm already late—but did you get what you needed?"

Carver went to stand. Sandling and Blackwood followed his lead and stood. "For now, I think so, yes," Carver said and extended his hand. Blackwood took it briefly and then let go.

"Let me get Abigail, who you just met, to get back in touch with any further data that might be useful, and, if there was anything—anything at all—that may be useful, you just let her know, and we can get right on it."

"You seem eager to help," Carver said. "We appreciate that."

"Oh, I am, I'm sure it's the least we can do. It's just such a thrill to think that our research may aid an investigation in some way. Perhaps there's an opportunity to have some details from the case for us to write another paper about it ..."

Carver gave a single laugh. This guy never quits. "Sure—if we catch him—but I won't be painting you any more Rorschach test pictures and passing it off as fine art," he said and smiled broadly to let Blackwood know it was in jest.

"Ha! No, I very much doubt that you will, Augustine," Dr. Blackwood said. "We'll save those for the mental patients, shan't we?" And winked at him. Carver furrowed his brow for a split second, a smile still on his face. An odd thing to say, but hey, touché.

Their eyes were locked with half-grins firmly fixed on their faces. It grew awkward.

"Should we go?" Sandling suggested.

"Here's my card," Carver said and slid a card from his wallet. Blackwood took it, held it up, and said, "We'll get back to you."

21

SANDLING LIFTED her hand and waved goodbye to the receptionist. Carver followed her out the front doors and down the red steps of the Psychological and Brain Sciences building. They were squarely in the middle of the vast campus. As she stepped out into the sunlight, she saw the ant-like scurrying of college students back and forth. Carver came up next to her and said, "I don't remember which way it was."

She said, "It's down here," and pointed to their right.

Even though it was a short walk through campus back to where she'd parked, she wasn't going to start the conversation with Carver. She preferred not to engage. She was still feeling hurt. Somehow, this man just had a way of encroaching into her life. The meeting they just had with her therapist was a case in point. How did she get herself in a position where Carver was sitting down and having a dick-measuring contest with *her* therapist? It just belied belief.

"You were quiet in there," Carver said as they walked. "Everything okay?"

"Uh-huh," Sandling said.

If she wasn't so annoyed by the whole situation, she'd be

enjoying the bright green leafy walk in the sunshine through such a beautiful place. She'd loved college; hell, she'd spent enough time there reading for her PhD. She'd had the full experience of each of those seven years. But somehow, now it seemed like another galaxy like she wasn't even the same person. It was hard for her to look back and think of all the hopes, dreams, and possibilities she had in college. And then, here she was, walking next to a man who betrayed her, and him having just given his business card to the man she entrusted to fix her.

"I know this great barbecue spot on the corner of Union and Ash," Carver said.

Sandling put on her dark sunglasses, about to step into the car, and said, "What?"

She looked at him like a teenager looks at their parents when asked to take out the trash. Perplexity and annoyance.

"What?" Carver asked. "It's only five minutes from here."

"I was thinking of heading back to Annapolis," Sandling said. "Are you all right to get a cab back from here?"

"Listen, I don't know about you, but I'm starving," Carver said. "And ..." He looked her up and down.

"And *what*?" She stopped opening the door, stood up straight, and waited for him to reply.

Carver climbed into the passenger seat and looked across at her standing there. Sandling stayed still for a second. She wished he could feel her frustration. Or understand the empathy and anguish of a child watching their parents argue. She opened the door and got in.

"So you're not taking a taxi?"

"You look like you could use a good meal," Carver said.

She shook her head. "Yeah, you're not the first person to tell me that this week."

"See?" Carver said, then unsure who she meant, asked, "Wait, who else told you that?"

"Who do you think?" she glanced at him and started the engine.

"Right, so you're putting me in the same category as Zimmer now?"

She lifted her eyebrow as she reversed out of the parking spot and didn't reply. Carver sat quietly. He seemed like he was finding those barbs a little hard to take, even if she'd said it tongue in cheek. Maybe he was right, she thought; calling him Zimmer was hurtful. She was still really angry with him, she realized. She knew she was upset, annoyed even, but to think of him in the same breath as the man who killed her father? That was too much, Caitlin.

"Where am I going?" she asked. Carver stared out the windshield and said nothing. She stopped, waiting to hear which direction the barbecue joint was going in. "Carver?"

"Huh?" he said and looked at her.

"Which way?"

"Oh, ah, go down here and then turn left onto San Martin."

SANDLING COULD SMELL it from the street. She leaned forward over the steering wheel to look through the windshield at a white building with large, dark-glass windows. It had more of a small factory look to it than a really good barbecue place. She pulled into a parking spot on the narrow street and got out.

"We're here," Carver said. He sounded excited, she thought.

"Wait, we're here?" Sandling asked. "I don't see any ... Oh! There it is. I see." She saw a small blue sign that said: *Blue Pitt BBQ*.

They went up a few stairs and inside. It took a second for

her eyes to adjust to the dankness. The air tasted of spices. The whole place, floor, ceiling, chairs, and tables were all made out of dark-stained wood. Even the restaurant was the color of barbecue, Sandling noticed.

Carver took a seat in a booth at the back while Sandling looked around before joining him. There was an outside area in the sun and she took her handbag off her shoulder and set it down on the floor. Sliding into the booth, she asked, "Wouldn't it be better outside in the fresh air?"

"I'm waiting," Carver said, prodding his index finger onto the table. "This is where it's at. Smoky barbecue, you know? You need to go for the whole experience."

"Sure, but I wasn't planning on having to try and clean this suit. Now I'm going to have to go and pick out another. I'll have to put that on the agency, right?"

Carver leaned back and gave her a single nod, kind of acknowledging the attempt at a joke.

After a long silence, she asked, "How did you hear about this place anyway?" She heard somebody shout, "Carver! Hey, Carver!" from the kitchen. Sandling saw a big gentleman, wearing a white apron, a white chef's hat, and black gloves, standing in the back and calling over to them. "Wait a second. I'm coming out," he hollered.

"You know the owner?" Sandling asked. He smiled and gave her a nod as he stood. She was surprised. A broadly built man with West African features came bundling onto the restaurant floor. He had to duck under one of the roof beams and put his dinner plate-sized hand out for Carver to shake. Sandling hadn't ever seen a man as big as him. She thought maybe a retired center from the Baltimore Bullets just stepped out of the kitchen.

"Special Agent Carver, as I live and breathe," the big man said. His voice was deep and husky. His accent sounded West African mixed with Texan, but Sandling couldn't be sure. Carver smiled, released the big man's grip, and pointed to Sandling. The chef changed the direction of his shoulders and put his hand outstretched under Sandling's chin.

"Caitlin Sandling, this is Big Mo Waller. He's the proud owner of the best barbecue ribs in all of Baltimore."

"Stop it, Mr. Carver, you are too much." He looked at Sandling. "Let me tell you something Miss Caitlin," Big Mo said, as he delicately took her hand. She felt like a toddler holding onto her father's finger when his hand enveloped hers. "Agent Carver is the best in the business. He was the one who found my daughter when nobody else could and brought her back to me. You must know that I'm forever grateful to him." He looked at Carver out of the corner of his eye, still holding onto Sandling's hand. "I'm sure he has told you the story?"

"No," Sandling said and shook her head and stared at Carver. She was still a little in awe of him and his career. Of course, he had a connection to a barbecue place because of a case. *Of course, he did.* So typical for this man. He was an agency legend, after all. She shook her head again. It was bewilderment.

"Whatever you want, it's on the house," Big Mo announced.

"Ribs," Carver said.

"Coming right up! Good to see you, my friend."

"Good to see you, Mo."

"Want a soda?" Carver asked as he went over to the fridge. He took out two cans of lemonade and came back, and put one on the table in front of Sandling.

"Thanks," she said and pulled the tab with her fingernail and cracked it open. She took a long pull on the sweet, bubbly drink.

"Cheers," Carver said and clinked his can against hers

"So he's a grateful father?" Sandling asked.

Carver studied her expression to try and read her meaning. He put his can down and smacked his lips. "Yep," he said. "Long time ago now but we're here because these are genuinely the best ribs within a hundred-mile radius, not because Big Mo thinks he owes me something."

"Must be nice to relive the glory days, though, right?"

Carver sighed and shrugged and looked over at the kitchen. He was thinking about it. He glanced back at Sandling. "I'm not gonna lie, it's a nice feeling to come back and find someone who is joyful now instead of being all torn up inside, that's for sure. It's not often we get to have that in this profession."

Sandling took a sip of her drink in place of having a suitably deep response to what Carver was talking about. She'd been thinking a lot more about that idea recently; Why was she doing the things she was doing? The truth was that if her father had been a bricklayer she probably would have been a bricklayer, and if he'd been a gardener then she would probably have been a gardener. But as it turned out, he was a special agent with the Federal Bureau of Investigation and he was also her best friend. She felt certain she would have ended up in the same place in her life because he died when she was so young. The picture of him—the profile—she had of him in her mind didn't go through the natural adjustment in perspective that children get of their parents as they advance in life, to then view those moments, situations, and life events retrospectively and assess them as adults. She never got to see her dad as a woman. She only had a child's view of the world as it was, back then. A moment frozen in time. The world to a child looks enormous and scary and something to be protected from, and guided through. She felt like other people who had that stability and knowledge and wisdom—even if flawed—in their lives were on a pre-plotted course with a full tank and fully charged GPS. She felt like she was trying to use a sextant to navigate by the stars while bobbing along on the open sea.

"It's funny how we end up doing what we do, isn't it?" Sandling said.

"How do you mean?" Carver asked.

"I don't know," she said. "In life, I mean. Like how you and I ended up here in the same place doing a similar thing but with nothing really in common."

"Ouch," Carver said.

"No," Sandling said, trying to explain. "I mean it more like nature versus nurture, you know? When I was in grad school, I was convinced it was mostly nurture. How you were brought up, as opposed to your genetics. Now, I'm not sure. I'd go so far as to say I think nurture has very little to do with it."

"Yeah, when you've seen what we've seen—you question a lot of your beliefs," Carver said. "It makes you reevaluate what you think you know about the world. What you understand."

"Right," Sandling said.

A waitress in a black polo shirt brought out two red plastic baskets and set them on the table. "Enjoy," she said, flicking her braids as she walked back to the counter.

"Thanks," Carver said and took a steak knife and a fork out of a paper napkin. It smelled amazing. She might even have to try it, she thought.

"You know, Zimmer once told me that killing human beings was more of a vocation, is how he described it. A vocation," she repeated. "Not an illness, not a sickness, not some depravity against society, *more than a hobby* he said. It's hard work, it requires planning, skill, fearlessness, and he's right, you know, Augustine, these guys we're hunting, it's an actual game for them, I'm sure some of it's compulsive, but what percentage? It's hard to say."

"You're right," Carver said, around a mouthful of sticky, brown barbecue rib meat. "They're all part of the same club, right? They all know about each other, they all study each other, it's like a competition, it's like a crazy underground chess competition, but the players don't know each other. Personally, they never sit opposite one another," Carver said and shrugged. "I mean, what you can do? You have to play one game at a time, and actually, I'd argue that maybe on a theoretical, bigger picture level, it's a who's-the-greatest-of-all-time kind of thing, they're competing, but I'd say that the main competition is against us, you know, witting themselves and their sexual desires against a society which shuns and derides and doesn't understand what they're doing, and rightly so, they are outliers in the human race."

"So interesting, isn't it?" Sandling said as she lifted a french fry into her mouth and took a small nibble. Carver was watching her intently; she knew what he was thinking, that she was gaunt and working herself to death, and she wouldn't even bring herself to have a decent meal.

"Remember that time we went to that burger joint after you met Zimmer for the first time?" Carver asked, clearly trying to draw a distinction to how she was behaving now. "A lot's changed," he said and indicated her plate with his fork.

She agreed quietly, "A lot has changed." She stared at the ground with a thousand-yard stare and unconsciously chewed the chunky French fry.

"Listen, Cate, I, uh, there's something I wanted to say," Carver said.

Sandling looked him in the eyes and furrowed her brow. The look on his face. The sincerity. Oh, God, here it comes, she thought and put her French fry down.

"I'm sorry for—"

She threw down her napkin on the table, raised her voice, and said, "No—save it—*I'm* sorry, Carver, but you don't get to ambush me like this. I didn't even want to be here—remember—and now you're trying to corner me into accepting your apology—again—no ... I'm sorry, but *no*," she said and went to get up.

"Hey, Cate, don't leave. At least finish your food," Carver said.

"The food is lovely," she said towards the kitchen as she slid out of the booth. "But things are hard enough as it is. I don't need this right now. What I need is a professional working relationship with no emotions and no hard feelings. Okay? I just need to focus on work. Can we do that?"

"Sure," Carver said.

"I'll wait in the car. Come when you're done. I have work to do."

22

CARVER TRUDGED, head bowed, up the stairs to the office and heard Sandling coming up behind him. He stopped and turned.

"You're coming up?" He was surprised. He'd done all the talking—again—on the drive back to Manassas while Sandling gripped the wheel too tightly, her lips firmly pursed.

"Just need to grab a few things. I won't get in your way."

"That's not what I meant, Cate, you know that. Happy to have you. Take all the time you need."

"Okay," she said and stopped on the stairs just below him. She looked up at him and waited for him to keep climbing.

"Who needs a StairMaster, right?" Carver said as he turned and kept going. He was out of breath by the top. He pushed open the office door, and it only went halfway before it bumped against something heavy. He pushed but couldn't budge it.

"Hey!" he yelled. "What gives?"

"Sorry, coming!" Maudmont called to him. Then he

heard her stomping over. There was a grunting sound and the sound of something heavy sliding over the rough office carpet. The door pulled open fully, and Maudmont stood there looking all smiley and flushed, fanning herself with her hand. "So hot," she said. Then she saw Sandling and got excited, saying, "Hey! Welcome. Come on in."

Carver stepped over a banker's box, and his eyes darted around the room. The whole team was there.

"We got another delivery," Underwood said, gesturing to the boxes. "Piles of evidence."

Frank Hornigen, Rachel Fox, and Toby Underwood were sitting at their desks, looking at the evidence boards.

"I see that," Carver said and gestured to the line of whiteboards in front of the office windows.

"That's what we've been working on," Maudmont said. "Psychological autopsies of the list of victims you gave us."

"Nice. Impressive," Carver said as he studied the whiteboards filled with photographs and notes. One wall was covered with maps, crime scene photos, and copies of personnel files. Carver stood there as if he was trying to absorb all of the information via osmosis.

"We were just getting everything laid out," Maudmont said. "So we could give you a briefing."

"Oh, that's good," Carver said. He was surprised with the work. It was well done. "Walk me through the boards."

The team looked at Penny Maudmont, and she sarcastically said, "Oh, okay then, I guess I'll do it." She walked over to them and pointed. "We've got two alleged victims per board. Three boards in total. These are pictures of each of the police-suicide victims. Beneath each photo, you can see a brief description and method of their supposed suicides." She glanced at him. Carver nodded. Maudmont continued, "The table here, in front of the whiteboard—it's a little cluttered right now—is all the physical evidence recovered from the scenes."

There were evidence bags, files, and various items from the different scenes.

"The hard thing," Underwood said, "is there were only so many of the police departments that actually kept anything. Most of the fourteen names weren't considered suspicious—"

"So we've had to focus on these five victims," Maudmont said.

"Alleged victims," Fox corrected.

"Alleged victims, right," Maudmont said.

Carver surveyed the table tops; the team had done a good job, for once.

"Looks like I might need to put in a requisition for more office space," Carver said. "Junk everywhere."

"Tell me about it," Hornigen said. "My desk is the unofficial dump site slash sorting bin.

"Our desk," Underwood said.

Maudmont stepped forward and caught Carver's eye. "Funny you should mention that, boss. Did you notice? The bail bonds business downstairs has gone under. Maybe we could look into leasing it, hmm? Girls downstairs and boys upstairs ..." she said and pressed her tongue into her cheek.

"What else we got?" Carver asked.

"Rachel's knack for cross-referencing data proved invaluable," Maudmont said. Fox was at her computer, pretending not to listen but absorbing every word. Maudmont pointed to the first image. A young-looking guy with a narrow mustache and a combover. "Detective Samuel Greene, late forties, was found in his locked car. Apparent carbon monoxide poisoning."

"Okay," Carver said.

"Greene was working on a missing persons case that

suddenly went cold," Fox said and spun around from her computer to look at the team. "No leads, no witnesses. It was like the person vanished into thin air."

"That's right," Maudmont said. She moved to the next image. A Latina-looking lady. Maudmont pointed at her picture, "Detective Maria Rodriguez. Mid-thirties, found in her bathtub with slashed wrists."

"She live alone?" Carver asked.

"Yes, except for her cats. The body was discovered when the neighbor downstairs complained about water leaking through the ceiling," she said.

"Maria left the water running? Hmm," Carver said and furrowed his brow.

Maudmont continued down the line of headshots. "Detective John 'Jack' Marshall. Early-fifties, ex-military. Appeared to have jumped from a bridge, or maybe fell, toxicology showed he was five times over the legal limit, body was found washed up on the river bank."

"Anita Shaw," Maudmont said. "Case was particularly troubling. She was in her early forties and overdosed on sleeping pills at home. Left a cryptic note. Shaw was a forensic science expert."

"Okay," Carver said.

"And finally, Detective Thomas Lee. Late-thirties, tech-savvy, found with a gunshot wound in his home office. Gun in hand. Colleagues said Lee was quiet but incredibly observant."

"Remind you of someone?" Underwood asked and glanced over at Fox. She stuck her tongue out at him.

"Good work laying it all out," Carver said, trying to take it all in. "Nice idea to narrow it down to the cases we had the most evidence for. Just to clarify, we aren't saying that the other nine suspicious suicides *aren't* murders; we're just saying that these are the ones that we have the highest likelihood of being able to prove were murders. Is that right?"

"Yes, exactly," Hornigen said.

"So what do we have?" Carver asked. "Physical evidence?"

"Yes," Hornigen said. "Personal belongings, evidence found at the scenes."

"Eyewitness testimony?"

"Hmm," Hornigen said. "Harder to come by, I checked through the reports. Most of the time it was a statement from a person who reported them missing or found the bodies. If this *was* someone carrying out murders, they were meticulous."

"Mercy killings," Sandling said. Everyone turned to look. She was sitting alone at her desk behind the team. "Sorry," she said.

"No, please, go on," Carver said. "I'm sure we'd like to hear it." He looked around the room. Everyone was listening, waiting for her to speak.

She cleared her throat. "Ah, well, if someone was killing these cops and making it look self-inflicted ..." She seemed like she was trying to work out how to explain it. "Well, why make it look like a suicide?" Sandling asked.

"Precisely," Carver said.

"Unless you believed they deserved to die, right?" Sandling said. "Typically, mercy killings are when the killer believes they are sparing the victim from suffering—in some way—by ending their life. In some twisted way, the killer views it as a compassionate act." Everybody was looking at her, listening. "But here's where it gets dark. Some serial killers adopt this idea, but they also distort it to justify their actions. They convince themselves that their victims are better off dead. They believe they're performing a mercy killing by taking their lives, especially when they perceive the victims as being in situations of hopelessness or failure."

"You're saying our killer thinks they're doing the world a favor by murdering these detectives?" Fox asked.

"Yeah, exactly, Rachel. Imagine a killer who sees these detectives as being more useful dead than alive."

"But how could that make sense?" Maudmont asked. Then, thinking out loud, she said, "So, it's like they think they're saving future victims of crime by getting rid of these detectives?"

"Something like that," Sandling said, suddenly conscious that she'd influenced their thinking. "But it's also more than that. They'd see themselves as judge, jury, and executioner. This is extreme narcissism—carrying out what they believe to be a necessary act to maintain a certain moral or ethical standard." Everyone was quiet. Sandling stood up. "I'm not saying that *is* what this is, obviously. I'm just saying that's one possible psychological explanation."

"Isn't it a stretch to call it mercy killings if the victims aren't febrile or incapacitated?" Carver asked. "None of them were sick."

"No," Sandling said and approached the boards. "They weren't *physically* ill. What I'm saying is—from the killer's perspective—say he does have this sense of doing *them*, and the world, a favor by putting them out of their misery. There would be something they've done to make them deserve it." Sandling looked at the first headshot of Samuel Greene. "You said this guy was working a missing person's case, right?" Maudmont nodded. "What about the other detectives? What cases were they working on?"

The team looked around at one another. "We haven't got that far yet," Underwood said.

"That's where I would start ..." Sandling said, looking at the board. Then, she seemed to stop herself. She looked around at the team. "I mean, if this was my case, you know, that's where I might start looking."

"Some sort of connection between the deaths?" Carver asked.

"Right," Sandling said. "That's assuming the mercy killing theory holds water."

"It's sound from a psychological profile, isn't it?" Carver asked.

Sandling shrugged and nodded. "We don't know that they were murderers yet, right? But assuming they were and we're looking for a motive—to me—that makes the most sense."

"People commit murder to cover up a crime, for personal gain, or just for fun," Underwood said. "But this does feel different."

The team turned and looked at Carver. He had his fingers on his chin and massaged it slowly. "Okay," he said, "but there's nothing to suggest the suicides are linked in and of themselves."

"Yet," Maudmont said.

"*Yet*, right," Carver agreed. "So what's the connection? Why target these detectives? If there's a pattern, we need to find it. Why these detectives, and what did they do that got them killed?"

The team looked at one another. "On it," Hornigen said. Fox spun around and started tapping on her keyboard.

"Here, Toby, help me with all the evidence bags. We need to lay them out nice and organized so we can see what we have to work with," Maudmont said.

"All right, come on then," Underwood said and slid off the desk he was sitting on.

"Thanks," Carver said under his breath to Sandling. She gave him a polite smile. She was tolerating him again. That was more than he'd got before. "You'll sticking around?" he asked. "We could really use you."

"No," she said and shook her head. "I've got to be heading back. My case isn't going to solve itself. There is something I need to discuss with you, though."

Carver's phone rang in his office. He looked at it and said, "Okay, give me a second to answer."

"Wait, Gust, here. I made you a coffee," Maudmont said as she came over with a steaming hot cup of black drip coffee.

"You're a star," he said as she gave it to him. He carried it carefully and went to answer his phone. He picked up the receiver and said, "Carver," and took a sip of his coffee.

"Hello, Special Agent, uh, Carver ...?"

"Yes?"

"Yes, hello. This is Abigail Abingdon. I'm Professor Blackwood's research assistant ... we met, um—"

"Oh, yes, hi, Abigail. How are you?" He said and set his coffee down.

"Yes, fine, thanks," she said. "Professor Blackwood asked me to call with the data you wanted about the methods of suicide." Her voice rose at the end as if she was asking a question.

"Yes ..." Carver said.

"Well, I have the information. Would you like me to share it over the phone, or what might be most convenient? I could come down ..."

Carver checked his watch and leaned forward a little so he could see the rest of the team. "I'll tell you what, I'm going to put you through to one of my colleagues—Penny—she's going to take it all down from you, and you guys can work it out; how does that sound?"

"Um, yes, fine. Thank you."

Carver cupped his hand over the mouthpiece and called out, "Penny. Penny!" He got her attention. He pointed at the phone. "Call for you. Can you take down what she wants to share and let me know if it's any good?"

Penny gave him a thumbs-up, and Carver removed his hand and said, "Abigail, I'm putting you through now."

CARVER HUNG up as Sandling leaned her head into his office. "You got a second?"

He always felt a twinge of anxiety at those four words. "Sure. What's up?"

Sandling stepped inside, holding a tightly rolled newspaper. She slapped it down on his desk and unfurled it.

"Have you seen this yet?" Her tone was clipped, her annoyance unmistakable.

Carver straightened and reached for the paper. The headline read: Baltimore Serial Killer Cleanses Victims. Below it was Jessica Webb's byline. His mouth tightened as he scanned the article.

"How did she get this?"

"Benson said she name-dropped you with the street cops and got a couple of uniforms to spill what they'd seen." Sandling crossed her arms. "But look at this." She jabbed her finger at a line in the article. "She's completely made up that we're questioning suspects within the department. That we think it's internal."

Carver's jaw set.

"You know what this does?" she asked.

Carver folded the paper carefully and set it aside. "Yeah. I do."

"They're talking about ending our involvement. Baltimore PD wants us out." Sandling leaned forward, her hands gripping the edge of his desk. "I can't have that, Gust. I need this case."

Carver's eyes narrowed. "We all need this case, Cate."

"Then deal with her," she snapped. "She's your responsibility, and you're still keeping her in the loop about the suicides, aren't you?" Carver didn't respond. "Next time, it could be something worse on the front page," Sandling pressed, her tone icy. "Something about the murdered cops. Something we can't fix."

"She's grieving," Carver said. "She's desperate for answers. I can't blame her for that."

"Doesn't mean you give her a free pass," Sandling shot back.

Carver rubbed the bridge of his nose, feeling a headache forming. "I'll talk to her."

"You'd better," Sandling said, straightening. "Because if she pulls this again, it's not just her name on the line. It's mine. It's all of ours."

Carver nodded silently.

"I'm heading back to Baltimore now," Sandling said. "If they even let me in the building." She turned on her heel and left without another word.

CARVER WAITED until the sound of her footsteps faded before picking up his phone. He stared at it for a long moment, then dialed. It rang twice before Webb answered.

Her voice was almost cheerful. "Gust! How are you?"

"Not too great," he said, tone dry. "I'm looking at your byline in the Baltimore Sun."

"Listen, I can explain—"

"No explanation necessary, Jess," Carver said. "But I can't keep talking to you about cases anymore. You understand, don't you?"

There was a pause. He could hear her breathing on the other end.

"I do," she said finally, her voice quieter. "But I swear, Gust, I wasn't trying to sabotage anything."

Carver leaned back in his chair, the tightness in his chest building. "I don't think you were. But you crossed a line."

"My editor—"

"Your editor isn't my problem," Carver said. "You know what's at stake here."

Jessica's tone softened, almost pleading. "Gust, please. I need this job. You know I do. I'm freelance. If I don't give them something, I don't get paid. I'm just trying to survive."

"Why'd they hire you?" Carver asked, his voice low. "Did you tell them you had an in with the FBI? Is that how you got the gig?"

Jessica hesitated. "I'm sorry," she said finally. "I'll behave. I promise."

Carver closed his eyes. He wanted to believe her. But hadn't she promised before?

"Jess," he said, his voice quiet but firm. "This is serious. You need to think about what you're doing. Think about Elizabeth."

Jessica's voice broke. "I am thinking about her, Gust. Every second of every day."

Carver exhaled, the tension in his chest easing slightly. "I know you are. But this isn't the way."

Another pause. Then, softly: "I'm sorry."

"You can't divulge anything we spoke about, Jess. It's off the record. Always."

Jessica sniffed. "I won't let you down, Gust. I promise."

Carver shook his head slightly, unseen. "Good. Take care of yourself, Jess."

"Gust?"

"Yeah?"

"Just ... find out who killed my father and my sister. Please."

"We're doing our best," he said, his voice steady. "But that's all I can say now. You understand?"

"Yes."

Carver hung up and leaned forward, elbows on his knees, head in his hands. After a moment, he looked up and reached for his coffee. It was cold.

23

"THE THING THAT HAPPENED—YOU SEE ..." Victor Crowe said as he stood in the shower under a scalding hot stream of water. He let the water spray from his mouth as he spoke like he was poking his head through a waterfall, and it garbled his words. "Everyone was jealous. Everyone was just *jealous* of him. Yes, that's it. That's why the Gospel of Judas was removed from the canon. He was the One Follower, he was the only one that the Son of Man shared his secrets with. The other twelve standing there gawping, looking at him—they were full of rage and jealousy themselves, they betrayed Judas with *their* words. He *didn't* betray them. What the people don't know, and they will come to understand, is that Judas was acting on Jesus' instructions! My God! It makes perfect sense. He *wanted* Judas to make him pay the ultimate sacrifice. Jesus wasn't betrayed by Judas. Judas, the *One* Follower, the first follower, the *one* truth, to whom Jesus spoke and gave him instructions, was betrayed by the other twelve who went to stab him in the back." Crowe moved his index finger back and forth, like the Pope, in white and gold robes, addressing his congregation. In his mind, he was. He was addressing the whole world with his words. He was a great orator. A man who could stand on the side of a mountain and speak to thousands of people and have his words heard and written down and talked about for centuries. "You see? You see!" Crowe's voice grew louder and more shrill. The truth was he had been born Hindu—even if the so-called authorities denounced it as fantasy—you see they'd locked him up. They'd taken him away and locked him up and made him *think* he was crazy. They were convincing, though. They were slippery like eels and their silvery tongues whispered like so many spies and thieves. But how could they deny—to his face—the sixth chakra, the Bindi mark on his forehead in the shape of the all-seeing eye, marking him out as an Aryan mystic from the Himalayas? He knew things they did not. He knew that like the cosmos, all things, all religions are but one. And he was the One Follower incarnate. That is why they turned his skin to soot and ashes. That is why they burned him from the inside. That he may burst into a flaming ball of fire at the time of the reckoning. And it was fast approaching, streaking like a comet across the night sky.

Crowe stepped out of the shower, his brown hair plastered to his forehead and covering his eyes. He moved straight out of the bathroom and put his hand on a faded hardcover book with no jacket. It was the long-hidden Gospel of Judas. The truth that has been hidden from humans for centuries. Sixteen sacred chapters reveal the profound teachings of the real Son of Man on the spirit and the stars. "Unlike the other disciples," Crowe recited, dripping water on the carpet, "Judas truly understood the divine wisdom imparted by God—simply a luminous cloud of light residing in an eternal, imperishable realm. It speaks of Adamas, the spiritual father of humanity, created in God's image and dwelling in this imperishable realm."

Victor picked up the book and opened to a marked page.

He held the gospel in one hand and swept the other as if he were blessing a crowd. To him, trumpets were billowing from the besieged wall of a great city as he spoke to them. "In the beginning, God created angels and lower gods, twelve of whom were destined to rule over chaos and the underworld. These angels crafted a physical body for Adamas, the first man, Adam. However, humanity soon forgot its divine origins, and Adam's descendants—like Cain and Abel—were drawn into what we now know as the universe's *first* murder. And so, the people began to believe that the flawed physical universe was the entirety of creation, losing sight of God and the imperishable realm." Crowe's voice rose in a high-pitched, frenzied scream. "Jesus, sent by the *true* God, not by one of the *lesser* gods, came to reveal that all salvation rests in the connecting with the God *within* us. It is only by embracing this inner divinity that we can return to the imperishable realm."

There was a thumping coming from the flat below. That old hag Ms. Wilkinson pounding on her ceiling again. It's fine, Ms. Wilkinson. The world might not want to hear the true account, but we'll make them understand. Not only will they hear it, but they will see it, taste it, feel it, and be stunned into obedience by it.

The thumping continued, and Crowe raised his voice even louder. "Yet ..." He cleared his throat. The ash. They'd turned his blood to ash. He needed to replenish his life force. "And yet! Eleven of Jesus' disciples misunderstood his teachings. So fixated were they with the physical world and continuing the apocryphal practices of animal sacrifice—which pleased only the lower gods—that they *falsely* taught that martyrdom would lead to bodily resurrection. No! No, I tell you!"

Crowe grew very quiet and solemn now. Playing to the

assembled crowd. He shivered, his thin, hairless body almost dry.

"But, Judas, blessed with an immortal soul, grasped the true essence of Jesus' mission. Humanity is divided into those with immortal souls—like Judas—who can know the inner God and enter the imperishable realm, and those—like the other disciples—who are doomed to perish not only physically but also spiritually." His voice rose again with gathering intensity. "And so say we, the Gospel of Judas condemns the rituals tied to the physical world—like animal sacrifices and the cannibalistic communion ceremony and the consumption of Jesus' flesh and his blood. We declare that Jesus' death was not a sacrifice to atone for humanity's sins to satisfy lower gods, but a *revelation* that the true God demands no sacrifice, for He is the most gracious and the most loving."

Crowe snapped the book shut, bowed his head, and finished his sermon, "Embrace this truth, understand the divine within you, and reject the false teachings that bind you to the physical world. The path to the imperishable realm lies within, as shown by Jesus to Judas and on to Jazazul—the being known by another form, we, together—Victor Harlan Crowe." My blood is becoming ashes again, Crowe thought. He needed to turn it back into blood. The thumping from below stopped. The thing was, if even the One Follower could be betrayed, then those doing the betraying deserved justice in the cosmos. A reckoning with the lower gods. A sacrifice of flesh and blood. If she were younger, Ms. Wilkinson would make a fine sacrifice. Now, it was time to find another messenger. Crowe sat down and fired up his aging desktop computer. It clicked and moaned and trilled as it connected to the source of all knowledge. The great oracle, his source of truth, showed him the way.

24

For Rachel Fox, trawling the dark side of the web was like being on the dark side of the moon, as if she were staring into a black void of space. She'd been crawling around this creepy-as-hell part of the internet for a few days. At work, she relied on gasoline-smelling energy drinks to stay awake. But all she was doing was waiting for the time when she could don her black cape and her mask, become *Hungry-Fox25,* and slip silently into the murky swamp that was the depraved side of humanity.

Maybe this was a bad idea, Fox thought. After all, she'd been starstruck by seeing Caitlin Sandling at the office yesterday. She'd so desperately wanted to talk to her about this side investigation she was working on and its merits. But, then she saw Sandling's genius while she was analyzing the whiteboard of police victims. Fox lost the courage. Somehow, she didn't feel like what she was doing matched the insight and depth of understanding about the human condition that Agent Sanding possessed.

Fox had planned to set herself up as bait and wait for someone—by her reasoning, the murderer—to contact her. The offers trickled in at first but now threatened to burst the dam. If her proposition or willingness to become a longpig was a carcass floating in the water, then the offers she was receiving were like a vicious school of pirañas zipping by and snapping meat off it. She had to deal with dozens of email messages and requests. It was nice to be popular. It gave her a strange sensation. She felt special and wanted and *popular,* which was something—because of her intense internal world—she'd never been. Even though she was flattered, she had a job to do. She needed to weed out the fantasists from the real thing. Even though this forum existed and seemed to have a disturbingly large user base, she couldn't believe more than one person there was the real deal.

As she sat in the low glow of her monitor, her hands hovering over the keyboard, she got a ping notification, and a new chat message popped up.

"How do I know you're the real deal, *HungryFox25*? Plenty of pretenders on this forum. Only a few real ones. And you know them when you see them."

"That's interesting," she said to herself. Her mind started whizzing, and she leaned forward. She sensed this was a challenge. This guy's handle was *BlackHand1914*. Pretty obscure, Fox thought. The Black Hand Movement had assassinated Archduke Ferdinand, sparking World War One. An ominous choice, Fox thought, but she wasn't sure. This didn't feel real. She thought she'd go along with it and see where it went.

"I want the rush of feeling my life slipping away by your hands," Fox said as she typed. "What would the last words I hear be?"

The cursor just blinked at her for what felt like ten minutes. Fox's eyes narrowed. Maybe she'd lost him already. Nope, there, he was typing. Fox read the message: "There's a difference between reality and fantasy—it's where they meet that is the real 'meat' of this." She let out a gasp-laugh. "Excuse the pun," it continued. She checked around the dark room to make sure she hadn't woken her grandmother. "Prove you're genuine."

"You first," she replied. These guys all loved talking in detail about their prowess and exploits. The writing it out was as close to the fantasy as most of them would get. What a hobby, she thought.

BlackHand1914 was typing ... "Whatever you have in your mind about how this goes, it's wrong. All right? You're thinking clean, cold, stainless steel. You're wrong. This is what it looks like. A secluded, derelict tunnel in an abandoned haunted house ride, designed, erected, and decorated by me for one purpose and one purpose only. The S&M decor doesn't leave much to the imagination. You know what that's for. Out there, you're alone. Nothing around for miles. No one to hear you scream, beg, and pray for your life. But there's no one else you should be praying to by then except me. I'm your God now. And your cells will live on in me. Becoming a part of me."

Fox bit the side of her cheek and covered her mouth with the sleeve of her hoodie. "Wow," she said. "This guy sounds truly insane." Her grandmother was stirring. It's alright, Bobo, go back to sleep, she thought.

"You still there?" *BlackHand1914* typed.

"Yes," she replied. "Go on ..."

"Okay ... tell me where you are?"

"Tell me where the amusement park is."

"That's a secret. I will say it's only about a 90-minute drive from Baltimore," she read, and her eyes went wide. Ding. Ding. Ding. Fox felt dizzy. It can't be, she thought. Her mouth was dry. She reached for the Dr. Pepper next to her computer and sipped.

"What else?" She typed with her free hand.

"It's the most terrifying place you've ever been. I'll chase you through the dark with a chainsaw and no one will know. The whole back portion of the House of Horrors is dedicated to the craft. Imagine: A hoist for draining your body of blood, I'll save that, nothing goes to waste. Every drop is harvested ... and I use that word specifically because that's all you are to me ... nothing more than livestock. The part you don't get to see is the real magic. The key is in the preparation, same as painting a house—any kind of handiwork—only this requires meticulous care in the slaughtering and cooking of you."

Fox's heart was thumping out of her chest. This guy means it. She felt it coursing through her. The details were disturbing in their precision.

"You've got me excited," she typed.

"Excited?" She waited for him to keep typing. "Don't get confused, baby. The animals don't get excited. They get scared. You ever seen a steer on the conveyor belt? They know exactly what's happening. That wide-eyed fear in their faces. Mouths open, slobbering everywhere. Now imagine you're that bovine. That's how you should feel."

Her heart was racing in her chest. She thought, *game on*. If you really like to string women up and butcher them, then you've just met the wrong one. She was going to get him. One way or another. She was onto something. She knew it. She doubted she was going to sleep after that. All it meant was she had time to make a plan and draw this guy into her trap. An abandoned amusement park just over an hour from Baltimore ... she did a search. Three possibilities from the list appeared. Enchanted Forest in Maryland, a nursery rhyme-themed amusement park, was open from 1955 until 1995. Gwynn Oak Park operated from 1893 until storm damage from Hurricane Agnes forced its closure in 1972. Lastly, Bay Shore Amusement Park along the Chesapeake Bay closed in 1947. She shook her head. Scouting these and surveilling them would take too much time. And, short of going caving with a flashlight and emergency rescue gear, she couldn't imagine walking down dark tunnels looking for a murder room. Plus, no way someone like this would allow himself to be exposed without some kind of security in place. So what could she do? she wondered. What about finding out where he lived rather than where he killed people?

Unless this guy was very clever and very security conscious, she might be able to track his computer's IP address. Every device had one. Like a fingerprint for each laptop, cell phone, or television. All she had to do was find out what his IP address was and use it to get his location. Fox typed quickly, pulling up a few useful tools on her screen. First, she hacked into the main server hosting the *Zambian Meat* website. Once inside, she could find the IP address registered to the hostname. Then, she used the WHOIS IP lookup tool to check public IP address information. Hmm, nothing came up. Maybe this guy was a little bit smarter than she thought. She wasn't going to give up that easily, though.

Fox's FBI security clearance gave her access to Baltimore's CCTV system, including private cameras registered with the CitiWatch Community Partnership. Fox brought up the IP-GPS tool and entered the address. The coordinates popped up: 39.30148, -76.63947. She put the coordinates into Baltimore's public surveillance system search tool, and it brought up a CCTV camera mounted on the Riggs Avenue and Carey Street bus stop, identification number 12180. She got a live feed from the camera. It was grainy, and there was a lag, but from what she could see, the camera was directly opposite a tall gray building with a white-neon cross. She cross-referenced the coordinates on a map. She was looking at the Wayside Baptist Church in Sandtown-Winchester. She started to feel nervous. This was a dangerous neighborhood. It is a poor community full of rival gangs, lots of drugs, boarded-up houses, and poverty.

It was also home to a practicing cannibal.

25

"Oh, Abigaaail ..." Blackwood sang from his desk. She realized some time ago that she was always listening for him, waiting for him to beckon her, when she was working in his office—which was almost every day. It was his siren song for his research assistant; he said he needed her near him, that she was his muse. She doubted that, but deep down, she wanted to believe it. It was also more than flattering to have such a prominent professor of forensic psychology tell her he needed her. Wanted her, even. She knew he listened out for her, too. The walls between them might as well not exist. Sometimes she daydreamed about ...

"Abigail!"

Shit! She pushed the chair back, and it scraped on the wooden floorboards. He hated that. He also hated calling twice. He hated saying anything twice. He was very exacting, very precise. Someone who, as long as everything was *just so*, was content—but the moment there was a slip or an aggravation, or something didn't go quite like clockwork, well, then there was a problem. He tended not to handle situations like that too well. It was almost as if he took it personally, as she'd once thought. But no, he was far too smart and savvy to be so wrapped up in himself.

She tapped lightly on the door, as always, and pushed it open. He was writing at his desk. He had his concentration face on. His lips pursed, and his brows furrowed, just so.

"Come in, Piglet. Close the door behind you."

He called her *piglet*, that was his pet name for her. She'd snort-laughed at one of his witticisms once—he didn't tell *jokes*—and from that moment, she was his little piglet.

"Come and stand here next to me." He said he liked to have her close. He liked her smell. She could sometimes sense him smelling her hair when he was standing nearby. When she could feel the heat radiating from his body. She went and stood next to his chair while he finished writing his letter. He signed with a big flourish of his pen. He brandished it like a fencer's foil. He pushed himself back in his chair and he looked up at her. She smiled. She couldn't help it. He was so handsome. She thought so, anyway. She was sure most people did. The outside of his knee was touching her bare thigh, and she felt funny inside but didn't want to move. Sometimes he did that.

"What did you find out from Agent Carver?"

Abigail's mind darted for an answer. "I, um, spoke to him, but he passed me over to his colleague, someone in his office, Penny Maudmont."

His expression changed. He wasn't pleased. "Who is she?"

"No, it was great, actually," Abigail said, trying to bring him back to her. "She was very talkative. I told her you and the special agent had met, and I told her how you were helping—*we* were helping—with the case. She couldn't have been more, I want to say, bubbly?"

"Okay, well, if she's so effervescent, then what did you talk about?"

"I found out quite a few things, actually," Abigail said and covered her smile with her hand. He laughed, sat up, and lifted his fingers like he was about to tickle her. Sometimes he did that. Just harmless fun.

"We talked for hours," she said, exaggerating. "We're besties now."

"You'd better tell me," his voice rising in mocking threat and lifting his hands like he was preparing to tickle a toddler. She giggled. It was silly, but she liked it. Anyway, she thought he liked it, so she played along. All she needed was pigtails and an oversized lollipop.

'Okay, okay! I'll tell you, professor ..."

"Go on, what did you find out for me?"

"*Everything.*" She grinned, knowing he would hang on her every word.

26

It had been such a long day. Hell, it had been a long week, month, and year. Toby Underwood sat with his hands on the steering wheel, staring out of the windshield into the night at nothing in particular. The neighborhood was quiet. Usually—back when things were good— he would have come home straight after work and relaxed with half a tumbler of his favorite Irish whiskey, he and his wife sitting on the sofa. Lately, he was in the habit of stopping at a three-star hotel near Dulles Airport and sitting in the hotel bar with some cheap whiskey. He'd dilute it with ice towards the end of his session when he'd had a few too many and couldn't face the music at home. He'd even spent the night at the hotel a couple of times instead of going home. There was no judgment in an empty double room at the La Quinta Inn. He'd had two stiff drinks this evening and felt like he was teetering on the edge of a diving board. He was still sober enough to handle the nightly fights and the icy welcome he received when he finally went home. Underwood opened the car door and stepped out.

He belched and lifted his hand to his mouth, blew away

the offending fumes, and said quietly to himself, "Pardon me."

He had his keys out and walked up to the front door, but when he put them in and turned the knob, it was unlocked. He took a deep breath and pushed the door open. All the lights were on, and he squinted against the brightness. His two little girls, aged three and four, were screaming in that pitch that only little girls can while chasing each other around the glass coffee table in the lounge.

Sigourney was in the kitchen unpacking the dishwasher and calling out to the girls over her shoulder, "How many times do I have to tell you two not to run around that goddamn coffee table? One of you is gonna trip one of these days, and we're gonna take you gushing blood to the emergency room." They kept running. His wife turned and stepped towards their daughters and said, "Kayla, goddammit, I've asked you to stop!" The two girls stopped and then saw their daddy standing there.

"Daddy, Daddy!" they yelled and raced up to him. He crouched down and took one in each arm, closed his eyes, and tried to savor the moment with his two precious angels.

"Where the hell have you been, Toby? God damn it, you left me here all alone all day with them. Do you have any idea what that's like?"

He opened his eyes and gave each of his girls a kiss on the side of their heads, stood up, and said, "Hi, Zig." That was his pet name for her, even though she hated it now. He said it partly passive-aggressively because he knew she hated it and partly because it somehow reminded him of how it used to be. "How are you? Sorry, it's been a long, stressful day."

"Yeah, well, you could have called or at least messaged me to let me know you were gonna be late. You know? I had to cancel plans."

"Oh, no. I'm so sorry," he said. His tone was flat and mechanical. He didn't feel what he was saying to her. He was saying what he needed to placate the situation and get to the part where he could go and have a shower and get another drink.

"Why don't you go and play in your room, girls?" he suggested. "Mommy and Daddy are going to talk."

The two little girls looked at each other and giggled and ran off down the corridor. Toby took off his jacket and hung it on a hook near the front door. He kicked off his shoes and left them under his jacket while he undid his top button, and loosened his tie, preparing for the nightly fight. He walked into the lounge which had the open plan kitchen off to the side.

Sigourney was back unpacking the dishwasher. "Even when you're here, you're not here," she said without looking at him. He'd heard it so many times before. He probably didn't even need the whiskey to numb his emotions, but it had become a comforting routine which he liked because it dulled his senses and made his wits a little slower.

"No, I'm sorry, Sigourney. I really am."

"God, stop apologizing. You sound so weak and decrepit. I'd rather you just crawl back under that rock you're hiding under than try and placate me. You know how hard it is for me with my mom going through her chemo, trying to look after *your* daughters, with your *God-knows-what* every day."

Underwood just watched his wife as she collected cutlery from the tray and moved it to the drawer. He would have gone to help her but she didn't like him being very close to her and it would have turned into an issue too. Better just to get yelled at for not helping. That was probably the lesser of the two evils. He wasn't even allowed to apologize in his pathetic state.

He'd thought about it a lot. He could pinpoint the exact

moment their relationship shifted. It was the morning he'd told her. They'd been sitting in bed having coffee, which was their beloved morning routine, and watching the early local news. Someone had tipped off a journalist. The fact that the police had botched an investigation into a suspected serial killer in the local area, and in a desperate attempt to try and relocate him, they'd gone public and shared the artist's rendering of a witness statement on TV, hoping that a tip or someone in the public had seen him. Underwood had sat staring open-mouthed at the TV. He couldn't believe that they'd highlighted the failure.

"What bloody goddamn *idiot* went and did that?" Sigourney said. He'd just started crying there in bed. She started hugging him and trying to console him and say, "There, there, what happened?"

He looked up at her through his tears and said, "It was me. I accidentally dialed the suspect and he heard our whole conversation about the plan to arrest him."

It was right after he'd said those words that her eyes changed. He'd seen the transformation happen right before him while he was sitting in bed. Her expression went from concern and comfort to wanting him to get away from her. The look of absolute disdain, bordering on hatred, is something he'd never forget. She'd gotten straight out of bed, gone into the bathroom, and closed the door. He was left alone to wallow. That was the last time his wife had ever looked at him with love in her eyes. Back then, they had just had their second daughter and she was in love with the man whose career was on the up. Yes, he had to travel and be away, but the way things were going and from what he promised her, a fast promotion track and a nice job in Quantico would be theirs in a few short years. The butt-dial incident, or Butt-Gate as it became known in the Bureau, changed everything for him. He was reprimanded, lost his seniority, and was given the only punishment worse than death. He was sent to the wastelands of the Manassas resident agency to tread water with no hopes of promotion or furthering his career until he either resigned, redeemed himself—which nobody had ever done—or died.

He'd broken the cardinal rule: Don't embarrass the agency. The institution still embodied the personality of its first director, J. Edgar Hoover, in that it had no sense of humor. Underwood, of course, couldn't blame them, but hell, fellas, you know? Come on. Show a little compassion. Show a little pity. So, he'd fucked up, he understood that, but to let the local police publicly come out and blame it on the Bureau. It was his mistake, but he felt like a fall guy, or at least like he'd served his penance, done his time in purgatory, and was in desperate need of revival.

"I'm sorry, Zig," he said again, leaning his forearms on the kitchen counter. It was earnest. He meant it this time.

"That's just the Scotch speaking, Toby," she said and looked at him with that doe-eyed, disappointed look she'd perfected over the past three years. "Every day, Toby, every goddamn day, I'm stuck here in this matchbox of a house with your daughters because their father has no prospects and no security. You promised me we'd see the country— *it was one of the perks of the job*!" She started to cry. He felt shame. He wanted to go to her and hold her, but she would just push him away. She held the back of her hand under her nose, and then her expression changed. It was alertness. Shock.

"What's that?" she said.

Underwood straightened. "What?"

"*That*. Out there!" she said.

He spun around to look out of the large, rectangular living room window. It was dark out there, the streetlights barely doing their job. He squinted and walked closer to the glass. There was a figure out there standing under a tree, staring in the direction of their house. Underwood went up the glass and put his hands up the window and leaned his head against them to get a better view.

"Don't just stand there, Toby, take your damn gun and go and see what's going on!"

She was right. He reached around his back and felt for his service weapon in its holster in his waistband. "Shit," he said under his breath. He'd left it in the glovebox of the car when he went into the hotel bar. "Screw it," he said. He moved towards the front door. The girls were coming running down the corridor. He pointed his finger back towards their bedroom and said in his stern voice, "Go back into your bedroom now, girls. Quickly."

"Come on, girls," Sigourney said and ushered them back down the corridor.

'What's going on, Mommy?" Lucy asked.

"It's okay, Luce, just go with mommy for a second, okay?" Underwood pulled open the front door and went onto the porch. He squinted towards the spot in the street where he'd seen the figure. It was clear now. His blood was up. His breathing was shallow. His heart kept pace like a fast-bass beat. He went down the stairs and onto the front lawn. His eyes were scanning all around. He looked over his shoulder and down a little alley at the side of the house. The neighbor's motion sensor spotlight came on. He scanned around the street, the trees, in between the cars. He couldn't see anything.

Maybe it was nothing? he thought. But they'd both seen it. He'd definitely seen something. Was it the booze? He breathed into his cupped hand and smelled his breath. Couldn't smell anything. He turned and went back into the house.

"Zig? It's okay," Underwood called.

"Who was it?" Sigourney asked from the bedroom.

"Dunno," he said. "No one out there."

He went back into the living room to look out of the window again. Now, there was a black car sitting on the opposite side of the street. It was dark inside the cabin. He couldn't make out if anyone was in it. It hadn't been there a second before. He was sure of it. Wasn't he? He went outside again. This time, as he stepped out of the front door, the black sedan drove off. No lights. He couldn't make out the plate. His vision was too blurry. No point in calling it in, he thought. After all, he was drunk.

"God damn it," he said. "What the hell is going on?" Underwood went back into the house and saw Sigourney with the cordless telephone in the living room. "What are you doing?" he asked.

"Calling 911," she said to him. "No, sorry, just talking to my husband."

"Hang up the phone," Underwood said.

"What? No, I'm calling the police."

"Hang up the phone," Underwood said, walking over to her. He snatched the phone out of her hand and hung up.

"Daddy!" Lucy screamed. "That wasn't very nice."

"What the hell are you doing, Toby? Somebody is lurking outside the front of the house, and I'm calling the police."

"No, you don't understand, Sig. We can't call them."

"Why not?"

"What am I going to tell them? We think that there was somebody outside. I don't have my gun because it's in the car. I've been drinking. The neighbors, all they're going to talk about is the stand-up shouting matches we have. And I'm drunk."

"*I'm drunk*? How many drinks have you had?"

173

"What does it matter? I'm drunk. I can't call the police, and they can't help, okay?"

"Well, they're probably going to turn up anyway because you've just hung up on the emergency line."

"Well, let them come then. We'll just tell them it was a mistake because it *was*. We didn't see anything, and we don't know what's going on. And I'm not getting in trouble again for something that I can decide on this time, okay?"

She just scoffed and glared at him with a hateful look. "Come on, girls, let's go and get ready for bed. Daddy needs some time to himself."

27

Rachel Fox didn't own a car. She didn't know how to drive, and she was petrified of the idea. Not of the act of driving a car, but the concept of human beings all just—somehow—agreeing to the rules and trusting other people to agree with them too. And then everyone just hopped into these huge, metal boxes with engines and sped around all over the place. The whole idea just freaked her out. She didn't trust human beings. So she was sitting in the back of the CityLink bus from West Baltimore to Lafayette Avenue.

She had her laptop in a shoulder bag and headphones on over the hood of her dark sweatshirt. She sucked on the curved crescent-shaped lip ring in the corner of her mouth like she always did when she was nervous. She'd taken two trains and two buses to get here. She was committed now, but she was also wondering if she was doing the right thing.

All she wanted—more than anything—she told herself was to boost her credentials in the field and emulate Caitlin Sandling—her oblivious mentor. If she could just prove herself, maybe she'd get out of being in the Sofa Squad. She loved them, she did. She was very affectionate to everyone as people, some of the few human beings she felt even slightly comfortable around, but she had this feeling that she owed her mother more. Something for the sacrifice she'd made for her by getting out of North Korea. If she could do this, she told herself, she could do anything. After all, the chances were that this was going to turn out to be nothing.

Although ... she thought, it could also turn out to be something. She felt afraid, but she was also excited. At least, she thought it was excitement.

Fox was the last one left on the bus. The inside was brightly lit, making it difficult to see outside. She got glimpses of what was out there in the night as they passed below the yellow street lights. The bus driver pulled into a bus stop and said, "Last stop," over his shoulder. Fox collected her things and walked unsteadily down the center of the bus and gave him a wave before she stepped out of the rear doors and onto the sidewalk. She glanced left and right. The streets were abandoned. She wasn't yet exactly where she needed to be. It was another 15 or 20-minute walk. She checked her watch, pulled the straps of her backpack a bit tighter, and removed her headphones. She left them hanging around her neck so she could hear what was going on around her. She started walking. She was making good time. All she could hear were distant cars and sirens. There was enough light for her to see from the almost full moon. She glanced up at the sky and saw a couple of stars and moonlight shining against the slow-moving clouds overhead. She heard bicycles behind her. She glanced over her shoulder and saw two youths on their modified BMXs. They wheeled up slowly, standing on the pedals and looking at her. She tried to pick up the pace to hurry along.

"Hey, lady, what are you doing here?" one of them said. She looked at him out of the corner of her eye but didn't respond. "Hey, you, lady, I'm talking to you. What the hell are you doing here?" the other one, with a slightly deeper voice, said.

"Leave me alone, please," Fox said, trying to sound tough. There was a several-second pause before they started laughing.

"Hey, you, this is our street. You can't be walking along here. You need to pay your taxes."

"This is a public sidewalk, I think you'll find ... now, I'm on important government business, so unless there's anything else, I suggest you make yourself scarce." She smirked and gave herself a mental pat on the back. She felt like she was channeling her inner Carver, doing what she thought he would do and saying what she thought he would say.

"Listen here, *bitch*, did you not hear what I just said? You owe us to cross this street." They pulled up onto the sidewalk and stopped in front of her.

"Listen, gentlemen ..."

"Hey, stop talking! Give me your backpack."

She touched her shoulder strap. "I can't do that. Listen, you guys are making a big mistake."

"I don't want to hear it. You owe us taxes. Now give me your fucking backpack." One of them lunged forward to try and get her backpack, and she twisted out of the way, swinging it around in front of her. She unzipped her bag and put her hand on her service revolver, showing it to them.

"Well, well, well ... take it easy. We just wanted your stuff."

"I'm a federal agent," Fox said, "And you are impeding an investigation ... so unless you want to end up in the emergency room with a GSW. I'd s-s-suggest you make yourself s-scarce."

"Yes, ma'am," one of the boys mumbled. The other stood

in front of her, glaring at her with a stone-cold look on his face. "It stands for *gunshot* wound," Fox said.

His friend slapped him on the shoulder and said, "Come on, man, let's bounce." They kept death staring back at her as they cycled off. She let go of her weapon, zipped her backpack closed, and slung it on her back. She checked which direction she was going and set off again for the Wayside Baptist Church.

She saw the white-neon shining cross on the church. This was the spot, she knew. To her right was the rubbly-looking brick wall of a building that had a faded white mural on it saying: Save the Salvation Army. To the side of the church were two brownstone houses with overgrown, dense trees and shrubs encroaching on an alleyway that looked as if it led all the way along the side of the church. She had coordinates but not an exact address. Having researched the area, the church had seemed like an obvious place to start. She went up the stairs and pulled on the front door and it rattled but didn't open.

She had to look around herself. The streets were still quiet. There was the occasional sound of a car driving on one of the side streets, but otherwise, she was surprised. She'd expected block parties and pimps and prostitutes to be hanging around—but it seemed like a nice neighborhood. She went back down the church stairs and looked down the dark, overgrown alley. She estimated that the person she'd been interacting with—*BlackHand1914*, the man who wanted to kill, butcher, and eat her—was now within fifty feet. One of the things that swayed it for her was the username. It couldn't have been chosen randomly. It was a clear insight into the person behind the handle. She knew that the Black Hand was the organization that assassinated

Archduke Ferdinand in Austria and was used by the Germans as an excuse to incite war with Russia. That wasn't the compelling thing for her, though. If she took the reference to the next layer down, *Franz Ferdinand* was also the name of a rock band. One of their most popular songs was called *Evil Eye*. No matter how much she tried, she couldn't see past the coincidence: the username and the song. It *had* to be him. Now she just had to find him.

Fox started walking around one side of the church, looking for any basements or boarded-up areas she could enter. There was nothing around the left-hand side. Her only option, she decided, was to go down the dark alley and see what she could find.

28

CAITLIN SANDLING STOOD with her arms crossed with her back to the wall of the dark motel room. The lights were off as the forensic team traced glowing purple, ultraviolet light around the corpse and the bed. Male this time. Overweight, hairy, chained by the wrists to the headboard. She could hear the cars whooshing by on the busy road outside. The white hazmat suits glowed magenta in the dull light. There was an open brown-leather briefcase to the side of the victim. It was still full of Polaroid photographs. The bed, body, and all over the motel room floor was a layer of pictures spread out like a dealer spreading cards at a poker table. The photographs were all lewd and illegal images of children. It made Sanding feel sick. Michael Benson stood next to her, twirling a lollipop in his mouth. It rattled off his front teeth as he moved it, but her thoughts were too far away to be annoyed by it.

Sandling glanced at him as he whispered, "What do you think?" and held his red candy out towards the dead body.

She shook her head, thinking, *do you have to do that?* And said, "We'll know if it was him as soon as they lift the body and check the mattress."

"Whether it's him?"

She nodded. "The same guy, yeah."

"Strange, though, isn't it?" Benson asked.

"What is?"

She saw him grimace as the light from a car sped past the motel. "Dunno, the *guy*, right? The others were women."

"Not all of them."

"No," Benson conceded. "Not all of them, but it just doesn't *feel* right somehow."

Oh, you're feeling now, she wanted to say sarcastically to the guy licking a lollypop at a murder scene.

"You think it's him?" Benson asked.

She shrugged. "I don't know, Mike. Guess we might have a better idea after the medical examiner checks his anus."

Benson stared wide-eyed at her. He whispered, "You think he sodomized him?"

She shrugged and shook her head. "I don't know, Mike. Seriously, I know as much as you do."

"Yeah, but you're the profiling wizard. Aren't you supposed to *know* this stuff?"

"Witch."

"Which what?"

"No, *witch*. As in abracadabra. I'd be a profiling witch. Not a profiling wizard." She waited for him to say, *more like profiling bitch*, but he never did. She took a deep breath. "I think it's him. We'll know when they check under the body," she said again.

"Because of the burn marks."

"Mm-hmm."

"But ..." she said without finishing her thought.

"But what?"

"You're right. It doesn't make sense. Not according to the profile, anyway."

"Why not?"

She thought about how to answer him in a way that a chimp might understand. "This doesn't look spontaneous to you, does it?"

"No, not really."

"No, not at all," she said. "He didn't stumble across him, right? He knew this guy—John Doe—was going to be here. He knew he would be here with that suitcase full of pedophilic material. Either the victim had those handcuffs with him, or the unsub brought them with him, which indicates planning."

"Yeah, and ...?"

"Paranoid schizophrenics who commit murders don't plan ..."

"So the profile is wrong."

Sandling scoffed. Not because it wasn't possible but because of the obtuseness of Benson's pronouncement. It was so *obvious* to him when, in reality, it was anything but. It was complicated.

Of *course,* the profile might have been inaccurate, but she knew it wasn't. The profile was dead on, at least according to the textbook. This case was anything but textbook.

"Why're you scoffing? You don't think the profile needs a tweak?"

"A tweak?" She shook her head and smiled at him. So innocent. So thick. "The profile is correct," she said. "The unsub's behavior is the problem. He's not following the script."

"How so?"

"There is actual motive behind these killings," she said. "He's not just fulfilling his insane paranoid psychotic fantasies. You know? This seems like punishment to me. He's carrying out some sort of ..."

"What?"

"I don't know—retribution."

"Okay," Benson said carefully. He was unsure of the implication.

Sanding helped him out. "We need to go back and look at the other victims. Something connects them. Something more than that, they were victims of some individuals with mental illness. We need to find out *what* it is and connect the dots so we can draw a line back to the perpetrator."

"How're we going to do that?"

Sandling let out a long sigh. "I'll have to go and ask someone for help."

One of the crime scene techs came up to them and pulled his face mask down. "We're getting ready to move the body," he said.

"Thank God," Sandling said.

"The coroner is here," the tech said and gestured to the door behind them. They stepped out of the way as the medical examiner's staff guys came in with a gurney. Sandling and Benson watched as the forensic team helped roll and lift the naked, overweight body onto the gurney. They all grunted and heaved and managed to get him off the bed. Sandling tried to avoid watching the body as it passed by, but she also couldn't look away. She'd never seen a corpse without a head before.

29

It was nearly dawn. Rachel Fox could see the gray light starting to lighten the sky through the narrow gap in the windows above her head. She was taped to a wooden chair in the back corner of a basement, panicking. She didn't know what she was going to do. Her hands were taped together tightly, and her mouth was sealed shut with duct tape.

Last night, Fox used her investigative skills and tried to locate the source of the messages; she'd made her way slowly, step by step, one foot after the other, down that alleyway. She twitched and jumped every time she heard a twig crunch underfoot or something scurrying in the night around her. She thought she'd moved 300 feet, but it was probably closer to 50 before she saw another light ahead. She'd come to a wooden fence. The garden behind the fence was overgrown with long grass and prickly plants trying to grab onto her arms. She was really afraid. She didn't want to use a flashlight in case she alerted the people she was looking for. She wanted to turn back but also felt so close to solving this thing.

She took a deep breath and swallowed and prepared to

step forward. In front of her was an old wooden house. There was enough moonlight to make out the shape and see the dark irregular patches where the paint was crumbling away. One quick look, and I'll leave, she promised herself. She made her way down the path toward the house, hyper-alert and listening hard for any sounds. A dog barked in the distance. The clouds were still moving overhead, silver and black in the moonlight. As she got nearer, she saw a glow coming from the basement and crept down some outside stairs to get a better look.

She saw a curtain behind the glass of the basement door, but a small gap let her see inside. It was a strange setup. Along the walls, she could see floor-to-ceiling metal and wood shelving. The floor looked like unpainted concrete, with an old, faded red rug. In the middle of the room, a glowing computer monitor was visible.

"I don't know ..." she heard someone say. She froze, sure she'd heard a noise above her head. She quietly put her backpack around her front and unzipped it again. She took out her cell phone and crouched low. She'd seen enough. She needed to tell Carver or Sandling. Then she heard another noise.

I have to go, she thought, but panic gripped her. Her eyes were wide, and she was hyper-alert. She quickly climbed in a low crouch up the stairs. She went fast but quietly and kept her eyes up and glancing around her. It's just a cat or a bird or a mouse, she told herself as she climbed. Some sort of animal, you don't need to worry about it. Plus, the street's right there. You can easily get out and get help.

She tried not to panic, her breathing shallow and quick. She reached the top of the stairs and leaned around to see. There was now a light on at the front of the house—not a spotlight. It hadn't come on automatically. Someone was standing there.

"Oh shit," she whispered. She was about to make a run for it, but someone behind her spoke before she could move.

"Oh shit is right," a voice grunted. He swung something at her head, and she felt a sharp pain on the back and side of her, and she crumpled to the ground. That was the last thing she felt as she lay there in the long grass.

SHE'D COME to while the man was dragging her across the same basement floor she'd seen from the window. As he moved her, she started squealing and kicking out and started to scream.

"Let me go! I'm an FBI agent. You're committing a felony."

"You're trespassing on my land," the man said gruffly. He placed her on the chair like he was lifting a child. He grabbed the back of her hair, tilted her head back, and looked into her eyes. His face was only an inch from hers. She forced herself to look at him. To remember every detail. She was looking into the eyes of a killer. She had no doubt. His teeth were crooked and yellow. Too many cigarettes. They were worn like smoothed-over stones washed by the waves. He was wearing a red and blue flannel with a white T-shirt underneath. He had long, matted hair on his face. His eyes were wide, wild, and bloodshot. Suddenly, Fox realized she was probably going to die.

"Listen ..." she said softly.

"Shut up! I'm warning you."

He let go of her and grabbed her wrists and held her still like he was holding a small bird just enough that it couldn't fly away. He took a roll of silver duct tape from the shelf behind her and put the end in his teeth to pull it loose. He wrapped the duct tape side around her mouth and hair.

There was no use fighting. She was just trying to get enough air through her nose to stay conscious through her panic. Once she was secure, he'd gone over and rifled through her backpack on the floor. He found her gun and her identification but not her cell phone. It was still in the long grass at the top of the stairs. She'd dropped it. Then he'd left and gone upstairs.

Now, sitting in the chair, trying to breathe, she could feel the throbbing lump on her head and the strange sensation of the caked blood and duct tape stuck to her hair.

30

Carver was standing in his office doorway, leaning against the frame. He checked his watch, furrowed his brow, and asked the team, "Where the hell is Rachel Fox?"

Maudmont looked up from her phone and said, "I don't know, Gust, it's unusual for her to be late." She got up and walked towards Carver. The others were at their desks and glanced at her as she walked by.

"Yes, I know," Carver said. "That's why I'm asking. I don't think she's missed a single day since I've been here. And she's usually the first one in and the last one out."

"Well ... I don't know about the first one *in*. Generally, I'm pretty good at ..."

"This isn't a competition, Penny. I'm just saying that it's pretty unusual. Wouldn't you agree?"

"Yes, very," Underwood chimed in from the back.

"And you've tried calling her?" Carver asked.

"Three times," Maudmont said.

"And?"

"*And* it goes to voicemail each time. No idea."

"All right, well, it's ten o'clock now. We have a duty of care to locate her. Just get her emergency contact number and home address from personnel records and we'll try and track her down."

"Okay," Maudmont said. "Anyway, I'm sure it's fine, she probably missed the bus and her phone died, or the bus is broken down and they have no signal, or—"

Carver nodded and said, "I'm sure it's *something*." He stepped towards the whiteboards. "How have you guys been doing with the background investigations into the detectives?"

"You mean the murder-suicides?" Underwood asked and leaned back and looked over his shoulder at the headshots.

"Alleged murder-suicide cases," Hornigen said.

"It's just us here, Frank," Carver said. "There's no jury of your peers. We're working under the assumption that these deaths are suspicious, right?"

"That's right," Underwood said and stuck the tip of his tongue out at Hornigen.

"Take me through it," Carver said and put his hands in his pockets.

"We did a lot of digging," Underwood said. "Penny was on the phone to all the departments. You might have heard it ... the fax machine has been churning out copies of investigations and reports."

"Oh, that reminds me," Maudmont said.

"What?" Carver asked.

"Oh, no, never mind, sorry! Toby just reminded me that I need to order more paper for the fax machine and maybe more ink ..."

Carver shook his head. "I can't believe we still use a fax." Carver waited. They looked around at one another. "Well?" Carver said to Underwood and raised an eyebrow.

"Oh! You want me to ... Sure," Underwood said and stood. He positioned his tall, lanky body to the right of the board and pointed with his long, bony finger.

"Detective Samuel Greene was working on what became known as the Anderson kidnapping, a case that was all over the press. Detective Greene was leading the investigation into the kidnapping of a teenage girl, Emma Anderson, who disappeared on her way home from school. The main suspect was a neighbor with a criminal record. They brought him in for questioning. After several hours of interrogation, he broke down and confessed to murder."

"Okay," Carver said. "So what happened?"

"His lawyer challenged the nature of the confession. Judge decided he failed to properly Mirandize the suspect before the interrogation began."

"Oh, no," Carver said.

"As a result, the neighbor's confession was thrown out. They lost their main evidence."

"What happened?"

"Without the confession, there was insufficient evidence, and he was released. Emma Anderson has never been found."

"How did Greene die?" Carver asked.

"Locked himself in his garage with a gallon of vodka and a hose running from his tailpipe into the back window. Suffered carbon monoxide poisoning and was pronounced dead at the scene."

Carver shook his head and sighed. He could only imagine the guilt and resentment the detective felt towards himself.

"I mean," Hornigen said. "You can kind of empathize with him, you know? It's a tough one to take."

"Sure is," Underwood said.

Everybody in the room had messed up on a monumental scale. They each felt a little of the self-deprecation and self-hatred that Detective Green must've felt.

"Who's next?" Carver asked.

"Detective Maria Rodriguez," Underwood said.

"Do you remember the Midtown Strangler case?" Hornigen asked Carver. He nodded. Everyone had heard of that case.

"Rodriguez was investigating a series of murders ... female victims being strangled in their apartments."

"Didn't they get the guy?" Carver asked.

Underwood nodded. "The pressure was cooking on this one. They sanctioned an arrest of a suspect—turned out to be based on circumstantial evidence at best."

"During the trial, the defense revealed that Rodriguez and her team failed to disclose a key piece of exculpatory evidence ..."

"What was it?"

"An alibi. The defense found a witness who placed the suspect somewhere else at the time of one of the murders. The suspect was acquitted, and the real killer remained at large, eventually claiming two more victims."

"Shit," Carver said.

"And the detective?"

Underwood paused and swallowed and looked at Hornigen while he spoke, "It wasn't pretty. She was found in her bathtub." He made a cutting motion on his wrist and shook his head. "She bled out."

They all took a moment. Such a sad outcome for the victims and Detective Rodriguez.

"A series of school bomb threats got Detective John Marshall involved. Everyone called him 'Jack'. Good guy by all accounts."

"Aren't they all," Carver said quietly.

"Marshall handled a case involving a bomb threat at a local high school. He arrested a student who'd made threatening comments online. I guess the technology side of things wasn't Jack's strong suit. He missed some digital

191

evidence that could have exonerated the suspect. The student was wrongfully charged, he was given a suspended sentence, and expelled."

"Life ruined," Maudmont said and shook her head.

"Meanwhile, the real culprit—a fellow student who tried to frame the bullied student—later confessed to a girlfriend, who turned him in."

"This was just pure negligence," Carver said. "What happened to the investigating detective?"

"Marshall jumped from a bridge. His body washed up a few days later. He was drunk and had enough anti-depressants in his system to put us all in the loony bin."

"What about the others?" Carver asked.

"There's a definite pattern," Underwood said.

Carver kind of moved his head from side to side and said, "Yeah, but there would be, wouldn't there? I mean, if you're so low that you decide to top yourself, then there has to be an extenuating circumstance, right? People don't do this to themselves for no reason. What happened with Shaw?" Carver asked.

"Failed to follow proper protocol in collecting and preserving evidence from the scene of a fire that killed two children. Contaminated evidence led to the case against the main suspect, a man with a history of arson, being dismissed. The suspect was released. Shaw took her own life. Later investigations suggested the fire might have been accidental, but the true cause was never determined."

"And her suicide?"

"In her garage at home. Sleeping pills and carbon monoxide poisoning."

"Another one?" Carver asked.

Underwood shrugged. He pulled a face and said, "Pretty common one, isn't it?"

"Maybe," Carver said. Then, "Last but not least?"

"Detective Thomas Lee. Investigating the murder of a tech mogul found dead in his mansion. The prime suspect was the victim's business partner, who was caught embezzling funds."

"So they had a motive."

"And good lawyers. Lee failed to secure a warrant for a crucial piece of evidence—it was deemed inadmissible. The suspect was acquitted due to lack of evidence, and the case went cold. Later, it emerged that the embezzlement was a cover for a larger criminal enterprise."

Before Carver could ask, Underwood looked at him and said, "Gunshot wound in his home office."

Carver touched his hand to his chin and said, "Elizabeth Webb was also found in her car. Alcohol and carbon monoxide poisoning." *Is that just a coincidence?* He wondered. *Her father was found in his home office, like Lee.*

Underwood looked at Hornigen, and they both shrugged. "I mean, there are a lot of similarities," Hornigen said.

"Correlation doesn't mean causation," Carver said. He wasn't sure. It sounded like a long shot. He was imagining trying to convince Deputy Gibson that there was something suspicious about these deaths, and he was having a hard time seeing how she might be swayed.

AUGUSTINE CARVER LOOKED around at the team. "What else do we have?" He asked. "Anything?" He indicated some evidence laid out in neat piles. "What's all this stuff over here?"

Maudmont was working on it. She said, "This is all of the evidence collected from the scenes while the detectives' deaths were being investigated. There's all sorts of stuff here."

Carver went over and stood in front of the table. She'd designated each case with a line of green string, sellotaped to the table, and stacked little piles of evidence in clear plastic bags under the images of each detective. Carver picked up an evidence bag from one of the cases and held it up to the light from the window. "Find anything interesting?" he asked as he squinted at the bags. He didn't feel confident there would be much.

"Not really," Maudmont said. "I was just in the process of collating and documenting it. I haven't—"

"What's this thing?" Carver asked, interrupting her. He was holding a small bag that contained keys, a wallet, a phone, rosary beads, and other small items.

Maudmont took a bag from him and read the label. "It's contents that were found on Detective Lee, so contents of his pockets, and on his person."

"No, I know that," Carver said. What's this?" He pointed to a small, square, red glass bottle with a gold top and a golden-colored chain.

"That's a car ornament. People hang them from their rearview mirrors," Maudmont said.

"What are they for?"

"It's like a St. Christopher's medal, isn't it?" Underwood said. "Some sort of religious thing for a safe journey."

"I always thought it was fragrance," Hornigen said. "Nice smelly for in your car."

"Nice smelly?" Underwood asked.

"Yeah," Hornigen said. "Nice smelly, you know?"

Maudmont laughed.

"Could be," Underwood said.

"Okay, but there's another one."

"Whose stuff is that?"

"Rodriguez's stuff," Carver said.

They all looked. There was another evidence bag with

another red glass bottle. Underwood shrugged and said, "I mean, they are pretty common, you know? You see them a lot in taxis and stuff."

"Okay," he said as he shifted through a few of the other bags. "Here's another one," Carver said. "This is Marshall."

The team gathered and picked up the others.

"Here's another one," Hornigen said and held it up.

"I found one, too," Underwood said.

"Okay, hmm," Carver said. "Now we're getting somewhere. Right?"

They didn't seem convinced. "It is a coincidence," Underwood said.

"Someone could have bought them in bulk. Maybe it was standard issue?"

"Oh, come on!" Carver said. "What are the chances of each of these detectives, all with similar failures in the cases before they died, all being found with one of these?" Carver opened the evidence bag and took one of the glass ornaments out. He held it up for them to see.

Underwood was looking at it, so Carver kept it there. He was holding it up like he was inspecting the color of a glass of wine. He felt like maybe he was trying to convince himself too. The evidence was thin. He guessed he just really wanted to be able to go back to Jessica Webb with something that could help put her mind to rest. Something that would help him feel less guilty that he was the one who lived and her sister was the one who died. Underwood came closer and leaned towards the bottle as Carver held it up.

"What? What is it?" Maudmont asked.

"There's ... Wait, am I losing it? Is there something in there?" Underwood asked.

"Yeah, the fragrance," Hornigen said.

"No, it looks ... it looks like something solid."

Maudmont stood on tiptoes to see, and Carver lowered it

for her. He was also looking. "I think he's right," Maudmont said. "There's something in there."

Underwood took the bottle from Carver's fingers and tried to unscrew the cap. It wasn't coming off. He was pulling a face trying to unscrew the golden cap like a guy trying to open a stubborn glass jar. "Give it here," Carver said and took it back.

"Wait, no," Maudmont said as Carver put it on the floor and stepped on it. He heard the glass crack.

"I'll get the hoover for all the glass, I guess, then, right?" Maudmont said out of the corner of her mouth and raised her eyebrows, annoyed.

Carver moved his shoe, and there was something that looked like a small button on the floor. He bent to pick it up. "It's paper," Carver said. "A tiny folded ball of paper."

"Let's unfold it," Hornigen said.

"Here," Maudmont said and went to her handbag. She pulled out two pairs of tweezers and held them out to Carver.

"You do it, Penny," Carver said. "My fat fingers won't hold steady enough."

MAUDMONT HELD THE TWEEZERS, one in each hand, with her face up close to the bit of paper on the table. Her eyes were wide and fixed on it. "Looks like it's been rolled and squashed," she said as she held onto the end with one tweezer and gently unfurled the other side. "It's like origami." She stuck the tip of her tongue out and kept it in the corner of her mouth. She unfurled it gently and then held it open to look.

"What is it?" Underwood asked as Maudmont stared. She furrowed her brow. "I don't know," she said. "It's ink. Some kind of drawing?"

"Give it here," Carver said, and she turned the tweezers and showed him the paper.

He squinted. "Can't be ..." Carver said under his breath.

"What, what is it?" Maudmont said, handling it now like a radioactive substance. She put it down on the table, and they all leaned over to look at it. Delicately painted in black ink, like Japanese art, was a human eye. Carver blinked rapidly. His eye twitched. He was thinking. He shook his head. They were looking at him now.

"Gust?" Maudmont said.

"Huh?" Carver said.

"What is it?" Underwood asked him. They were all expectant.

Carver sighed deeply. I'm too old for this shit, he thought.

"I ... I'm sorry," he said. "It's just ... what does it look like to you?" he asked.

"It's an eye," Maudmont said.

"An evil eye?" Underwood guessed.

Carver started nodding, "So I'm not seeing things. That is really there, right?"

Underwood glanced at Hornigen. "We need Fox to do the analysis, don't we?"

Carver looked relieved. He even smiled. Finally, someone had come up with something useful. Something that gave him an out. Fox was the one who could tell with certainty whether what they were looking at bore more than a passing resemblance to the burn marks Sandling found at the crime scenes in Baltimore.

Carver looked at Maudmont, and she glanced at him. She shook her head with a questioning look. "I tried to call her!" Maudmont said.

"Call her again," Carver said. He looked at Underwood. "Toby?"

"Yes, boss."

"Get Rachel's next of kin and emergency contact details off the system."

"On it."

"Caitlin might know," Hornigen said. "Fox worked with her on the Incubus case."

Carver made a finger pistol at Hornigen. "Good thinking, Frank. Let me give her a call."

31

SANDLING STOOD SIPPING LUKEWARM, stale-smelling drip coffee from a styrofoam cup in the makeshift kitchen on the seventh floor of Baltimore PD headquarters. She saw Benson rush past the kitchenette, and their eyes met. He came to a sudden halt, grabbed the wall to stop his momentum, and came back. He looked her up and down and said, "There you are! I've been looking everywhere." He held out some printouts for her. "We've got some information back about our guy, the child predator murder victim."

Sandling raised her eyebrows and said, "Charming." Then she set the Styrofoam cup down on the counter beside her and took the papers. "What have we got?" she asked as she scanned the report.

"Get this, right?" Benson said as she read. "Our third victim is named Howard Clarke; he's a middle-aged man who also happened to be convicted of child exploitation." Sandling looked up at him, trying to slot the details into the bigger picture. This sounded odd.

"He did his time and survived," Benson said as Sandling furrowed her brow. "You know how those prisoners hate convicted sex offenders, right? Especially child offenders." Benson winced.

"Got it," Sandling said and looked back at the report.

"Anyway," Benson continued. "He managed to convince the justice system he was rehabilitated. Changed his name and moved to Maryland. Blending himself back into society. The guy really made a go of it, too; he even became a motivational speaker at something called 'Starting Fresh: The power of beginning again.' He got quite big on the juvie offenders circuit."

She shook her head and thought: these guys were attracted to youth offenders. She knew that Zimmer, when he was still a preacher, also used to make the rounds at juvenile offenders centers. Captive audience. Easy pickings, she thought. Benson was still talking. "Seems everything wasn't quite up to snuff with old Howie, and in his secret alone time, he just couldn't stop being naughty. Behind closed doors, he continued being a pervert. Forensics found thousands of indecent images on his personal devices with chat histories from pretty sick and creepy interactions in online forums." Benson's eyes were wide and he had an intense glare on him as he waited for Sandling to respond. When she didn't, he said, "Pretty sick, right? I hate that."

"Hate what?"

"I don't know ... that we give a guy like that a second chance, and he goes and ..."

"He what?"

"... *Betrays* us like that."

"You see it as a betrayal?"

Benson glanced over his shoulder to check who was listening to their conversation. He turned and asked, "Don't you? Well, maybe it's 'cause I'm a dad and all that, but this shit just makes me *sick*. I mean, little kids, come on!"

Sandling was studying his face. He started to get frustrated with the lack of interaction. He changed the subject.

"Want to know what else I found?" Benson asked.

"About Clarke?"

"About our other victims."

"You've been doing some homework?"

"Hell, well, your witchy-voodoo stuff wasn't cutting it, so I figured I would try some old-fashioned—real—detective work."

Benson was being sarcastic about her profiling methods. "You went out for doughnuts?" she snapped back.

"Yeah, yeah ... laugh it up, Ms Wits. Wait 'til I break this case wide open."

"What've you got?"

"We think our unsub might be some kind of religious nut, right? With the iconography. You said yourself, this Eye of Horus stuff is linked to all sorts of omens and things, right?"

"What did you find?"

"I just started thinking, what if we looked at everything through some deranged religious nut point of view."

"Such as?"

"Our lady of the night in the Clorox bath. If she was a harlot then would a body left in bleach not be some kind of downtown purification ritual? Cleanse the wicked of their sins, sorta thing."

Sandling raised an eyebrow and shrugged. "Could be. So he thought she was a sinner?"

"Yeah, sure, but aren't we all? There must be something about these people—"

"If he's selecting them ..."

"Right, *if* he's selecting them, there's something that connects them in some warped way."

"Zany?"

"Yeah, you know, whacky. Some sorta mentally sick kinda logic."

"Right," Sandling said. "So far, we've got the divorcee Evelyn Monmouth—"

"Not divorced, separated. And she was having an affair with Robert Rimsby."

"Hmm," Sandling said.

"Which brings me to Alice Waters, aka Candy Floss. She was also married, did you know?"

"No," Sandling said. "Don't think I did."

"Not a popular choice for a prostitute, but she was."

"And so you think this is punishment?"

"What's the Eye of Horus about?" Benson asked rhetorically. "It's the All-seeing Eye, right? Or ... a version of it. What's the perpetrator saying?" He raised two fingers and pointed them into his eyes. "*'I'm watching you'* ..." he said. "Isn't it possible—and I'm not saying plausible because I know it's thin—but isn't it possible that he's wrapped up some kind of religious mythology into his paranoia and view of reality?"

"Sure, it's possible. It just doesn't sound like any paranoid schizophrenic I've ever heard of."

Sandling's phone started buzzing. He checked it. Carver.

"Sorry, I've got to take this," she said.

"I'm going to brief the chief," Benson said. "Catch you later."

"Hi Gust, I'm just in the middle of something ..."

Carver spoke quickly and got right to the point. She hadn't heard him like this before. When Carver told her about Fox and asked for help, Sandling said, "Of course! I'll be right over."

32

It was almost 10 P.M. Caitlin Sandling hung up her cell phone and turned to the minivan parked under a streetlight opposite the Wayside Baptist Church in Sandtown-Winchester. Carver and the rest of the team were sitting in the van. There were some kids on BMXs cruising by, watching them closely, wary of the new presence in their neighborhood. Sandling kept an eye on them as she walked back to the van and slid the passenger door open.

"Any luck?" Carver asked and looked back at her from the front seat. Maudmont was holding a map of the neighborhood open on her lap in the middle of the back seat. Hornigen and Underwood were flanking her and looking down at it.

"No, no luck. Gibson says that she can't justify leaning on the local police department."

Carver slammed his palm on the wheel and said, "Damn it."

Maudmont jumped at the aggression and said, "Jesus, Gust. Calm down."

"Hold the map steady," Underwood said.

Maudmont glared at him. "All right, Mr. Bossy. I would if our supreme leader didn't *explode* like that."

Sandling had been trying to find a way to get some local SWAT team support on-site, but they were struggling with jurisdiction issues and no warrant. As she looked at the team, she felt they weren't a hundred percent sure what they were looking at.

"Need some help, guys?" Sandling asked. Maudmont glanced up at her.

"Yes, we're just trying to work out where the cell towers are, over here," Maudmont said and pointed.

"That's the last ping that we got from Fox's phone. Could we triangulate with that?" Sandling asked.

"Well, we need three points of contact for triangulation, and at the moment we've just got the cell tower," Underwood said.

"What about the coordinates?" Sandling asked.

"Two points is not bad," Hornigen said.

EARLIER THAT AFTERNOON, Sandling had rushed down to Fox's apartment. Fox's grandmother didn't really speak English, but Sandling showed her ID and spoke gently. The granny had let her in. The apartment was small but tidy. The dining table was covered in stacks of books on programming and cyber warfare. It was Fox's desk. Through gestures and a little bit of dictionary translation, Sandling managed to make herself understood. She explained that she was looking for her granddaughter. The grandmother had immediately stood up from the sofa and hurried over to the small kitchen of the open-plan living room. She pointed to a green post-it note stuck to the door of the fridge. It was just a random number. Her grandmother was gesticulating and chatting rapidly in Korean.

Sandling took the Post-it note off the fridge and studied it. There were dots and apostrophes on the numbers "... coordinates," Sandling said, "You think this is where Rachel went?"

Sandling used Fox's family name: Lisa Chung.

"*Ye, ye, ye, ye, ye,*" her grandmother had said. "Yes, yes. She go there. She say, 'Call police if I no come.' Here, I tell the police."

Sandling thanked her and left. She immediately called Carver and told the team about the coordinates. They brought them to this spot opposite the church.

"But we are already standing in the spot where the coordinates brought us to, aren't we?" Sandling asked.

Underwood took out the coordinates again and squinted at them in the low street light. Sandling used her phone as a flashlight and joined them studying the map.

Just then, Sandling heard bicycles pull up beside them, and two kids saying, "What you doing here, honkies? You the cops?" one asked.

The other sniffed the air and said, "Smell like bacon up in this mother."

"Hey," Carver said, opened the door, and climbed out of the front seat. "Go on," Carver said as he walked around the back of the van, "This is police business. Nothing to do with you."

"Police, huh?" One of them spat on the ground. "You're not welcome round here."

"Get out of here," Carver said. There was a tense standoff. The boys looked at one another and pushed on their pedals ready to cycle off.

"Hey, wait," Sandling said.

They stopped and one said, "What?"

"Did you guys happen to see an Asian lady around here the past couple of days?"

The boys looked at one another. The one closest to Sandling lifted his chin and said, "What's it to you?"

"She's our friend and she's missing."

He sucked on his tooth. "Yeah, we seen something ... but it's gonna cost you."

Carver stepped forward. "Cost us? How about the next time I see you around I don't bust you and confiscate your bikes, huh? How about that?"

"Man, you tripping," one said and waved him away. He looked at Sandling. "Twenty bucks."

"So you sayin' you saw her?"

"I said maybe."

"I don't pay for maybe," Sandling said and turned back towards the map.

"Okay, sweetness, yeah, I saw her ... what of it?"

"Where'd you see her?" Sandling asked, turning towards them, her eyes narrowing. The boy lifted his chin towards the church. "Over there walking along the sidewalk."

"By the church?"

He didn't say anything. Then, "Where's my money?"

Sandling glanced at Carver. He huffed and took out his wallet. "Here's ten," he said and the younger of the two snatched it from him. "We said twenty."

"You get the rest when you tell us what you know," Carver said.

"Did you talk to her?" Sandling asked.

"Uh-huh," the older one said.

"What about?"

"Nothing. Same as you. Told her this was our street and she had to pay to play."

"You tried to rob her," Carver said.

"Hey man, screw you, we tried—"

"What, did she pull a gun on you?"

The boys glanced at one another.

"Hey, keep the change you filthy animal," the younger one said and they turned their bikes and rode off laughing.

They shook their heads.

"Okay, so we have eyewitnesses that place Rachel at the church," Sandling said.

"Yeah, but we checked all around there and there's nothing."

"No," Sandling agreed. She took the map from Maudmont and put it flat on the sidewalk, beside the open van door. She got on her knees and studied the map under the light from her phone, at the same time as she double-checked the coordinates. "This is the church," she said, pointing at the map. "Three-nine, three-zero-one ... " she said. "I think that the coordinates are slightly behind the church, a little bit further north."

The rest of them got out to look at where she was pointing. As Underwood moved past her he said under his breath, "Wonder Woman does it again ..."

"Huh?" Sandling said and realized she smelled alcohol on his breath. She watched him.

"You take the lead," Underwood said. She kept staring at him. He closed his mouth and stepped away from her. He'd noticed her reaction and reached into his jacket and pulled out a box of Tik Tacs.

"Want one?" Underwood asked her and held them out. She hesitated. Had he been drinking? She wondered.

He was looking at her expectantly.

"Eh?" He promoted as he popped a few into his mouth and smiled. He crunched down on them.

"Err, no thanks," Sanding said.

"Come on," Carver said. "Let's go."

THE TEAM WAS CROUCHED LOW. They were shoulder to shoulder, looking at a house thirty or forty yards away. The garden was overgrown and branches hung down from the trees above them. "There're lights on in there," Maudmont whispered. They could see them glowing from behind the curtains.

"What are we gonna do?" Underwood asked.

Sandling stood up and touched the cold metal frame of the wire fence surrounding the property. The front gate was hanging off its hinge and ajar. "I'm going to ring the doorbell," Sandling said.

"Are you crazy?" Maudmont asked. "What if there's a killer in there?"

"We'll soon find out," Sandling said.

Carver stood up from his hunched position, and the others followed suit. Maudmont brushed off her skirt.

"What about us?" Hornigen asked.

"You're our backup in place of any local blue and whites," Carver said and gave Sandling a nod. "You go to the front door, Caitlin. I'll come with you. Toby and Frank, you guys wait here. If you hear anything ..."

"Like what?" Underwood asked.

"Like gunshots, numb nuts," Hornigen said and gave Underwood a light backhand to the chest.

"Right," Carver said. "If you hear anything like gunshots, screaming, cries for help, you come running, okay?"

They all nodded.

"Everybody check their service weapons and make ready," Carver said. "And unclip those holsters."

"What about me?" Maudmont asked.

"Penny, you're our connection to the outside world,

okay? If anything happens, you go back to the car and call 911, okay?"

"Got it," Maudmont said.

SANDLING'S fists were balled up by her side. She walked, stiff-armed and jaw-locked, towards the front of the house. She was hyper-alert and her heart raced. She wiped beads of sweat from her brow.

"How do I look?" she asked Carver as she straightened her suit jacket.

"Ready," Carver said.

She went up the small set of stairs to the front and banged on the door with the back of her fist. They could hear intense heavy metal music coming from somewhere inside. Then a woman yelled, "Brandon! Brandon! Someone's at the front door!"

They glanced at one another.

"Here we go," Carver said.

They heard her complaining, "Goddamn boy. Inviting people around at all times of the night." The door vibrated as the metal music from inside thrummed through the wood. Sandling unclenched her jaw and tried to look more relaxed. She could hear blood whooshing in her ears. It was fight or flight. She wanted to run but she fought to keep her nerves steady. Her heartbeat seemed to match the thudding beat of the music.

She glanced at Carver. He gave her a half-grin. "Slipknot," he said.

She didn't know what he was saying. "The band," he clarified.

She shrugged and heard the latch drag from inside. Whatever it was, this wasn't going to be easy. The woman's voice came again, louder, closer this time. "Brandon! You hear me, boy? Damn, music gonna blow your brains out." Then the door opened to reveal an elderly woman with wild white hair, her face creased, and a cigarette burned nearly to the end in her right hand.

"What do y'all want?" she asked and crossed her arms.

Sandling held her badge up for the old woman to see. "Hello, ma'am. We're from the FBI."

"Am I in some kind of trouble?"

"No," Sandling said and smiled, trying to look nonchalant. "You're not in any trouble, Mrs. ..."

"Sachs."

"Right, Mrs. Sachs. I just need some details, please."

"Details about what?"

"It might be easier if we step inside," Carver said. "It'll just take a few minutes."

"Who're you?"

"I'm also with the FBI," Carver said and showed her his ID. "Special Agent Carver."

She looked at his credentials without seeing. She blinked at them with her watery eyes. Carver glanced over his shoulder, indicating the night air, and said, "It's kinda cold."

"Sure is," Mrs. Sachs said. "And you got me here in my nightie with the door open. Whole goddamn neighborhood listening in."

"Should we step inside?" Sandling asked and moved towards her. She pushed the door open with the palm of her hand and the old woman moved aside.

Carver closed the front door behind him. Sandling's eyes scanned the house. It was a relic. The decor reflected years of neglect. Brown tones made the room feel smaller and darker. An old armchair sagged under its weight, clutter gathered on the table next to it—an ashtray full of cigarette butts, a couple of wine bottles, a deck of worn-out playing cards. The whole place felt old and forgotten. A television flickered in the corner, some kind of trashy talk show where guests yell over each other. It was barely audible over the throaty screaming coming from the music in the basement.

"We're looking for a young woman," Carver said. "We have reason to believe she might be in danger."

The old woman furrowed her brow, but her lips twitched into something like a sneer. "Ain't nobody here but me and my grandson." Her eyes narrowed. She leaned forward slightly, peering past Sandling and at Carver. "You boys always pokin' your noses in around here, thinkin' we're up to no good. Well, let me tell you somethin'—he's a good boy. Whatever you're accusin' him of, you got the wrong one."

Sandling glanced at Carver. "You've had trouble with the police before?" Carver asked.

Mrs. Sachs pursed her lips and refused to answer.

Carver softened his voice. "Ma'am, we're not here to accuse anyone. We just need to talk to Brandon. Could call him up here."

The old woman squinted, her eyes darting between them. There was a pause, just long enough for Sandling to notice the tremor in the woman's hand, a show of fear behind her bravado. A doubt.

"Fine," she said. "But he ain't done nothin'. You'll see." She pushed past them. They followed her through the living room, past the open-plan kitchenette, and down a dim, dank corridor to the end. She stopped and stamped on the floor and hollered at the floorboards. "Brandon! Turn that damn music off and get up here!"

No response. The music kept going. Sandling's hand drifted toward her hip and the handle of her service revolver.

"Brandon!" the woman screamed again, stomping on the wooden floorboards. Sandling's stomach tightened. She could barely breathe. This wasn't right. Something was off. Carver stepped beside the woman, his voice calm but firm. "Ma'am, we need you to turn the music down and call him again. It's important."

The old woman huffed, but there was a glint of worry in her eyes now. "He's got that music dialed up," she said, finally softening. "Won't hear nothin' till I bang on the pipes." She reached into a nearby cabinet, pulling out a rusted wrench.

As she clanged on the pipes beneath the sink. Sandling took a deep breath. The music stopped. Silence. Then, they heard a voice yell, "Fucking hell! What!?" Then heavy footsteps up wooden stairs.

The old woman moved aside, and said under her breath, "See? Told you he'd come." She seemed proud.

Outside, Toby Underwood stood with his eyes trained on the house. His fingers were drumming impatiently on the metal tube of the wire fence. He could feel Hornigen watching. "What, Frank?" Underwood asked as he shifted from foot to foot. The minutes dragged on for him. He checked his watch for the seventh time.

"You seem a little jumpy," the former Secret Service agent said. He was more nonchalant.

"Come on, Frank, it's been ten minutes, let's go and see what's going on."

Hornigen stood still, his arms crossed. He glanced at the house but shook his head. "No, wait here. Carver said to stay put. Why are you so nervous?"

"Not nervous ... excited."

"Why so excited, then?"

Underwood gave a little shake of his head. He wasn't sure. Maybe it was the chance to finally make up for screwing the pooch the last time he was tracking a serial killer. The time he was undercover, trying to get evidence of an alleged serial killer, and butt dialed the suspect. The guy was in the wind. Vanished. Probably still killing people in other states. Or another country.

"Dunno," Underwood said.

"Anyway," Hornigen said. "They told us to wait, so we wait."

But Underwood wasn't listening anymore. He felt the need to act. Not wait. He couldn't stand around any longer. He stepped away from his colleague and started walking towards the house. He figured Hornigen would join him. He would, right? Wouldn't just leave him hanging, Underwood thought as he walked. They were practically partners. The overgrown path that led up to the house was dark and uneven. He moved carefully. Fine, whatever. Frank can come if he wants, Underwood thought. He kept his eyes on the house and didn't look back. Then he heard shouting from inside and saw Sandling, followed by Carver, run across the front of the house.

THE WOODEN HATCH door to the basement opened. Brandon Sachs came into view. His eyes were downcast, and his skin was pockmarked and acne-ridden.

"Who the hell are you?" he said when he saw Carver and Sandling.

"This is the police, Brandon. They need to speak to you."

"And you let them into the house?" he said furiously

through clenched teeth. His face was red with anger. The old woman lifted her hands to protect herself.

"Get out of here!" Brandon said to Carver and stepped towards him.

"Whoa," Carver said and raised one hand and put the other on his hip. "Stop right there, Brandon. We just want to talk."

"I ain't doin' nothin' wrong."

"Brandon, I'm Special Agent Carver with the FBI. We only want to ask you a few questions."

"I ain't got nothing to say to you."

"Where's the girl?" Sandling asked.

His head swiveled towards her. "Get out of my house!"

"Brandon, listen to me," Carver said. "Is this your house? It's your grandmother's, right? She invited us in."

"Yeah, well, I'm uninviting you. Get out."

"Doesn't work like that, son."

Brandon was standing between them. His chest heaved up and down. His hand twitched. Sandling tightened her grip on the handle of her weapon. She glanced at Carver. He furrowed his brow and gave her a slight nod, telling her to keep calm. Then they heard something fall over underneath them. Everyone except Brandon glanced down at the floorboards. Then they heard a glass break and a muffled cry. Brandon panicked.

"Freeze! Don't move!" Sandling yelled. The old woman screamed. Before they could grab him, the suspect opened the hatch and ducked under it and into the basement. Carver bent to pull it open but it wouldn't budge.

"He's locked it from the inside," Carver said.

Mrs. Sachs was up against the wall, wailing and shaking.

"Mrs. Sachs, ma'am," Carver said, imploring her, "Do you have a spare key to the basement?"

Her hand was shaking. "There's a backdoor to the basement," the old woman said, pointing towards the front of the house. "The key is in the lock."

SANDLING GRABBED the keys out of the front door and ran hard. Her chest heaved. She was out of breath as she reached a set of concrete steps at the back of the house. She held the keys tightly like she was afraid they'd leap out of her grip into the long grass. The dirty metal dug into her palm. She bounded down the stairs two at a time and got to the back door. She stopped outside and held the bunch close to her eyes trying to find the one that looked like it would fit.

Behind her, Carver said something like, "Hurry up!" before adding, "Be careful." She gritted her teeth and blocked him out. The last thing she needed right now was a micromanager. The heavy metal started blasting again from the speakers in the basement.

"Shut it, I've got this," she said to herself. She knew the stakes. The only thing on her mind was Rachel Fox. She imagined her somewhere in that basement, terrified, waiting for them to get her out. A curtain covered the small window, and whatever lay behind it, she hoped, wouldn't be the last thing she saw. She heard Carver on the phone to Maudmont.

"Penny," Carver said. "Call 911. A suspect is holding a federal agent hostage."

Sandling tried another key, her fingers steady despite the nerves. She felt the key turn and glanced at Carver. He nodded and hung up the phone. Sandling's grip tightened on the knob. Just as she was about to open it a crack, she heard Hornigen whisper from behind her, "What's going on?"

He was out of breath. "Shhh," Sandling hissed as she

opened the door a crack. From inside she heard Brandon Sachs shout over the music, "Stop! I'll kill her, I swear!"

This guy's crazy, Sandling thought. "Brandon," Sandling called out over the noise while pulling out her service weapon. She surprised herself, her voice sounded steady and firm. "This is Special Agent Sandling, FBI. We're coming in. We're not going to hurt you."

She pushed the door open and raised her revolver as Brandon screamed, "Get away! She's dead! You're all dead!"

She stood there, aiming the weapon at the suspect, and felt like she wasn't in her own body. She was watching herself like in some sick play. An amateur theatre production of a horror movie. The air hit her first. It tickled her nostrils—thick and sour with chemicals. Along the walls, shelves reached from floor to ceiling, stacked with jars. Inside the jars, the shapes were unclear, rotting white masses floating in alcohol or formaldehyde. Were they human body parts? She didn't know. Didn't care. She couldn't process anything at the moment. Her attention was zeroed in on the suspect.

Brandon stood at the bottom of the stairs with a long, sharp, shard of glass in his right hand. The tip was against Fox's neck, right where her Carotid Artery was. Sandling saw a light-colored pinkish liquid running down Fox's arm. He'd cut himself, or he'd cut Fox. Sandling felt her adrenaline spike. She wanted to kill him. If he'd hurt Fox, she wanted him to suffer. The blood flowed down in a trickle. Fox was in front of him, duct tape covering her mouth, wrists bound, legs taped at the ankles. Her dark eyes were wide with fear. Her nostrils flared. She was crying and sweating. Fox was shivering. Specimen jars were lying shattered all around them with broken glass all over the floor. The chemical smell was overpowering. It stung Sandling's eyes, and they started to water, but she wouldn't let herself blink. Her entire view of the world had shrunk down to Brandon Sachs, that blade of glass, and Fox's terrified eyes. Sachs looked as scared as Fox did. The whole situation was seconds from exploding. She kept her voice low and steady and said, "Brandon, we're not here to hurt you. Please ..."

"You have a gun! You all have guns!"

Sandling needed to de-escalate. She took a risk. She took her aim off him and raised her hands by her head. There was a glint in Brandon's eyes. He immediately seemed less tense.

"There," she said. "See?" Sandling got out of the half-squat she'd been in when ready to fire and stood more upright.

She took a deep breath. "Let's make a deal, Brandon, all right? I'll put my weapon down, and you do the same; how about that?"

His eyes looked up and left at the ceiling. He was thinking. The tip of the shard moved about an inch away from Fox's neck.

This was working, Sandling thought. "Okay, good ..." she said, then something else caught her eye. She saw two black leather shoes coming down the stairs behind the two of them. It was Underwood. Sachs noticed her looking past him. He must have seen the panic and surprise on her face.

"What is it?" Sachs asked and went to turn.

"Wait, no!" Sandling yelled.

The last thing she saw as she screamed was Special Agent Toby Underwood's eyes and the strangely determined look he had on his face as he brought his weapon up. It was like it was happening in slow motion. Brandon opened his mouth and started to shout as he turned around. The shard of glass went back towards Fox's neck. Carver and Hornigen pushed past her, hands raised, yelling at Underwood to stop. It was too late. His finger pressed the trigger. A single dull shot rang out, and the thud echoed around the concrete basement. Sachs' body spun to his left as he was knocked off balance by the bullet. Fox fell the other way and slumped to the floor.

Sandling screamed, "Nooo!"

Underwood stood with his weapon trained on the suspect's body as it lay on the wet concrete floor. Everyone was still. Motionless for a moment as they tried to process what had just happened.

The angry heavy metal was still blasting. Hornigen went to turn off the music. As he did, Sandling heard the distant sound of sirens getting closer.

33

SANDLING REMOVED HER NITRILE GLOVES. The forensics team was still taking pictures and bagging evidence as she walked toward the flashing blue and red lights. She saw Mrs. Sachs standing in front of her house, sobbing into her hands, as a policewoman took her statement. Sandling sighed. She saw Carver coming toward her. Everyone was in a hurry, but he didn't slow down as he approached.

"Would you have shot him?" he grunted as he brushed past her.

Now that her heart rate was level, her weapon was in its holster, and her mind more clear ... She didn't know. Should Underwood have shot him? No, she thought. Not in her opinion. Was the situation under control? Who knows, she thought. She pushed the wonky garden gate open and walked past the side of the church. The street was full of emergency service vehicles. Rachel Fox was sitting in the back of an ambulance wrapped in a gray blanket. She had her chin lifted as a paramedic dabbed the wound on her face with a cotton ball. Sandling smiled to herself. Fox was safe. But her joy quickly turned to loathing. What role had she played in sending Fox to that house? She wondered.

Then she saw Underwood standing between two uniformed policemen. He was animated, describing the shooting. Underwood lifted his arms and hollowed his body and said something and the cops laughed.

"Toby!" He glanced at her, and his smile faded. The local cops turned towards her. "Shouldn't you guys be manning the perimeter?" Sandling asked them. They glanced at one another and said, "Ma'am," and moved off to help with crowd control. Sandling walked up to him.

"Hell of a night," Underwood said.

"Yup," Sandling said. "Hey, Toby, you sure you should be talking to those cops about the shooting?"

"What, those guys?" He asked and gestured over his shoulder. "Sure, why not?"

He seemed pumped up. Sandling glanced past him, put her hand on his arm, and took him aside. She lowered her voice.

"The inspection division will investigate the shooting, Toby. Baltimore PD internal affairs might too."

"INSD, really? How come?"

"Well, for one thing ..." she lowered her voice again. "For one thing, you shot him in the back."

"Yeah, but he had Fox. Besides, it was his *side*. You telling me you wouldn't have done exactly the same thing."

"Thing is though, Toby, the situation was under control. He was lowering his weapon ..."

Underwood pulled a disbelieving face and said, "Come on! Don't give me that. No way was it under control. He had a knife to her throat."

"Not a knife ..."

"Well, a blade made of glass, but still a knife."

"No, it's not, and you'd better get your story straight."

"Why?"

"You know why, Toby. I smelled your breath. I can see

220

the outline of the hip flask in your jacket right there," she said and pointed to it.

"Oh, what? Come on! You're not seriously going to rat me out, are you?"

"Listen, Toby," she said earnestly and took his arm again. "Quieten down, all right? Have you had more to drink since the incident?"

"*Incident*?" Underwood repeated incredulously. "What the hell! I saved her life. I probably saved your life."

"No, you didn't."

"Yes, I did, and you know what? I don't need a story for the firearm investigations teams, you know why?" Sandling just stared at him. "Because you were there, Sandling."

"What are you—"

"You and your little phobia were there. A special agent too scared to fire her weapon? Give me a break. I saw you. You couldn't even point it at him, let alone fire—I know you—maybe if it was to save your own life, but a colleague? *Please*."

"I'm not going to tell you again, Toby. Keep your voice down."

"Why? Are you scared what I'm saying is the truth? Is it too real for you? Yeah, I fucking shot a guy. Yeah, he wasn't facing me. But you know what? I'd do it again ... and you? You'd fold. Again."

"You've been drinking, Special Agent Underwood."

People were looking at them. The din around them had quieted down. Underwood's eyes darted around. Faces and eyes were staring at them from the darkness lit up by the flashing red and blue lights.

"You didn't have to shoot him," Sandling said quietly and walked away.

Underwood yelled after her, "You have no idea what's going on in my life, Sandling!" She was gone, and he was left standing alone, encircled by police cars and ambulances. Sandling's fists were clenched by her side. She was so frustrated. She decided to go and find Fox and apologize. She hadn't seen her since the ambulance arrived. It had all been a blur since the shooting, like floating in a dream. It didn't seem real. Just then, she felt her cell phone vibrate in her pocket. She looked at it and saw Deputy Director Bronwyn Gibson's name lit up her phone. She hesitated, knowing this wasn't going to be a simple conversation and one she wasn't sure she wanted to have now. But there was no avoiding it. She put her hand to her forehead and massaged her temples as she answered.

"Special Agent Sandling," Gibson said. Her voice was formal with a hint of excitement. "First of all, congratulations on wrapping this up."

"Thank you, ma'am," Sandling said.

"Bronwyn. We're on first-name terms now, Caitlin. Besides, it's been a heavy night, I'm sure. Carver tells me the suspect was killed … that's a shame."

"Yes, ma'am," she said. She didn't feel like being informal. The whole situation carried too much weight. It was like a solemn procession for her. It deserved a measure of ceremony.

"I must say, though, I expected better judgment from you than getting the Sofa Squad involved in something this delicate."

Huh? Sandling thought and pressed her lips together. "With all due respect, ma'am, the lack of resources—"

"I know," Gibson cut in. "You were under pressure. I understand that. But it's over now. You've done well. I promised you something if you succeeded; we're getting you out of there. You don't belong in that place with those screw-ups and outcasts anymore, right? I think you've proven that tonight."

Sandling felt a swell of pride. She glanced over at the ambulance where Fox was being treated. She looked devastated and exhausted. Then Sandling felt guilt. This was what she wanted, wasn't it? To get out of Sofa Squad, to be seen as something more than a flawed agent? But Underwood was right, and his words played over and over in her head. The smell on his breath and the outline of the hip flask in his jacket wouldn't leave her.

Should she mention it? It was survival or self-immolation. She wanted to bring it up—to tell Gibson about his drinking—but something stopped her. If she mentioned it now, Underwood could drag her down with him, and she'd be no better than him. After all, wasn't that why he was at Grant Avenue in the first place? He was a screw-up. She needed to get away from these people. Plus, she just wasn't sure she had the emotional energy left for that fight. Not tonight ... Gibson continued, her voice lighter now. Everyone was getting a buzz out of stopping a maniac.

"The media will be all over this. You've helped catch the guy who's been terrorizing the residents of Baltimore. It's finally over, and we'll announce it by morning. Good work, Special Agent Sandling."

"Ma'am," Sandling said, her voice low. She paused, trying to find the right words. "What do you mean? This isn't the Incubus Killer. I'm not sure we've caught the right guy."

There was quiet on the line. Gibson's tone shifted. She was sharper now. "This man .... this ..."

"Brandon Sachs," Sandling said.

"This suspect is in his mid-thirties, a single white male who lives at home with his mother. He was active on a cannibalism website, for god's sake. His basement is filled with body parts."

"We don't know from what animal ..."

"They're human according to forensics ..."

Sandling was quiet. They wouldn't know for sure until they were tested.

"He took Rachel Fox hostage, didn't he?" Gibson said. "She was investigating him, correct? He was a prime suspect, I understand. And she was taken by him, during an investigation *you* were leading. Am I correct so far?"

Sandling didn't answer. She was thinking about the symbols. Did Brandon Sachs seem like a guy with a strategy? Obviously, his mother would vouch for his whereabouts but that didn't mean she would be lying. "That's what happened, isn't it, Special Agent Sandling?" Gibson's voice cutting now. This wasn't death by a thousand cuts. This was a guillotine. "It sounds to me like you have your man. Doesn't it? What am I missing?"

Sandling's chest tightened. Maybe Gibson was right. Now she was unsure; her confidence knocked. This constant battling ... She glanced back at the ambulance where Fox was being checked over. Brandon was dead. The pieces fit together neatly enough, but that sick feeling in her gut wouldn't leave. It was all too easy.

"Yes, ma'am," she said finally. "You're right. That's what happened."

"Good," Gibson said, her tone easing back to its earlier confidence. "Take a breather, get some rest. I'll make sure the paperwork is taken care of. We'll talk about your next move once this blows over."

Sandling hung up, staring at the shadows caused by the flashing lights around her. Some rest? Yeah, *right*, she thought.

She'd done what she set out to do. Yet, something still felt wrong. She needed guidance. A moment of quiet reflection. She dialed her therapist's number. She knew it would go to voicemail but if she did it now, she wouldn't try and talk herself out of it when she woke up tomorrow. She needed to speak to *someone*. Dr. Blackwood's phone went to voicemail. "You've reached the voicemail of Dr. Edmund Blackwood's office. Please leave your name, number, and a short message, and my secretary will get back to you."

"Hi, Dr. Blackwood. It's Caitlin Sandling. I think I'm ready ..." she said. "I ... I think I'm ready to continue. Would you be able to see me this week? I could really use it. Let me know, please. Thanks. Bye."

She hung up. She felt better. She'd be able to get it off her chest. Everything would be fine, she told herself. Let's go and see Rachel now. Put this thing to bed. Bed, God, I wish, she thought and yawned as she walked over.

34

THE NEXT DAY, Caitlin Sandling lay on her back, staring at the ceiling. Dr. Blackwood sat behind her in his sparse downtown Baltimore office. She couldn't see him, but she felt his presence, like a shiver at the back of her head. They were downtown, not at the university. It was the first time she'd been to these premises. It was a low-rise block of offices rented out to small businesses. On different floors, there was a tailor, a physiotherapist, and a hatmaker. The sensation of lying on her back under fluorescent lighting reminded her of being at the dentist. And, while it wasn't quite the same as having her head tilted back with her mouth open and someone's latex-gloved fingers prodding inside her mouth, it felt similar enough. Except it was the top of her skull, her therapist was prying open. Her innermost feelings and fears, and it made her uneasy. She felt the nervousness and uneasiness, this time about divulging too much or saying the wrong thing.

It was an uncomfortable subject.

"You were saying," Dr. Blackwood prompted. "You feel guilty—tell me more."

She could hear from his voice he was reading from his

neat cursive notes. "Guilty ..." she repeated and sighed. "You can say that again. I don't know what it is. I thought I knew what I wanted ... now ... now I'm not so sure."

"In what way?"

"You know I never felt I even needed therapy?" Sandling said, scoffing at herself.

"Most people don't."

"But since we started, I feel like I need it more than ever. It's so strange, isn't it? Like how accountants are the worst people with money?"

"Most psychologists I know are emotionally wretched. Occupational irony," Blackwood said. Sandling sighed—it didn't help. "That's why we all have assigned mentors to help through this type of thing."

Yeah, Sandling thought, I sure could have used a mentor in life. Was her lack of a father figure something to do with why she couldn't form strong mentor-like relationships with senior colleagues? She'd always shied away from using her dad's death as an excuse, but she always felt like she had to do it alone.

"You called me in a panic very late the other night ..."

"Yes," she said and closed her eyes. She didn't want to think about it.

"What happened? It's the reason you're here, right?"

She felt a lump in her throat and choked as she said, "Yes," and coughed. "Sorry."

"Do you need a tissue?"

"No, I'm fine."

"You were saying ..."

"God, where to start?"

"There was some kind of incident. Tell me about that."

"I'm not sure what I can disclose," Sandling said. "It's an ongoing investigation."

"Oh, really?" Dr. Blackwood's voice, usually even and

monotone, now held an inquisitive edge. She found his lack of judgment comforting—until now.

"Did you read something?" Sandling asked and wanted to half-turn to look at him. Her eyes were locked, looking at her peripheral vision.

"No," Dr. Blackwood clarified. "I thought you'd reached some closure ... with the case, I mean."

"Well, we have—sort of—but something feels off to me ..." Sandling was processing her thoughts as she spoke. "Anyway," she changed tack, "Some of the guilt is about what happened to my colleague, and some of is what happened to the suspect."

"Did something go wrong?"

Mildly, she thought sarcastically. "You could say that."

"You know this is a safe space?" Dr. Blackwood clarified. "I can't disclose anything to anyone about what we talk about here."

"I know," Sandling said. "And it's not that I don't trust you, I just don't feel comfortable talking in too much detail about ongoing cases. I know you probably wouldn't report to anyone, but since I was referred here by the Inspection Division, I want to be careful with what I say."

Dr. Blackwood didn't respond. The silence lasted until she started to feel uneasy. "Is something the matter?" Sandling asked.

"No, of course not," he said.

She heard Dr. Blackwood's fountain pen scratching on the paper, and the sound gave her mild fingernails on a chalkboard sensation. Perhaps it was because she already knew what he was going to say.

"I understand," he said. "And acknowledge your feelings. If I may, though, I am aware—conscious—however, that although you came here on referral to deal with any trauma you might be dealing with after having discharged your weapon." He means shot a suspect, Sandling thought. Dr. Blackwood said, "Yet, we haven't even broached the topic." He paused. Sandling said nothing. He waited. She felt her hands and jaw tense.

She heard Blackwood inhale, and he said, "Do you feel remorse?"

"Yes, of course."

"About both suspects?"

She opened her mouth to reply but stopped to think. If she was honest with herself, she didn't feel remorse for stopping Edward Derange. Did he get justice? That was a different question, but she'd managed to overcome her phobia and react when it counted, and that meant something. Carver, Ruth, and who knows how many other victims were alive now because of what she did. Did she have a guilty conscience about what happened to Brandon Sachs, the Incubus Killer suspect who kidnapped her colleague? She swallowed, thinking about it. She was sorry he was dead. He was a weird guy with a deeply embedded fantasy about cannibalism, but that's all he was. Just a fantasist. The bottles and jars he kept on shelves in his mother's basement were the organs—eyes and all that stuff—from animals, mostly like sheep and goats. He was into voodoo and some other occult practices. He'd been arrested for running an illegal butcher shop without proper permits. But he was not the guy. How could she tell? He was online on the nights of the murders. He was in the basement—chatting. And his mother vouched for him.

What she felt remorse for was not challenging Toby Underwood when she had the chance.

"You're right," she said. "I've been feeling ... off like everything's out of balance. There's a lot of stress." She sighed. "My work life has been a mess lately." As if she had any other sort of life outside of work, she thought.

"You've been under a lot of pressure. It sounds like you've had more than usual."

"Yeah," she said, feeling some self-pity. It was comfortable and warm in that mental space, like snuggling under a soft blanket. Dr. Blackwood then ripped it right off her.

"Are you not taking any personal responsibility for the outcome the other night?"

She was taken aback. A little stunned at the bluntness. She'd been warm under her blanky, and now she was standing outside in the cold.

"Yes," she admitted. "Rachel ... I should've kept her safe, or at least looked out for her more, but I didn't know what ..." she stopped herself from making an excuse. Instead, she said with resolve, "That's on me. It should have been my responsibility. But Toby ..." She trailed off, closing her eyes. Underwood's name still made her feel anguish.

"Toby Underwood?" Dr. Blackwood said, prodding her.

"Yes," Sandling said.

"He..." She paused, feeling herself grow tense again. "He shot the guy even though he didn't have to. I'm adamant he didn't have to. The suspect was putting his weapon down, okay? He wasn't a threat anymore. But Toby... I don't know, he's reckless."

There was a lingering silence again.

"He wasn't supposed to shoot," Sandling said more firmly. "I saw it. The guy was dropping his weapon. It was done."

"So, why did Underwood shoot?" Blackwood asked, his tone neutral, still focused on her.

Sandling hesitated. She could feel the weight of her guilt creeping up on her again. Was it her fault? She was questioning herself now. "He told me I wouldn't do what needed to be done. He thinks I freeze up when things get tense. He said he did it *because* of me ..."

"Would you have done it?" Dr. Blackwood asked. "What needed to be done?"

She swallowed. Honestly, she wasn't sure. She was sure that the suspect was cooperating, though. It wasn't relevant as far as she could see.

"Do you think if we'd worked through your trauma more, you might have been able to prove to people in your life that your phobia wasn't a liability?"

His words hung in the air between them, and Sandling's eyes darted as she thought about it. Was it true? She was still scared of pulling the trigger. Was she in denial about how far she'd come?

"Possibly," she conceded, though Dr. Blackwood didn't seem interested in her hesitation. His next question cut right to the core.

"How do you know Toby thought you'd freeze up?"

She blinked, caught off guard. "Why do you ask?"

"Why does Toby think you'd freeze?" Blackwood's voice was steady, unassuming—a surgical question cutting through her defenses.

"I don't know," she answered, avoiding the question's significance. "He's just ..."

"Do you believe him?" Blackwood asked.

"I ..." Sandling stopped. She had been about to say no. Of course not. But the memory of that moment, of standing there as the situation unfolded, haunted her. The suspect was lowering his weapon, the blade of glass reflecting the bright light, and Toby confidently pulling the trigger. Had she hesitated?

She could hear Blackwood scribbling notes again, the sound breaking her train of thought. He was waiting for something. She stiffened her resolve and said, "I was in control. Sachs wasn't going to hurt her. But Toby... panicked or jumped the gun. He's been waiting for an opportunity to make up for his mistakes. And now I can't stop thinking about it." She swallowed hard. "This isn't the first time he's messed up. There was this case... he was undercover, tailing a guy. A serial killer." She shook her head. "He let the guy escape."

Blackwood didn't react, just kept writing. "And you think this reflects on his competency now?"

"Yes," she replied, the word sharp and certain. But as she said it, she questioned herself again. Was this about Toby? Or was it about her? Her thoughts scattered, and she kept second-guessing Dr. Blackwood's motivation behind this probing.

"It sounds like you're carrying a lot of weight with you," Dr. Blackwood said. "Have you ever thought that perhaps this isn't just about your colleague?"

Sandling shifted uncomfortably. The way he said it, the way he turned it back on her—was too precise.

She was getting nowhere. "I don't know."

Dr. Blackwood didn't push. Instead, he glanced at his watch, setting the notepad aside. "I'm afraid we'll have to end here for today."

She felt frustrated. "Already?"

"Yes. We'll pick this up next time." He stood, signaling the end of the session. "Take care of yourself, Caitlin. We'll continue to work through this."

She nodded, still feeling like there were too many words left unsaid. Too many loose ends hanging there. She stood slowly, walking toward the door in a daze. Sandling pressed the button to call the elevator and waited, watching the floor numbers above the doors. "Come on," she said and pressed the button several times quickly. "Screw it," she said and decided to take the stairs. On her way down, she saw a man coming up. She was hurrying, but his disheveled appearance caught her eye. He held a cardboard box in his hands.

He wasn't looking at her. He avoided eye contact. There was something unsettling about him. His clothes looked worn, his hair matted. As she passed him on the marble staircase, a faint but putrid smell wafted toward her. She wrinkled her nose and kept descending, avoiding eye contact.

35

Dr. Edmund Blackwood quietly wrote notes from his session with the special agent. He glanced at the clock above the door, frowned, and checked his watch. His next patient was late. He was a stickler for punctuality. He'd come to see it as a marker of trust and dependability—a sign you'd do what you promised. Nothing was more important.

There was a light tapping on the office door, and it opened. The first thing that hit Dr. Blackwood was the smell. He sighed as the disheveled being shuffled in carrying a battered cardboard box under his arm.

"You're not who I expected to see," Dr. Blackwood said, curious but unfazed. The man opposite him was twitchy, like a drug addict tweaking for their next fix. Dr. Blackwood leaned forward and slowly lifted his hand and said, "Victor, hello!" and clicked his fingers. Victor Crowe glanced at him and locked eyes with his old psychologist.

"Who were you expecting?" Crowe asked. "Not that fat kiddy fucker again."

Blackwood watched him, thinking, trying to insert himself into the wild paranoia storming through the rotting mind opposite him.

"Do you know something about why Howard is late for his session?"

Crowe lifted his hand to his mouth and snickered. Blackwood shook his head and sighed.

"Is he going to miss his appointment?"

Crowe dropped his hand unconsciously, touching the box. "He ain't missing shit."

"Please don't tell me ... Um, you haven't been taking your medicine, have you?" Dr. Blackwood said.

"So?" Crowe said, his eyes darting around the room as if following a housefly. Dr. Blackwood observed the telltale signs: dilated pupils, rapid blinking, and the stench of unwashed clothes. Crowe was deep into a paranoid schizophrenic episode, off his meds, and spiraling.

Dr. Blackwood sighed and asked casually, "Did you see anyone leaving while you were making your way up?" Dr. Blackwood hoped this homeless-looking specimen took the elevator and the special agent the stairs, or vice versa.

Crowe's eyes flicked toward the door. "Yeah," he muttered, voice low. "I seen a woman. Smelled nice."

"You liked how she smelled?"

"Yeah, but she looked strange."

"Strange how?"

"Her eyes ..."

Dr. Blackwood was patient with him like he would be with a toddler. "What *about* her eyes?"

"They were made out of electricity and made my brain sparkle when she looked."

"I see," Dr. Blackwood said, unimpressed. "Did that bother you?"

Crowe's lips twitched. "Is she watching me? Are you? Are you working her? You have to tell me, remember, that's the rule. They're all in on it. You and her, right?"

"Why don't you come and sit down, Victor?"

He shook his head, standing in the middle of the office, shuffling like he needed to go potty.

"What's in the box, Victor?"

Crowe glanced down at it and moved his arms to protect it.

"No one's watching you, Victor. I don't want what's inside —I just want to know what it is." Dr. Blackwood leaned back in his chair and rested his hands loosely on his lap, showing his paranoid patient that he wasn't a threat. "You know I'm bound by confidentiality. You're safe here. But I need you to focus."

Dr. Blackwood could see the agitation brewing in his patient's eyes. If he wasn't reined in, he'd slip into a full break. "You're holding that box pretty tight. Why don't you set it down and come and sit?"

The room seemed to shrink. Both men stared at the box, Dr. Blackwood sensing the weight Crowe bore.

"He didn't want to miss his appointment."

"Who didn't"

"Kiddy fucker."

Dr. Blackwood let in a sharp intake of air. Please tell me this isn't real, he thought. "What's in the box?"

"Want to see? You should know."

"No ... no, I don't think I want you to open it in here. Please just tell me it's not what I think it is."

"What do you think it is?" Crowe was treating it like a game. A childish game. He could barely control his excitement.

"Put it on the floor and tell me what's in it. It'll be right there. Safe," Dr. Blackwood coaxed him. "Or put it on my desk where you can see it. Just for now."

Crowe reluctantly came forward towards the desk and set the box down on it. He sat in the chair opposite but stayed leaning forward flicking his eyes between the box and Dr. Blackwood. "The soap's been listening again," he said and bit his thumbnail.

"Why don't you take off your jacket? It'll help you feel more comfortable. You can relax."

Victor reluctantly obeyed and unzipped his jacket, revealing a once-white T-shirt, now stained the color of a used teabag. It was caked with blood, old sweat, and something fouler. The smell hit Dr. Blackwood like a wave.

"On second thought, zip it back up. Did anyone else see you come here?"

"They see everything."

"Is that why you're not washing, Victor?"

"I don't bathe because of the soap. It's listening to me. They hear everything through the pipes. It's all connected. Don't you see?"

Dr. Blackwood didn't react. He simply nodded and, standing up slowly, said, "I understand." His voice feigned sympathy.

"You haven't been taking care of yourself like you said you would. You aren't taking your medication," Dr. Blackwood said.

Crowe shook his head. "It turns my blood to ash."

Dr. Blackwood sighed. Not this *ash-blood* delusion again, he thought. It was under this delusion—that his blood was turning to ash—that Crowe became violent. He thought he needed to drink human blood to save his own life. To stop his blood from turning to ash. For completely logical reasons—that only made sense to himself—he was drinking blood to stay a human being.

"I do wish you hadn't come here, Victor," Dr. Blackwood said.

"I brought Howard for you."

"You thought I'd be pleased about that?"

Crowe didn't respond.

"Who was the woman?" Victor asked. "With the electric eyes."

"Well, that's part of the problem, isn't it? She's the police, son. And she's looking for you."

"Why'd you bring her here?" Crowe was perplexed. His anxiety kicking off. Dr. Blackwood wondered if he should restrain himself; after all, he'd immediately noticed the signs of Crowe being in the depths of a bottomless paranoid schizophrenic episode.

"I didn't bring her. If anything, you brought her with your little game." Dr. Blackwood had known Victor Harlan Crowe for years. He'd even been his doctor and treated him for a few of them. Back then, Crowe was just a confused kid. Susceptible to manipulation and easier to please. But he also had a severe mental illness. Not one that couldn't be treated at that stage, but the combination of no familial support and a refusal to manage his medicine intake meant he'd spiraled. It was a deep, almost bottomless abyss he'd fallen into.

"It's not a game. It's a mission. They've sent me. The three Gods."

From what Dr. Blackwood could piece together over the years, Victor Crowe grew up in a deeply religious household. His father was an authoritative and devout man. A lay minister in their local church. Victor like most children, worshiped his father and sought his approval in everything he did. When Victor was ten, he caught his father having an affair with a member of their congregation. It shattered his worldview, like a mirror dropped from a great height. His faith and trust in his father was gone. Victor felt deeply betrayed and had to question and assess what he saw as the lies of the religious ideals he'd been so desperate to embody and uphold.

Betrayal forces you to reevaluate not only the betrayer

but yourself. The embarrassment of being so blatantly deceived without realizing it cuts deep. The trauma of this betrayal caused Victor to develop a distorted view of the meaning of trust. Betrayal for him became entwined with moral corruption. Already displaying paranoid schizophrenic tendencies, it wasn't a leap for him to begin questioning the sincerity of everyone around him, as Crowe himself had once told Dr. Blackwood in one of his more lucid moments, "I believe that hidden sins lay behind every righteous facade."

Crowe's illness left him fixated on betrayal. It became like a new religion to him. When he discovered the Gospel of Judas—in this gospel, Judas is not a traitor but someone acting under Jesus' instructions to help bring about his sacrifice, which would free his divine soul from the human body—it made complete sense to him.

Dr. Blackwood interpreted the reversal of betrayal and redemption as a mirror held up to Crowe's internal struggle. Delusional, he saw himself as a Judas figure—misunderstood and acting under higher orders. The idea of betrayal as a form of spiritual duty had become intertwined with his paranoia.

If nothing else, it offered a way for his mind to reframe its chaotic, guilt-ridden existence. The idea that Judas, often labeled as the greatest betrayer, was, in fact, following a divine plan spoke to Crowe. He saw Judas not as a villain but as a misunderstood martyr, chosen by fate to bear the weight of betrayal for the greater good. That sense of twisted redemption resonated with a sick person who, since childhood, had been abandoned and betrayed by those who should have cared for him.

It wasn't long before Crowe's obsession expanded beyond Christian texts. He began studying ancient Egyptian mythology, finding mysterious and labyrinth-like connections in ancient mythology. In Crowe's mind, the All-Seeing Eye represented a divine justice, like Judas—an ultimate authority that decided who lived and who died.

Crowe, in his chronic state, perceived himself as a tool of divine justice and believed he had been chosen to restore balance in the same way Horus avenged his father. Betrayal became an instrument of that justice, a way to test and purify the world.

And so, in the twisted and dimly-lit maze of Crowe's mind, betrayal became a justification for extreme brutality and violence.

"The soap is telling me things," Crowe said again, his voice rising in agitation. He kept glancing at the box.

"Yes, but Victor, there's something much more important we need to talk about. You've been having the thoughts again, haven't you? About people who betray you?"

"No," Crowe said vehemently. "I don't have the thought. The thoughts are planted there, like an Easter egg, waiting for me to reach up and grab it. When I have it, then I am told what they say."

Dr. Blackwood leaned in, his voice lowering as he carefully threaded his words like a needle into the patient's mind. "I know you've been working through this. How long is your list?" He paused, watching Crowe's paranoia swirl visibly in his eyes. "But it's not just about you anymore, is it? People are investigating you, Victor. They're watching. They think they can stop you. And we both know what happens to people who betray the truth, don't we?"

"They can't know. You're not allowed to tell them. You said so."

"I know a way we can stop them," Dr. Blackwood said and smiled thinly. "You want the voices to stop, don't you? To see your mother?" Blackwood spun the day's newspaper around for Crowe to see and tapped his finger on the headline: FBI makes major arrest in Baltimore killings.

"They're getting too close, Victor. They're onto you. If you don't stop them, someone else will betray you. You have to act before it's too late."

Crowe's eyes flickered with pained panic. He glanced at the box again. Dr. Blackwood followed his eyes. There was a soft, wet patch forming in the corner, and maroon-colored goop seeped out.

"Victor?"

"Yes?"

"Is a piece of Howard in that box?"

"His head."

Dr. Blackwood closed his eyes and let the strangeness of the words settle over him.

"I thought you'd want to see him so you could have your session," Crowe said. "Don't you want to speak to him?"

If Crowe had been a psychological experiment, Dr. Blackwood would have said he'd never seen anything like it before. On the plus side, by using basic suggestive and behavioral techniques, Dr. Blackwood could get Crowe to listen to him, if not obey. The pure irony was the way someone so lost could be steered in almost any direction. It really was true. No wind is favorable if a man knows not which port he sails unless someone else sets the destination. Dr. Blackwood knew where he was going and precisely how he was going to get there.

36

Caitlin Sandling was sick of motels. She'd picked up Minx, her fluffy white Turkish Angora, from the cattery and gone home to her apartment. As far as the Baltimore Homicide Unit was concerned, the case was closed. She sat in the warm, dim light of her one-bedroom walk-up apartment and turned on the television. Minx hopped onto the sofa to join her, stepped quietly onto her lap, and started purring. Sandling hated using the damn remote but stuck her tongue in the corner of her mouth, glancing at the buttons as she pushed them. She scrolled through the channels until she found the one she wanted. It was the local Baltimore news, where Baltimore's mayor, Scott Dixon, was standing on a podium behind a lectern covered in microphones giving a speech. He was in a tan pinstripe suit and smiling broadly.

"People of Baltimore—finally—our nightmare is over. For too long, citizens of this fine city have been traumatized by what the media dubbed the Incubus killer well—tonight—I'm ..." He looked down and cleared his throat like he was choking back tears. He put his hands on the sides of the lectern. Sandling rolled her eyes. Typical showman. The mayor looked up and continued, "We're proud. Grateful!

We're *blessed* to announce that, thanks to the resolute and steadfast determination of our very own Baltimore Police Department and," his voice quietening and quickening, "With some input from," he checked his notes, "Special Agent Caitlin Sandling of the Federal Bureau of Investigation, the man suspected of carrying out these horrible, horrible crimes has been stopped."

"Oh, God," she said under her breath as she stroked her cat. Gibson would have loved the shout-out to the FBI there, but she wanted to crawl under a rock. Gibson would be dining out on that line for some time to come. No doubt, Sandling thought. Even if the man they'd shot dead didn't seem to fit what she knew. She still didn't think Brandon Sachs was the guy.

Dixon continued, "Our city can rest easier knowing this individual is off the streets. A quick and effective response from Baltimore's law enforcement has proven again that crime is our number one priority. And why my program of tough, community-driven leadership through our *Hugs not Thugs* campaign is working."

The camera cut to the press pool, and reporters started shouting questions. Sandling's phone buzzed, and she muted the television. She looked at it and saw it was Deputy Director Gibson. She didn't want to answer. She wasn't ready, not yet. The phone kept buzzing, and she groaned and picked it up.

"Caitlin," Gibson's voice carried the rare pitch of cheerfulness. "Pack your things ..." Gibson said. Sandling frowned, rubbing her eyes. "Sorry, what?"

"Pack your things, Special Agent Sandling. You're out. Congratulations. I'm moving you out of Grant Avenue and back to Quantico. You've proven yourself here. I said I would help, and I'm keeping my word," Gibson said. Her words were smothered in pride.

Sandling didn't respond right away, unsure of what to say. She felt happy; her ears were ringing with the news, but she was so full of doubt. She realized she was nobody in the context of this case but how could they be overlooking the obvious? She watched the screen as Mayor Dixon continued to field questions, her mind still lingering on the dead suspect.

"Sandling, hello?" Gibson said.

"Yes, ma'am, I'm here. Look, I—ah—I just don't think it's him."

Gibson paused a second and said, "What?" Her tone had shifted.

Sandling wasn't sure if she didn't hear her, so she said, "I don't think it's Brandon Sachs. The suspect we put in a coffin, he was …" Sandling was trying to put words to her gut. "He doesn't fit the profile. Besides, he has an alibi."

"Nonsense," Gibson said, brushing her off. "What's his alibi, his mother?"

"But—" Sandling tried to interject.

"Agent Sandling, listen. He had a federal agent hostage. He has a record. He fits the new profile. The police are confident, he's the guy."

"But—"

"He's one sick puppy by all accounts," Gibson continued. "Look at the evidence. We found things at his place. The symbols, the photos on his hard drive, his cannibalistic tendencies, it all points to him."

Sandling's pulse quickened. "You've seen the report?"

Gibson paused, then her voice softened, like a parent talking to a child. "Caitlin, there's a lot at play here. You know, the public perception of it all. The mayor's office … donors … politics—people in high places are banking on this case being closed. They need this win, and we've given them one. Let's not rock the boat, hmm?"

Sandling stared at the TV, watching the mayor shake hands with police officials. Gibson's words felt weighty. Layered with meaning. Sandling was silent. Gibson said, "Enjoy this moment. You've earned it. Pack your bags—Quantico is calling." Her tone was final. She hung up. Sandling didn't feel any better about it. Even as the city and the FBI celebrated, she couldn't feel like the victory was hers.

"Come on," Sandling said to her cat and scooped her up. She went to the kitchen, pulled open the refrigerator, and scanned the empty shelves. She pulled half a bottle of pink rosé from the door and put it on the counter. She slammed the fridge door, opened a cupboard, and took out a large wine glass. If you can't beat them, join them. A saying had never seemed more apt as she put the cork between her teeth and pulled and poured almost the rest of the bottle into the glass.

"Cheers," she said to Minx, her cat staring at her, and took a big gulp.

Toby Underwood slumped at the teak bar, his fingers loosely around a tumbler of whiskey, staring at the selection of green and clear bottles in front of him. His reflection swayed back and forth in the mirror behind the bottles. His half-closed eyes were bloodshot, and he was working hard to keep them open. The bartender stood nearby, cleaning a glass, though the dishcloth in his hand had worn out from use a long time ago.

Underwood glazed at the bartender and grunted. His words slurred together. "Why are you bartenders always drying glasses?" he asked and lifted the tumbler to his lips. The bartender glanced at him and smiled politely.

"You've been ... been doing that forever, man," Underwood said.

"Old trick of the trade. Makes folks feel like I'm busy doing *something*. No one's comfortable if I'm just standing here, doing nothing."

"Huh," Underwood said. He lifted the tumbler again and, before sipping the last of the Scotch, mumbled, "I've know a few tricks of the trade myself." Inside, he didn't believe it, though. He knew he was hiding away here. Drinking alone. He thought he would've escaped the embarrassment and shame, but now the burden of his actions felt more like they were pressing down on his chest.

The television perched above the bar flickered with the local news. Underwood gazed at it and then said, "Hey, turn it up. I worked on this case ...." The bartender looked at the TV and pressed a button on the remote control. Mayor Scott Dixon was standing at a podium. The news was a rerun of him delivering his politically charged announcement about the capture of the Incubus Killer. "A special thanks to the FBI special agents who assisted with the case," the mayor said.

"Hear, hear!" Underwood said and lifted his empty glass. "How about another one to celebrate ..." he belched, "... our success."

"Congrats," the bartender said. "You part of that?" He gestured toward the news and lifted his chin.

"Sure was," Underwood said. "I got him."

The bartender set the glass he was polishing down and snatched a bottle of Laphroaig from the shelf. He uncorked it and sloshed some of the rust-colored liquor into Underwood's tumbler.

"Much obliged," Underwood said and nodded slowly. His eyes were narrow, and his smile was thin and without joy.

"Cheers," the bartender said. "Maybe business'll finally pick up. No more folks scared of a serial killer and coming to Baltimore."

"Yeah, maybe," Underwood agreed. He stared at his drink. Twisting the glass under his fingertips. He was drunk. He knew he was. Time to go home. He could just about face it now. The hum of the bar's low conversations filled the silence between them. Underwood took another long sip from his whiskey. The alcohol hardly burned now—he barely felt it. A figure appeared to his right. He barely glanced up. His vision was blurry and lazy.

"Mind if I join you?" the man said, his voice cutting through the silence.

"Help yourself," Underwood said.

"What'll it be?" the bartender asked.

"What he's having," the man said.

"I was just leaving," Underwood said.

"Come on, stay! I overheard your conversation about catching the killer. Let me buy you a drink."

Underwood blinked and looked across at the man, trying to focus.

"All right," Underwood said. "What the hell. One more."

He was just another guy, one of hundreds in the city, blending into the dim lights of the bar.

The bartender poured their drinks.

"I couldn't help but overhear," the stranger said, lifting his glass to salute Underwood. "You're the one who shot Brandon Sachs, right?"

Underwood's lips twisted into a half-smile, though it lacked warmth. "I didn't say that."

"Sure, but it was you, wasn't it?"

The stranger's eyes flicked up towards the television. The news had moved on to other issues. "It must've been quite a moment," the stranger said, glancing over his shoulder. Exhilarating, right?"

Underwood shrugged, his shoulders heavy with alcohol and regret. "Just doin' my job."

"Funny, though," the stranger continued. "That guy Sachs. Not exactly the monster they made him out to be, was he?"

Underwood's brow furrowed, but his reaction was dulled by the whiskey and his tired mind.

"How about we toast to your big win?" he said.

There was something off in the way the stranger talked, but Underwood couldn't put his finger on it. He wanted to leave. Was Sachs the monster they made him out to be? Was he really the killer?

Underwood had thought bringing Sachs to justice would ease the guilt of letting the other serial killer escape. But the hollow feeling inside him hadn't shrunk. They clinked glasses, and Underwood looked into this man's eyes. He was grinning. Something about it made him feel uneasy. Underwood drained his drink and coughed. He made a move to stand. He wanted to go home.

"How about one more?" the man said. "My treat."

37

It was 10 A.M., and Augustine Carver rested his head against the glass of his office window, staring at the street below. He was tired. What had he gotten himself into? Every morning, he felt like trying to shake off the weight of too many unanswered questions.

Something just didn't feel right. Brandon Sachs was neutralized, sure, but it felt too ... neat. Penny Maudmont tapped lightly on his open door. Carver pushed himself away from the glass. He turned towards her and she said, "Toby still isn't in yet."

Carver nodded. "Could you call him?"

"I have. His cell phone goes straight to voicemail."

"Okay," Carver said. "Call his wife. Let's check on him."

Maudmont nodded and left. Carver followed her out. The rest of the team was sitting in front of their terminals, working. Carver saw Rachel Fox sitting at her desk.

"Rachel, what are you still doing here?" Carver's voice was softer than usual. Fox had been at her desk all morning, though she should've been at home recovering. She glanced up from her screen but didn't respond. Carver furrowed his brow. Maudmont caught his eye and mouthed, "Let her be."

Carver relented and sat on a desk at the back of the office. Something didn't sit well with him. The team had been fraying at the edges lately. He sighed, covered his mouth with his hand, and listened as Maudmont phoned Underwood's next of kin. Maudmont's expression told him something was wrong. Mrs. Underwood's panicky voice carried through the receiver. Maudmont put her hand over the mouthpiece and said, "He had a custody hearing today."

"Hmm," Carver said. Something about this bothered him. Underwood never missed a beat when it came to his kids. As unreliable as he might've been sometimes, he wasn't about to let a custody hearing slide. Carver folded his arms.

Maudmont took her hand away from the receiver and said, "Hang on, Mrs. Underwood, I'm going to put you on speaker." She pressed mute and said, "Gust, you're going to want to hear this." She switched to speakerphone. "Mrs. Underwood, can you hear me?"

"Yes," the woman said.

"Can you please repeat what you just told me for Special Agent Carver?"

"He didn't come home last night. That's not like him. We've been having problems, and he's been staying out late, but he always comes home. I don't know where he is. Toby missed the hearing. His phone's off, and I have no idea where he is. Honestly, it's not the first time this has happened. But this hearing... I just can't believe it. He loves his kids, Penny, I know he does. This isn't like him."

Carver exhaled and felt a knot in his stomach. Underwood might've had his demons, but he would've shown up for that hearing. Carver had seen the pain when he talked about losing his kids.

"Mrs. Underwood, it's Augustine here."

"Hello."

"Hi—do you have any idea where he may have gone?"

She thought for a moment. "He's been drinking," she said more quietly. "He thinks I don't know, but he comes home stinking. I found a receipt in his jacket last week. I didn't confront him about it. He's been acting strangely recently—you know how he can be, right, secretive? He's been under a lot of stress."

Carver stood, the rest of the team listening intently. He took a few paces towards the telephone. "Have you noticed anything strange recently or out of the usual day-to-day?" Carver asked.

"There was this one thing ... but no, Toby said it was okay."

"What was it?" Maudmont asked.

"Someone was parked outside the house the other night. They drove off in a hurry when Toby confronted them."

Carver raised his eyebrow and looked at Hornigen. He furrowed his brow and sat back in his chair. That was odd. Carver exchanged a glance with Maudmont.

"We'll look into it," Carver said. "You'll hear from us soon ..."

"Okay," Mrs. Underwood said.

"Wait, one more thing. Are you still there?" Carver asked.

"Yes."

"What's the name of the bar?" Carver asked. "From the receipt you found."

"He said it was from a case he was working on. The La Quinta Inn, near Dulles."

"Okay, thanks," Carver said.

Maudmont took the phone off speaker and picked up the receiver to finish the call with Mrs. Underwood.

"Sounds fishy to me," Hornigen said to Carver.

"Yeah, something's wrong. He's not the type to just disappear, not when it comes to the kids," Carver said.

Rachel Fox tapped on her keyboard.

"Can we get a BOLO out on his vehicle and person," Carver said, more an instruction than a question.

"On it," Hornigen said and picked up his phone.

"Also, see if anyone at the hotel remembers seeing him," Carver said.

"I'm checking CCTV from bars around the airport," Fox said quietly.

"Here's his car," Fox said as her screen flickered with footage from the previous night. Carver went over to have a look. A grainy image of Underwood's Prius pulling into the hotel parking lot. Fox stopped it on his license plate.

"Here," she said. "That's it. I found him."

Stilted grainy images showed the lanky Underwood getting out of his car and heading for the hotel entrance.

They were joined around the screen by Maudmont and Hornigen. The footage was grainy, the kind of low-quality video they would've expected.

"Skip to the end of the night," Carver said.

"I will, but it's buffering super slow," Fox said.

"There," Maudmont said and pressed her finger on the screen. Fox glared at her. "Sorry," Maudmont said, "but that's him, right?"

"He's not alone," Hornigen said.

Underwood was unsteady on his feet—and clearly intoxicated—as he exited the hotel. A man was beside him. Underwood had his arm around the guy's shoulders. The stranger was wearing a baseball cap with the brim low and obscuring his face.

Underwood stumbled, and the stranger helped him up. Underwood was laughing. They didn't head back to the Prius. The stranger helped him into another vehicle.

"Can we get a plate?" Carver asked, leaning over Fox's shoulder.

"Yes," she said, typing swiftly. Then, she zoomed in on the vehicle, copied the license plate, and entered it into the DMV database. They waited silently as the system processed the request.

"Come on," Hornigen said, biting his thumb.

"It's stolen," Fox said after a moment. "Reported missing three days ago."

Carver raised his eyebrows. "Three days? Dammit," Carver said.

"This is bad," Maudmont whispered, taking the words out of his mouth.

Carver's eyes stayed fixed on the screen, the knot in his gut tightening as he stared at the side of the man in the ball cap's face. "We need to find him. Now."

38

CAITLIN SANDLING FORCED herself up the last step to the Grant Avenue offices, her thighs feeling like lead. Using the last of her strength, she turned the handle and kicked the door open. It slammed loudly, making them jump. "Sorry," she said, sucking in air.

Everyone was huddled around Fox's desk, staring at her. Sandling stood just inside the threshold, watching them. She could feel the perspiration forming on her forehead. She hated being sweaty in her suit. Panting and rosy-cheeked, she said between breaths, "Why the hell is no one answering their phones?"

Carver patted his pockets and seemed to realize his phone was in his office. "What are you doing here?" he asked. "I thought you were moving up to Quantico today."

She was flushed and puffing and bent over to catch her breath. Sandling shook her head. "No, something came up."

They watched her and waited, and she stood up.

"Brandon Sachs didn't do it," Sandling said.

"We know," Carver answered, and she walked towards them.

"How do you know?" she asked.

Carver indicated the screen. "We've just seen Toby abducted by a man outside Dulles," he said. Then, "Wait, how do *you* know Sachs didn't do it?"

"Wait—what? Someone has Toby?" Sandling asked.

"We're just working through it now," Carver said.

Sandling felt a ringing in her ears. The shrill tinnitus grew louder as she tried to make sense of what she'd just heard. She gasped at the realization and covered her mouth. Toby? How? Why? It doesn't make any sense. She felt a sudden foreboding twisting into guilt. What did she miss? She thinks back to their last conversation, replaying his tired smile and his unspoken frustrations. She felt a pang of regret and clutched her heart.

"What's that?" Carver asked, gesturing towards her hand. Sandling looked down at her chest, where her hand was covering her heart. She was scrunching a clear evidence bag. "What makes you think Sachs didn't do it?" he asked again.

"Call it a hunch," Sandling said, holding up the evidence bag with a handwritten letter inside. "He's communicating with us now."

"Communicating with *you*, you mean," Carver said.

He was right. This sicko was talking to her now. What had she done to deserve this?

"Can I see it?" Maudmont asked.

Sandling held it out for her. The contents were visible inside. Blue-blotched ink on lined stationery. "It's from him—the real Incubus Killer," Sandling said as Maudmont took it. She placed the bag carefully on the desk, tapped the letter with the edge of her finger, and asked, "What does it say?"

"It's a confession," Sandling answered. "More like a taunt. He admits to everything. Claims responsibility ..."

"Read it, Penny," Hornigen said.

Everyone stared at her. "I'm not sure I want to ..." The room fell quiet as she cleared her throat.

"The handwriting is erratic," she said. "*To the so-called authorities ...*" Maudmont paused for a second, her voice lower. "I don't think I can do it." She looked up from the letter for a moment, her eyes meeting Carver's.

"Give it here," Sandling said. "I've already read it."

> To the so-called authorities,
>
> So, you think you've trapped me, caught me like some rat in a maze? Adorable. You wish it were that easy. I watch as you congratulate yourselves, thinking you've solved it all. But how wrong you are. You don't have a clue—none of you. I'm still out here. I always have been. I always will be. I will die in infamy.
>
> The ones I took? They weren't innocent. No. They begged for mercy, but I gave them grace. More than the world ever would. They didn't deserve to walk among us, not with the lies they carried in their hearts, the sins they refused to atone for. You wouldn't understand, though, would you? Because you're one of them. Your entire system is built on corruption, feeding the weak while the rot festers.
>
> Isn't that what you always tell yourselves? "Just one more body." "We're getting close." You're not. You never were.
>
> I am cleansing this world. You, all of you, are just too blind to see it. The police, the detectives, the pathetic men and women you send my way, they're

just as guilty. They are failures of justice. They betray the people they swear to protect. They deserve what's coming to them.

And now, I've taken one of your own. He's next. You know him, don't you? You better find him. You better pray you get to him before I do what must be done.

You think you can stop me, but you can't. Because I'm not alone.

Yours in Heaven,
Incubus

"He's asking us to stop him," Maudmont said, her voice cracking.

Carver's expression hardened.

"He's got Underwood," Sandling said. Maudmont gasped. Fox covered her eyes and cried. "He's taunting us. Telling us to stop him, but we don't even know where to begin. He's playing with us, and now, he's taken Toby."

"Can we be sure?" Hornigen asked.

Carver stared at the letter, Sandling could see his mind twirling like hers had. The implications started to hit the team, and a sense of dread hung over them. Just then, Maudmont's desk phone shrilled loudly, and they all jumped.

Jesus!" Carver exclaimed. The phone kept ringing. They all stared at one another. "Is somebody going to answer that?"

"Let it go to voicemail ..." Hornigen said.

They waited as the phone rang and rang, then the line clicked, and Maudmont's high-pitched voice told whoever was calling to *'please leave a message after the beep and we'll get back to you ...'*

They all listened, hoping it would end so they could focus. There was dead air, and then a voice—distorted and crackling—came through the line.

"*Hellooo*, Agent Sandling. Pick up, pick up, wherever you are ..."

Sandling furrowed her brow and glanced at Carver. He was stone-faced. Then the voice said, "I assume you've received my letter by now."

Their eyes went wide. Sudden panic. Should they answer? Sandling went to pick it up. "Wait!" Carver said, his eyes darting as he thought. "Trace it," Carver said to Fox. She spun around and started tapping on her keyboard. They listened.

"You already know who this is. And it's not over yet," the voice said. "You think that man in the basement was me? Ha! No. Brandon Sachs was an error in judgment. I'm still out here, all alone. But now I have your colleague."

Fox's lip quivered, and she bit it. The words hit Sandling like a hook to the liver, and her heart rate spiked.

"By the way, he's still alive ... but for how much longer, I can't say. That now depends on you."

Sandling swallowed. Her hand was trembling. She took some deep breaths to try and stay calm.

"That is to say, you should've figured it out by now, Agent Sandling. What a poor, poor investigator you are. If you ever figure it out, you'll also know exactly what happens next ..."

There was a loud bang on the other side of the line.

"He hung up," Maudmont said.

"No," Fox said. "He put the receiver down, but the line is still open." They leaned in to listen to the machine, which was still whirring away. There was no more voice, only the faint hiss and hum on the open line.

"Is he still there?" Carver asked.

They all turned to Fox. She was typing rapidly. "He put the phone down but didn't hang up," Fox said again, her voice low but urgent. "Give me a second."

Carver was pacing. He went up behind Fox, peered over her shoulder, and said, "Where is it coming from?"

Fox jumped and yelled, "Shit!" Then, "Don't do that to me, Gust."

"Sorry, sorry, I forgot. Sorry."

Fox shook her head and turned back to the screen, "I'm working on it. He's bouncing the signal, probably using a payphone with a scrambler."

Sandling's fingernails were digging into her palms as she clenched her fists. Underwood was out there somewhere. The open line gave them a chance, but they were racing the clock—and didn't even know how much time was left. "There," Fox said. Her voice was sharper, more determined now. "Got it."

Carver stepped closer again. "Where?"

"A payphone in West Baltimore," Fox said and pointed, her eyes on the screen.

"Let's go," Carver said. But nobody moved. "What?" he snapped.

"We don't have a choice, do we?" Hornigen said.

"No, we don't," Sandling answered. Her tone was forthright. "Grab your things and hurry! Toby's depending on us."

39

CAITLIN SANDLING KNELT behind a squad car, silently cursing as the rough gravel bit into her knee. The spinning, flashing lights of the police cars lit up the abandoned industrial site around them. They were in front of a cluster of derelict warehouses on the outskirts of West Baltimore. An eerie silence hung in the air. A couple of abandoned warehouses sat derelict in front of them. Under fast-moving clouds and the white light of the moon, all Sandling could see were exposed bricks and shattered windows. The local police had surrounded the area, their patrol cars forming a jagged perimeter. Carver had called in a favor and they'd gotten snipers positioned on the adjacent rooftops, their rifles trained on the warehouse. Rachel Fox's trace had led the team to a bank of pay phones on a concrete railway station opposite the industrial park. They'd been confused at first, but seeing that the derelict buildings were the only outposts nearby, they decided to sweep the industrial park. After all, they couldn't just leave the area they'd been drawn to, not with the suspect who'd said he'd kidnapped Underwood on the loose. The site was massive, and Carver called for backup. Teams of local policemen helped them clear the site, checking inside warehouses and derelict buildings until they came to the final warehouse at the far end of the park. A patrolman had walked in to inspect it and backed out of there, saying he saw a wild-eyed crazy guy holding a man—suspected to be Toby Underwood—by his neck and threatening to stick the knife he was holding to it in. The copy said the guy was screaming at him about how his blood was turning into ash. Now, it was a hostage situation, and there was a media presence.

Sandling waved away an insect flying around her head, attracted by the lights. It struck her as a strange choice for the killer. After all, if he was communicating with them, he wanted fame. He wanted the credit. But his notoriety was fading because the mayor told the world Brandon Sachs was responsible for the reign of terror. Surely somewhere more public? Somewhere, people would see and feel his presence. But out here, there was nothing. Just the broken down warehouse, standing alone in the industrial zone, hundreds of yards from anything resembling life. There was no traffic, no people, just rusting containers and disused machinery scattered around the place. Sandling pulled out her service revolver and squinted in the dim light as she checked the chambers of the cylinder. Underwood had been missing for hours. The thought of him in danger—or her role in it—gnawed at her. He'd been reckless lately, though, throwing himself into the case without thinking, and part of her wondered if she should've seen it earlier. After all, she was a psychologist. What was it about their last conversation that had unsettled her? Why didn't she recognize it for what it was? A cry for help. She'd failed him. She shook her head, chastising herself as their argument replayed in her mind. She was being sharp and unforgiving to herself. She knew she'd been hard on him, and now she wondered if it had been too much. Just then, the wind picked up, carrying the sound of someone shouting orders at the far end of the warehouse. Sandling flinched and moved into a crouch. Sandling kept her eyes on the building, trying to ignore the pain in her knee from the gravel. Then she saw the local police chief stride up to Carver, his heavy boots crunching on the ground as he marched, oblivious to any danger from the warehouse. His hands were on his hips, a scowl chiseled into his face. Carver stood up and crossed his arms. He didn't flinch. The chief came right up to him and started talking, standing close to Carver's face.

"Listen, special agent, I've got SWAT in position. My men are ready to go in. We've been out here long enough already, you know what I mean? The longer we wait, the more dangerous this becomes."

Carver glared at him but stayed calm. "You're not going in until I give the word," he said. "This is my operation. I have tactical command which supersedes your rank. You don't go to the restroom without my say-so. We go when I say we go."

The chief's face flushed red in the spinning white light. He looked like he was going to take a swing. He took a deep breath and said. "With all due respect, my men are trained for this. We're not sitting around waiting for someone to get killed."

Carver didn't flinch. "I've got a man in there, and we don't know the full situation. Stand your men down. We're not going in guns blazing until we're sure what we're dealing with."

The chief let out a frustrated sigh and took a step back. "You're putting people at risk," he said, waving his finger in Carver's face. "My guys are clocking overtime just standing here."

"I don't give a shit about your budget," Carver said. "I care about getting everyone out of there alive."

The chief glared at him, but Carver was stone-cold. It was something Sandling could still admire about Carver and how he held himself. She felt a flicker of pride she hadn't realized was still there. Carver had always been rough around the edges, someone who used her and the team when it suited him. But here, in the middle of this desert of concrete and broken glass, she could see that maybe, just maybe, he cared. The chief threw his hands up, shoved his bullhorn into Carver's chest, and said, "Here, take it since you're so high and mighty. The SWAT team is stacked and ready, and they aren't going to wait forever." He turned away and walked off, shaking his head and cursing. Sandling stepped closer to Carver as the local officers moved back into position. Their eyes met. He didn't say anything, but Sandling understood implicitly *why* she needed this team—needed him—to keep herself going. Thunder rumbled in the far distance, the sound low and ominous.

Augustine Carver looked at each one of his team. Their faces were expectant and concerned.

"Storm's coming," Carver said, looking up at the darkening sky. He gestured for Sandling to get down and knelt on one knee, eyes scanning their faces as he spoke. "He's not wrong, you know. We can't just sit here."

Sandling glanced at the rest of the Sofa Squad, waiting for someone to chime in. Hornigen shifted his weight, wiping the sweat off his brow.

Fox opened her mouth, hesitating briefly before blurting, "I'll go take a look." Her bottom lip quivered, but Carver could tell she was determined.

"No, I'll go," Sandling said.

"Rachel, in the best possible way, you've just come back from the hell of the Sachs case; this isn't the time for you to be throwing yourself into any more danger," Carver said and sighed and rubbed the back of his neck. "Listen, we all need to agree on this, but we can't be too reckless." He looked at each of them in turn. They nodded. "Okay, then. We're going to see if we can talk him out." Carver stood and signaled to the others. They rose, checking their weapons. Maudmont looked unsure and Sandling saw Carver notice. He took pity on her.

"Penny ..."

"Yeah?"

"... I need a liaison with the local police and the SWAT commander. It's a big job, but can you make sure they don't do anything stupid, *like open fire while we're doing recon*?"

Maudmont's face visibly relaxed.

"Do you have any final thoughts or feelings?" The rest of them shook their heads. "All right," Carver said, "I'm going alone."

"Wait, what?"

"I thought you said—"

"I changed my mind. Make sure SWAT don't shoot me in the back," Carver said and started walking out in the open, across the concrete parking lot to the front of the warehouse.

"Wait, Gust, your bullhorn!" Sandling called after him, but he didn't break stride. He walked towards the warehouse, holding his FBI-emblazoned jacket open so that whoever was in there would see that he wasn't armed.

"Screw this," Sandling said and looked at Hornigen. "Come on, Frank, we've got to help him. This is crazy!"

"He told us to wait."

"No, he didn't, he didn't say a goddamn thing. Just started walking over there."

"Okay, so what do you want to do?"

"Come on, we've got to get closer. We can't do anything this far back."

"I'm coming too," Fox said.

"This way," Sandling said.

They moved off from their position, hunched low, looping around the side of the warehouse, out of view. Sandling's butt burned from the crouched run, and cursed herself for not keeping fitter. Behind her, she could hear the footsteps of the others as they ran. Sandling kept checking on Carver out of the corner of her eye.

WHAT THE HELL am I doing? Carver asked himself as he walked across the glistening concrete. He tried to steady his breathing. His adrenaline was up. He felt his heart thudding against his ribcage. He was hyperaware of the long-range sniper rifles trained on his back as he walked. There was a loud bang, and he jumped and stopped dead. It wasn't a gunshot—thank God. More like someone slapping a sheet of metal. Oh, shit. Here we go. The heavy front door swung open, and a wire-thin man with scraggly hair, clutching his side, poked his head out. He stepped forward, dragging his right foot. He seemed injured. He looked up and blinked big blinks like he couldn't believe what he was seeing.

"They've come for me," the man muttered.

"What?" Carver asked.

The man didn't respond; he just stood there.

"Hello?" Carver called out. "This is the FBI—we're here to help." Silence. "Sir? Are you okay?" he tried again, clearing his throat. He sounded nervous. That would be a bad signal to send.

"What do you want?" the man asked.

"To help you," Carver replied.

"No one can help me ..."

"I'm sorry about that," Carver said. "I'm Augustine. Who are you?"

"Who are any of us but a lump of meat with a heartbeat?" the man said, lifting his hand from his gut to inspect it. Carver could see the shimmer of moonlight glistening off the black-looking blood on his skin. "I'm hurt," the man said and looked up.

"I see that," Carver said. "Who did that to you?"

The man shook his head and covered the wound in his side again.

"No one can help me."

"What's your name?"

The man glared at Carver and then said quietly, "Victor."

"Pleasure to meet you, Victor. I'm Gust."

The warehouse loomed over him.

Carver saw a blur of movement to his right. The suspect saw him notice. Victor's head snapped around. "What's that? Who's there? You're trying to trick me!" He stepped back toward the door.

"Shit," Carver swore to himself. Then called out, "No, wait!" Before Victor made it back inside the door, there was the *snap* of a bullet and then a *crack* of the shot from behind him. Carver instinctively ducked. Victor's back arched, and he yelled out in anguish. Carver ran forward, arms up, and shouted back at the snipers, "Cease fire, you fucking morons! Cease fire!"

The metal door slammed shut behind him. Carver saw the team step out from around the side of the warehouse.

Now wasn't the time for admonishment, he decided. He took a deep breath.

"Holy shit, right?" Carver said, trying to make sense of what had just happened. "Right?" he said and looked around. They stared back at him sheepishly. "The guy's bleeding. We need to get in there."

"Do we send the SWAT team in?" Fox asked.

Carver shook his head. "There's no time. We need to go now."

With their weapons drawn, the team moved quietly towards the metal door. Carver could hear his blood rushing in his ears, his heart pounding in his chest. The adrenaline had kicked in with the gunshot and he was laser focused on the job at hand.

"I'll go first," Hornigen said. "First one through the door always gets it in the teeth, and you've got lives to live still." Nobody said anything.

Hornigen reached the entrance, the rest of the team stacking up behind him, backs pressed to the wall. The rumble of thunder rolled across the darkening sky, growing louder as the storm crept closer. Every second felt like it stretched out, the anticipation twisting in Carver's stomach.

Hornigen looked back at Carver and nodded. "Okay, we're going in. No shots unless absolutely necessary," he whispered. The rest of the team nodded back, weapons raised, as they prepared to breach the door. Carver moved first, his hand reaching for the handle. He glanced over at Hornigen, giving him a quick nod before he slowly turned the handle, careful not to make a sound. The door creaked as it opened. They saw nothing but darkness inside.

40

CAITLIN SANDLING TIGHTENED her grip on her gun. She held her issued flashlight next to the barrel, just as she'd been taught—ensuring she'd hit whatever the beam pointed at. Her heartbeat echoed in her ears, her focus narrowing as her eyes adjusted to the dim light filtering in from the warehouse windows. She stepped forward, following Hornigen in, and moved cautiously into the wide, empty space. The air was thick with mildew and something else—something familiar. It was blood. The metallic tang hung in the air, sharp and unmistakable. The room was large, cavernous, and cold. Old, dust-covered shelves lined the far wall, but her attention was drawn to the center of the space. The suspect Carver had spoken to outside lay face down, his cheek and chest pressed to the cold concrete. He groaned softly.

Sandling had her flashlight trained on him. "He's alive," she said.

"Fox ..." Carver said, "Someone! Find a light switch." Their torch lights cut across the dark, open space. The back of the warehouse was filled with boxes, and the front, where Victor lay, seemed about the size of a double garage.

"Found one," Hornigen said from behind them. He flicked it, and there was a groan and buzz of beam-mounted fluorescent lights as they popped on. As the white tubes flickered and warmed up, they started to see the full scene unfold in front of them. Sandling lowered her flashlight and went to the suspect's side. She touched his neck—it was warm. She put her fingers under his nostrils. "He's breathing," she said. "We need EMTs! Rachel, relay to Penny. We need an ambulance."

"Okay," she said, and Sandling turned back to the suspect on the ground.

"He did this to me," Victor hissed.

"He's trying to say something," Sandling said, kneeling next to the suspect. When no one responded to her, she glanced up and saw Carver standing to her right side with his mouth open. He was motionless. She followed his gaze. In the heat of the moment, she hadn't fully taken in her surroundings. Behind a stack of boxes, in the center of the room, sat Special Agent Toby Underwood. He was strapped to a chair, his head slumped to one side, his clothes torn and stained with blood. Sandling's breath caught in her throat as she took in the sight of him—still, lifeless, pale. He was clutching a cheap curved-bladed fish knife covered in blood in his right hand.

"At least he got his own back," Carver said dryly. His voice sounded sad. Sandling was stunned. She didn't know what to say or do. She wanted to scream. She felt the cold knot of dread tighten in her stomach. This was wrong. All of it. She shook her head. Her eyes locked on Underwood. She couldn't look away. A wave of nausea hit her, and she swallowed hard to keep it down. For some reason, she kept expecting him to sit up and greet them. He didn't.

"Are you okay?" Carver asked. She put her hand over her mouth, nodded, and forced herself to stay in control. She went to her training: stop, assess the situation. Her eyes moved from Underwood to Victor and back again.

"Help me roll him on his back," Sandling said to Carver. He knelt next to her, and they rolled the limp body. Victor groaned. "Where the hell is that ambulance?" Carver yelled. Just then, the big metal roller doors to the warehouse started grinding open.

"On their way," Hornigen said. Looking down at the slender, raggedy man in front of her, Sandling could see the knife wound in the suspect's lower abdomen and the dark, beet-clouded blood seeping out of it onto his clothes. Sandling forced herself to assess the scene forensically. There was a dead body and a nearly dead suspect, but there was more. This place had been a hideout for some time. The walls were covered in murals, and a large, jagged emblem of red paint—or blood—was smeared on the boxes behind Underwood's body, forming the Eye of Horus. There were burned-out white candles placed haphazardly on the floor at the corpse's feet. The more Sandling examined, the more she stepped back from the emotional reality and into the analytical mind space she forced herself to create. No room for sentiment there. Bits of paper, maybe letters, some grainy-looking photos, and other objects were scattered on the ground, thrown around like someone in a rush. Either that or the workings of a paranoid mind. The scene felt suffocating. Sandling's eyes were drawn back to the giant Eye of Horus. The symbol dominated the warehouse, an ominous presence watching over the chaos.

"The symbols match," Carver said without emotion.

Surrounding it was a disturbing collection of items—blood-stained rags, scattered letters, crude drawings, and what appeared to be religious artifacts, all arranged in a way that felt both random and deliberate. The scene screamed of ritualistic sacrifice, with Underwood at its heart, a helpless victim of whatever madness had unfolded here. But something gnawed at her. Just then, she heard the metal roller door clunk as it opened fully and the rush of footsteps coming behind them.

His eyes fluttered open. "Watch out," Carver said, but he was too late. Sandling looked down and saw his eyes wide, staring at her. He was wild and unfocused. His arm shot up suddenly, grabbed Sandling's hair behind her head, and pulled her down to him. She shrieked and screamed, "Ah! Let me go!"

Carver drew his weapon, stood up, and shouted, "Let her go!"

Victor started to whisper into her ear, his words garbled and barely coherent.

"There's a night adder watching you," he hissed. Sanding stopped struggling as she took deep breaths and listened. "You're seeing a painting in the sky. Mirror, mirror on the wall. Who is the craziest of them all? That's right ... it was me. It was us. Except I didn't do it, you see? I used my nails and knuckles like snail trails to create what he revealed to me. Inside a message is a message, hidden to the world by all who cannot see." He winced. "Ah ... It reveals itself to those who are backward, like me." Victor's breath hitched, "They'll know. They'll know it was me. Please ... stop me before I ... before I ..." He trailed off, his body trembling as he clutched his side. The hand holding her hair went limp. He let her go, and she pushed herself free. Victor's body exhaled its final breath.

"Move, ma'am! EMT coming through," a medic said, pushing past her. "Sir? Can you hear me? What's your name?"

"Victor," Sandling said quietly, still hunched near the floor, in shock. Carver glanced at her, then moved closer.

"Are you okay?" he asked as he helped her up. Sandling looked up into his eyes. She saw concern on Carver's face.

"This wasn't the work of a mastermind," she said, her voice distant. "He looked terrified, lost."

"It's okay," Carver said and led her out as swarms of people rushed into the scene. "We'll figure it out."

"Toby ..." Sandling sobbed as Carver guided her outside. "How could I? Oh, God, Toby!" she said as tears streamed down her face.

41

THE TEAM SAT in the back corner of Kelsey's Irish Pub in Ellicott City, west of Baltimore, looking dejected. Caitlin Sandling slumped on a heavy stool at their keg-shaped table, a thick hospital blanket draped over her shoulders. The pub was warm, but she felt ice-cold like the chill had seeped into her bones.

On the drive back from the crime scene, Hornigen spotted the bright green neon sign for the bar from Route 40 and pulled in. Giant screens mounted under the ceiling showed sports. Around them, people chatted loudly, dipping barbecue wings into the blue cheese dip.

No one in the Sofa Squad spoke. Each was lost in their own world, processing what had just happened. Just then, a perky, tank-top-wearing waitress bounced up to them and plastered her best smile on for them. She had her pen and little notepad ready to go and said, "How're y'all doin'? I'm Molly, and I'll be your server today. I see you've already got your drinks from the bar. Our barbecue chicken wings are world-famous! Can I get some for the table while you choose your—"

Sandling suddenly sat up, staring at Hornigen across

from her. "Tell me you don't think any of this makes sense," she said loudly, ignoring the waitress standing beside her. The waitress looked embarrassed and stopped her routine. Sandling seemed to become aware that the girl was standing behind her, and Carver said, "I think we just need a few more minutes, okay? But could you bring another pitcher of beer for the table and a Coke for my colleague, and how about some breadsticks?"

"Breadsticks ... right," Molly said and turned on her heels.

"Thanks, Molly," Carver said after her.

"Can I just say," Hornigen began, his voice catching, "before we start talking about the case ... to Toby Underwood. He was sometimes a difficult guy, but he was part of our team. He was trying his best to make up for what got him sent down here." He raised his half-empty beer glass.

"Cheers," Carver said and touched Hornigen's glass. Fox did the same with her Coke. Penny too. Sandling just stared at her untouched drink on the table. She felt like she was floating in a dream. Like none of this was real. It couldn't be real. How could this be happening? It wasn't, she decided. She was certain it wasn't happening. Someone was calling her name from far away. *Caitlin. Caitlin.*

"Caitlin?" Carver said again.

"Huh?" She wanted to apologize but her mouth wouldn't open and close properly. She just gazed at him.

"Are you okay? I mean, I know you're not, but you know what I mean ... *are* you?"

She started breathing faster. Was she? "They fucking murdered him, Gust. They killed him."

"What do you mean by *they*?"

She didn't know what she meant; she just had this strong sense of injustice. "When they told us to go along with the

Sachs as a suspect story ... they are complicit. Aren't they?" She wiped a tear from her eye. "Someone is culpable. They have to be, right? This doesn't just happen. Does it? Tell me it doesn't."

Carver shrugged and swallowed, and said, "I don't know." He sounded like he meant it. "But Victor Crowe ... he's the guy, right? So, maybe his death means something now. We got the guy, right?"

Sandling furrowed her brow and cocked her head, and asked, "Why did he leave the payphone off the hook, hmm? Why do that?"

"He was taunting us," Hornigen said. "He wasn't going to be there, was he? But Toby, in his final—you might even say redemptive—act stabbed him in the liver and put an end to it."

"Toby was tied up ..." Sandling said.

"Yeah ...?"

"So how did Toby stab him? Did the suspect tie his arm after he was stabbed?"

Hornigen took a sip of his beer. He didn't know.

"What are you suggesting?" Carver asked. She felt like he was just giving her a chance to vent. She was going to take it because she couldn't help herself. She was so angry, full of rage, torment, and frustration. How could this have happened?

"It doesn't add up," she said simply.

"Doesn't sit right with me either," Maudmont said quietly and glanced up at Carver sheepishly like she didn't think her opinion mattered. She gave it anyway. Sandling felt a flicker of pride. It quickly dissipated into darkness again.

"Do we think Victor Crowe was behind the suicides?" Sandling asked, her tone flat. She took a sip of her beer and recoiled. Blergh. She hated stale pub beer.

"Murder-suicides," Fox said. Sandling could tell she hadn't meant to correct her, but she had anyway.

"Yeah, those ..." Sandling looked at Carver. "You think Crowe was behind those too?"

"I don't know," Carver said. She was sure he was trying to placate her without antagonizing her. "We need to take some time to process what's happened."

"That's what we're doing, isn't it?" Sandling asked. She was intense.

"Is it?" Carver asked more calmly.

"Why'd he do it?" Maudmont asked, put her beer down, and twisted the beer glass so it was sitting exactly in the middle of the cardboard coaster. She looked up. They were all looking at her. "Target Toby, I mean. Why'd he target Toby?"

"That's right!" Sandling said. "What did Toby have to do with it? Why Toby?"

Fox closed her eyes like she was forcing her thoughts through a narrow tube and blurted out, "The murder-suicides were targeted killings, weren't they? The policemen and women had each made their own mistakes in their career, right?" She opened her eyes and looked at Carver. "Isn't that right, Gust?"

"Wait," Hornigen said. "Are we saying Toby's death was meant to look like one of the cop killings?"

"That's what I'm asking," Sandling said. "Do we really make this ..."

"Victor Crowe," Maudmont said, helpfully.

"This Victor Crowe, do we make him for the suicides? *Murder-suicides*," Sandling corrected herself and gave Fox a little nod. Fox smiled shyly.

"What are the facts?" Carver asked, then said, "Look, I'd really rather prefer we take a beat here and try to regroup, but if we aren't going to do that, then—what do we know? He was there ..."

"He told me he didn't do it," Sandling said, staring at a spot on the table top.

"Like a suspect has never pled innocence when they're caught red-handed," Carver said and took a sip of his beer, then said, "Sorry."

"I make Crowe for the Incubus killings," Sandling said. "He fits the profile to a tee, but what doesn't fit is this ... this whole deal, you know?"

"Like what?"

"Like the location ... the planning. He never kidnapped anyone. There were a lot of moving parts to getting Toby from the airport bar to the warehouse. Was he capable of doing that? Did you see him? Would Toby—our Toby—even blackout drunk, would he have left with someone like Crowe?"

"What do you mean?" Fox asked, confused.

"Did you see the state of him? Or smell the state of him?" She shook her head. "I got a full dose. He was unwashed. Disturbingly bad hygiene," Sandling said, trying to be careful with her words for Fox's sake.

Fox leaned down, pulled her laptop from her backpack, and flipped it open. Just then, the waitress returned with a pitcher of beer and a basket of breadsticks. She set them down on the table. Before she could say anything, Fox said, "What's your wifi password?"

"Um, excuse me?" Molly said.

"Never mind, I'll just hack your network."

Molly, the waitress, stood there very confused. Carver waved to get her attention. "Five more minutes," he said, holding his hand up.

"What are you doing?" Maudmont asked Fox.

"Getting the facts," Fox said. "Here," she pointed at the

screen. "He has a rap sheet. It's long. Victor Harlan Crowe. In and out of psychiatric hospitals, it seems like, for years. His mother is his next of kin. History of schizophrenia ..."

"I'll say," Sandling scoffed.

"... He was treated at Napa State Hospital in California, and they had him for a while at St. Elizabeths Hospital in Washington, D.C. too."

Caitlin nodded. "What else?" she asked.

"Started young. Juvenile detention at fourteen. Assault charges. Pops up on the grid here and there. Started small, petty violence, arson. Then it escalated."

"Fits the profile," Sandling said. "What about for your unsub?" she asked Carver. He didn't say anything. She looked around. There was silence. Carver's voice was heavy, tired, "We need DNA," he said. "That's the only way we'll know if we're right about any of this. For now... It's still just guesses. Educated guesses, but guesses nonetheless." Carver shifted in his seat. "We also need to tell Toby's wife and family."

Maudmont covered her mouth. "My God ... his daughters."

Sandling looked down as her phone started buzzing on the table. Gibson's name. She swiped right, hit the speaker button, and said, "Hello."

"Special Agent Sandling," Gibson said, warm and confident. "I have to say—well done again—you've done it. You've cracked it."

"Ma'am?" Sandling asked, surprised by the tone.

"Two busts in one," Gibson said, her voice tinny against the background noise. Everyone was listening. "Brandon Sachs, *and* this whole thing with the voodoo guy—it's the triple-double. And, your reward is in. Pack your bags. Quantico is calling—and not just to desk duty. Name your post.

Full field agent, consultant, anywhere you want." Sandling felt sad. She couldn't help feeling sick inside. She could feel them looking at her and she closed her eyes. The silence grew awkward. "Congrats, Caitlin. You're back in the big leagues. You're out of that Sofa Squad and into the real game now. The others don't need to know until you're ready to make the move. You've earned it. It sounds like you're busy celebrating, so I will let you go."

There was a pause. Sandling nodded silently. "Yeah, I guess."

The line went dead before she could say anything else. She stared at her phone for a moment. This was the opportunity she'd dreamed of since leaving the Behavioral Analysis Unit—since falling and failing.

"You're not leaving us ..." Fox said.

"What's a triple-double?" Maudmont asked.

"I dunno," Sandling sighed. "Is it a basketball thing?"

She looked around the table—Penny, Rachel, Frank, Gust—she suddenly realized how much she needed them. Her failures still gnawed at her. Fear of how her phobias still held her down. She kept looking at Carver. He couldn't hide his disappointment.

"Gust ..." she whispered. "I ... I was going to talk to you about it. Can you forgive me? For everything." Tears welled up in her eyes, and she felt them spill over. "I wouldn't be here without all of you. I'm sorry." She got herself under control. "I'm going home," Sandling said.

"I can drive you," Hornigen said.

"No ..." she got off her stool, took the blanket off her shoulders, and left it where she'd sat. "I want to be alone. I'll get a taxi. Bye," she said.

"Bye," Maudmont said.

Sandling left them sitting there and went to the bar to

ask them to call her a cab. She stepped outside to wait and huddled under the awning at the front. It was raining and cold and she hugged herself and looked at the black sky and shivered.

CAITLIN SANDLING FUMBLED with her keys as she unlocked the door to her apartment. She felt exhausted, like she was dragging an invisible weight behind her. She stepped inside and turned on the lights. Her phone buzzed, and it went to voicemail again. She had five missed calls from Benson. She couldn't face him. Not now. She tossed the phone onto the sofa and stood still, rubbing her temples. Her muscles ached from tension. Gibson's compliments made her cringe. Alone in her empty apartment, she had never felt more lost.

Minx meowed, padded over silently, and weaved between her legs, but Sandling barely noticed. Everything about Underwood's death gnawed at her. The way he had been found, strapped to the chair with the Eye of Horus looming behind him. The symbolic ritualization was different than Crowe's other crime scenes. Everyone seemed convinced, though. Two killers—Crowe and Sachs—were caught. Case closed. Another notch in her belt. But it didn't fit. Not for her.

Sandling picked up Minx and sank onto the sofa. She wanted a drink. She wanted a bath. But she had no energy for either. Curling onto her side, she held her cat close. Her phone buzzed again. It was Benson. She sighed and answered it, her voice tired. "Hey, sorry, rough night."

Benson cleared his throat. "We got the DNA."

"What, already?" Sandling said and sat up.

"The mayor's all over this thing," Benson said. "They want to be sure."

She scoffed. "This time they want to be sure?"

"Yeah," he said and she imagined him shrugging. "It matches though. Crowe's DNA. It's him, Caitlin. We got him. You got him. The Incubus Killer."

She blinked, and put her head in her palm, trying to process the information. Crowe's DNA on the Incubus victims.

"It's a hollow victory, Mike," she said quietly.

"I heard about your colleague. Sorry," he said.

"Yeah, that too. I mean, *definitely* that, but also ... who the hell was Brandon Sachs then?"

"What do you mean?"

She sighed. "Well, if Crowe killed Evelyn Monmouth, her ten-year-old son, Derek, Robert Rimsby, Alice Waters—"

"Yeah," Benson said.

"Well, if Crowe did it then who the hell is Sachs?"

Benson hesitated, "I don't know."

There was a brief, awkward silence. Sandling knew she shouldn't take it out on Benson but she was so angry. Anyone would do.

"What else do we know about him?" Caitlin asked, pulling herself back into focus.

Benson sounded like he was checking his notes. "His mother's been footing the bill for his apartment and everything else. Dude's got a history of schizophrenia, pretty severe."

"I know."

"Oh, yeah? How?"

She wanted to say '*I'm in the Federal Bureau of Investigation, remember?*' instead she said, "One of my colleagues is a computer whizz. She got his hospital records from his time at Napa State Hospital and St. Elizabeth's Psychiatric too."

"Hmm. Interesting, that explains why his mother was

protecting him. Paying for him to live on his own in this rundown apartment. Forensics are over there now."

"Anything else?" she asked.

Benson paused on the other end of the line, then said, "Why didn't you call me?"

"When?"

"When you went to arrest Crowe?"

"*Jesus*, Mike, are you serious? You can't seriously be pissed about that ..." her tone was harsh and she immediately regretted it but it was done. He didn't respond. "There was no *time*! They had ..." her voice caught in her throat. "He said he had Toby. We went as fast as we could ..."

"Yeah, no, I mean, I just wish I could've helped ..."

"Yeah," she said quietly, calming down now.

"I'll keep you posted if anything new comes up. But for now, that's what we've got. A sick man with a vendetta. Hey," he said, sounding more chipper, "at least you were dead on about the profile right? I guess this stuff does kinda work, huh?"

"Thanks, Mike," Caitlin said quietly through gritted teeth. "I appreciate it."

"Anytime, Cate. And... try to get some rest, huh?"

She hung up and groaned. For some reason, she craved a beer, of all things. Maybe the idea of the ice-cold glass bottle. She stroked Minx absentmindedly, her fingers moving through the soft fur, her mind elsewhere. She wanted to feel pleased, even relieved after hearing Crowe's DNA matched the crime scenes. He *was* the Incubus Killer, after all. There was a void where her sense of accomplishment should've been. Instead, something gnawed at her. What was it? Something she'd read, or something she'd heard. She felt like she'd just forgotten what she was thinking of and was trying to remember. The more she tried the more elusive it was. Maybe Mike was right, she thought, she had done her job. The profile was dead on. They finally got the guy ... okay, they'd lost Toby but at the end of the day no one else was going to die. In that sense, they'd won. She'd won. She'd managed to diagnose him in absentia purely from his chaotic crime scenes. He'd even been committed. But that was weird, wasn't it? Napa State Hospital in California. She furrowed her brow. Then, it hit her. She sat up.

"Napa State ...," she said and the cat sat up too staring at her. "No! It can't be." But there it was, right in front of her.

She got up from the couch, the cat meowing in protest, and she rushed over to the big stack of boxes piled underneath her dining table cum workspace. She got on her knees and yanked box after box out from underneath. She found the one she was after stood up and dropped it on the table. She pulled the lid off and it clattered to the floor as she rifled through the disorganized files, her fingers flicking through page after page, file after file.

"Come on, Caitlin. I know you know this," she muttered, her father's voice coming out of her mouth. She pulled out the file she thought she was looking for. Her hands trembled as she opened it. "Is this it?" she whispered to herself. The top of the printout read: Hermann Zimmer. The man she believed had killed her father in the line of duty. She ran her index finger down a column of Zimmer's location and address history, his assignments, his work as a priest in juvenile detention centers, time he'd spent in psychiatric wards. Her finger stopped on the line. Napa State Hospital. Her breath caught in her throat as she scanned the dates. Her pulse quickened. She grabbed her phone from the couch and called Fox.

"Hey, it's me. When was Crowe at Napa State?"

There was a pause on the other end as Fox checked. "Ten years ago. Why?"

Sandling glanced back at Zimmer's file and double-checked the dates. Same time.

"Hermann Zimmer was there too."

42

EVERY TIME CAITLIN SANDLING visited Hermann Zimmer, visceral memories of her childhood and her father flooded back. Since learning Zimmer was the prime suspect in her dad's death, the brightly lit prison waiting room triggered the same sensations. The familiar buzz of fluorescent lights hummed overhead, accompanied by the distant screams and the echo of slamming cell doors deep in the building. She bounced her knee and straightened her jacket. Did she need to be here? Maybe she should just call the whole thing off. After all, they'd got him. What difference did it make?

Her hands fidgeted in her lap, rolling the hem of her jacket between her fingers as a clock ticked on the wall, marking each second that passed in time with the thudding in her chest. A fleeting thought crossed her mind—she didn't *have* to know the truth. She could live without it, but then who would she be? Her father's voice was in her head. His broad, warm smile when he'd say, "You'll be an even better detective than me one day."

Sandling exhaled slowly. Zimmer was the only one who knew what really happened to her dad. The door's seal hissed as it opened, and a guard stepped in, nodding to her under his black cap. "We're bringing him up. Follow me? This way."

By now, she knew the way to death row. The guard led her down narrow corridors, the sterile white walls seeming to close in around her. Their footsteps echoed as they walked. She felt unsteady, the space claustrophobic. They got to the main gate that led onto the old death row. He opened it and swung his arm out for her to enter. She walked past the row of empty cells on either side of her, the beds neatly made up with rigid hospital corners and rough blue blankets, as if they were waiting for their next guests. She got to the end, to the cell converted into the Chaplain's Quarters, and the guard stopped.

"You'll be okay?" he asked, his eyes staring blankly at her face.

"Sure, I'll be fine, thanks," Sandling said, her voice steadier than she felt.

The guard gave her a nod and left her standing there in the silence. She felt suddenly cold and very alone again. Zimmer would be there soon. She could hear the echoing clang of gates slamming, the clatter of chains, and footsteps approaching. A familiar kind of dread settled in her stomach. It was all a mind game. She knew it; he knew it. She turned up late at inconvenient times, and Zimmer wanted to put her on edge. She still had the bitter taste of their previous conversations on the tip of her tongue. Before she'd met him for the first time, Carver said he was like a snake toying with a mouse. And how he'd toyed with her. No matter what she could have done, he knew something she didn't know. The one thing every child wants to know when their parent dies. She could never win. She was the mouse.

She glanced up—and there he was. The Ripper, shackled at the wrists and ankles, was being led down death row. His eye locked on hers, a faint smile tugging at the corner of his mouth, his expression almost serene. She went in and sat down and waited. He ducked as he came into the space and it felt smaller, more cramped. Sweat beaded on her brow. The guards sat Zimmer across from her, his metal chair screeching as he adjusted himself. They didn't talk for the first few moments. The guards left. She cleared her throat and tried not to squirm in her seat.

"It's late, Cate," Zimmer said, his voice sounding hoarse, "But a little birdie told me you'd be back."

"Did you receive your writing tools, Hermann?"

A smile formed at the corners of his mouth. "Yes, I did. And welcome they were, too. I'm working on my memoirs ... some details even you might find interesting."

"Yeah, well, I'm here to talk about something else."

"Yes, indeed, you're here at the witching hour - it must be important. Otherwise, why else drag me, an old man, from my bed, hmm? Did you think I might be up to go pee anyway? Or is it because people only visit priests when they're about to die?"

Sandling wasn't going to let him dictate the pace. "Let's skip to the end, Hermann, hmm? You know why I'm here."

"Shame on you," Zimmer grinned. "You've grown so cold since we last talked. I miss the old you. The old *us*."

She scoffed. "Us. There is no us. Do you want to see me break? Sorry to disappoint." She leaned forward, her eyes narrowing. "I want to talk about Victor Crowe."

Zimmer's snarl didn't fade, but there was a twitch in his eye—something annoyed him.

"Who?"

"Don't play dumb."

Zimmer watched her closely. "So you got your man, finally. I suppose some congratulations are in order, and by your demeanor, perhaps some condolences too?"

"You taught him to paint," Sandling said, her voice carefully even.

"Did I? I suppose I may have. I taught him many things. He was so impressionable. They all are at that age. What's he been painting?"

"The Eye of Horus. The evil eye. Like I showed you."

"So presumptuous of you, Cate. What gives you an inkling that I even know of him?"

She reached into her jacket pocket and pulled out a black and white photograph, "Because here you are—in Napa State Psychiatric's annual magazine—sitting right next to one, still healthy-looking, Victor Crowe."

"How interesting ... so we shared time at a facility, so what?"

She could tell Zimmer was getting annoyed. She was beyond caring.

"So, it's just a coincidence?" She asked.

Zimmer glared at her and then smiled ruthlessly at her. "Are you here at," he glanced at the wall clock, "ten to three in the morning to ask me to do your job for you?"

"Oh, you don't want to play this game anymore?"

Zimmer's gaze sharpened, and the playfulness in his voice dropped away. "It's all about perspective, Cate, my dear. Perspective is all. What you see depends on how you choose to look at the world. We create our own reality. That's a part most people never learn."

"Is that what you taught Crowe?"

Zimmer scoffed and shook his head, then leaned forward, his voice becoming gruff. "I prefer guidance. The human species are desperate for someone to guide them; show them the truth they're too blind to see." Zimmer cocked his head, "Why are you really here?"

Sandling sighed.

"Did you kill my father?"

Zimmer smiled like the Cheshire Cat and leaned back again. She hadn't meant to ask it, but it just popped out of her mouth. He must have seen the look of dismay on her face. Laying her cards down flat like that.

"You surely aren't still looking for closure, Cate? Are you? Forgiveness is the key to eternal peace. You know as well as I do, *closure* is a myth. There are only answers, and they're never as satisfying as you think ..."

"Does that mean *be careful what you wish for*?"

"What do you want?"

"I want to hear it from you."

Zimmer just stared at her.

"Answer me!" she said and slammed her open palm on the table.

"Tsk-tsk," Zimmer said. "Your father's fate was sealed long before he and I ever crossed paths," Zimmer said, his voice soft. "He was chasing shadows, truths he wasn't prepared to accept."

"Tell me what happened ... "

Zimmer's eye sparkled. "I merely ... what did I do?" he looked up and asked himself. "I merely illuminated the path for him. He walked it himself."

Sandling gritted her teeth. She wouldn't give him the satisfaction of seeing her breakdown. "You manipulated him, just like you've been manipulating me."

"You're not as easy, though, are you? Not like you at all that way. You have a better grip on your mind, even if you're still lost in it."

"Fine. Tell me about Crowe then," Sandling said, redirecting him. She could feel her rage boiling under her calm exterior, but she wasn't about to let Zimmer see. "He worked under your *guidance* too, didn't he?"

Zimmer's grin returned. "He had so much potential. Much like you."

"I'm nothing like him."

"Are you sure?" Zimmer's voice was velvet, smooth, and dangerous. "We all wear masks, Cate. Even you. Especially you. We choose what we show the world, and what the world sees depends on where they're standing."

"Why was the Eye of Horus at the Peninsular Killer crime scenes—and now here in Baltimore, decades later, on opposite sides of the country?"

"That would be the million-dollar question, wouldn't it?"

"Well, money is no use to you but your gingivitis is looking worse. You're looking cold, Hermann. Don't you miss those Napa winters?"

Zimmer scoffed. "Don't run your mouth writing cheques your lowly rank can't cash, Cate ..."

She dropped the corners of her mouth. "But I'm moving up, Hermann. You helped me get this far, right? So why wouldn't I keep the cosmic balance in our relationship going."

Zimmer's chains clinked as he touched his chin. Did he believe she was as career-focused as Gibson thought? Would he take the bait? Would he bite? She put on her best poker face. A blank stare. He watched her with his one watery, good eye.

"Medical attention," Zimmer said. "And you *personally* handle the request for my relocation back to California," he said. "I have eyes and ears everywhere, Cate. I'll know if you don't. I want my medical review board reinstated."

"I am like this with Deputy Gibson," Sandling said and crossed her middle finger over her index finger. "Thanks to your help, she thinks I shoot rainbows and ice cream sundaes out of my backside—we should keep this good thing going."

Zimmer was eyeing her, but he had no reason to doubt

her. His flaw was that his megalomania prevented him from thinking she was smarter than him or more manipulative.

"And like the cat," Zimmer said. "I have nine times to die." Sandling frowned. Before she could say anything, Zimmer continued, "How deep does it go, Agent Sandling? Let's not pretend you came here for Crowe. Or even your father. You need to know how deep this goes, don't you? As if your career depended on it ... hmm?"

"Think about my offer, Hermann," she said.

"The world doesn't move on without me, Cate. It never has. I live in every action and every decision people make. Just like I live in your father's memory. Whether you like it or not, I'm always with you."

She checked her watch. It was nearly 4 A.M. "I'm going to go now, Hermann. Thank you."

Zimmer frowned. "Have you got what you came here for?" He seemed incredulous.

Sandling stood up and turned to leave. Zimmer sat looking at her and said, "Be careful, Cate. You should take a long look in the mirror. Sometimes, they show you things you otherwise would never see."

SANDLING STEPPED out of the exit to the prison and into the cool early morning air. She hugged herself as she walked. The sky shifted from black to purple, dawn a thin wisp on the horizon. "And like the cat, I have nine times to die," she murmured to herself. Where had she heard that before? Or had she? It gnawed at her. She reached her car but didn't unlock it. Instead, she leaned against the cold metal, staring at the empty parking lot. Her frigid fingers fumbled for her phone, and she dialed Carver.

After a few rings, a Carver's voice answered. He hadn't been asleep.

"Hey, Caitlin," he said, calm, as if he'd been expecting her call. "What is it?"

"I went to see Zimmer," she said, her voice low as if the Ripper might be listening. "He said something to me that sounded weird."

"Okay."

"Have you ever heard the phrase, 'and like a cat, I have nine times to die' or something like that? Ring any bells?"

"It's from a Plath poem," Carver said. She sensed tension and waited for him to continue. There was a pause on the other end, and then Carver's voice said sharply, "It was part of Elizabeth Webb's suicide note."

Sandling's gasped and her breath caught in her throat. "Wait, *what*? How could Zimmer know about that?"

"I don't know. Did you mention it to him?"

She looked up at the purple sky, trying to think. "I don't think so. Why would I? I didn't even remember what it was from myself."

"Hmm," Carver said. "Coincidence?"

She shook her head silently. Hermann Zimmer was nothing if not calculating. It couldn't be a coincidence. It meant *something*. "This is the suicide they suspect of being murder?" Sandling asked.

Carver sighed. "Yeah, it's Jessica Webb's sister. They found the same note, same stationary, on her father and her person."

"What about the other suspected cop murders?"

"No," Carver said. "The others only had the Evil Eye."

Sandling rubbed her eyes. "God, Gust. I'm so confused." Carver didn't reply. Before he could tell her to get some sleep, she said, "So we have potentially eight murders, two of them with Plath quotes, six of them with the Eye of Horus at the scene. And we're meant to believe that Crowe did them all, including the murders we *know* he did."

God, what is going on? she thought. Then, like seeing lightning flash across the sky, she had an idea. She said, "I gotta go," and hung up. She started walking back towards the prison and then broke into a run. The night-duty officer looked up from his desk as she burst through the door, heart racing and moving with purpose.

"I need to see the visitor sign-in book," she said, her words tumbling out. "For Hermann Zimmer."

The officer raised an eyebrow but pulled out the ledger, flipping to the last page. She grabbed it from him and put it on the counter. She flicked through the pages, scanning the names as she ran her finger down the columns. Then she saw it. Her hand started to tremble. She glanced at the duty officer and quickly ripped the page out.

"Hey, you can't—"

"Too late," she said as she was already halfway through the door. Gripping the torn-out page tightly as she ran back to her car.

43

Sandling gripped the steering wheel, her knuckles white. She was on autopilot, not entirely sure where she was headed or what she'd do when she got there. Her phone was on speaker, and Fox's voice was distorted against the road noise.

"Sorry for calling so late," Sandling said.

"Could you say it again?" Fox asked.

"Can you pull any Chesapeake Prison CCTV footage from last week? I need footage from the visitors' entrance."

"I can try."

"Thanks."

"What am I looking for?"

"A man. There's a name on the sign-in sheet that … it's tiny writing, but I need to be certain. I need to know who was there."

"Leave it with me."

"Okay, bye …"

"Caitlin?"

"Yes?"

"Are you okay? You sound… different."

Was she okay? No.

"Uh-huh, yep, totally fine."

"Okay."

"I'm fine," Sandling said again before Fox hung up.

She looked around. The buildings around her became familiar: Johns Hopkins University. She frowned and parked in front of the Department of Psychological and Brain Sciences. She checked the time—too early to be here. She cut the engine and sat there for a moment. The quiet campus seemed to sigh. It was so quiet. Morning mist still hovered over the lawns.

She thought she recognized the handwriting on the sheet, but she had to be sure. Even if it was his, there ought to be a rational explanation. But then again, what would they have been talking about if that specific Sylvia Plath line came up? The thought seemed too surreal, too far-fetched for her to take seriously. And yet, here she was. She'd been replaying her conversations with him over and over on the drive. Trying to remember what she'd said. What he'd written. How he'd responded. Did he and Zimmer know one another? Everyone knew of Zimmer the Ripper, but how were they acquitted, if indeed they were?

She opened the car door, stepped into the quiet campus, and shivered. Just then, a campus security guard pulled up on the brick path in a golf cart.

"Good morning," she said.

"Morning, ma'am. It's a little early, mind if I ask what you're doing here?"

She paused. Hmm, she thought. She felt offended. She was tired. A little crabby, sure; she hadn't slept in a couple of days. Screw it.

"FBI," she said and flashed her badge. "I need you to unlock the psych department. It's a federal investigation."

"Um, I think I should check—"

"Sir? Listen to me, what's your name?"

"It's, uh, Bob ..."

"Listen, Bob, campus is quiet, and that's a good thing. I'll make a note for commendation. Right now, I just need you to help me open the offices. You're welcome to escort me ... Please?"

The guard raised an eyebrow, nodded, and pulled a set of keys from his belt. "Sure thing. Follow me," he said.

As they walked, he made light conversation. "I used to be a volunteer in the police force, you know? Oh, a long time ago now," he was saying.

Sandling walked in silence. The guard fumbled with the key but unlocked the department door and held it open for her. In the dim light, it seemed bigger and more ominous.

"Want to come in?" she asked. The guard looked uncertain.

"You can wait here?" she suggested. He looked relieved.

She moved through the dim hallways without turning on the lights. Her shoes tapped softly on the polished floor, her breathing steady. When she reached Dr. Blackwood's office, she paused outside, looking at the brass nameplate.

She took a deep breath, opened the door, and stepped inside. The office was lit by lamps from the open quad outside the bay windows. It was tidy and orderly—the kind of space befitting a man of his stature. She found a light switch and turned it on, then moved to his desk. You're here to confirm or disconfirm. That's all, she told herself. Look at the handwriting. See if it matches. Then go.

She went behind his desk and sat in his chair, her fingers brushing across the surface of his desk as she opened each drawer one by one. Nothing immediately jumped out at her. She looked for his calendar, then sighed and leaned back in his leather chair. She was exhausted. She closed her eyes for a moment. She felt the nauseating swirl of exhaustion, her brain ready to shut down. She jerked awake and opened her eyes—falling asleep here wasn't an option.

When she opened her eyes, she was looking at the ceiling. Something caught her attention—a shimmer. A reflection. She squinted, her eyes tired. At first, it seemed like a blur of purple and blue. But something seemed strange. She stood up and moved to the other side of the desk. It was the painting Dr. Blackwood talked to her and Carver about. She stood, staring up at it. Why did he have a mirror up there? She went back around, sat in his chair, and leaned back like she had before. The painting was visible in the mirror, but it didn't look the same. She blinked and rubbed her eyes. The blobs of color that were abstract before now ... weren't. It wasn't just the messy oil painting that Blackwood bragged was an impression of mental illness. From this angle, something took shape. An image. And then she saw it more clearly than she'd ever seen anything before.

An eye was staring at her.

SANDLING burst through the door at the Grant Avenue offices without stopping to catch her breath. She was breathing heavily as she saw the rest of the team already there.

"Thanks for coming," she said between breaths.

"We got your message," Carver said, walking towards her. "What's up?"

She held up the piece of paper she'd torn from the prison's visitor sign-in book. "I think Dr. Blackwood has something to do with it," Sandling said. She looked at Fox. "Did you manage to get the CCTV footage?"

"Yes, I have, right here," Fox said and pointed at the screen. The others gathered around. She pressed play.

"That's grainy," Carver said.

"Yeah, but that's him, isn't it?" Sandling said, leaning in to see the video. "I'm pretty sure I recognize the tie he's wearing ... and the penmanship in the prison visitor book matches."

"Okay, that is strange," Hornigen said, "But why is it *suspicious* that Blackwood visited Zimmer? They already met at his medical hearing in California, right?"

Sandling glanced at him as she thought about it for a second. Three or four different thoughts were going through her head at the same time.

"Caitlin?" Carver said, snapping her out of it.

"Well, they'd crossed paths before," Sandling said. "That part isn't strange by itself, but I checked the records. Their paths crossed on several occasions at different hospitals."

"We know that Zimmer used to profess to be a priest. That was a time he used to visit and run religious clubs, and even multi-faith denominational extracurricular activities at prisons and psychiatric hospitals all over the state," Carver said to Hornigen.

"Right," Sandling said. "Double-checking Blackwood's history, he always boasts about being a clinical psychologist, not just an academic."

"Okay?" Hornigen said, sounding unsure.

"There were three instances where their paths crossed at various psychiatric hospitals," Sandling said. "Blackwood was consulting at Napa State Psychiatric while Hermann Zimmer was being treated there."

"Right," Hornigen said. "But that doesn't prove anything, though, does it?" He seemed to be playing devil's advocate.

"Not in and of itself," Sandling conceded. "But they were also both there at the *same time* as Victor Crowe."

"So you think there's a link between Blackwood, Crowe, and Zimmer?" Carver asked. Sandling glanced at him.

"Whether there's a link or not is not in question. We *know* there's a link between them, and I have proof," Sandling rested her hand on the back of Fox's chair. "We found a photograph of the patients from a psychiatric hospital's annual magazine showing Crowe and Zimmer together. We also know from his records that Blackwood was posted there at the time."

"Sure," Hornigen said. "But I'm still trying to work out what the theory is about the link to the cases. Was Zimmer responsible? Were Zimmer and Blackwood responsible? And then Crowe went rogue?"

"I don't know," Sandling said. "All I know right now is that Blackwood is involved *somehow*."

"Yeah, but what do we actually have on him? We can't place him anywhere. There's no DNA evidence," Carver asked.

"Do you remember that painting he was so proud of when we went to his office, Gust?"

"Of course. The one he said was painted by a patient's impression of his mental illness."

"Check this out," she said, showing him a photo on her phone.

Carver looked at it and frowned. "I don't understand."

"Blackwood has a mirror above the door—opposite this painting. If you sit at it at a particular angle and look at it, it shows the symbol we've found at every crime scene." She passed the phone so the others could have a look too.

"I don't get it," Maudmont said.

"Have you ever looked at one of those old-school 3D posters, Penny?" Sandling asked. "The ones you put your nose close to and stare at to reveal the hidden image?"

"Yeah," Maudmont said. "But I never got it to work."

"Me neither," Carver said.

"It's like that, but Crowe's brushstrokes create a visual trick. You can only see it reversed in a mirror and ..." Sandling suddenly stopped talking and stood there stunned with her mouth open.

"And what?" Maudmont asked.

"And ... when I saw Zimmer early this morning, which feels like three days ago already ... He told me to *look in the mirror*, to have a good look at myself." She looked at Carver. "He was *telling* me that Blackwood was involved."

Carver looked at the ceiling.

"What?" Sandling asked. "You know Zimmer as well as I do ..."

"Not as well as you," Carver said. "You two are something ..." He left the sentence unfinished. "But you do understand how his brain works better than anyone," he conceded.

"You think it's too big of a stretch?"

"And he's covered himself in a courtroom, that's for sure," Hornigen said and shrugged. "It's tenuous at best."

"Nuanced, open to interpretation," Carver said.

Sandling said, "I mean, it can't be a coincidence, right? He said it while we were discussing the crime scenes."

"May I see?" Hornigen asked. Fox handed him the phone.

"How did you get this?" Carver asked.

Sandling shrugged. "Tricks of the trade?" she said innocently.

"So it's inadmissible in court?" Carver asked.

Sandling noticed that Maudmont looked concerned.

"Yes, I suppose so," Sandling said.

"Dr. Blackwood is a respected academic and physician ..." Carver said and looked at Sandling. "We don't have anything on him," Carver said. "It'd get really political, really fast. What do we have proof of? That he visited Zimmer? That he has a painting by Crowe in his office?"

Sandling swallowed and said, "I couldn't see through it ... until tonight. It's all there. Blackwood had access to everything—Zimmer, Crowe, us. I mean, goddamn it, I even told him about Elizabeth Webb's suicide note! And *he* told Zimmer. It's the only way Zimmer could've known about the Plath poem. He's been in my head this whole time."

"Wait, Plath poem?" Carver asked.

"Oh, no!" Maudmont suddenly said and covered her face with her hands.

"What? Penny, what? What happened?" Sandling said, concerned about her reaction. Maudmont dropped her hands away from her face and stared at the floor. "I ... I messed up, guys," she said quietly.

"What do you mean?" Carver asked.

"I ... it was only a coffee! But I met with Dr. Blackwood's research assistant a couple of times. And we talked on the phone. She used to call me to check in, like a friend would. I thought ... I thought it was harmless. She asked questions about the case, but she was helping us, right?" She looked up at Carver. "That's what you said, Gust? Or at least, I thought she was ..."

Sandling and Carver exchanged an uneasy glance. Carver's brow furrowed, "What did you tell her about the case?"

"Not intentionally ... I mean, she just seemed ... nice. I didn't realize she was feeding information back to him. I'm so sorry ..."

"It's not your fault," Sandling said. "We've all been played."

"Okay," Hornigen said, "Just so I'm clear. To recap, we have a known link between Hermann Zimmer, Victor

Crowe, and Edmund Blackwood. They've either been seen together or shared time at different psychiatric hospitals and prisons, right?" Sandling nodded. Hornigen carried on, "We've also got three crime scenes where Crowe and an Eye of Horus were placed at the scene."

"Yes," Sandling confirmed.

"And six suspected murders of police detectives with the same symbol," Carver said.

"Hmm," Hornigen said. "Could it be Zimmer?"

Sandling shrugged. "I doubt it, but Zimmer was free."

"Not for the most recent one," Carver said. "Zimmer was already locked up by then."

"Right. So, it wasn't Zimmer."

"It wasn't Zimmer," Sandling said. "It doesn't fit his MO."

"So that leaves Blackwood," Fox said, looking up from working on her computer.

As Fox flicked through different programs on her screen, she said, "You're not going to believe this."

"What is it?" Sandling asked.

For a few seconds, Fox kept working on her computer without replying. Just as Sandling was about to prompt her, she said, "I realized that, although we had connections between three suspects, and one of the suspects to one series of murders, we had no connection—other than a dubious one via the symbol—between any of the suspects and the suspected police murders," Fox said. The team looked confused.

"And what did you find?" Maudmont asked, prompting her. Fox turned around on her chair. Everyone was staring at her. "I only found one right now ..." Fox said.

"One what?" Sandling asked.

Fox glanced at her, a little annoyed. "One connection."

"Okay."

"Guess who was a psychiatric consultant on the Detective Maria Rodriguez's prosecution?"

"Dr. Edmund Blackwood," Sandling said flatly.

"Yes," Fox said. "I found an invoice made out to the LLC Dr. Blackwood ran his psychological consulting business out of. He used to provide expert testimony in criminal cases."

"What was the case?" Carver asked. Fox glanced at him and spun back to her screen. She typed a search and said, "The Midtown Strangler case."

"Rodriguez withheld exculpatory evidence that led to a wrongful arrest. The real killer escaped justice," Hornigen reminded them.

"And Blackwood testified?"

"Yes," Fox said. "The case fell apart, and the suspect walked. The killings continued before suddenly stopping. Nobody knows why."

"So we have the motive," Carver said.

"It's thin," Hornigen said.

"Is it?" Carver asked. "I met him. He's a serious guy. I'd go so far as to say he's a megalomaniac, or at the least showed megalomanic tendencies ... would you?" He glanced at Sandling.

She didn't say anything.

"I'm checking for links to the other cases," Fox said. "Whether Blackwood consulted on any more of them."

"So we have Blackwood linked with the case a murdered detective worked on. And Blackwood is linked to Crowe ..."

"And Zimmer," Sandling added.

"And Crowe killed Toby," Hornigen said.

"Supposedly," Sandling said. "While his hands were taped to a chair ..." She didn't mention what she also suspected, that she might have seen Crowe once before at Blackwood's midtown offices. She didn't know why she couldn't tell them. Was it embarrassment? The guy was wearing a baseball cap, and she didn't get a good look, but the smell ... She was afraid if she mentioned it, they might blame her. After all, if she'd realized sooner, maybe Toby would still be alive.

"I'm convinced," Carver said. "Anyone else?"

They looked at one another. Hornigen gave a nod and shrugged.

"So what do we do now?" Maudmont asked.

"We still have no evidence against Blackwood," Hornigen said.

"Nothing that would convince a jury," Carver said.

"But what about ..." Sanding started to say.

Carver shook his head. "None of it is good for an arrest warrant, let alone a conviction," he said.

"So we just let him walk?" Sandling asked. "This could be the guy who took Toby."

"No ..." Carver said. "But we need to think of something."

"What evidence would be enough?" Maudmont asked.

"A confession?" Fox suggested.

Hornigen laughed. "That would be good enough! But what are we going to do? Ask him if he did it and hope he says 'yes' and confesses to the whole thing?"

Fox looked hurt. Sandling pulled a stern face at Hornigen, who tried to recover. "I just meant, it's harder to do than it sounds, Rachel. It's a good idea, though."

"I mean ..." Carver said with his hand on his chin. "She's not *wrong*. We practically have to get him to admit it."

"I know!" Sandling said. Her expression was serious. "We *use* it."

Carver furrowed his brow. "Use what?"

Sandling looked at Fox. "We make Penny a double agent," Fox said.

"That's right," Sandling said.

"Me? What? Why're you all looking at me?" Maudmont protested.

"You want to make this right, don't you?" Sandling asked her. "Blackwood doesn't know we've figured it out yet ..."

"Figured what out?"

"Blackwood killed Toby," Sandling said profoundly in realization.

"I thought it was Crowe ..." Maudmont said.

"No, look, think about it. After the Sachs screw-up, we all of a sudden received a letter from the alleged killer claiming responsibility," Sandling said and turned to Carver. "And you were already investigating murders Blackwood never ever dreamed would even be discovered—let alone investigated."

"And he had a mole," Hornigen said.

"Abigail," Maudmont said, her cheeks flushing.

"That's right," Sandling said. "It's not your fault, Penny, okay?" Maudmont nodded. "Abigail told Blackwood what she managed to find out about the investigations."

"Do you think Abigail knows what Blackwood was up to?" Carver asked.

Sandling thought for a second. "I doubt it, but ... it's irrelevant. Blackwood *knew* you were onto him, Gust," Sandling said.

"And he had the perfect patsy in Victor Crowe," Hornigen added.

"Exactly," Sandling said.

"Also," Hornigen said and lifted his finger. "Toby was too good a target to miss."

"How so?" Carver asked.

Hornigen shrugged. "He was a screw-up, wasn't he? As far as Blackwood was concerned. He let a serial killer go, just like in Rodriguez's Midtown Strangler case. Underwood's killer escaped justice, and then he shot Brandon Sachs, an innocent man."

"Oh my God," Sandling said. "You're right! How did I miss that?"

"Blackwood killed Toby," Carver said. "And framed Crowe."

Maudmont said, "Blackwood probably stabbed Crowe in the stomach and put the blade in Toby's hand too."

They were all silent for a few moments.

"Has Abigail been in touch lately?" Sandling asked.

Maudmont looked ashamed. "Yes, we're meant to be meeting for coffee."

"When?"

"Tomorrow."

Sandling looked at Carver.

"She said he has more information for us!" Maudmont said in her defense.

"Blackwood wants more information," Carver said.

"I'd say he's already laying low after the Crowe incident ..." Sandling said.

"So what do we do?" Hornigen asked.

"Turn Penny into a double agent," Fox said.

"What does that mean?" Maudmont said.

Sandling knew it was risky, but they were out of options. "We feed misinformation to Blackwood's research assistant—something about what Zimmer told me," Sandling said. "Make it sound like Zimmer is ready to flip on Blackwood and make a deal with the federal government. It doesn't matter what—immunity or better accommodation, but we *know* Blackwood and Zimmer speak ..."

Carver folded his arms and stared into the distance. "They might be working together," Carver said.

"They probably are," Hornigen agreed.

"Could you do that, Penny?" Sandling asked. "Go along

to your coffee date, as usual, and give her some misinformation. It'll help us."

Maudmont was unsure, and then her expression hardened. "Yes," she said, pushed her lips together, and nodded. "Yes, I can do that."

"Then what?" Fox asked.

Sandling said, "Leave that to me."

44

Penny Maudmont sat at an outdoor table at the café, her fingers wrapped around a half-empty coffee cup. She felt nervous and laughed a little too hard at Abigail Abingdon's conversation. Abigail was the type to always have her phone in hand or on the table, constantly checking notifications. Maudmont felt like she had to strain to hold Abigail's attention. She put on her most anxious-looking expression. Abigail noticed.

"Are you okay, Penny? You seem a little ... on edge."

"Oh, no, yeah, I'm fine. Fine!" Maudmont said, waving her away. Abigail went back to scrolling on her phone, and Maudmont sipped her coffee so she could think. "There is one thing," she said.

Dr. Blackwood's research assistant looked at her. Abigail furrowed her brow and rested her hand on the table, showing concern. "What is it? Something to do with the case?"

Maudmont smirked, leaned forward slightly, kept her tone casual, and dropped the bait. "You won't believe what I found out," she said, her voice low and conspiratorial.

"God, tell me!" Abigail said and put her phone face down. She was very interested. "I love all this FBI stuff." She put her hands under her chin.

"You remember how my colleague Augustine Carver caught Hermann Zimmer?"

"Mm-hmm." Abigail nodded.

"Well, Zimmer's going to make a deal. He says he has information about the case Carver is working on, the one with the dead cops. He is going to help us catch the suspect in return for a transfer back to California and a state psychiatric hospital instead of being stuck in a supermax prison during our winters."

Abigail's eyes sparkled, her hand twitching toward her phone. "I ... um, that's, uh, kind of genius, I guess, right? I mean, Carver using someone he caught before like that, isn't it?"

"I'll say," Maudmont said and sat back, looking at her coffee.

"So you think he'll do it? Zimmer, I mean. Would he turn state's witness?"

Maudmont sighed and shrugged. "I'm sure Gust will see what Zimmer knows. He's made it clear he knows who's behind it and is willing to spill for a transfer, so we'll see ..." Abigail nodded silently. "Anyway, did you get anywhere with the research materials you mentioned last time?" Maudmont asked.

Abigail stared blankly for a moment before sudden recognition lit her face. "Hold on a sec ... I just need to check my diary; I have a feeling I'm late for something."

"Sure," Maudmont said. "I'm just going to the little girl's room. Be right back." Abigail was already focused on her phone. Maudmont slid out of the chair and gave her a smile. She shrugged her shoulders and said, "One sec."

IN THE SURVEILLANCE VAN, Carver watched the live feed on a bank of screens. Sandling sat beside him, eyes glued to the monitor, fingers drumming on the console. Fox typed on her laptop, ready to trace any calls. Carver's phone rang, and he picked it up and said, "Stay calm. You're doing great."

"She's looking around—she's about to leave," Sandling said.

"Better head back to her, Penny," Carver suggested. "Make sure she understands the urgency."

"Okay," Penny said.

Carver hung up. So far, so good, he thought. We might pull this off.

PENNY MAUDMONT SWALLOWED HARD, put her phone away, and walked back to the table, careful not to seem too surprised.

"Oh, no, you need to leave?" Maudmont asked as Abigail stood and stuffed things into her handbag.

"God, yeah, I'm so sorry ..." she said. I totally forgot about this really important meeting I have on campus and I'm going to be in *so* much trouble if I don't make it."

"Well, that's okay. It was nice to talk to you. Let me know where we are on those police suicide studies when you get a second."

Abigail leaned in for a hug, air-kissing Maudmont on both cheeks. "Mwah, Mwah. Lovely to see you, darling. Thanks so much for the coffee ... I always feel bad making the FBI pick up the tab, but it was a work luncheon, so ... you know?"

"Okay, bye," Maudmont said. "Don't forget, you can't tell

anyone what I said about Zimmer, right? It's highly confidential."

Abigail scoffed, "What? Me?" And touched her chest. "I would never, Penny darling, never."

"Good, because I could lose my job."

"Don't be silly." Abigail turned to leave, then paused. "By the way, when did you say this was all happening? I just want to make sure we can get everything to you in time to help with the case."

"It's happening," Maudmont checked her watch. "It's happening this evening. Carver is going to see Zimmer about it later on today. The governor has the transfer paperwork ready to sign as soon as Zimmer tells us what he knows about the painting."

"The painting? What painting?"

"Oh, shoot!" Maudmont said, acting flustered. "I've said too much. I really must be going, too."

"See you, kisses. Mwah, mwah." Abigail blew two kisses and hurried away, phone in hand, typing. When Maudmont was sure Abigail was out of sight, she went across the street and opened the sliding door to the back of the van. Sandling helped her in and slammed the door shut.

"You got her," Carver said.

Fox's fingers tapped on her keyboard as she monitored the research assistant's movements via the street cameras. "She's calling," Fox said, her eyes darting between the laptop feed. "Wait ... there it is." A signal pinged. "Got him," Fox said. "Blackwood's on the call with her."

"Can you track it? Find out where he is?" Sandling asked.

Maudmont took a deep breath, exhaled, and shook her hands in front of her like she was trying to dry them off.

"You okay?" Sandling asked.

Maudmont exhaled shakily. "Yeah. I'll be fine. Just a little flustered—I can't believe it worked."

"You did great," Carver said again. "Let's go to the prison."

Hornigen started the van and pulled out of the parking space.

45

CAITLIN SANDLING SAT ALONE in the Chaplain's Quarters on Death Row. The ticking clock and her breathing were the only sounds. Her phone buzzed on the table. She picked it up.

"Hey," she said, her voice low.

"Blackwood's coming," Carver said carefully. "He's heading to see Zimmer."

Sandling closed her eyes for a moment. She was terrified. This was what they'd planned, but now that it was happening, her anxiety gripped her and wouldn't let her go. "Okay," she said, her mouth dry. She stood and walked to the small window, staring out at the empty, barren courtyard below. "How far away is he?"

"Thirty minutes, maybe less. We're keeping a distance but will be outside when it happens. Stay calm, champ. And don't forget how dangerous he is."

Sandling allowed herself a thin smile. "You think I don't know that?"

Carver sighed on the line. "Yeah. But you're unarmed. Just ... remember what we talked about, okay?"

She gripped the phone tighter, feeling her pulse in her

temples. "I've got this, Gust," she said, her voice low and confident, though inside, metal butterflies flapped in her stomach.

"Good luck," he said.

"Thanks. You too." She hung up. This was it—now or never. She watched the clock tick by. Her heart thumped as she walked to the open cell door. It had been years since she'd felt this vulnerable—alone, unarmed, waiting for a suspected killer to walk through the door. She hadn't expected this level of tension—not with a man she'd once trusted, someone she'd shared her deepest secrets with. Sandling closed her eyes and breathed in, steeling herself for what was coming down the corridor. One last check. She'd installed listening and recording devices in the Chaplain's Quarters.

She sent an SMS to Fox and said aloud, "Testing, testing, one, two, three, four."

Fox messaged back: Loud and clear.

46

CAITLIN SANDLING WAS ALONE NOW. Everyone had worked together to put her here—within touching distance of justice for Toby. She moved softly on the balls of her feet down the white, blank walls of death row. The plan was in motion. They'd bugged the meeting room. Zimmer, for his part, thought he was being hauled to the abandoned wing to meet her and finalize the details of his transfer deal. He was told she'd come around. His visitor tonight would be Edmund Blackwood.

She trusted Carver. She trusted the team. Surveillance was in place. The listening devices were working. Every detail was accounted for. All she had to do now was wait.

She slipped into a disused utility closet along the empty block. It reminded her of playing hide and seek as a child. But back then, getting found meant giggles and being "it." Now, it felt like being hunted. The closet smelled of disinfectant and dust. A mop bucket sat in the corner. She squeezed into the shadowed space and held her breath, her back pressed against the cool cinderblock wall.

Distant gates slammed open. The metallic clang reverberated through the wing, and her pulse quickened. They were bringing Zimmer up. Her ears strained to pick up the low murmur of voices.

"Where is she?" Zimmer snapped, oozing contempt. "I don't have all bloody night for this. I expected her to be punctual. Constantly getting dragged hither and thither ... pathetic."

The guard stifled a laugh. "Yeah, what can I say, huh? Good luck with that. We're all rooting for you, Father Zimmer."

Zimmer snorted. "Save your prayers you heathen. You'll miss me when I'm gone."

The guard chuckled. "Can't say I'll miss the sermons."

Sandling could picture Zimmer's scowl as he shuffled forward in his restraints, already trying to calculate his next move. The sound of the gate unlocking carried through the wing. The guard escorted Zimmer past her hiding spot, the faint metallic clink of chains accompanying their footsteps. Sandling didn't move. Didn't breathe.

They reached the chaplain's quarters. She heard the guard's keys jingle as he locked the door behind Zimmer. Then came another set of footsteps—a different rhythm. Slower. Steadier.

"Right this way, sir," a guard called.

"Father Zimmer, is it now?" Blackwood's smooth voice carried through the corridor.

Sandling's breath hitched.

"This way, sir," the guard repeated.

"No need to babysit me. I can handle myself," Blackwood said.

"Suit yourself," the guard replied. "Press the buzzer when you're ready." The gate clanged shut.

Sandling silently swore. The guard was supposed to stay.

She carefully leaned forward, peeking through a crack in the closet door. Blackwood's dark silhouette moved down the hall, his gait unhurried, his demeanor calm. She slipped deeper into the shadows, her pulse roaring in her ears.

Inside the chaplain's quarters, Zimmer's restraints clanged against the table. "Blackwood? What the hell are you doing here?"

"Hello, Hermann," Blackwood said smoothly, the scrape of a chair indicating he'd sat down. "Nice to see you too."

Zimmer laughed once, humorless. "I wasn't expecting you."

"Oh? And who were you expecting?"

Zimmer didn't answer immediately. "Doesn't matter. What are you doing here?"

"I had to see it for myself," Blackwood said.

"See what?"

"The man about to betray me."

Zimmer chuckled. "You think I'm Judas now, do you?"

"I think I had no choice but to come and confirm it."

Sandling stayed perfectly still, listening intently.

"You're on a wild goose chase," Zimmer said dismissively. "The Feds are clueless."

"How can I be sure?"

"You worry too much."

"That's easy for you to say. Your days, your meals, even your toilet breaks are planned for you."

Zimmer sneered. "You should try it, *Blacksin*. Might suit you sooner than you think."

"Is that a threat?"

Zimmer leaned back. "Why are you really here? Do you think it's wise to be seen here?"

"I had no choice," Blackwood said again, his tone tighter.

"Why?"

"A little birdie told me you were about to cut a deal."

Zimmer laughed softly. "Pfft. Don't concern yourself. We all play the game."

317

"And what's your game, Hermann?"

Zimmer didn't answer.

"Who did you think you were meeting?" Blackwood asked.

Zimmer was silent for a moment, then said, "The FBI bitch."

Sandling's stomach twisted.

"You think she's coming?" Blackwood asked.

"That would make for an interesting ménage à trois," Zimmer said, voice dripping sarcasm.

Blackwood went quiet. The scrape of his chair against the floor made Sandling flinch.

"Are we alone?" Blackwood asked.

"The Lord watches all things," Zimmer said dryly.

"Besides him."

"I did smell something sweet when I came in," Zimmer said.

"Chanel No. 5?" Blackwood mused.

Sandling's chest tightened. Her lavender body cream. She cursed herself. She hadn't even thought about it when getting ready.

"Hello?" Blackwood's voice echoed through the corridor. "*Hellooo*? Caitlin, are you with us?"

She froze, her breath catching in her throat.

"I smell your cheap perfume, Caitlin," Blackwood called, his voice taunting. "Why don't you come out and join us?"

Sandling pressed herself against the wall of the closet, heart hammering. She felt trapped, like prey in a snare.

"Caitlin," Blackwood said again, his footsteps drawing closer. "Don't make me look for you. We'd just like to have a little chat ..."

Sandling closed her eyes. She couldn't let him find her. Not yet. Not like this.

47

"Boo!" Blackwood screamed as he flung the metal door open. Sandling cowered and lifted her arms to protect herself. His eyes were wild and frenzied. She'd never seen this person before. He was a predator, his fangs showing through his snarl.

"Come here!" He shouted and went to grab her. Sandling couldn't run, so she had to fight. She kicked off the back of the metal box and rammed into him, trying to push him out of the way. Blackwood had removed his shoes, and she hadn't heard him coming. His socks slipped on the shiny floor and he fought for friction under his feet. He grabbed at her and got hold of her hair, and she screamed again. She tried to get away, but his arm went around her chest and lifted her. She went to scream as loudly as she could, but he covered her mouth and muffled her cry. Her eyes widened as she realized he was cutting off her breath, carrying her back to the chaplain's quarters where Herman Zimmer waited. She kicked and flailed and thrashed wildly from side to side, but he didn't relent. Her lungs burned and she pushed her head back, opened her mouth, and got one of Blackwood's fingers between her teeth. She bit down with all the force she had left. She felt the skin on his finger compress.

There was a crunch, and he lowered her slightly and grunted loudly in pain, but he didn't let go. Didn't try and pull his finger out of her teeth. Her heels skidded on the slick floor as she dug them in, trying to gain leverage. Blackwood was still dragging her backward. He was hunched over and swearing, but she was fighting a losing battle. She wanted to sob. She wanted her father to come and save her. She wanted to go home. But she knew she would be joining Toby Underwood soon. She couldn't breathe. Fighting for air was all she could do now. She stopped biting him. She was physically drained. Her body went limp. She stopped fighting and closed her eyes, letting her head slump to the side. She let him do what he wanted.

THE HEAVY, wooden chair felt cold as Blackwood used his necktie to strap her wrist to the armrest. She could taste blood. It was Blackwood's. His finger dripped red drops on the polished wood and onto the floor.

"You'd better not have killed her," Zimmer said, reflecting his annoyance.

"I know what I'm doing," Blackwood said. He was breathing heavily. "Why don't you make yourself useful and get me something to tie her down?" She could feel Blackwood standing over her.

Zimmer said nothing, then asked, "Pray tell, *Blacksin*, what's the plan here?"

"Just get me the fucking twine, will you?" Silence.

"I'm shackled to the desk, you imbecile. I can only move so far ... Zimmer demonstrated. He could stand and get a few feet but the restraints snapped tight. He was close enough to reach for her, though.

"Fine, watch her. I'll get it." She felt Blackwood move off and Hermann Zimmer over her left shoulder. Please ... please ... she started to think to herself. Please let Gust or Rachel or Frank be listening. Please send help. *Please* help me. God, please help me. She heard Blackwood opening the wooden drawers of the chaplain's desk behind her. She forced herself to open one eye. There it was. The buzzer. She only had one hand free. She lunged. At the same time, Zimmer's chains scraped on the metal table as he jumped after her.

"No!" she shouted as he grabbed her from behind. "No!" He pulled her backward and she stuck out her leg. Desperate, she kicked the red button on the wall. "Aargh! No! Hermann, stop!" she yelled as she heard the familiar buzzing sound far away. Zimmer pulled her back into the chair. He breathed heavily and said, "You shouldn't have done that, young Cate."

Blackwood smiled. He held a ball of twine for wrapping parcels and a roll of yellowish Scotch Tape. He looked at Zimmer, who sat back down in his fold-out metal chair.

"What's their average response time?" Blackwood asked.

"Ten minutes," Zimmer said. "Depending."

Blackwood set to work tying her down properly. First, he tied her already secured arm and then removed his tie. He stuffed it in his jacket pocket. While he restrained her, she gathered herself. She knew from her training in hostage negotiation that captives who humanized themselves were much more likely to survive than those who did not. She had to say her name. She had to make him see that she was human.

"Hey, Edmund," she said, "It's me, remember? Caitlin? We know each other."

"Shut up," Blackwood said as he yanked the twine around her wrist.

"You're hurting me! Dr. Blackwood, please!" The rough string bit into her soft skin and cut off blood flow.

"Shut your mouth before I suffocate you with this sticky tape."

She had to make him see sense. "What do you want, Edmund?"

"For you to shut your gob before I shut it, permanently."

"Is this the real you?" she asked, glaring up at him. She had tears in her eyes and sniffed. "Or was it the man I lay on the sofa talking to? Hmm. Who is pretending?" Blackwood got down on his knees and started tying her ankles to the chair leg. It's okay, she told herself. Keep him busy. The team was on their way. She hoped they were. She *prayed* they were. And sooner rather than later, the prison guard would turn up. What was Blackwood going to do then? How was he going to explain this to him?

"It's over, Edmund, don't you see?" Sandling said, looking down at him. She grimaced as the twine bit into her calf. "The guard is going to come, and he's going to see me tied up, and ... it's over! Let me go, and we can work this out." Blackwood moved to her other leg and started wrapping the thin rope around it. "Tell him, Hermann," she said, looking over her shoulder. Zimmer had been particularly quiet, watching the whole scene unfold from his one keen eye. He shook his head once. "This could be bad for you, too," she said to Zimmer. "You were on your way to California, remember? We have a deal. I was going to show it to you. The paperwork is done. It's all—"

"Shut up!" Blackwood shouted and bashed her in the back of her head with his palm. Her head snapped forward, and she moaned in pain. Blackwood yanked her head back by her hair and pulled out a strip of clear tape. "Hold still, you dumb bitch," he said and started violently wrapping the tape around her face. It was haphazard, and Sandling's eyes went wide as one line of tape went over the top of her nose. They all heard a gate clang in the distance. Oh, thank god, she thought. Someone was coming. *Hurry, hurry. Please hurry.*

"They're coming," Zimmer said.

Blackwood went silently to the other side of the chair, put his hands on the armrest, and leaned back. He started dragging her out of the chaplain's quarters and into the open corridor. He was heaving, and her weight on the wooden high-backed chair squealed and slid slowly out into the white walls lit up by the fluorescent lights. Sandling squinted and turned her head from the glare. She fought for air as Blackwood stood in front of her. He glared at her. The prison guard would be at the main gate to death row at any moment. He bent a little at the waist, staring directly into her eyes. She felt shame, pity, and hopelessness. She was sore, exhausted, and in pain. Then, without warning, Blackwood raised a balled-up first up to the side of his face. He opened his eyes wide, looked sideways at his fist, and then punched himself right on the nose. He put real force behind it and hit himself again.

"Eurgh," he grunted as he stepped backward. He smiled and touched his fingers under his nose. He was bleeding. It dripped onto the floor. He gave a single laugh and said, "Watch this now!"

Sandling wanted to look away but couldn't. She watched on in disgust as Dr. Edmund Blackwood, her therapist, started punching himself in the face. He grunted as he did it. "Ugh, ugh, ugh." Then he started shouting. "Ah! No! Please stop! Don't hurt me!" As he flung himself full force into the metal bars of the adjacent cell. He had blood running out of his lips and nose. He put two hands on the bars on either side of his head, looked back at Sandling, and grinned. He had blood between his teeth. He looked like a wild animal feeding on a carcass. Thump! He smashed his head into the bars. Clunk. Clunk. Clunk. He was bashing his brain in head-butting the metal bars. It didn't take long before he had a welt and blood vessels rising to the surface of his skin. He kept going, grinning like a madman, hitting himself again and again, harder each time, until his face was a mess of blood. Sandling couldn't take it anymore and looked away, but the sickening thud of his flesh and bone on metal made her nauseous. Finally, he stopped and slumped to the ground. Down the corridor, they heard the guard yell, "Hey! What the hell is going on down here!?"

Blackwood winked at Sandling and rolled onto his front. Blood was dripping from his face. He pushed his hands and knees through it as he crawled towards the guard. The keys jangled and scraped as the guard frantically tried to unlock the gate. Blackwood was crawling towards him and lifted one of his arms weakly to reach out to him and cried, "Oh, God, thank God! Please, help me! Help me! He's gone crazy." His voice was garbled and blood ran from his mouth as he spoke. The prison guard pulled the gate open and it crashed against the bars. He ran in, slipping a little on the slick floor, and slid into help Blackwood.

"What the hell happened?" he shouted, running toward Blackwood. "Where's Zimmer?" he yelled. Blackwood raised his arm and pointed behind himself at Sandling. The prison guard left Blackwood and rushed towards Sandling. What he couldn't see was Blackwood get to his feet and run towards the open gate. Sandling started yelling, but the tape around her mouth just came out like a frantic scream.

"I'm coming, I'm coming," the guard said over her. "It's going to be okay." He checked to see if Zimmer was still secured to the table and then crouched in front of Sandling. "I'm going to get you free. How did this happen?" the guard called over his shoulder to Blackwood without looking.

Sandling could see Blackwood heading for the gate. He stopped and turned towards her. Her nostrils flared as she struggled to warn the guard. Her chest heaved with the effort of trying to get free. She watched as Blackwood calmly pushed the gate shut with a clang. He gave Sandling a glance over his shoulder as he put his hand on the bunch of keys. The guard glanced back at the Blackwood as Sandling tried to scream to warn. Blackwood was about to stop Sofa Squad—or anyone else—from getting into death row to help her. Then, she stopped struggling. She was exhausted and watched as Blackwood leaned back and kicked the key with his heel. He put his hand on the damaged key and yanked it. She heard a high-pitched shriek as he strained, pulling hard, and the metal gave way, the key snapping off in the locked gate. He was breathing hard, turned, and smiled maniacally at Sandling. She saw blood staining his teeth. He raised his hand to his mouth and, like he was trying to get a bit of food out, pulled pieces of his chipped teeth out and sprinkled the bits like salt on a salad. She couldn't believe it. What was he going to do now? He hadn't escaped. He'd done the opposite. He'd boxed himself in. Now, he *couldn't* escape. But neither could anyone else get in. As the guard started unwrapping the Scotch Tape from around her face, Blackwood, still shoeless, padded up behind the prison guard with his tie wrapped around each of his fists. Sandling squealed, trying to warn the prison guard, and as he removed the tape from her mouth, she screamed, "Watch out!"

The guard turned, but as he did, Blackwood slipped the necktie over his head and yanked hard on it. Immediately, the guard's hand went up to his throat, and he tried to force Blackwood off. His eyes bulged, veins popping at his throat and temples. His face went red. Blackwood fell backward, pulling the prison guard down on top of him. The guard struggled for purchase under the silk cutting into his neck. His legs flailed, boots screeching across the floor and leaving black streaks as he gasped for air. In his last moment, the guard began walking sideways over the floor, kicking out and trying to escape the death grip. He gargled, and he started bleeding from the mouth. His body started jerking in place. The guard's wide eyes pleaded with Sandling. She could do nothing but look on in horror. Then, the body stopped moving. Blackwood didn't let go. He held on, forcing his weight forward and into the guard's back to wring the last drop of life out of him.

48

Caitlin Sandling watched as Dr. Blackwood rolled the prison guard's limp body off him and got himself to his feet. He was breathing heavily. He looked savagely beaten. His suit was torn and his shirt was stained with blood. He wiped his mouth with the back of his hand, and his chest heaved as he fought for breath. He put his hands on his knees as he rested and glanced over at Zimmer.

"Hell, *Blacksin*, I never knew you had it in you ..."

"Yeah, well ..." Blackwood said between breaths without finishing his sentence. "Listen, Hermann, this is what I was thinking ..." Blackwood took the bunch of keys out of his pants pocket and started sorting through them.

"You're looking for the small padlock key first," Zimmer said, leaning forward a little to see. Oh, no, Sandling thought. Don't free Zimmer. Don't let the Ripper loose on me. Where was Carver? Where was Hornigen? Where was Fox? She needed them now more than ever. She was alone, locked in a prison with a pair of sadistic serial killers. "Unshackle me," Zimmer said, his voice smooth, like he was ordering a coffee.

"And then?" Blackwood asked.

"I'll take care of the FBI agent."

"I can do it," Blackwood said.

Zimmer shook his head. "Best stay out of this one ... for forensic's sake. After all, you've already had your fun today ... it's my turn now."

Blackwood smiled his broken-tooth smile.

Sandling's heart pounded in her chest, her gaze darting from Blackwood to Zimmer. She felt dizzy and tested the tightness of the twine around her wrists. It dug deeper into her supple skin.

"What then?" Blackwood asked.

Zimmer shrugged and smiled gently at him. "I need you on the outside, Edmund; one of us should at least be free to carry on. With the FBI out of the way, we'll restart my medical review proceedings. But I need you on the outside for that. You're no use to me in a cell ... Anyway, who's to say what happened? We pin it on the guard."

Blackwood's eyes flickered toward the dead body lying splayed in an unnatural position in the corridor. "You'll be the hero," Zimmer said. "Imagine the publicity. The man who survived Zimmer the Ripper. You'll walk out of here a free man. It's the perfect cover. And there's a book deal in it too."

Blackwood moved to unlock the shackles and hesitated. He held the key suspended just above Zimmer's hands with his back to Sandling and said, "That's what's in it for me. And what's in it for you?"

"The chance not to rot in here ... which is what will happen unless I help you. Anyway, what option do you have, Edmund? You're in a prison. You're only walking out of here in a body bag or on a gurney."

Blackwood leaned in, voice raspy. As he put the key into the padlock and turned it, he said, "Deal. You scratch my back, and I save your life. Yes?"

Sandling realized Zimmer's eye was staring, unblinking, at her. He grinned, flashing his rotting teeth. "But," he said and glanced up at the man standing over him, "Edmund ... you can't watch, okay?"

"This your sick fantasy?" Blackwood asked absentmindedly. "No, otherwise, they might be able to prove you were part of it. Turn your back."

"Let me just unlock your handcuffs," Blackwood said as he flicked through the keys. Sandling had given up—out of ideas. The only way she was going to be saved was if Carver and a SWAT team arrived at the gate and shot Zimmer from range before he suffocated her.

"Damn thing," Blackwood said and went to hold the keys up in the light coming from the small window. As he did, Zimmer pounced like an old tiger. His grin morphed into a grimace of hate and loathing. Sandling's eyes widened and she gasped. The force of Zimmer's body knocked into Blackwood, and he wrapped the chain of his restraints around the psychologist's neck. Like the guard, Blackwood's hand went straight to the chain pulled tight against his neck. Zimmer got behind him and yanked his head and neck backward. As he did, he lifted his knees into a fetal position and threw himself down. Zimmer was a big man, much bigger than Blackwood and they went to the floor. Blackwood writhed, trying to get leverage from his fingertips under the taut chain. From the force Zimmer applied, Sandling realized he wasn't trying to choke Blackwood out. He was trying to snap his neck. Sandling screamed and thrashed against her restraints as Blackwood's eyes bulged. Zimmer snarled, pulling tighter. Blackwood's face turned red, his legs kicking out as Zimmer grunted.

She finally saw it. Zimmer was the beast now. The pure primal nature of his illness. She heard a crunch, like pulling a chicken leg off a carcass, as the nickel-plated chain bit into

Blackwood's windpipe and compressed it. Zimmer only pulled harder. Just as Sandling couldn't take anymore—the shrill, high-pitched whine in her ears, the disgusting guttural sounds of a man being choked—the chains tore into Blackwood's skin. His artery exploded in a red spray across the ceiling, the table, and the floor.

"I always despised you," Zimmer said into Blackwood's dead ear.

Sandling turned away and mock charged. She heard Zimmer roll out from under Blackwood's limp body. When she looked up, he was standing over her. "No, Hermann, please ... I'm begging you." She flinched as his large hand reached for her face, but instead of striking her, he wiped away a tear running down her cheek. She heard shouting coming from behind him.

Zimmer smiled at her. "Step away from her, prisoner! Step back now, or we will shoot!"

"Don't ever forget, Caitlin. The Lord giveth, and the Lord taketh away. Today, he saved you. Tomorrow, you save me. Understand?" She nodded frantically. Zimmer raised his handcuffed hands and said, "Tell them you're safe."

She looked wide-eyed at the guards trying to pry open the gate. Their voices boomed through the narrow corridor, ordering Zimmer to *back away* and *get down* before they shot him full of holes.

She cleared her throat and tried to shout, "I'm fine! I'm fine! Don't shoot!" She started to sob, looked down, and said, "Please, don't shoot..."

Zimmer took a step back as instructed and got down carefully on his hands and knees before sliding forward onto his chest. Sandling was looking out of the corner of her eye at Dr. Blackwood lying in a shimmering pool of black-looking blood.

"Never mind him," Zimmer said, glancing up at her

from the floor as the guards rushed toward him. "He was arrogant. People like him are crazy ..."

The guards jumped on his back and pinned him down. "Don't move, Zimmer, don't move!' one of them shouted in his ear. Another guard crouched in front of her. 'Are you hurt? Anywhere hurt?"

She shook her head as he started to get her loose. As he freed her wrist, she saw Carver running up to her, followed by Fox and Hornigen.

"Oh my God," she said and touched her free hand to her mouth. She burst into tears. She'd never been so happy to see anyone in her life. Her lip quivered, and she said, "I'm alive. I'm alive. I thought I was dead for sure ..."

Carver crouched in front of her, put his hand on hers, and said, "You're alive. You're alive."

The guards pulled Zimmer up from the ground, and Carver glanced at him. Zimmer smiled and said, "Augustine ..." as they dragged him away. Carver sighed and opened his mouth to speak.

"Don't say anything, Gust. Please, just don't say anything."

49

A few weeks later

CAITLIN SANDLING STOOD LOOKING DOWN at Toby Underwood's grave inside the wrought-iron-enclosed Manassas Cemetery. She watched the pinewood box as it lowered. The steady creak of the winch ropes sounded like nails on a chalk board to her. She imagined Toby lying there with his eyes closed, his face ashen white, and his fingers interlocked on his chest. She didn't feel anything—worn out of emotion. She'd spent one night in the hospital under observation after the hostage situation at the prison.

She hadn't spoken to anyone about what had happened since the FBI's Inspection Division took her statement. She'd also heard the prison was investigating why the guard had abandoned his post. Sandling suspected Zimmer's influence. Carver thought it was an oversight. Either way, she'd suffered. She'd considered speaking to a therapist. She'd even been appointed one by the Bureau but she couldn't bring herself to do it. Blackwood had robbed her of something basic you need to function as a human being: the ability to trust without fear.

Underwood's widow stood opposite, holding a tightly folded ceremonial American flag, flanked by her two children. They were being buffeted by the cold breeze, and Sandling breathed through her mouth as she tried not to think of the last time she'd seen Toby Underwood alive. This should never have happened—not like this. Sandling zoned out as the priest spoke, retreating into her thoughts. Unraveling this case had been almost as hard as solving it. Victor Crowe's DNA had matched the scenes of the Incubus killings, and Blackwood, though absent, was suspected of murdering at least six police officers over two decades. Each officer he killed was methodically punished for their perceived failings.

The casket came to rest, and the chaplain said his final words. Sandling felt an overwhelming sense of dread as they started shoveling soil on top of the wooden box. She looked away and saw Carver watching her. The only missing puzzle piece was what started Carver's investigation. The Sylvia Plath quotes found at Elizabeth Webb's and her father's scenes were unique. And, while it seemed plausible that they were part of the series of murders Blackwood had carried out, it became apparent that they weren't. Carver had had the uneasy and disquieting responsibility to tell a disbelieving Jessica Webb that her sister and her father had simply taken their own lives. It would have been easier if they were Blackwood's victims, easier to process, simpler to be angry about, and more straightforward to understand. But the harder question to answer was why. Why'd they done it? That was something Carver and the team couldn't answer.

For Sandling's part, the confrontation she'd had with Underwood replayed incessantly in her mind. She told herself that she should have noticed he was spiraling. If she'd been a good teammate, she might've. If she hadn't been so focused on escaping from herself, she could have. She might have done more to help him. Now, instead of finding him drunk at a bar, they were laying his body to rest forever.

Meanwhile, Zimmer was getting what he wanted. After Blackwood's failed tribunal and the shocking revelations about his manipulation of both Zimmer and Crowe, the authorities had little choice but to review every decision Blackwood had ever influenced. As a result, Zimmer's request for a transfer to California was granted. His original trial, meanwhile, was now to be reexamined. Carver said that Zimmer had played his hand perfectly. She couldn't fathom that it was all an elaborate game. And she couldn't shake the feeling that she owed Zimmer her life. How warped her reality had become. Saved by the hand of the man who'd condemned her father.

She wondered, standing there, whether Zimmer's twisted sense of cosmic justice mandated that he achieve Maat, knowing he'd destroyed her life once before. Perhaps, in his twisted perception, sparing her was his version of absolution. She suspected that he'd realized she was more valuable to him than Blackwood and decided to go home with the person who'd brought him to the dance. So far it was working out for him.

After the whole picture became clear, the media didn't quite know what to make of Victor Harlan Crowe. Just saying his name was shorthand for madness. Even in insanity people needed a reason for the murders. Something to explain how a man could come to believe he is anointed to expose betrayal and punish people with blood. Sandling could empathize with the public. How did the son of a devout family become a killer leaving biblical symbols painted in blood at his crime scenes?

Overall it was the Eye of Horus symbols that captured the media's imagination. They leaned into the sensationalism. Morning talk shows gave plenty of airtime to academics and religious figures adept at linking their delusions to shadowy myths and ancient conspiracies. True crime shows couldn't get enough. Religious commentators debated whether his warped belief in the Gospel of Judas was a corruption of their faith or a product of a lost truth. Psychologists spoke at length about the cycle of trauma and mental illness. None of the experts could untangle the threads of his life with much certainty. Sandling and Benson had pieced together most of the puzzle.

Crowe grew up in rural Ohio, the only child of a devout Christian family. His father, Pastor Warren Crowe, was the spiritual center of their small community. According to those who remembered him, Victor was the quiet boy in the front pew, hands clasped, with eyes only for his father. To anyone on the outside, the Crowes were a model family, but inside, the house was filled with resentment and violence.

Crowe's mother, Linda, bore the brunt of his father's ferocious temper—all the while teaching Victor to obey and endure. As Warren Crowe's sway of his congregation grew, his slip into alcoholism and dogma grew. His father preached a doctrine of fear: sin lurked in every corner, and the righteous must be ever vigilant against betrayal by their neighbors, their families, and even themselves. When young Victor overheard an argument—his mother accusing his father of infidelity with a young congregant, he became disillusioned. Victor didn't understand the words, but the betrayal was clear. The man who demanded perfection from his family had failed them. Linda grew silent after that, her strength hollowed out. Victor began to see hypocrisy everywhere—in his father's sermons, in the parishioners' forced smiles, and in the quiet complicity of the church. He retreated into himself, developing an obsessive fixation on the concept of betrayal. Victor's mania encompassed ancient symbols and grew alongside his developing paranoia. He told his classmates about the eye of a god who saw all sins, even the ones buried deep in the soul. Teachers reported his drawings of eyes, pyramids, and crosses on every surface.

By fifteen, Victor had his first documented psychotic break. His mother found him in the barn, muttering passages from the Bible while carving a crude altar from scrap wood. He claimed he could hear the voices of betrayers, that he had been chosen to bring their sins to light. His parents sent him to a psychiatric facility, where he stayed for three months before being released with a diagnosis of schizophrenia and a bottle of antipsychotic pills. It was during this time that Victor met Hermann Zimmer, then still a preacher visiting psychiatric wards. Zimmer claimed to see a divine spark in Victor, a young man who understood the burden of judgment. Zimmer introduced him to the Gospel of Judas, a controversial text that recast Judas not as a traitor but as a necessary instrument in Jesus' divine plan. As his psychosis engulfed him, he saw himself as a Judas figure, both victim and agent of a higher truth. Zimmer's twisted sermons planted the seeds for Victor's later crimes. They spoke of the Eye of Horus as a divine watcher, a symbol of balance and justice. To Victor, it became an emblem of his holy mission. He moved from job to job, city to city, living in rented rooms and storage units. He avoided medication and fell deeper into his delusions. His crimes began a few years later.

Crowe would latch onto a victim by chance, but view each interaction as ordained and tied to his mission. He looked for signs of betrayal in his victims—real or imagined. A husband's secret affair. A prostitute's dual life. A pedophile's exploitation of children. He believed he was purging the world of falsehoods, one sinner at a time. The thing that struck Sandling was how he manufactured some of the situations, for instance, they found a hard drive filled with photographs Crowe had secretly taken while working his job at the fun fair working as a carousel operator. They'd matched some of the photographs Crowe took with those at the scene. Crowe had made contact with headless Howard Clarke on some dark websites and agreed to meet him to sell the pictures. It was the first time on record that a paranoid schizophrenic killer seemed to display planning behavior.

His crime scenes were a tapestry of judgment. The violence committed against the adulterer. The Clorox bath for the prostitute. The beheading. Each act was a ritual. Watching them bury Toby made compassion difficult. While the media labeled Crowe a monster and stigmatized others suffering from schizophrenia, Sandling saw something more tragic beneath the insanity. His life was a series of betrayals, which played a role in his psychosis and left him chasing an absolution he would never find. He had been both victim and perpetrator, a man consumed by the very sins he sought to punish. Something that she realized through her off early in the investigation was the murder of the Clorox bath prostitute's pimp. Someone with Crowe's sick state of mind shouldn't have been able or cared about planning. And yet he'd first killed the procurer to make sure he'd be undisturbed with his main target. Crowe was as strange and disorienting psychologically as he'd been during his spree.

Even in the pursuit of justice, truth could be elusive,

fractured by perspective. Crowe's alleged final victim, lying in a box in front of her, hadn't fit the pattern. No one could make sense of Dr. Edmund Blackwood. His guilt was in doubt. Sandling had become a target for some people who believed she was in league with Hermann Zimmer. She was there after all, and people couldn't wrap their heads around how a man so revered in his field could've orchestrated the alleged detective killings. To the public, Dr. Edmund Blackwood was the embodiment of academic brilliance. A forensic psychologist, behavioral consultant, and adjunct professor at Johns Hopkins University, he was celebrated for his work in criminal profiling and his incisive lectures on the complexities of the human mind. His sharp suits, silver-streaked hair, and piercing blue eyes gave him an aura of authority that few dared to question. But beneath the polished exterior lay something far more sinister.

Blackwood's colleagues admired him for his intellect, but even the most seasoned officers who worked with him on cases felt an unnameable discomfort in his presence. There was an edge to Blackwood, a sense of detachment that hinted at a darker side.

Those who tried to dig into his past would have found little more than a carefully curated facade: a middle-class upbringing, academic excellence, and a sterling career. But the truth was far more fractured.

Blackwood's origins were a mystery to even those who thought they knew him well. He was born Edvard Dunkelweldt, the son of immigrants who fled Eastern Europe during the height of the Cold War. His parents settled in Illinois and anglicized their surname to Blackwood in an attempt to blend in. Blackwood's father had been a failed police officer turned bitter security guard, whose frustrations with his inadequacies bled into every corner of their home life. His father's constant berating and emotional abuse planted a deep disdain for authority in Blackwood, a seed that grew quietly as he climbed the academic and professional ranks. To Blackwood, law enforcement was a field rife with incompetence and hubris. His father's failures had shown him the fragility of the badge, while his years as a consultant revealed how often justice was a matter of chance rather than skill. The system, as Blackwood saw it, was irreparably flawed. And when he encountered his first major failure—a serial killer wrongly accused and convicted due to police negligence—it shattered whatever faith he might have had in those sworn to uphold the law.

The case, which led to the exoneration of the accused only after their death, became the turning point for Blackwood. He began to see himself not just as an analyst but as a corrective force. If the system couldn't root out its own corruption and ineptitude, he would. His descent into vigilantism wasn't born from rage but from a calculated sense of justice. Blackwood's attacks on police officers weren't random. Each victim was chosen with precision, their pasts meticulously dissected for failures that Blackwood deemed unforgivable. A detective who pinned a series of murders on an innocent man. A lieutenant who ignored evidence, leading to more victims. A profiler who rushed to judgment, leaving an actual killer free to roam. It was enough for Sandling to wonder if leaving the Eye of Horus at the scenes was a kind of insurance policy for Edmund. Had he planned to frame Crowe all along? She'd never know. Only that he'd tried to use Victor Crowe and Toby Underwood as cover to distract the FBI from the real culprit.

His academic credentials gave him the perfect cover. As a respected figure in the field of criminal psychology, Blackwood was often consulted on the very cases he orchestrated.

He used his insights not just to deflect suspicion but to sow confusion. Sandling did not doubt that Blackwood thought he'd get away with it. In the end, his belief in the incompetence of the police was his downfall.

Blackwood lived a fractured personal life. He was divorced, estranged from his children, and maintained few close relationships. Those who knew him socially described him as private, enigmatic, and intensely focused. His world revolved around his work, both legitimate and otherwise, and his ability to compartmentalize allowed him to maintain his dual existence. While he wasn't a prolific serial killer, his crimes stretched over a decade or more. Each murder was a statement, a meticulously crafted message that only the most astute would ever decode. The profile Sandling was working on showed that his disdain for law enforcement wasn't just professional; it was deeply personal. His father's failures, the injustices he witnessed, and his god complex combined to create a man who saw himself as the ultimate arbiter of right and wrong. To her, Blackwood was the most dangerous kind of killer: someone playing a secret game while believing he was righting wrongs that made the world a better place. In his mind, every life he took was a necessary step toward a greater good. He used his sessions with her to stay ahead of the investigation, mining her for information while maintaining his facade of concern.

The scene at Chesapeake Detention Facility was the stuff of nightmares. The intelligentsia, however, refused to accept the story. Conspiracy theories spread online. Commentators questioned why Zimmer, a convicted serial killer, had been allowed to assist in an FBI investigation. They speculated that Blackwood had been framed, his crimes exaggerated to cover for Bureau incompetence. Sandling—hailed by the mayor—became the face of the criticism.

Then there was Blackwood's assistant. After the fallout, she had resigned, claiming ignorance of Blackwood's true intentions, but Sandling wasn't so sure. She had been in too deep for too long not to have seen the darkness. Perhaps she was another victim of Blackwood's manipulation, or perhaps she had been complicit. Either way, the Bureau had closed that chapter.

For Sandling, the case left more questions than answers. Had Zimmer saved her out of remorse for what he'd done to her father, or was it simply another move in his endless game of power and control? As Sandling stood there watching, she thought of Blackwood's last breaths. Victor Crowe and Dr. Edmund Blackwood were dead, Zimmer was heading back to California, and Sandling—once again—was left to pick up the pieces.

The service ended, and the mourners started drifting slowly away or making their way to Underwood's widow to offer condolences. Sandling was just sad. She looked over at her team as they walked away and realized how much they'd changed. Gibson had called again, offering her the chance to go to Quantico despite the media fallout. But standing looking at the rectangular hole in the ground, she knew she couldn't leave them, not now. They'd gone through hell. And for what? To walk away now would be abandoning them. A betrayal. After everything they had been through, she couldn't stand on the shoulders of their suffering to save herself. It was all of them or nothing. Turning down Gibson still felt like the right decision. She didn't want the fame, promotions, or headlines anymore. What she needed was to stay with the team that had become her support. Penny Maudmont had been crushed after realizing how Blackwood had used her for information. She'd almost quit but was slowly coming around, rebuilding her confidence. They had lost a colleague, a friend, and now it was up to them to continue without him. She wiped away a tear, stood straight, and as the others started to walk away from the cemetery, she lingered for a moment longer. Her journey wasn't over yet. But one thing was clear—she wasn't going to do it alone. Not anymore.

50

AUGUSTINE CARVER WALKED AWAY from the grave, flanked by his agents Frank Hornigen, Rachel Fox, and Penny Maudmont. They spoke quietly. Carver was silent, hands in his pockets, his mind elsewhere. He had spent weeks untangling the threads of Elizabeth Webb's life, combing through every detail. Yet, as much as he hated to admit it, the truth was clear—just not the truth Jessica Webb wanted to hear. Elizabeth Webb had been a decorated detective, the type of officer others wanted to emulate. She was sharp, driven, and, by all accounts, committed to justice. But beneath her accolades lay a quiet, personal struggle. In the months leading up to her death, Elizabeth had been unraveling. The signs were there for anyone willing to look: missed days at work, uncharacteristic lapses in judgment, and a string of appointments with the department psychologist.

Carver had reviewed her files. She'd struggled with a recent case—a missing child who was never found. Elizabeth had been the lead detective, and Carver could see how she would have blamed herself for the failure. Her notes from that investigation painted a picture of a woman fraying at the edges, obsessed with finding answers that refused to materialize. Her personal life didn't provide much solace. Elizabeth had been living alone since her divorce three years before. Friends described her as private, almost reclusive, and her ex-husband noted she'd become 'distant, and consumed by work' in their final months together. She had no children. Her few close friends were mostly colleagues, equally burdened by the stresses of police work.

Then there was the matter of her father, retired Detective James Webb. He'd been a man of the old school, known for his stoicism and uncompromising approach to the job. But Carver had uncovered a quieter side of him, too—years spent hiding his struggles from the people around him. Records suggested James Webb battled severe depression in his final years, exacerbated by his retirement and his inability to let go of the cases he never solved.

Carver considered every angle, looking for something that would link Elizabeth and her father to the broader conspiracy they'd uncovered. Jessica still clung to the idea that her sister had uncovered something damning, some connection between the murdered detectives that led to her death. But Carver couldn't make the pieces fit. Elizabeth's work files showed no signs of her pursuing anything unusual in the days before her death, and forensics found nothing to suggest otherwise.

What the team did find was a troubling pattern—Elizabeth had been spiraling long before her father's death. Notes revealed that Elizabeth had confided fears of following in her father's footsteps, both professionally and personally. She felt the weight of his legacy pressing down on her. Jessica, of course, refused to accept it. She was convinced that someone—something—was responsible for her sister's death. She hounded Carver and the team, presenting scraps of evidence that never quite held together. He understood her desperation. Losing Elizabeth had left a void Jessica couldn't fill, and believing in foul play gave her purpose. To accept that Elizabeth had taken her own life meant accepting that she hadn't been able to save her sister.

Perhaps there was something deeper, some genetic predisposition or shared trauma that linked Elizabeth and her father's paths. Carver wasn't sure. What he did know was that the system they both served had done them no favors. The relentless grind of police work, the unspoken expectation to shoulder the burden without complaint, took its toll.

In the end, there were no villains, no grand conspiracies in Elizabeth's story. Just two people, father and daughter, weighed down by the unrelenting pressures of their lives. Carver doubted Jessica would ever accept that, but for him, it was the only truth that fit.

Some questions didn't have satisfying endings. Some stories ended not with revelations but with heartbreak. Elizabeth Webb was one of them. He walked down a grassy bank and fished his car keys from his pocket. The others lingered nearby. As Carver reached for the door handle, the whirr of a bicycle caught his attention.

A cyclist in a spandex suit and sunglasses coasted up to him. "Special Agent Augustine Carver?" the man asked, his voice muffled behind a sleek helmet.

"Who's asking?"

The man didn't answer. He pulled a small parcel from a saddlebag, handed it to Carver, and said, "No need to sign." Then he rode off. Carver held the parcel and watched him go. The package was small, wrapped in brown paper, and tied with a plain piece of twine. He walked around to the back of his car, set the parcel on the trunk, and began untying it. The Sofa Squad wandered over to him. Carver tore it open. He looked inside. There was a small figurine. He held it up, inspecting it. Beneath it, he found a Polaroid photo of a crime scene: a body slumped against a graffitied wall, a plea scrawled across concrete in blocky letters: *For God's sake, please stop me before I kill again.*

A note was folded beneath the Polaroid. Carver opened it, his eyes narrowing at the familiar handwriting.

It read: *He's done it again.*

Carver held the figurine up to the light and turned it slowly. His phone buzzed in his pocket. He put the wooden carving back in the parcel and took out his cell phone—Mitch Roberts.

"Got your package," Carver said, no greeting necessary. "What do you make of it?"

Roberts' voice was gruff. The sound of a man running on fumes. "No idea. That's why I'm asking you. It's a weird one," he said. "I was beginning to think it looked a lot like that other case you worked ..."

Carver frowned, his fingers tightened on his phone. "And what's the setup?"

"No leads, no clue, no idea."

Carver leaned against the car. "Isn't that just an average day for NYPD?" he asked dryly.

"Yeah? Well, this ain't average, Gust," Roberts said. "The political pressure is piling up, and we've got Jack. We need you."

Carver sighed. "You were pretty disparaging the last time we talked, if I recall."

"That was then. This is now. You understand? I changed my mind. We need you guys out here."

Carver paused. "What's the biggest concern?"

"Panic," Roberts said. "Sheer bloody panic. You should have seen it ..." his voice trailed off, then came back. "We can't have the whole of the greatest city on earth afraid of their shadows."

Carver looked at the Polaroid again, the scrawled plea on the wall. *Stop me before I kill again.*

"So what do you say?" Roberts asked.

Carver let the silence hang before replying. "I'll call you back," he said.

"Don't wait too long, Gust," Roberts said, then hung up.

Carver pocketed his phone. The team was standing within earshot and now drew closer, sensing something was up.

"What's that about?" Maudmont asked, nodding toward the parcel.

Carver sighed. "An old cop buddy sent it over. Mitch Roberts. He's chief of station in Manhattan now."

Rachel Fox leaned in to see inside the parcel. "I heard about this," she said.

Carver arched an eyebrow. "Why haven't I?"

"It came up on some pretty dark underground threads about serial killings that aren't getting media coverage. Speculation about cases the police aren't sure are connected ..." Carver's lips tightened. Fox shrugged. "The forums don't have a lot of detail, just rumors ..."

"What are we going to do?" Hornigen asked.

Carver glanced at each of them. "I guess we're taking a case in Manhattan," he said.

THE SERIES CONTINUES...

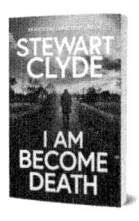

IN A CITY OF MILLIONS, A KILLER MAKES HIS MOVE. BUT WHAT ARE THE RULES?

The first victim is found meticulously posed, a chess piece placed on the body. Then another. The deeper Carver digs, the more unsettling the sequence becomes - because something doesn't quite fit.

Special Agent Augustine Carver knows killers, but this pattern is like nothing he's ever seen. When a fingerprint matches a missing child who vanished seven years ago, the case takes a chilling turn.

Carver is starting to wonder if he's chasing a killer or hunting a hidden secret no one could ever see coming ... before it's checkmate.

Press here: Grab yours now.

ALSO BY STEWART CLYDE

Discover the Stirling Hunt thrillers:

Blood Feud

Black Beach

Red Vendetta

Zero Hour

Printed in Dunstable, United Kingdom